Then the ground rumbled fiercely, a real shock wave.

Slaves screamed in terror and many followed Direfang, who stumbled to his knees as the ground shook harder.

Steel Town . . . Hell Town now . . . the place had gone berserk. Steam spewed up from a wide rent in the earth to the south. Behind him a woman screamed shrilly. A man called to her, then both voices were silenced in a thunderous crash.

Grallik N'sera had always feared the greater number of slaves. He had nightmares about the slaves rising up and crushing the Dark Knights, and dread gripped him now as he neared the closest pen.

His wall of fire lit up the whole camp, revealing the scale of the destruction that Steel Town had suffered from this second quake. Nothing stood, not a single wall or post. A cloud of dust, bigger and higher than the first quake, rose up and shadowed all the knights and laborers who were picking themselves up and shuffling around the camp. Grallik imagined this was what the Chaos War in the Abyss must have looked like.

"Hell," he said. "Hell's come to Neraka."

THE STONETELLERS

The Rebellion

Death March
August 2008

Goblin Nation

THE REBELLION

THE STONETELLERS
VOLUME ONE

JEAN RABE

The Stonetellers, Volume One
THE REBELLION
©2007 Wizards of the Coast, Inc.

Published by Wizards of the Coast, Inc. DRAGONLANCE, WIZARDS OF THE COAST, and their respective logos are trademarks of Wizards of the Coast, Inc., in the U.S.A. and other countries.

Printed in the U.S.A.

Cover art by Matt Stawicki
First Printing: August 2007

9 8 7 6 5 4 3 2 1

ISBN: 978-0-7869-4280-0
620-95946740-001-EN

U.S., CANADA,
ASIA, PACIFIC, & LATIN AMERICA
Wizards of the Coast, Inc.
P.O. Box 707
Renton, WA 98057-0707
+1-800-324-6496

EUROPEAN HEADQUARTERS
Hasbro UK Ltd
Caswell Way
Newport, Gwent NP9 0YH
GREAT BRITAIN
Save this address for your records.

Visit our web site at www.wizards.com

ACKNOWLEDGMENTS

Thanks to Margaret Weis, Jamie Chambers, Sean Everette, and Cam Banks for providing invaluable resources and suggestions regarding Krynn's goblins and their cousins and for making sure my Dark Knights remained well within the bounds of the Order. And thanks to medieval chef Daniel Myers for his lessons on how to properly feed fantasy characters.

DEDICATION

This one's for
Ben, Brent, Corey, Dean, Jonathan, Miya,
Ryan, and Urgoth—Saturday's warriors

1

MOON-EYE'S HEART

The ground shuddered and a rumbling began—the sound had no direction, seeming to come from nowhere and everywhere deep in the Neraka mine. It was a soft sound at first, almost comforting. But it quickly grew in intensity, becoming hurtful and blotting out the clang of pickaxes being dropped and miners calling to one another in panic. A great breath accompanied the quake, the earth exhaling in a thunderous *whoosh* that belched centuries-old dust the color of cinnamon from its depths.

Moon-eye's throat grew painfully tight as he clung to a support timber. The lantern hanging from a spike directly overhead jiggled. Its light sent shadows careening frantically along the shaft walls. The young goblin peered through the dust, which was falling like a steady rain, and flinched when fist-sized chunks of the ceiling came loose and struck him. He fought the urge to run toward the surface, instead edging away from the timber and making his way deeper into the collapsing mine.

Fleeing goblins brushed by him as he went, some

begging him to turn around and leave with them. A few carried guttering torches, which helped Moon-eye make out the jagged tunnel walls and avoid the largest pieces of stone littering the floor. Some struggled with bulging sacks—fearing their whip-wielding taskmasters more than the quake and therefore not willing to abandon the precious ore they'd mined. One dragged a diminutive goblin with a crushed skull.

"Feyrh!" Moon-eye heard a large goblin shout at him. Run. Escape. Flee. The single shouted word was almost lost amid the continuing tremor and the slapping of the swarm of goblin feet against the floor.

Twice he fell when the mine shook violently. Both times he got back up and pressed deeper, only to fall again when a burly hobgoblin running in the opposite direction pushed him out of the way. *"Feyrh!"* the hobgoblin spit at him. *"Feyrh, dard!"*

Flee, fool!

Moon-eye shook his head and got up slowly in relief as the ground grew still and the rumbling quieted.

"Feyrh!" the hobgoblin called a last time before lumbering out of view.

"Cannot leave," Moon-eye said to himself. "Not without Graytoes." Broken shards of rock cut into his bare feet as he continued on. Then another tremor struck, and more falling debris bombarded his back and shoulders and set his small body to bleeding and aching fiercely. At a side tunnel, he waited for another group of fleeing miners to pass; then he sniffed the dust-choked air.

Moon-eye's sense of smell rivaled the finest hunting dog's. He sorted through the tang of the goblins' sweat and terror, the scent of the old bracing timbers, which were threatening to split at any moment, and the odor the very stone gave off. He sniffed the sweet traces of water. Rivulets always trickled down walls in parts of the mine from some hidden stream. He also picked up the disagreeable stench of waste. Permeating everything, blood was heavy in the air, and Moon-eye knew it was not just his, that many other miners had been injured.

How many injured?

How many dead?

"Graytoes!" He called twice more, then inhaled deeper and smelled the fetid odor of something rotting, a hint of sulfur, and the stink of a Dark Knight. One of the taskmasters was down that side passage, and he hoped the vile man didn't make it out alive.

Moon-eye disregarded all those scents and continued probing. He drew as much of the fusty air into his lungs as he could, over and over, finally finding the familiar scent he'd been searching for.

"Graytoes." His quest led him farther down the main tunnel. He started off at a careful lope just as the ground bucked even more strongly, once more sending him to his knees. The rumbling was like the sustained growl of some maddened beast, and it came from a specific direction.

Moon-eye looked over his shoulder and picked through the shadows to see a wall of earth and rocks rushing at him. Broken goblin limbs and a helmet that must have belonged to a Dark Knight roiled in the churning mix. The mass moved with a torrential speed, forcing the dank, dry air of the mine howling before it, bludgeoning the support timbers and shattering them and gathering the falling ceiling into itself before rushing on.

Moon-eye sped deeper down the main shaft, forcing himself to ignore the rocks biting at his feet and trying unsuccessfully to shut out the roaring cacophony so close behind him. He concentrated on the familiar scent; it came from yards distant. He turned at a side passage, then another, the second one angling upward and well away from the racing wall of earth. He leaped into the passage just as the ceiling gave way in the tunnel behind him.

"Graytoes!" Moon-eye thought he heard a reply to his call, though a part of him feared it was his imagination.

The ground shook again, and the odors all around intensified, settling in his mouth and threatening to overwhelm him. The dust filtering down was as thick as a curtain, and all Moon-eye could see were bands of black and gray. This tunnel was a more recent excavation, he realized, and the timbers were strong and fresh and—so far—holding.

"Graytoes!" Moon-eye crawled ahead, focusing on the remembered scent, constantly wiping his left eye with one hand while the fingers of his other hand felt along the wall to guide him. His right eye was a solid milky orb, oddly large and protruding from his leathery orange face. It was wholly worthless. The feature inspired his name, his father telling him that the eye reminded him of a full moon. Moon-eye had been born on a night when Krynn had only one moon, before the War of Souls. On the very night that Solinari, Lunitari, and Nuitari mysteriously returned, his family was captured by ogres and sold to the Dark Knights. When he was old enough to work, he had been sent to the mines, where he'd been toiling for years. He had no idea what had happened to his parents and siblings, lost like the single, large moon.

He passed a fissure in the stone, and through it came muted screams and the sound of rocks falling. He pressed his face into the crack and inhaled, registering and discarding one horrid odor after the next, before continuing down the passage.

It felt like an eternity, though he guessed it was only seconds, before the quaking took another pause and he stopped to catch his breath and steady his nerves. Moments later he reached a chamber filled with mounds of ore, buckets, picks, and crumpled bodies under chunks of stone. The nearest form was the only one breathing, a young female goblin whose legs were pinned by a fallen beam. A lantern that hung precariously from a crooked spike cast a soft glow on the scene.

"Graytoes." His voice caught as he moved toward his mate. Her skin was the color of sunflower leaves, but it looked dead and ashen from the stone dust. Her once-delicate features were marred by deep welts. "Moon-eye's Heart," he whispered as he knelt by her, smoothing at her cheeks with his calloused fingers, his gaze darting from her face to her trapped legs.

The blood he smelled in that place was not hers, so perhaps she was not too badly hurt. He gently touched her slightly rounded stomach, covered only by a canvas rag of a shift; she carried their first child.

"Moon." She sighed. Her eyes fluttered open, filled with pain and fear, and her thin, shaking fingers grabbed at him.

"Moon-eye's Heart," he said. "Must escape this place."

2

STEEL TOWN

One day earlier

Grallik rose just before dawn and stared across Steel Town. The buildings and the men blended in shades of gray and brown, as if someone painting the scene had used so much water that everything ran together to create a drab spectacle. The air was colored dully, too, from the dust swirling thickly. And it was heavy with sweat and waste and dirt. No amount of spitting could rid Grallik of the foul taste.

The Dark Knight mines were an extensive labyrinth, and piles of debris from the excavated tunnels lay everywhere, including right outside Grallik's door. The largest piles formed the northern and western boundaries of the camp, one the size of a hill, rising nearly a hundred feet and occasionally luring goats from the eastern mountains.

Grallik breathed shallowly and kept his eyes on the debris hills as he strolled to the center of the camp. He passed neatly maintained residences of wood and stone with colorful curtains at the windows, dingy shops that looked as if a strong wind would blow them over, and men

6

and women scurrying from one place to the next, all of them haggard-looking because of the dust and grime and stink that blew everywhere and stuck to them.

Grallik coughed and held a hand to his mouth. The cough had developed a year earlier, but came more frequently in recent weeks; he sometimes worried that it signaled a serious malady.

He did not have to be up at that early hour. He could stay in what passed for his home and wait until perhaps the breeze stilled and at least some of the dust settled. But long months ago it became his habit to rise early and watch the men, a mix of Dark Knights and paid laborers. The latter worked in hot, dry, and desolate Steel Town because the coin was good; the knights were posted there. Long before sunrise, the knights and workers were swinging heavy mallets at mounds of ore, smashing the rocks in a perfect, ceaseless cadence. The smaller chunks were easier for Grallik to deal with.

Grallik was Steel Town's resident wizard. A Thorn Knight, or a Gray Robe as some called him, he would have preferred a posting in Neraka or with an army in a more hospitable clime. But he'd taken the Blood Oath decades past and recited it every morning: "Submit or die," obey the will of his superiors and put all personal goals behind the aims of the Order. He accepted his duty in Steel Town because he believed in the words, and in the Code, the strict set of rules by which all the Dark Knights lived. He just wasn't as fervent about them as he had been in his younger days.

Grallik's ash-gray robe was always spotless, save for its hem, which was permanently colored brown by the clay and dust that spread from one end of Steel Town to the other. He wore his blond hair cropped so short that the slight points of his half-elf ears showed conspicuously, and he allowed not the faintest hint of stubble on an angular face that would have been handsome were half of it not horribly scarred.

Not only was the left side of Grallik's face disfigured, so was the entire left side of his body, his left hand twisted and the skin on that hand oddly shiny and forever looking wet.

There were scars elsewhere, but none so bad or notice-able—especially with his robe covering most of his features. All of them were the result of a fire that took his home and his parents and twin sister when he was little more than a child. His magic couldn't heal him. Not even prayer to Takhisis and Zeboim helped. And in all his years with the Dark Knights, serving alongside their priestly Skull Knights, and before that with the wizards, no one had been able to provide any relief.

Grallik no longer entertained any thoughts of improv-ing his appearance. He was intent merely on bettering his arcane knowledge and on doing his job, which at Steel Town entailed heating the rocks the Dark Knights and laborers were breaking up and forcing the iron out of them. The same fire that had taken his family and forever marred his appearance was part of his job. Fire fascinated him and served him well.

The wizard, using spells and charcoal, melted off the impurities and turned the ore into carbon steel so black-smiths—some of the best in that part of the country—could pound it out and fashion swords and armor for the Order.

There was never any halt in the work and never a change to the routine . . . not in the thirty-eight months he'd been there.

In the years before Grallik's arrival at Steel Town, the Dark Knights had used wagons to haul the ore to the capi-tal city, Jelek, and Neraka, where the ore was processed in forges with flues as tall as three men. Later the knights grew to rely on a smelter built at the camp to cull the iron ingots that were transported to weaponsmiths in the north and east. The smelter had fallen into disrepair, serving only to provide shade for one of the slave pens. It would likely never be used again, and that was because of Grallik and his skills.

One of the knights Grallik observed that morning acted sluggish, raising his mallet once for every two times his fellows did. The wizard noted the knight looked pale; perhaps he had acquired some ailment. Grallik took a few steps back to distance himself. He did not want to catch something in that desolate place where there were only four Skull Knights available for healing and none of them able to mend his scars or stop his cough.

Grallik dug his slippered foot into the earth as he continued to watch the Dark Knights and workers labor to turn large rocks into small ones. Sweat plastered their tunics and tabards against their bodies and slicked their hair against their faces. It was hot already, though the sun was not yet up. But it was not nearly so hot as Grallik would soon make the stone.

The rocks and stones had to be very hot indeed for him to leech the precious iron from them.

"Look," a knight said between swings. He pointed to a small volcano to the north of the camp, its cap glowing bright orange. "One of these days it's going to bury this place."

"The gods won't let that happen," another knight said. "Steel Town's too valuable to gods and men."

"Hell Town," Grallik muttered, thinking that was a better name for the camp. "Aye, Hell Town is far, far too valuable."

The commander currently in charge of Steel Town, a decorated veteran of the Chaos War, Marshal Denu Montrill of Solace, approached and stopped at Grallik's side. Montrill also rose early to supervise the knights and laborers.

"Marshal Montrill," Grallik said, greeting him. "The slaves have been collecting richer ore from the deep part of the mountain, and I pull more iron from those rocks. But I do not believe all of our efforts should be spent on that shaft. There is still iron in the older sections, and it would be a waste to leave it there. We should mine the older sections until they are dry. Leave nothing useful behind."

Montrill nodded. "True enough. Still, I've had the youngest and strongest slaves assigned to the new shaft. And I've sent word to the Nightlord that we need more blacksmiths. They cannot keep up with you regardless, Guardian Grallik. They can't forge the swords fast enough."

Montrill's eyes sparkled darkly as he added, "More blacksmiths and armorers for the fine, fine steel you provide."

The knights and laborers backed away from the rubble they'd created, took several deep breaths, then started shoveling it into a cart, mindful not to splash any stone or dust on the commander and Grallik.

"Thank you. And now I think I must go about my business, Marshal Montrill, rather than waste too much time. If you will excuse me." Grallik respectfully withdrew to his workshop, mentally preparing himself for the spells he was going to cast on the rocks. He hoped to finish at least one cart before the sun came up and the daily ritual began again.

⸻ ຣ ⸻

Grallik participated in the ritual that morning. He recited the words perfectly, though merely by rote on this occasion. His mind was elsewhere—on the second mound of ore waiting for him in his workshop; on his talon, which had been grumbling about the lack of water and being assigned a shift of digging the new well; on the mine, which he feared would be rich with ore for an eternity; on being trapped by his usefulness, there in Steel Town.

He did not eat breakfast with the officers, instead heading straight to his workshop after the ritual and starting work on the ore. He had no appetite, and he ignored his thirst. He concentrated on the fire he summoned to swirl around the damnable rocks.

The furnace made the workshop impossibly hot and drenched the wizard in sweat. His eyes, pale blue under the sun, shone as he worked, and his scarred skin glistened as the iron began to drip from the rocks and pool beneath them. It was not terrible work, he had to admit. Playing with the fire pleased him.

Grallik did not leave his workshop until the horn was blown for the evening meal, his empty stomach convincing him that it was finally time to eat. The light had gone out of his eyes, giving his angular face a forlorn cast, an expression that told the others in the crude hall to give him a wide berth. He was exhausted, but not physically in the way the knights who also sat at the tables were. His muscles didn't ache from pounding rocks as theirs did, though his chest ached from his coughing bouts. Still, he was fatigued to the point of collapse. Fire magic drained him. Grallik demanded too much of himself and the magic. It was a point of pride with him that he nurtured the flames until he could scarcely stand or breathe.

He sat at the end of a long table, two lengths of his arm separating him from the nearest knight. He caught the glance of a young man, the tavern owner's son, who desired to be a squire to the Dark Knights and who often worked the hall. The boy immediately filled a plate for him, bringing it while it still steamed. A half-filled mug of water, which was rationed even for officers, quickly followed. Dinner was some sort of meat pie, served in an appealing golden-brown crust. Grallik savored the smell of it before cutting it open. He suspected the recipe had been intended for venison or beef, but there were no deer in that part of the country, and the Dark Knights did not keep cattle at the camp. So mutton had been used instead, and not liberally.

The pie was mostly made of chopped prunes and dates, with raisins lining the bottom. The fruits were readily available at Steel Town, as knights coming in for rotations brought wagons of supplies with them. There was a small side of a spinach pudding, and though it was reasonably tasty, Grallik thought the cook had used too much fennel. Dessert consisted of pears poached in wine and covered with a sweet syrup. All of it was passable, he decided. For the knights, the food was not bad at Steel Town.

When he was sated, he returned to the ore and went back to work until he nearly passed out, emerging before midnight in search of a bit of welcome coolness. But there was none. Despite the lateness, it was still uncomfortably hot.

It was darker than he expected, as the clouds had grown thick since dinner and stretched in all directions as if they were sealing Steel Town and the mine away from the stars. Lightning flickered through the thunderheads, and Grallik could see curtains fluttering in open windows. He heard the pine trees shaking—no doubt shedding their needles.

He was irritable for a reason he couldn't define and blamed his foul mood on the starless sky. He lifted his head until he was staring straight up, feeling dizzy as he continued to watch the lightning fingers. Grallik breathed deep, hoping to find the scent of water in the clouds, something to cut the heat and override the odors of the knights and the stable and nearest livestock pen—and the worse stench that wafted from the slave pens.

Grallik faintly smelled the pine trees, and wood smoke coming from the chimney of the tavern, even the iron nuggets in his workshop. He could always detect the smell of iron. The air that stirred the scents around him seemed trapped under the clouds, however, and made the world feel suffocating and cloying.

The thunderheads continued to pulse with lightning, and faint booms chased each other. The ground shuddered slightly under Grallik's feet, but not a single drop of rain fell. His scarred flesh tingled with anger and anticipation.

There must be a storm, Grallik prayed. Something to relieve the hell of Steel Town, to drown out the stench that swelled under the cloud dome, to turn the damnable dust into damnable mud, to clear the air, however briefly, so he could breathe easier and stop coughing.

If he had the right magic, he'd try something to coax the clouds into giving up the rain. But he didn't, and his magic was all but spent that night anyway.

He heard the crack of thick lightning and the rumble that followed it. He heard the guttural conversation of goblin and hobgoblin slaves, the whinny of horses, the laughter of someone in the tavern, the clink of mugs, the growl of the massive hatori—the huge digging beast kept near the base of the southern mine. He wished to hear the drumming of rain.

Water might be at a premium, but the proprietor across the way had wine and ale and liquor aplenty. He dropped his gaze to the warm glow that spilled from the tavern window. He would buy something strong with the coins in his pocket, and he would sit in a corner by himself.

3

THE LISTENER

The rising sun colored the mountains the shade of ripening plums and the flat expanses between the peaks a deep rose. Clouds scudded across the sky, too high to cool the ground, however, and cruelly scenting the air with the possibility of rain. There'd been no rain for too long. The Dark Knights' crops had withered, and the pines that grew in the fertile earth at the base of volcanoes had started to drop their needles.

The camp's well had dried up four days earlier and crews were working to dig another one. The Skull Knights cast spells to create water, but there were not enough of them to supply what the population of Steel Town needed. The knights drank first, then the hired laborers and the horses. If there was any water left, the slaves and livestock shared it. Sometimes the slaves were allowed one sip, and so they sought places in the mine where the walls were wet from hidden streams.

Mudwort had not had a swallow of water in more than a day. She should have looked forward to her stint in the

14

mine, where she could lick at the rivulets running from cracks in the ceiling. But that day, though she was terribly thirsty, she didn't care to be anywhere in the deep tunnels and chambers.

More than five hundred goblins, toting thick canvas bags, picks, and shovels, wended their way up a narrow trail lined with jagged black rocks toward a gaping hole in the mountainside. Already three times that many were at work in other areas of the mines, and one thousand more were either just returning from shifts or sleeping in the pens, waiting to be woken up for their next turn in the mines. Always, there were goblins working, working.

Only Mudwort knew for certain that disaster would touch that day.

She angled her face to the sun then glanced down the mountain to take in a sweeping view of all Steel Town. That was not the camp's true name, but it was what the Dark Knights and the laborers had come to call it. The camp sat in the shadow of three volcanoes, which were usually glowing, the smallest making a grander show than the others. The volcanoes were an impressive sight, especially at night, and sometimes ribbons of lava would twist down their sides. But the lava never reached the camp, and the steam that rose from the domes never did more than tinge the air with sulfur.

Originally, the camp was called Iverton, after Rudger Leth-Iver, a little-known commander with scant military ability, but who had—three decades past—discovered rich deposits of magnetite and hematite southwest of Jelek in the foothills of the Khalkists. The ores, rich with iron, were superior grade, and Leth-Iver named the camp in his own honor.

In Iverton's first years, only knights worked the mine. But as time passed, laborers were hired from various towns in Neraka; then goblin and hobgoblin slaves were brought in. Finally, slaves, aided by priestly magic and by great beasts such as the hatori, which were chained in places below the earth, dug the tunnels. Only a handful of knights had to venture into the mines with each shift under their charge.

In the beginning, the camp consisted of a sprawl of tents, but in time those gave way to crude barracks and finally to permanent buildings of stone and imported wood and pens and shanties for the goblin and hobgoblin slaves. Iverton even boasted a tavern and gaming hall, a stable and blacksmith's shop, a trading post, and a dozen houses for the families who operated the businesses. There were large pens for goats, pigs, and sheep, a coop for chickens, and a long, tilled section for a garden when the weather cooperated.

Iverton's population nowadays hovered between two hundred and three hundred fifteen knights—from five wings to a full compgroup. The number varied according to the rotation and the amount of ore mined at any given time from the shafts. In addition, there were forty hired laborers, a half dozen business owners, and three thousand slaves. Nearly all of the latter were goblins, who were small creatures that could be easily herded into pens.

From her mountainside perch, Mudwort snarled at the Dark Knights standing before Marshal Montrill. In perfect lines and in full armor, they were kneeling with bowed heads.

After a moment of silence, their voices rose as a sonorous hum. Mudwort picked her way through the drone and recognized some of the words. It was the knights' Blood Oath, she knew, and they would repeat it five times. Interspersed among the words was something the knights called the Code—but neither ritual interested the goblin. In fact, Mudwort considered it all a blather, a useless waste of time and saliva.

THE REBELLION

The Dark Knights should listen, instead, to other words, words that truly mattered: Mudwort's words.

Mudwort had tried to tell the Dark Knights about the coming earthquake, though she didn't call it a quake. Mudwort had no word for what was imminent because she didn't know precisely what *it* was. She only knew that something bad was going to happen, as the stones she recently had touched in the mine felt . . . *nervous.* Yes, they were nervous stones, almost as though they were living things.

Mudwort became frightened by the way the rocks seemed to tremble in her hands, and so the previous day she'd told a Dark Knight taskmaster that something bad was going to happen and that everyone should leave the mine and not come back until the bad thing had passed. But the stupid knight would not listen to her, nor would the other knights she risked speaking to when her shift ended. She should have known better; the knights only pretended to listen to the goblins' snuffling pleas for mercy or their begging for extra rations and water; they thought goblin words were all twaddle and worthless.

The knights treated all the goblins as worthless.

And when she tried to tell the knights a second and a third time about the coming *something*—even using a smattering of words in their own ugly-sounding tongue, shouting them out from the slave pen—they still dismissed her and, later, beat her for the noise she had made. The lacerations from the whip still burned her back, and the wounds opened and bled freshly as she trundled with her fellows into the shaft and to a deep chamber and stretched with the pick to begin work on her section of the wall.

She had warned her clansmen too, whispering to them late the night before and encouraging them to pass the word to the other slaves working in the other shafts and chambers, including the smattering of hobgoblins among them.

Only a few goblins believed her. Some said they did, but she knew they were just being respectful. Most called her mad behind her back and some even to her face, laughing when she claimed the rocks were nervous. In the dozen years Mudwort had been a slave in the Nerakan mine, she'd never been sociable and had talked more to herself and the walls of the mine than to her fellows.

She couldn't fault them for thinking her crazy.

In the slave pens, she usually claimed a corner, where she sat, back against the post, meditating or at least making the pretense. The others gave her as much space as possible. Mudwort had something special about her, and they alternately feared and revered her—the latter particularly when it was cold and she did something to warm the ground beneath them.

At dinner she was usually last in line. She was overly skinny for a goblin—food held little interest for her. A one-eared hobgoblin often forced her to eat to keep her strength up. He was called Direfang and was the closest thing Mudwort had to a friend. Direfang was probably the only one who honestly halfway believed her when she told him that something bad was going to happen to the mine.

But the broad-shouldered hobgoblin told her ruefully that there was nothing he could do about the coming *something*. There was nothing he could do about anything; hob and gob slaves had no power in that world. Though he had advanced to the position of foreman, he couldn't order the goblins out of the mines, not even to keep them safe from whatever it was Mudwort was predicting. And he wouldn't dare argue with the Dark Knights over the matter. Mudwort had gotten nowhere by calling to the knights, and Direfang had no desire to be whipped as she had or to make the knights so angry that they revoked his meager foreman privileges.

Mudwort became certain of the coming *something* just

the previous morning. In one of the shafts in the very deepest part of the Nerakan mine, she was chipping with her pick at a wall of iron-heavy ore when a shiver passed through her. She picked up chunks to put in her sack, and felt the *difference*. It was like the stones were trying to tell her something, warn her about something bad that was coming. But she admitted she couldn't thoroughly understand the warning.

"Mad, maybe," Mudwort had said to herself at the time. "Mind-breaking, maybe. Mind-sour and sad."

She was working at that same station, pausing because the whip marks still hurt and because she was doing her best to listen to the stones. She pressed her ear against the wall. Mudwort always had been interested in rocks, as a youngling playing with them, sucking on them, or arranging them into patterns that others thought nonsensical. Until she'd been enslaved, she hadn't known that rocks had names.

But they did, according to the knights. At that moment she was mining for hematite. It was a metallic gray stone, occasionally earthy brown, with thin, bright red streaks in it. It was relatively brittle, as far as rocks went, and sometimes there were crystals in it that sparkled in the lantern light. She'd previously mined in a higher shaft for magnetite, a black stone with a shiny luster. It was heavier and broke at uneven, sharp angles under her pick. She preferred mining for hematite. Her sacks were not quite so heavy when filled with the metallic stone, and her arms did not ache so badly when carrying the sacks to the mine entrance.

The shaft wall felt cool to her ear, the sensation washing through her and easing the pain of her back. She stuck out her tongue and tasted the wall, finding the ore dusty and not unpleasant. Then she ran her fingers across the wall, ignoring the complaint of a stoop-shouldered goblin behind her.

"Trouble, Mudwort," he lectured. "Whip, no work. Work, no whip."

She dismissively waggled her fingers at him then ran her hands across the wall again. The stone felt *different* that day too, even more anxious, almost shivering. Worse than the previous morning, she decided after a moment.

"Trouble, yes," Mudwort agreed. "Trouble here. But trouble what?"

The stoop-shouldered goblin shook his head in disgust, spitting in Mudwort's direction. He turned back to his wall and found a spot where the hematite was particularly dark and started swinging his pick energetically at the spot.

The chamber they worked in had a low ceiling, like nearly every place in the mines. But goblins could easily stand upright there. The walls were dark and the lantern light meager, and that chamber—like most of the others—appeared to be closing in on the slaves. The closeness of the walls kept them in a constant state of skittishness. The air was perpetually stale, the stench of the miners' sweat so strong it often caused them to gag and work even faster so they could fill up their sacks and carry them to the mine entrance, where they had a chance to suck down better air.

It was easy to get lost in the tunnels, there being so many of them and all of them having a similar appearance—dark, narrow, braced by timbers that never appeared thick enough to be safe support. There wasn't a day when some goblin miners did not make it out at the end of their shift and were found by slaves in the next rotation. But Mudwort prided herself on the fact that she had never gotten lost.

"Saying what?" Again Mudwort put her ear to the wall. The ore sounded as if it were purring, and she imagined that it was trying to speak to her—her and her alone because only she would listen. "Stone is saying, saying what?" After several frustrating moments, she stepped away from the wall, head hung in defeat. "Saying nothing. Mind sour and broken."

She fixed her gaze on the spot still wet from her tongue. Wielding her pick, she struck at that place again and again until chunks started dropping to the floor. "Saying nothing. Saying nothing." Mudwort forced away thoughts about the nervous rocks and focused on striking the stone, knocking loose only the darkest, smoothest pieces of hematite. She knew the heaviest deposits of ore were in the darkest rocks.

Sometimes slaves were rewarded with food or water when they brought out sacks with prime ore. Mudwort was very thirsty, so she kept hammering at the wall, striking harder and faster as if she were angry at it. Perhaps the knights would give her water if she found some very fine ore.

Perhaps they would give her more than a sip.

She should have taken a sip the day before or that morning. She should have stood in line for it.

She'd already made four trips to the mine entrance where other slaves waited to take the mined ore down to the camp. Each time she received another empty sack to fill. There'd been talk for months that the knights would start using carts to take the ore down to the camp to ease the slaves' workload. But so far that rumor had not materialized. Mudwort had to drag her sack to the entrance each time because she'd filled it so full.

On the fourth trip to the entrance, she noticed the first significant vibration. Suddenly the stone rumbled softly against the bottoms of her feet. Mudwort shivered and tried taking her full ore sack down the mountainside herself so she could get away from the mine and the *something* she believed was coming soon. But that was not her assigned task that morning, carrying ore down the mountain, so the knight stationed at the entrance pointed her back inside.

She was making her seventh trip to the entrance, again

with a full sack, when the vibrations grew stronger and the mountain gave a jump beneath her. She grabbed the support beams at the mouth of the mine before she could be sent careening down the side of the mountain. The notion of death didn't scare her. That would be a welcome end to slavery. But she didn't want to bounce on rocks all the way down. She detested pain.

She lurched outside the mine entrance, holding her breath, knees bent to help keep her balance, sack of ore at her feet. There were plenty of sacks nearby, some that she and other slaves had brought out that had not yet been hauled down the trail. The Dark Knight taskmaster at the edge of the trail looked down at Steel Town with a worried expression.

Curious—Mudwort was always curious—she crept forward to see what he was watching, sucking in a deep breath and stopping when a crack appeared between her feet and splintered, looking like a stony spiderweb spreading forward to the trail and behind her to the beams at the mine entrance. It might not be terribly painful to be swallowed by the mountain, she thought, certainly not as painful as bouncing down the rocky slope. Being swallowed would be a fast death. The crack grew wider, and Mudwort scampered forward to stand directly next to the taskmaster, ready to grab his leg for support. He didn't notice her. He was intent on keeping his own balance and watching the camp below.

Mudwort followed his gaze.

People were scurrying like insects roused from a nest. They rushed from building to building, some grabbing the young ones and holding them tight. She imagined the knights were shouting to each other, the laborers and their wives and children screaming in fear. But she couldn't hear them over the rising rumbling sound of the mountain and, she realized, the worse rumbling of the ground far below the mountain. All the land within Mudwort's line of sight shook. Perhaps the flat expanse between the volcanoes, where Steel Town rested, was faring even worse than the mine.

As she watched, a barracks collapsed in on itself, the roof caving in first then the walls buckling. Puffs of dirt rose up, obscuring the jumble of stones and wood. She hoped that Dark Knights were caught inside and killed, but she suspected they would survive because the roof had not been made of material heavy enough to break their skulls.

Across from the ruined barracks was the stone and wood tavern, which she'd many times dreamed of visiting. It had been years and years since Mudwort had a decent meal and something strong to drink. The tavern seemed to bounce up in the air, the stones spat out of its walls, and the wood planks splintered and broke. The thatch roof burst apart, some of it dropping inside, the rest blowing in clumps across the camp in a hot wind that had suddenly picked up. A man ran out a side door, dragging a goblin-sized boy behind him. The doorframe collapsed, and what was left of the walls heaved inward. The man and boy dropped a few feet from the ruins, hugging each other.

More people were on the ground as the world bucked like a wild beast intent on throwing off its rider. Despite Mudwort's keen vision, it was difficult to pick out everything that was happening. She was too far away, and the quake was sending up clouds of dirt and dust that were blocking her sight. She suspected the dirt clouds were choking the people and hoped all the Dark Knights choked and died.

Everything became a jarring blur. Mudwort watched many horses bolt out of the stables and jump the fence, scattering and losing themselves in the dust clouds and the foothills. The other animals moved like a wave from one side of the pens to the other. Goats and sheep made sounds shrill enough that the ruckus carried up to Mudwort. Chickens flew from the big coop that had been ripped apart by the shuddering land.

The ground buckled in the center of the camp. Even from her mountain perch, Mudwort felt the throbbing pulse. The ground lifted walls and men, pitching them over. Geysers of sand erupted, stretching eighty or more feet high. Above them, clouds of screeching birds flew in all directions.

Sulfur clouds appeared, their stench spreading over the camp and up the side of the mountain. In the distance, through the dusty, gassy haze, Mudwort spotted flashing lights emitted by rocks being squeezed and smashed together.

Blessed chaos, she thought, a smile playing across her leathery, flat face. The Dark Knights' precious mining camp was collapsing into a ruin before her watering eyes. Not a building stood wholly intact as the quake intensified. A fissure yawned, starting between the abandoned well and the trading post and racing to what was left of the stables, widening and deepening as it moved and sucked in Dark Knights and laborers and any animals in its path. Bodies disappeared in the roiling ground, a few hands scrambling for a hold along the edges of the fissure then disappearing. One Dark Knight held on for a moment, and Mudwort feared he might save himself. But then the edge of the fissure crumbled, and his gloved hands dropped out of sight.

The forms were tiny, so far below her, and the dirt and dust continued to billow. Still, one figure managed to distinguish itself from the others, and Mudwort knew that it was Marshal Montrill. The feared and despised commander shouted orders that only the closest Dark Knights could hear.

Who cares? Words. More useless words, she thought. Only what the earth spoke mattered at that moment.

It spoke of vengeance, she guessed, angry about what the

Dark Knights had done to it—digging their wells and digging their mine, reaching into the belly of the world and pulling out precious ore meant to stay safe and buried. Or perhaps it spoke of sadness, that the mountain had been pierced and robbed and hollowed out, that once-perfect tower from ancient times.

Mudwort listened to the mountain cry and the ground far below answer.

The earth spoke of sadness and pain, she recognized, hearing each word emphasized against the soles of her toughened feet. It spoke of retribution against every living thing that walked across its face—the Dark Knights and townsmen and goblins and hobgoblins. The Dark Knights in the camp were driven to their knees, then to their bellies, the earth demanding they stay down and humbly prostrate themselves.

The finest-looking building, the residence for Marshal Montrill and his officers, had fared well up to that point, but Mudwort watched with glee as, finally, the tile roof swayed and rattled to pieces; one of the walls collapsed outward, burying a knight under a pile of stone and boards. The dust swirled too darkly for her to tell if the man was killed.

"By the Dark Queen's heads!" the knight beside Mudwort cried in anguish. His hand clasped the pommel of his sheathed sword and his gaze flickered from the destruction below to the path he stood on. More spiderweb cracks shot under him, lacing up and down the mountainside. "By all the . . ."

In that moment Mudwort moved behind him and threw her shoulder against the back of his legs. He dropped off the side of the trail and started rolling down the mountainside. Mudwort grabbed at the edge to keep from following him, spreading her arms and legs flat against the trail as the ground heaved. Her teeth clacked against each other, and she feared her bones would shatter, but she peered over the edge, watching the Dark Knight carom over jagged rocks, bouncing up with arms and legs flailing, coming down and rolling some more. His helmet flew off and his tabard shredded and flapped away like a blackbird taking flight. She thought she saw his sword come free, glinting in the bright sun and disappearing in the dust. He landed unmoving, speared on a rock spike.

Mudwort hated the Dark Knights more than she hated anything, and she wished them all dead. But she hadn't thought herself capable of killing one of them. Had she been a god-worshiping creature, she thought she might have felt a moment of regret for her deed. She heard some of the gods frowned upon killing and promised punishment for any of their followers who committed murderous acts. Good thing she was a godless creature, she decided, smiling wider when she saw another fissure open up wide down below and turn into a chasm that swallowed another barracks, what was left of a residence, and several futilely-fleeing souls. A heartbeat later the chasm closed, like a great dragon snapping its jaws shut. She struggled to hear the screams, hearing instead the groan of timbers behind her, wood snapping and rocks tumbling. Then there were more screams, but those were goblin and hobgoblin voices, coming from behind her, in the mountain itself.

She looked over her shoulder to see goblins rushing out of the mine, falling as the trail pitched and the mountain shifted. Some of them crawled past her, others picked themselves up and hurried down the trail, dropping sacks of ore as they went and pushing their slower fellows aside. One of them tripped and fell off the side of the trail, arms flailing. A few of them called to her, urging her up. But she stayed on her stomach, gripping the edge of the trail even tighter.

They would probably die in their race down the trail, she thought. Better to die high on the mountain, watching the Dark Knights go first to whatever hell their gods summoned them to. She leaned her ear against the ground, listening to the earth alternately purr and shout angrily. She hadn't expected the rumbling to stop, not while she still breathed. But it did.

Mudwort was disappointed, preferring that all of Steel Town should have been swallowed, every last brick and Dark Knight. But a small part of her was relieved that the ground was sated, and that she and many of the goblins and hobgoblins she knew were safe. She forced herself to relax then pushed herself to her knees, looking over the side.

The dust clouds thinned and settled, giving her a better view of the carnage. All of the buildings were broken and a few dozen armored knights were dead. Goblins were dead too, the ones who had been sleeping at the northern end of the largest slave pen. A hole had opened up there and sucked them down. Many more goblins were crushed and dead in the mine—she'd heard the screams and the rocks and timbers falling.

Then another tremor shot through the mountain, dropping Mudwort so hard her chin struck the trail and she bit off the tip of her tongue. Blood filled her mouth and she spit it out as she pushed herself to her feet and backed away from the edge. She put her back to the mountain near the mine entrance, continuing to spit out the blood. She cursed at the sharp pain that was strong enough to make her forget her aches from the lash marks from the taskmaster's whip.

More goblins rushed from the mine, most of them injured, with blood running down their arms and legs. A hobgoblin foreman toted a goblin over one shoulder and cradled another small one to his chest.

"Direfang . . ." Even as Mudwort spoke his name, she realized the hobgoblin wasn't her familiar friend. That foreman was not quite big enough, and he had two ears.

"Direfang is below still," the hobgoblin told her. "In the mine still. Helping still." The goblin he cradled tried to say something too, but only blood came out of his mouth. He was broken on the inside, and Mudwort knew he wouldn't live to see the bottom of the trail.

The ground shuddered more fiercely and belched more sulfur into the dirty air.

From far below, she heard a cry that the hatori had been loosed.

4

THE DIGGING BEAST

The Dark Knights called the great digging beast a
hatori, but the goblins and hobgoblins referred to it
as a dragon of the earth. Nearly thirty feet long—half the
size it could eventually grow to—the one at the camp was
acquired from ogre merchants two summers past at the
same cost as three hundred goblin slaves.

It resembled a crocodile, but it had a scaly hide as hard
as granite, pebbled brown and gray in hue, and pupiless eyes
the color of eggshells. It looked like a stretch of uneven rock
when it rested. The only thing that hinted it was alive were
its eyes, which never seemed to close, and the faint rise and
fall of its flanks from its breathing.

A thick chain was wrapped around its chest and neck,
like an elaborate dog harness, the end of it affixed to a thick
post that had been driven deep into the ground. The chain
was short, no longer than the length of a big horse. The
hatori liked to dig, and if the chain were longer, the beast
would bury itself under the ground and be hard to unearth.

It had two handlers: the Dark Knights Ramvin and

Ostan. They and a handful of other knights led it by the chain, like a man might tug a fighting mastiff, and they brought it into the mines each day. The knights would not have been sufficient to hold the creature—it was all muscle and teeth—but they teased it along with chunks of mutton and fat rats, both of which the hatori considered a delicacy, and they kept it constantly drugged with elixirs that were concocted by a priest who lived in Jelek. It was drugged just enough to be sluggish, never so much that it could not do its work.

Its claws were harder than the stone of the mountain, and with coaxing and prodding, the hatori dug the deepest tunnels for the knights—excavating more in a few hours than it would take a hundred goblins working several shifts to manage. The beast was treated better than the hobgoblin and goblin slaves, and the Dark Knights were more leery and respectful of it. The hatori never dug more than a few hours a day. The knights did not want to risk drugging it too much and inadvertently killing it. Neither did they want to tax it; the beast was too valuable an asset, and there were more than enough goblins to widen the tunnels the hatori had started.

The handler Ostan was just outside the hatori's pen when the quake first struck. The knight was pitched to the ground. He hadn't seen the cracks appear in the dry earth, one of them running through the ground where the post stood in the hatori's pen. As the cracks widened, the post tilted.

And the great digging beast stirred.

Ostan picked himself up just as the post slipped into the crack. He had the presence to yell for help and the sense not to venture into the pen alone to try to stop the hatori.

The creature watched the post sink out of view, tugging the chain with it. The hatori was so massive that for long moments the post dangled in what had become a crevice, held by the chain wrapped around the creature's chest.

"Trelane! Bring as many men as you can spare," Ostan hollered. "The beast is breaking loose!"

Indeed it was. The crevice was closing; the ground was continuing to rumble and causing the slats of the pen to bounce and rattle. Ostan nearly fell over again.

"Trelane! Be fast!" Ostan held tight with one hand to a top slat and drew his sword with the other, furtively glancing around and watching Steel Town begin to disintegrate around him. "The beast, it—"

It growled then, a sound Ostan had heard only a few times before. And though the quake was causing a considerable uproar, the growl of the hatori could be heard above it. The sound started as a low rumble, mimicking the upheaval of the earth, then rose in intensity until it became so high-pitched that Ostan had to drop his sword and hold his hands to his ears.

There was a snap, the sound of the chain breaking as the crevice sealed itself, with the hatori helping by rearing back at the same time on its stubby crocodile legs. The end of the chain swung back and cracked against the fence where Ostan stood.

Ostan couldn't hear the pounding of feet as a dozen knights and two laborers, the latter carrying coils of rope, raced toward the pen. The men vaulted over debris spilled from rock piles and widening cracks in the earth as they approached, some shouting words that were lost in the cacophony.

"We can't lose the hatori!" cried the first knight to reach the pen. "Slaves, they can die, and they can be replaced. We might never gain another one of these."

He slipped between slats, the knights and men following him, Ostan squeezing in from the other side after he regained his sword.

The creature growled again, the sound so hurtful it was

like a punch to the stomach of the two laborers, and the knights nearby scooped up the ropes, gritting their teeth and charging forward.

"Get a rope around its neck!" Ostan shouted. He tossed a chunk of mutton in front of the hatori; he'd pulled it from a pouch that was filled with such treats.

The hatori momentarily ceased growling. Distracted, it snapped at the meat. Then it raised its head on its stubby neck, opening its jaws wide to growl again. One knight darted in and looped a rope around its neck and tried to jump back.

But the ground bucked beneath him and sent him to his back, and before his fellows could grab the rope, the hatori swung around and bit the knight in half.

The beast swung toward the other handlers. Already close to the ground on its short legs, it didn't seem bothered by the quake. It lashed out with its tail, striking Ostan in the thighs with enough force to slam him back into the slats of the pen. The knight burst through and hit his head hard on the earth, his helmet worsening the blow and rendering him unconscious.

Eleven knights were left on their feet to swarm the digging beast, looping another length of rope around its neck. Four threw themselves across the hatori's tail so it couldn't flail easily, their weight helping to pin the beast.

"We've got it!" one of the knights called. He gestured with his head to the hatori's back, and three of the knights jumped on the back of the creature, trying to subdue it with their weight.

But the quake kept going and going. It seemed to go on forever, though in truth the disaster took only a few minutes—but it was long enough to spread more cracks in the ground and to tear apart what was left of the hatori's pen.

The ropes around its neck were thick but not as strong as the thick chains that usually held it in place. And the drugs that normally dulled its senses had been shaken off by the excitement of the quake and its near escape.

It thrust its claws into the still-shaking ground and thrashed its head back and forth. At the same time, it pushed itself up—enough to knock a few of the men off its back.

"We're losing the beast!" One of the knights on its tail clung desperately as the creature thrashed. "We must . . ." The rest of his words were lost as the hatori lurched forward and dug furiously with its front claws, thrust its snout into loose earth, and dived underground.

Most of the knights were sent flying as it whipped its tail back and forth, rolling over once as it continued its dive, crushing the sole knight who had managed to hang on to its back. Then it was gone, disappeared into the ground, ropes and chain with it.

The quake continued as the knights fought to regain their feet and rushed to see if Ostan was alive.

5

DIREFANG

Mudwort grabbed onto a thick timber at the mine entrance. Cracks ran along the length of the wood, and a piece had peeled away at the top. Splinters pierced her fingers as she held on tighter and stared into the maw of the mine, hearing more screams and more rocks crashing. The air that wafted out was stale and filled with stone dust and the smell of dying goblins.

"Direfang!" Mudwort shouted with as much volume as she could summon. "Direfang!"

There was no answer, just more screams and the loud crash of falling rocks and the groan of the timber to which she desperately clung. The bottoms of her feet still registered the heated words of the earth, but she was too preoccupied to pick anything out of the snarling and shouting. She was worried for her friend, Direfang, because if the hobgoblin died inside the mountain, who would force her to eat? Who would share stories of the time before they were slaves?

She would not miss the other goblins and hobgoblins

who were dead or dying—though she would feel some remorse at their passing since more work would be assigned to her and the other survivors.

But she would actually miss Direfang. Better to either save him or die with him, she decided after a moment's reflection.

She drew a deep breath, and when the rumbling eased, she took a first tentative step into the mine . . . then another and another. There were split bracing timbers and cross-pieces, and a place where part of the ceiling had collapsed, almost blocking the shaft. But it wasn't blocked enough to prevent a small goblin from squeezing through. Mudwort went forward, deeper, eyes peering into the shadows and fingers running along the stone wall to her left, tracking the faint vibrations.

Scarcely aware of her surroundings, she plodded on, instinctively stepping over rubble. She paused once and put her ear to the chest of a fallen goblin whose head was hidden by a jumble of rocks: no life. She paused again at a goblin and a hobgoblin lying curled together in the center of the tunnel, as though they'd fallen asleep. Scratches were deep on the hobgoblin's arm, but there was not much blood and no sign that rocks had crushed them.

Dead from fear?

She searched their bodies to see if by some wonder either had possessed a waterskin or if there was something tasty in their pockets that she could give to Direfang when she found him. They had nothing.

She knew where her hobgoblin friend had been assigned that day. She had spotted him toiling in a winding, narrow side tunnel when she hauled out her fifth or sixth sack of ore. She followed the main tunnel down until she reached a branch that would take her to Direfang's workstation.

The ground purred ominously as she went, and stone dust filtered down and caked her eyes. There were many piles of rocks and broken beams and crosspieces to wend her way around, and she stumbled and tripped more than once. Mudwort cursed in the old tongue; she was normally so sure-footed.

She squeezed through a crevice that hadn't been there before the quake and paused to press her face against the wall. Water ran down the wall, but not the thin rivulets she often saw—no, a wide stream that thrilled her. She drank more than her fill, not stopping until she feared her belly would burst. Then she cupped her hands to the stream and splashed it over her, turning until her back was flat against the wall. The water eased the pain from the whip marks.

She thought she could stand like that forever. The stream of water was more pleasant than the infrequent rains and she did not have to share it with anyone. The water pooled around her feet and ran into a thick crack. Mudwort listened to the soft splash it made against her shoulders and neck and believed there was nothing more wonderful in all the world than that very spot in the accursed Nerakan mine. The glorious water, all hers. The knights would not be back for a long time. Oh, eventually they would use their priests and wizard to move the rocks and order the slaves back in with their picks and shovels. But that would take time because they had no digging beast anymore.

Perhaps it would take forever.

She momentarily forgot about the whip marks on her back and about Direfang, forgot she was a slave and that she was hungry and could well starve if she stayed put. She thought only about the glorious water and the way it felt running wetly over her. She stretched her bony arms above her head and let her fingers play in the water then touched the backs of her hands to the stone and felt the rocks stirring again.

Mudwort bent to the faint tremor, trying to discern a meaning in the gentle vibration that pulsed through the stone. The grumbling ground had caused so much destruction already, had made some tunnels barely passable, had made other tunnels not passable at all, and had killed so many goblins.

What more destruction could the ground demand?

She concentrated, able to put more effort into deciphering the words since the water had filled her and lulled her. She could hear distinct words, in her own language. Mudwort slipped back around to face the wall, held her breath, and pressed her nose and mouth against it.

"What say?" She'd not tried talking to the rocks before. And she did not really expect them to reply. Still, she put her ear to the stone, all the while reveling in the feel of the water sluicing over her. "What say? Please say again."

She heard more words, soft yet sounding horribly urgent. A moment more and she realized she recognized the voice. It wasn't the rock speaking, it was her friend Direfang, and somehow his words were being transmitted through the wall of the mine. Taking a last long gulp of water, she pushed away from the blessed stream and followed the narrow shaft.

Another turn, another short passage, and she caught the flicker of a lantern ahead. Direfang was holding the lantern in one hand and clawing at a jumble of rocks with the other. The ceiling had entirely collapsed on that part of the tunnel, and from behind the rubble came the cries of trapped slaves.

Direfang was nearly seven feet tall, the largest hobgoblin in the slave pens, easily twice Mudwort's height. He had to stoop in a tunnel that was at best six feet high. His hairy dark gray hide was covered with chips of stone and dust, and there were places on his upper arms and chest where the hair had been ripped away and blood glistened fresh. His broad face was covered with dark splotches that would soon become ugly bruises, his pug nose and his chin were badly skinned, and the pair of trousers he wore—some of the hobgoblin foremen had clothes—were shredded.

"Mudwort help." Direfang cocked his head, the side without an ear toward the goblin, and gestured with his hand that held a rock. "Mudwort!" It came out as an order, in a stern voice he typically reserved for the slaves he supervised, and Mudwort's narrowed eyes and curled lip made it clear she did not like his tone. "Help now, Mudwort." This repeated order was even sterner and punctuated with a growl.

Mudwort, still wonderfully wet and refreshed, glared at her friend and turned to face the collapsed tunnel he stood near. She did not pull out rocks, as Direfang continued to do, but studied them. For a moment she considered returning to the place where the water ran freely down the wall, then her gaze locked onto a large stone shot through with blood red veins. She touched it then another stone and another.

None of the rocks there felt *different*. Neither did the flat of the stone floor or the intact sections of tunnel walls she brushed with her hands. But the purring had stopped. She couldn't ascribe any emotions to the stone, certainly not the nervousness she'd sensed before. They seemed to be . . . at peace, she decided after a moment. So the mountain was finally sated and the mine was done—done shaking. She released a great breath and closed her eyes in relief.

Mudwort didn't see Direfang scowl at her, but she did hear him shuffle away and, with a *tink*, set his lantern down somewhere behind them.

She leaned forward until her chin touched the jumble of rocks. She tasted one, spitting out the dust that thickly covered it, then placed her damp palms against a few of the smoother stones.

"Here," Mudwort pointed to a section as close to the ceiling as she could reach. "Rocks thin." Mudwort ran her fingers over the rubble again to be sure, stretching as high as she could. Then she let out another deep breath and started plucking the smaller rocks out from a spot just over her head, careful not to cause a cascade that could bury her. She carried the rocks away from the collapsed pile, setting them against the wall near the lantern. She saw spatters of blood on the base of the lantern, starting to dry and turning dark, and she glanced at Direfang. Both of his clawed hands were bleeding from pulling at the rocks. Her back bled fresh too; she'd opened the whip marks with her stretching.

The lantern oil had burned out by the time they managed to create a hole in the rubble big enough for a lean hobgoblin to squeeze through. Though the mine was black as pitch, Mudwort and Direfang could still see well enough to help the first slave through, then another, one after the next. All of goblinkind saw reasonably well in the dark, but the lanterns made things easier, and they'd been relying heavily on them in the mine. One of the goblins on the other side also had a lantern and carefully passed it through. It cast an eerie glow on the debris and battered survivors.

Mudwort recognized only a few of the slaves. None of them mined in her tunnel and perhaps were not even from her pen. One she knew for certain, though, a pot-bellied older goblin named Saro-Saro. Direfang pulled him through the hole and roughly sat him down then turned to grab another one.

"Mudwort was right about the bad something coming to the mine," Saro-Saro said. He brushed furiously at the stone dust covering his leathery hide. He couldn't manage to get it all off, finally giving up with a disgusted grunt. His back and shoulders bled in numerous places, and a deep gash on his belly glistened in the light. "Squeezed through," he told Mudwort as he pointed at the worst wound. "Hurt to squeeze through." A sad expression claimed his face. "Squeezed bad and walked on the smashed ones. Walked on broken brothers."

Direfang was helping the last trapped goblin, one cradling a broken arm. Then he pulled down a dozen more stones so a larger hobgoblin could fit through with two ore sacks she refused to leave behind. "How many smashed?" Direfang demanded of the final survivor to be saved.

She shrugged and positioned the ore sacks over her shoulders, shook her head brusquely, and started up the tunnel that would take her by Mudwort's blessed stream.

"How many?" Direfang repeated to the goblins clustered around him. There were more than two dozen who had crossed from the other side.

Saro-Saro sucked on his lower lip. "Broken? Smashed? Many, Direfang. Too many goblins have been smashed and broken. Should have listened to Mudwort. Should have believed Mudwort about the very bad something."

"Quake," Direfang replied. "It's called an earthquake, Saro-Saro. And knowing it was coming would not have changed anything. The taskmasters would still have sent goblins to the mines. Goblins would still have been smashed." He paused, a smile playing at the corner of his mouth. "Of course, it probably smashed a lot of Dark Knights too."

"Many knights dead too," said Mudwort. "Many, many."

"Not enough of them Dark Knights," Saro-Saro grumbled. "Too many goblins smashed, broken. Not enough knights broken." He spit a gob of mud out on the ground. "Not enough water." He looked up the tunnel. The hobgoblin with the ore had trundled out of sight. Then he looked up at Direfang, cocking his head. Saro-Saro obviously didn't want to stay in the mine any longer, yet he didn't want to go outside either. "Ore lost," he said. "Back there. Left it. Trouble, trouble, trouble."

Direfang reached out a clawed hand and almost touched Saro-Saro then gestured up the tunnel. "Go outside. Safer there. There will be no trouble for escaping the mine and leaving the ore behind. All must go now. Make certain a knight does some mending, one of the skull men."

"Yes, find a skull man."

The Skull Knights were usually quick to heal goblins and hobgoblins injured in the mine—not out of any sense of compassion or because their priestly order required them to help, but for the economic reasons. If they let the goblins die, there would be a smaller slave pool. A smaller mining force meant less ore would be mined each day, and that would not be acceptable to Marshal Montrill. Direfang knew the Skull Knights would see to their own first, but once Saro-Saro and the others got outside, they would eventually be helped.

"Hurry," Direfang ordered. "Hurry now. Take Leftear too. The skull men help heal."

Saro-Saro glanced at the goblin with a broken arm then gave Direfang an uncertain look. "Trouble, trouble, trouble," he muttered. "Should have listened to Mudwort." Then he turned and headed up the tunnel, the rest of the freed goblins and the other hobgoblin slowly following him.

When they were gone, Direfang picked up the lantern and checked the oil, turning the wick down to conserve the light.

Mudwort watched the rescued miners as they headed toward her precious stream, knowing they would stop and drink and enjoy the water that she thought of as her own discovery.

"Mudwort goes first." Direfang interrupted her thoughts. He pointed with his free hand toward the gaping hole through the rubble. "Help find more goblins not smashed. Do not let the mountain win by keeping the bodies."

He spoke to her in the goblin tongue. She knew he was fluent in man's language—perhaps in others too. He'd been around men longer than she had, practically raised as a slave, he'd told her once. He had escaped and been recaptured more than once. Mudwort knew that with a little effort she could learn much more of man's ugly speech. But she had more important uses for her mind.

"Mudwort goes first," he repeated.

With a sigh, knowing she could not refuse her only friend, Mudwort thrust the thought of the cool water to the back of her mind, climbed up the rubble and through the hole, and waited on the other side for Direfang. She sniffed the air, finding it fusty and dust-filled and choking. She wanted to be in the water or outside where the air was better, looking down the mountainside and delighting in the destruction Steel Town had suffered. She cringed when she heard some rocks tumble and saw stone dust filter down from the ceiling. She half expected to be buried by a cave-in, but only a few rocks were disturbed as Direfang forced his broad shoulders through the gap and joined her, his lantern held gingerly in one hand.

He stank of sweat and blood, and she moved away from him but found the air no better a short distance ahead. She reached her left hand to the wall and gingerly touched the stone, then pressed her palm against it before moving deeper and repeating the gesture. Once, she put her ear to a spot, but heard nothing other than Direfang's breathing and the pounding of her heart. At another place she paused and put her mouth to the wall where a rivulet of water ran down from an underground stream just overhead. A half mile later, they stopped where a shaft had collapsed. Caught in the rocks were easily a dozen slaves, arms and legs protruding at sickening angles, picks and scraps of canvas from ore sacks in the mess.

Blood pooled at the base, and Direfang stepped in the sticky puddle when he tugged on a pick until it came loose suddenly and brought several chunks of stone down near them. He stepped back again to get a better look at the collapse.

The Rebellion

"Tarduk!" Use care, Mudwort warned. She sensed that the mass might be unstable and could tell that at its top was a slab of ceiling filled with thick cracks. She tipped her chin up and got Direfang's attention. Another crack appeared and thickened as they watched, spreading in all directions. "All smashed, the goblins here. All dead, Direfang. Nothing to save."

"But Direfang could break the dead to save the spirits." He made a move toward the wall of rubble again, bowed his head almost reverently, then reached out and clutched an arm protruding from the jumble of rocks. He tore it off, and the next and the next, flinging the limbs against the wall behind him. Then he made a move to start grabbing the rocks to clear the corridor but stopped when Mudwort tugged at him and shook her head, mouthing *smashed smashed smashed.*

To convince him to leave that place alone, she touched the rocks warily, avoiding the jutting limbs that looked as though they were grasping at her.

She continued brushing across one rock after another, finding one chunk especially smooth and dark and with a winding red vein that suggested a rich ore content.

"Thick here, this collapse," she told Direfang after several moments. "Too thick. Rocks deep behind here. Rocks forever."

The hobgoblin stayed an arm's length away but held the lantern close. A line of drool spilled over his lower lip and onto the floor. "Goblins trapped behind it, dead or not."

"Maybe," Mudwort admitted. "But nothing to be done now."

Direfang snarled. "Later, then."

"Maybe."

"No maybe. Come back with more help later. Dig the goblins out."

Mudwort entertained the notion of leaving the tunnel

right then and visiting her wonderful stream on the way to looking down on the Dark Knights' ruined camp again. "Later come back, Direfang. With more goblins to help dig out the dead."

Direfang turned, straightening and knocking his head against the ceiling. He snarled again and stooped to retrace his steps until they came to a place where another shaft bisected the main one. There was a collapsed section several yards ahead that did not completely seal off the tunnel. He crept closer.

There was blood on the wall, streaks that could have been made by goblins and hobgoblins squeezing themselves through. Direfang would not be able to fit through that tight spot, so Mudwort turned to retrace her steps.

Then she heard the *tink* of him setting the lantern down and the crunch of rocks being moved out of the way.

"*Tarduk*, Direfang!"

He ignored her, working quickly and clumsily until there was a space big enough for him to fit through. He picked up the lantern again and stared at her.

"Mudwort needs to help with this." Then he disappeared through the opening. "Mudwort needs to help now."

The goblin shook her head and rubbed her belly, feeling it slosh pleasantly with the water she'd drunk. "Mudwort help," she glumly parroted. Then she followed him through.

6

CHAOS TOWN

Grallik doubled over coughing, unable to get the dirt out of his mouth. His chest felt so tight and hot, his lungs like charred wood. His eyes were filled with dirt too, burning so fiercely he could make out nothing with his vision. Everything was a blur of gray and brown and pain.

The misery sent his mind back more than sixty years to when he was a child in the great Qualinesti Forest. His parents, both half-elves, lived in the village of Willow Knot, in a small house, in front of which was an herb shop.

It had been a cold night, and a fire burned in the hearth.

Grallik's parents and his twin sister hadn't known there was magic in him or that he'd been testing his growing abilities when no one was looking. They didn't see him crook a small finger at the hearth that night and coax the flames to lick outward and grow brighter and higher. He'd only intended to make the room warmer. They didn't see him flee when the flames spread to the rug and flowed up the walls, stretched out to burn the left side of him before

45

he fell out the back door, gasping for air as he was gasping at that moment.

He heard his family's screams that night. They were worse, he thought, than the cries of the laborers caught in the quake. The roar of the fire in his house and his trapped parents' and sister's screams were always in his memory, louder than the rumbling of the ground, and had risen over the voices of everyone in Steel Town just minutes ago.

Chaos Town should be the camp's new name, he mused as his eyes finally watered enough so he could see, though dimly. The dirt that caked his face had turned to a clay muck that stung and felt heavy and hurtful. There was nothing to be done for it at the moment, he knew. But he'd get to a Skull Knight soon and have the man tend his eyes and to his tender ribs.

Grallik was on his hands and knees outside what was left of his workshop. A cloud of dust and dirt hovered around him and above the ground for as far as he could see, as persistent as the early morning fog that usually wrapped itself around the tall grass of the Qualinesti Forest. Shapes moved in the haze; knights, he recognized, by their posture, heads held high. They wore helmets despite the awful heat and the dust cloud, and Grallik imagined that their sweating faces must be covered with dirt that lined their eye slits. He brushed at his face, managing only to smear the dirt around.

Breathing slowly and shallowly, he got to his feet, leaning against the crooked stone and wood wall of his workshop. His fingers flitted across the cracked mortar; his had been one of the sturdier buildings in Steel Town, and he feared the remaining two walls would topple at any moment. He tipped his head up, hoping for cleaner air, but found none. The mountains and volcanoes that ringed the camp were hazed by the dust too, looking faded like an old painting.

THE REBELLION

He heard a nervous whinny and turned just as a frightened horse shot past him, eyes wide and foam flecking its mouth. A knight chased the beast, the sun glinting off his armor and making his shoulders and arms glow as if he'd been ensorcelled. Grallik watched him catch the reins and saw the horse toss its head, nostrils flaring and front hooves coming off the ground as it fought against the knight.

Grallik stepped away from the wall, arms in front of his chest as if warding off the choking dust and dirt. When the wind changed, he caught another mouthful. He spit it out again and cursed, coughing so hard that his shoulders bobbed. When the spasms stopped, he turned back to see the knight leading the horse behind the remnants of the stable and into a pen that was one of those that had largely survived the quake. At the edge of his vision, the wizard saw the pines on the slope of one of the volcanoes, their branches looking bare and pale, like the skeletal remains of long-dead creatures.

It hurt, physically and emotionally, to gaze upon the wholesale destruction. Grallik stumbled around the wall and into what remained of his workshop. Only the northern and western walls were intact. The front of the building had crumbled and the thatch roof was caved in. He'd hidden a flask of water behind some books on a shelf. He wanted to find it and flush his eyes. He choked back a bitter laugh as he pulled at the thatch to clear the floor, looking for the flask.

His worry always had been the volcanoes. He'd never considered the possibility of an earthquake, and yet it made sense. Land dotted by volcanoes was prone to quakes, he'd heard, and tremors had been recorded in the camp before his arrival. There had been rumors of faint ones just a few days ago. But something of the magnitude he saw that day had never occurred to him.

It took him several minutes to pull the thatch away and several more minutes to find both his breath and the water flask. He held it to his chest as though it were a priceless treasure and then against his face, finding some coolness to it. He kissed the cork then gingerly tugged it free, sniffed the water, and poured some in his eyes, finding only a little relief. Then he took a small mouthful and held it, savoring it as if it were fine, aged wine, finally swallowed it, and replaced the cork. Once more he held the flask against his chest, then he thrust it in a deep pocket so none would see that he had it. He turned too sharply at the pop of a timber and gasped in pain, instantly worried that his sore ribs might be more than bruised and responsible for the heat in his lungs.

His vision slightly improved and he took inventory. His workshop, which also served as his home, was largely destroyed. He was fortunate that the shelf and his precious water flask survived, both being on one of the standing walls. Benches and tables and his prized bookcase carved of walnut were so much kindling, torn apart as if a herd of maddened bulls had trampled them. The frame he heated the ore on was broken, the pans beneath it lost, and behind the frame—where his bed and meager possessions had been—stretched a wicked-looking crevice in the ground. The jagged crack extended south of the building and had pulled men and animals underground, including everything of value he owned—lost in the depths.

Grallik's throat grew tighter, and he fought for air in his grief and fury. He stumbled forward, kicking aside pieces of wood from a shattered bench and kneeling at the edge of the crevice. Without any roof, the sun shone down brightly over his head and the wizard could see that the bottom of the gash was dozens, perhaps hundreds, of feet below. A mailed arm jutted out of one side, a leg farther away was from a different knight's body. A piece of tangled blanket was caught between two large rocks, and a post from his bed poked up from what looked to be the deepest point. Everything was charred, with smoke rising from a few pieces still burning.

He'd been heating the ore when the quake struck, and when he ran outside to see what was happening, that ore had caught fire and spread to his precious possessions. He noted that pages ripped from one of his books were burning at the edges, as if someone were blowing on them. A section of the crevice's far wall had collapsed, but he knew nothing down there was worth recovering.

Grallik eased back from the edge and sat heavily, unmindful of the debris that jabbed at the backs of his legs. Everything he had nurtured and treasured was gone. In his mind, he likened his sense of loss to a close relative dying.

Again he thought of his family.

"Everything." The word came out as a harsh whisper, his mouth instantly dry again from all the blowing dust. "By the fading memory of the Dark Queen's heads, it is all gone."

He would have cried, but it was not in the nature of a Dark Knight. So he silently mourned and forced down a sob. The half-elf had never been one for burdening himself with personal objects, so he hadn't lost a considerable amount of goods. The Order provided clothes and food and more coin than he could spend—particularly at his posting. He disdained knickknacks or jewelry or art objects. He was a relatively simple man in terms of physical trappings.

But his magic—his scrolls and spellbooks and vials upon vials filled with prized arcane powders and enchanted liquids—that was all lost to the quake. Years of research had been sacrificed, notes on arcane experiments and diagrams of magical objects he'd intended to fashion—those were all gone. A tome of spells—a singular copy—from decades ago when he studied as a Black Robe with the Conclave, obliterated. He felt the color drain from his face and his chest constrict. His life was in ruins at the bottom of that crevice.

The rare magics learned while he was with the Conclave, the ones from before he joined the Dark Knights, those and much more were in the crevice. The spells that allowed him to call lightning from the sky and let him read passages in ancient, foreign languages, the spells that created spheres of acid out of air, helped him to breathe water, or stay awake for days at a time, the one that summoned an invisible force to clean his workshop and bring him food—he hadn't cast some of them in years. Without that tome and his other spellbooks to consult, to stir his memory and to renew his knowledge, he doubted he could ever cast such magic again.

"All of it lost. My research."

The destruction of his notes might extract the greatest toll. He'd so meticulously written down his evolving theories on strengthening steel and giving it arcane properties. He'd been so very close to an amazing breakthrough, something that would benefit the entire Order and propel him to fame and a prime posting and promotion up the ranks. Grallik was certain he could recall many of his notes, but it was years and years of note taking, and his memory couldn't absorb everything.

For nearly five decades, Grallik had served the Dark Knights, a long time even for a half-elf. A Thorn Knight, he commanded only one talon, nine men, all of them Lily Knights. But given the years, his title should have been marshal or warder, and he should have been assigned to a place where no silly act of nature, no earthquake, would have deprived him of his research and diagrams and books, especially the old Conclave tome. He deserved a more favored post.

"Sir N'sera?"

The half-elf didn't stir until he'd heard his name and title spoken a third time. He looked up to spot a member of his talon standing where the doorway had been.

"Sir, the commander—Marshal Montrill—is injured. Skull Knight Ramvin is tending to him. But until Marshal Montrill is able . . ."

The Rebellion

The rest of the words were unimportant, so Grallik shut them out and rose up, brushing futilely at his robe and picking his way out of the remains of his workshop.

Until Montrill was able and fit . . . until that time . . . then Grallik, because of his seniority, would take charge of all of what he thought of as Chaos Town. It was the responsibility Grallik had dreamed of even a moment ago, but in truth he was not prepared for it. At least the demands of the new job would keep his mind so busy he couldn't dwell on his utter loss.

"How many wounded?" Grallik asked, deciding that taking stock of his charges was the first proper order of business.

The knight drew his lips into a needle-thin line. "At least a third, Sir N'sera. Wounded or dead, all of that's being sorted out now. Between the quake and the hatori, falling buildings and the like . . ."

Grallik straightened and squared his shoulders, gesturing for the knight to move aside. "Then I place you in charge of the tally. See to it immediately. We must know our current strength." He paused. "And our weakness," he added under his breath, too softly for the knight to hear. He raised his voice to a normal level. "Marshal Montrill. You said he is hurt. How badly?"

A part of Grallik wanted Marshal Montrill to be very badly hurt, so he could at least be heartened by his promotion, but he shoved those malign thoughts away. For the good of the Order and the good of the annihilated camp, Montrill needed to survive. He was a capable leader.

"I don't know, Sir N'sera. Shall I . . . ?"

"Find out?" Grallik shook his head. "No, I'll see to Marshal Montrill. Start with the others. Begin your count." Grallik watched him go, wondering how the knight would approach the task and knowing whatever numbers he came up with would not be wholly accurate. The once-orderly mining enterprise was gone. In its place was a void of death, injury, and destruction that would take time to calculate.

No building stood truly intact, with unruly mounds of rubble replacing the familiar structures. Laborers and their families either milled about listlessly in disbelief or were rushing around in panic. Raised voices and shrill bleats and whinnies filled the air. Knights were assembling into formations on the west side of the camp. To the east, more knights were rounding up goblins and hobgoblins and repairing one of the five slave pens.

He'd cast warding spells and laid glyphs on the ground outside the slave pens shortly after his posting there and had refreshed them every third or fourth month as a precaution. But the quake tore up the ground they'd been placed upon, rendering some of the wards and glyphs useless.

Possibly all of them.

Grallik would have to pray for the precise warding enchantments so he could cast them correctly again. It would take days to restore all the enchantments to keep the slaves from escaping. Several of them, he recalled fondly, shot pillars and walls of flame into the air, incinerating potential escapees.

Of course, no slaves had tried to escape for several months. The Dark Knights had made examples of offenders in the past, catching those not burned to death by Grallik's wards and glyphs and torturing them before slaying them in front of the others. The Dark Knights had sufficiently beaten down the goblins' and hobgoblins' spirits and tore away their sense of self-worth to the point that likely none of them entertained thoughts of fleeing anymore. The threat of ogres, and some minotaurs, in the nearby mountains further hindered them.

My precious pillars of fire.

He'd have to replace all of them to be certain the pens were escape-proof. But he couldn't start doing it during the day when the slaves in the pen could clearly see what he was doing. He didn't dare risk letting them figure out that the wards and glyphs might have been rendered useless.

Their numbers were too great . . .

Grallik looked to the pens and shuddered. There were far more slaves than knights, ten times as many, and without the wards? Were the goblins smart enough to realize the wards might be gone? Just the day before, he'd heard a skinny female goblin hollering in the common tongue about something bad coming to the mine. He hadn't paid any attention to her babble.

Had she been babbling about the quake?

How smart were the goblins?

Out of the corner of his eye, he spotted two knights carrying a badly injured knight on a makeshift stretcher. Grallik set off after them, hoping they would lead him to the infirmary and the wounded Marshal Montrill.

7

DEATH SEARCH

Direfang managed to squeeze through one passage after another, at times stymied by cave-ins, forced to retrace his steps, stopping to brace sagging timbers with broken ones he'd picked up along the way, tearing off goblin limbs that protruded from rock slides, and demanding, again and again, that Mudwort help him with his laborious rescue mission.

"Cannot save any more goblins," Mudwort insisted finally. "Not here. Not in this part of the mine. Too much of it has collapsed. Why Direfang not give up?"

The hobgoblin bent until his face was close and even with hers. The scars and lines on his visage were thick and his expression hard, as if his head had been carved out of rock from the mine.

"Everything dies, Mudwort. Goblins, hobgoblins, death comes to all—from the quake, long years, sickness. But not everything has to be enslaved."

She raised an eyebrow, and he growled in response, a ribbon of drool spilling over his lower lip and plopping to the floor.

"Save goblins here, save slaves. Save other goblins in the hills from being made slaves. Understand?"

"Dark Knights bring in more slaves no matter what," she answered, fists on her hips. "Saving nothing by poking around here, Direfang." Her expression softened. "Saving spirits, though." She shuffled away from him, pretending to look for more oil and lanterns.

There was only a little oil left in the lantern Direfang carried, and they'd not found more. A niche where barrels of oil and other supplies were kept was buried under rocks. The air had grown fouler the deeper they went, and it was filled with the sounds of timbers groaning and rocks falling. Some collapsed tunnels they passed smelled thickly of death.

"All goblins left in this mine are smashed," she said after many minutes had passed. Her eyes flitted nervously to a split beam overhead. "Direfang be dead too if . . ."

"Don't know that, Mudwort. Might be more goblins alive." He forced his way through a choked passage, adding more cuts to his badly scratched chest and arms and scraping the top of his head. "Should not leave any goblins here, alive or dead."

"*Shalbo,* Direfang. Certainly bad, this place is. *Shalbo, shalbo* indeed. Give up, Direfang. Give up now! *Feyrh!*"

Direfang had been moving as quickly as possible, hesitating only at cave-ins and places where he couldn't hope to fit through. But he stopped at another blocked shaft and let out a great sigh. From somewhere beyond the blockage, the earth rumbled. It sounded like a new cave-in happening.

"Give up," she repeated. "Direfang, just give up for now. Please."

He glowered at her, and a bubble of drool spilled out of his mouth. He batted it away with the back of his free hand.

"Slaves always give up, Mudwort. Always give in." He scratched at a deep scar on his chest. His scar-ridden body attested to his years in service to the Dark Knights. The palm of his right hand was smooth, not having any of the blister scars and ravages of his left. When he was younger, his left arm had been thrust into a campfire because he'd been tardy bringing a commander his dinner. He'd not been tardy since.

His ear had been cut off ten years earlier when he'd tried to escape with a small band of slaves. The Skull Knights used their magic and determined he was not the instigator—he had been a follower, not a leader—and he was valuable in the mines because of his size and strength. So they only sliced off his ear and for a long time made him wear it on a cord around his neck until it had shriveled to a black and unrecognizable thing and finally rotted off. The other captured escapees were goblins, and their lives were slowly extinguished in full view of the pens. Only a few of the offenders escaped death.

Direfang's hair covered up most of the scars he'd received from various whippings. But some were so thick and deep that no hair grew over them and it looked as if his skin carried a disease. A jagged scar on his face ran from the outer edge of his left eye down to the tip of his chin. It was from an accident in a shaft the previous year, from a crosspiece falling down and clipping him. A fresh scar, on his right forearm, came when he was struck by an angry, thirsty, pick-wielding goblin, just three days earlier.

Scars crawled all over him. His appearance gave him an intimidating mien that helped make him an effective foreman. At that moment he looked even worse, coated with blood and stone dust.

"Maybe give up," he said finally. "Maybe Mudwort right." He turned and looked behind him, took a step in that direction, then stopped. "Maybe one more look." The hobgoblin pressed on through another crack, edging by broken, bloodied limbs that stuck out from shattered stones and timbers. By the time he reached a chamber where he could stand, his trousers were soaked in blood—his own and that from the victims he'd passed.

He sagged against a wall, exhausted, and fought for breath.

"No further." Mudwort shook her head, made a tsk-tsking sound. "No more tunnels to search. *Gart!* Give up. Or die here and rot."

It seemed as though they'd been through every tunnel they could fit through in that section of the mountain, and the chamber they stood in ended in another cave-in. They'd not encountered any live goblins for some time, so the prospects of finding any more were fading.

Direfang shook his head. His shoulders slumped in defeat. "Maybe here all gone, but try other places. There are other places in the mountain we can search for goblins."

There were two other entrances to the mines on their side of the mountain and two more elsewhere—five in all. Direfang stroked his chin, considering his next move.

"Tunnels done here, Direfang."

"Here," Direfang admitted. "Yes, done here." He pushed off from the wall and paced in a tight circle, crouching low as he paced so he wouldn't strike his head on the ceiling.

The lantern had so little oil left, it gave off only a faint glow. The light might not last long enough for them to return to a main tunnel. They might have to feel their way out.

"Go now," Direfang said. He yawned and looked over his shoulder at the crack they'd last squeezed through.

Mudwort cocked her head and listened to something Direfang could not hear. "Wait to leave." The goblin eased herself to her knees, then splayed her fingers across the stone floor. She put her ear close to the ground and listened more intently. A moment more, and she crawled across the chamber floor like a youngling, all the while her face pressed to the stone. Occasionally, she stuck her tongue out and licked it, only to spit out the horrid-tasting stone dust.

"Hear something, Mudwort?"

She nodded, continuing her inspection. "Singing," she said. "Hear singing." A pause. "Bad singing. Bad sounds. Same song over and over again. Hear a familiar voice, bad voice, and—"

In that instant the oil burned out and the chamber went black. Still, Mudwort continued to shuffle around, thumping the floor with her thumbs and rubbing her chin against the stone. Suddenly, she brightened.

"Direfang, *tarduk.* Stone is thin here. Weak. *Tarduk!*"

The hobgoblin carefully found his way to her, raised the pick, and started hitting the floor. Despite her claim that the rock was thin, it took him quite some time to knock a hole large enough to poke his head and shoulders through. The chamber beneath them was equally dim, but after a few moments, a lantern was lit from below.

Moon-eye looked up at the hobgoblin, relief spreading across his small, tear-streaked face. He'd been conserving the lantern oil, hoping against hope for a rescue. He turned the wick up so Direfang could see him better. It illuminated a passage below that was not completely blocked and which Moon-eye could have found his way out of. But the one-eyed goblin wouldn't leave the other figure outlined by the light of the lantern—his fallen mate, Graytoes.

"This beam," he called up to Direfang. "This bad beam fell across Moon-eye's Heart." The goblin had been unable to move the huge timber that still pinned his mate's legs. "Direfang move this beam, please. Save Moon-eye's Heart."

Direfang snorted, swinging his legs over the opening

and dropping down. He'd bent his knees to lessen the impact, but hitting the rock floor jarred him and forced out a moan.

"Mudwort help too," the hobgoblin said, glancing up. "Mudwort help now." He held out his arms, indicating he would catch her.

With a dusty sigh, Mudwort jumped down.

8

Wounds and Healing Hands

Grallik watched the knights carry their wounded fellow behind the lone, still-standing wall of the largest barracks. Rounding the corner, he saw several men assembling beds from pieces of broken cots. They were ripping sheets and blankets into strips to use for bandages and clearing away debris to make room for more men. Miraculously, the camp's four Skull Knights had survived the quake, though one of them was propped up against the wall, his tabard off, revealing a large red splotch on the center of his chest where something had struck him. The wife of the tavern owner tended him.

Another Skull Knight hovered over Marshal Montrill, who rested on a mattress laid flat on the ground. The third priest, a large Ergothian, was moving from one injured knight to the next and would soon have more patients to be concerned with as Grallik heard the crunch of boots and moans of pain coming from behind him. The fourth priest was gesturing where to place the arriving injured.

Laborers and their wives were helping, cleaning wounds

with what remained of the water supply. Some of their older children also worked at tugging off bits of armor, cloaks, and tabards and carrying off the blood-soaked bandages. The smallest children huddled together, some crying.

It seemed as if no one had escaped some injury. Added to the usual awful smell of Steel Town were the odors of blood and charred wood and the waste expelled from the dead.

In his younger years, Grallik had been in many skirmishes, and he'd heard vivid accounts of the war in the Abyss against Chaos. He'd been stationed far away at the time and hadn't reached the great cavern before the war ended. The injured in the camp looked as if they'd been in as serious a battle as the Chaos War. But the enemy there had been a force of nature, not an opposing military force or an angry god.

He worked a kink out of his neck, stifled a yawn, and strode toward Montrill, the Skull Knight leaning over the commander but glancing up to acknowledge him. Montrill was bare from the waist up, his chest, neck, and right arm already showing the beginnings of ugly bruises. His left arm was broken, with a piece of the bone sticking out and looking sickly as it glistened in the sun. The bones in his left hand had been shattered, the fingers an ugly, pulpy mass. To add to the misery, Montrill's nose was badly broken, his lip split, and a flap of his scalp was loose. He was glad the commander was unconscious and could not feel the pain.

One of the officers was just finishing telling the attending priest what had happened. The commander had been resting in that very barracks when the quake struck and a wall collapsed on him. The commander managed to crawl out from under the wall, then proceeded to pull free two other knights who were trapped. He went back in to check for more men when the next tremors brought down more of the building, again trapping Montrill. That time he was knocked unconscious, and knights had to go back in to rescue him.

The Skull Knight dipped a cloth in a small bowl of water and dabbed at Montrill's face. The commander's eyelids fluttered but did not open, and his jaw worked silently. The priest's free hand roamed across the commander's chest as he intoned a healing enchantment. The words were soft and comforting, sounding like a musical chant.

Grallik had always marveled at the Skull Knights' type of magic, so different from his own and beyond his ken. The spells were not as flashy as his, not very devastating in a battle. But in an instance such as this, the priests' magic was more effective. The Skull Knights gained their spells through prayer and meditation, drawing from themselves and the earth.

Again Grallik thought ruefully about all his lost powders and research notes. He rubbed at his eyes, which were burning worse than before. He would have to put up with the irritation because he knew it would be hours before the priests could see to him. He would pour a little more water on them from his hidden flask when he was alone. With Montrill unconscious, he was in charge. He could certainly order the priests to soothe his eyes right away and tend his sore ribs. But other knights had life-threatening injuries.

"For the good of the Order," Grallik mouthed. He would wait before asking the Skull Knights to look to his needs.

Movement to the north caught Grallik's attention. He stepped around Montrill's mattress, still listening to the priest's spell. Knights were laying their dead brethren near the dry well. Dirt still swirled in the air and, coupled with the piles of rubble, made it difficult for him to assess just how many dead bodies were in the immediate area. Twenty or more, he guessed, as he returned his attention to the priest and Montrill, perhaps as many as thirty. But there would be more dead and dying elsewhere; certainly some knights had been lost among the various crevices that had opened in camp and subsequently closed. And some had not returned from the mine.

A pale orange glow spread out from the Skull Knight's free hand, settling into the commander's chest and flowing outward, until all of Montrill's skin took on the color of dying embers. Montrill was sweating profusely. Grallik realized it wasn't a sweat caused by the heat of the place, but from a fever that accompanied his many wounds.

"Will he live?" Despite the careful ministrations of the priest, Grallik was worried. Please let him live, the wizard prayed. The aftermath of the quake would be an ordeal to manage, and though Grallik craved power, he did not want to inherit such a mess. "Will Marshal Montrill survive?" The glow was fading from Montrill's skin, showing a clammy paleness. The commander breathed evenly but shallowly.

The priest continued his healing chant for several moments before answering. "Marshal Montrill will live, I believe, though his wounds are grievous." He turned his attention to the commander's broken arm. "Hold his wrist, please, Guardian N'sera."

Grallik squatted and wrapped both of his hands around Montrill's wrist. The priest motioned to another knight, who grabbed Montrill's arm just below the elbow.

"Pull, gently," the Skull Knight instructed. He walked around to the other side of Montrill, leaned over him again, and worked the bone back below the skin. "More. That's it." He smiled at the sickening pop as the bone fit back in place.

Though still unconscious, Montrill arched his back and moaned from the pain. The priest steepled his fingers over the bone break and spoke words unfamiliar to Grallik. Again, the orange glow spread across Montrill's skin, brightest over the broken bone, and Grallik knew the bone was magically fusing. He'd watched the Skull Knights heal limbs that slaves had broken in the mine, but he'd never paid close attention before.

"So much dirt," the priest said to himself. Looking up, he met Grallik's gaze. "There could be an infection that my spells cannot reach. This I worry over. I believe the commander will live, but he needs time to rest, and I cannot vouch he'll be able to use his hands as before."

That the priests could repair broken arms and heal bruised ribs and worse was a credit to their craft. Grallik failed to comprehend how they could do all of that and yet not be able to erase his scars from his own burning. The rent in Montrill's arm was already disappearing, showing no trace of having been punctured and broken. How could that be possible—and still the priests could not repair his fire-scarred flesh?

"The commander's hand is especially bad." The Skull Knight frowned. "The bones are not simply snapped, they are broken like shards from a dropped pot. All splintered, like they'd been beaten by a hammer. I will do my best, but that hand will never be the same. I fear he will never regain full movement." He paused. "And it is his sword hand. You are witness, Sir N'sera, to the condition of his hand." The priest seemed nervous, perhaps worried that when Montrill awoke he would be angry at his condition and blame the healer.

However, Grallik knew Montrill and knew the man would instead be grateful to the priest who had saved his life. He knew Montrill was the kind of man who would shrug off his bad luck and simply learn to wield a sword with his other hand. The wizard released Montrill's wrist and nodded. "I am witness," said Grallik. "Do what you can for him and the rest. See if the trader, Thomas, can salvage some herbs to ease the pain. I will speak with the commander when he is awake."

The wizard stood and brushed his hands on his robe,

smearing some of Montrill's blood. Then he took another look at the wounded and dying and the chaos all around him.

"Then, if you and your men have anything left," Grallik said after a moment's hesitation, "any spells or supplies, do your best to see to the wounded slaves. We lost a considerable number, I am sure, and we need the rest healthy so they can reopen the mine and help rebuild the camp."

The Skull Knight replied with a noncommittal grunt.

9

DARK TIMES

It was shortly past midnight, nearly eighteen hours since the quake struck, before a priest tended to Grallik's eyes. And that had been at the priest's insistence, not the wizard's. The Skull Knight had noticed Grallik furiously rubbing his eyes and argued that the man currently in charge of Steel Town needed to properly see the devastation so he could best determine how to deal with the crisis.

His eyes felt much better, and the horrid headache he'd nurtured throughout the day was starting to recede. His ribs still throbbed, and the priest worked on them too; the faint orange glow that had spilled across Montrill's broken arm flowed over Grallik's side and chest. The warmth was so soothing that that the wizard had to struggle to stay awake.

"Broken," the priest pronounced. "Three or four ribs. But they should not trouble you any longer. Go easy, though, lest you undo my work."

In truth, the pain was gone, as though there'd never been a problem. Again, Grallik was amazed by the divine magic.

66

"Thank you," Grallik said. "I appreciate your diligence, brother."

The priest was mildly surprised at the comment. He was not used to being commended for his healing.

"And I also thank you for the hours you've spent with the wounded men. No doubt you'll be spending hours more before you've a chance to rest."

"Aye, indeed, Guardian. I suspect I'll drop from fatigue while there are still patients to see to."

The wizard wondered if he, himself, might keel over at any moment. He had spent hours organizing a better place for the wounded, away from the barracks wall that he feared might topple; ordering the laborers and their families to comb through the rubble for salvageable clothes and furniture; directing the blacksmiths to recover any steel, iron, and raw ore that was salvageable; commanding slaves to get to work on the new well; dispatching messengers to Jelek and Neraka to inform Dark Knight commanders about the disaster of Steel Town. His letters, written on soiled and rumpled pieces of parchment—that was all he could find—detailed requests for men and supplies, especially clothes and wood.

In those hours, Marshal Montrill showed no visible sign of improvement, though the Skull Knights seemed encouraged by his stability and assured Grallik that in time he would indeed recuperate. The priests believed that two knights with even worse wounds would also survive.

"The best medicine is a tincture of time," Grallik recalled the Ergothian priest saying. Montrill had had a close escape from death. "He will show definite improvement in a few days, perhaps. A week or more at the longest. But he will not be getting up out of bed right away. We all will look to you for orders until the marshal is able to resume his command."

Days and days in charge of this chaos, Grallik translated the prognosis.

The responsibility he once so craved had dropped in his grasping hands. He watched as a detail of knights and laborers, their clothes dark from sweat despite the coolness of the early day, dug graves and laid their fellows into the ground. Another grave-digging shift would take over later in the morning, and the burials could take some time, given the number of the dead and the protocol the Order demanded for burying knights. One of the Skull Knights was with the burying party, reciting words Grallik knew he would hear far too often before the cleanup of Steel Town was completed.

The bodies had to be washed, as part of the ceremony, and dressed in their finest armor and cloaks. Knights had to be buried with their weapons all polished. But Grallik had ordered the water conserved for the living, and he set even more hobgoblin and goblin slaves to work in earnest on three new wells, supervised by the former tavern owner and his wife. One of the three would have to strike water soon or their situation would become precarious. Water was a priority. The Skull Knights were too fatigued to create any with their enchantments—all their energy had been devoted to the injured.Commanding the men and slaves to perform all those odious tasks was far preferable to working alongside them, Grallik realized. He knew that if Montrill were healthy and giving orders, he would either be aiding the wounded or sorting through the ruins right alongside the others. Montrill could be counted on to give example in dire times.

It wasn't as if Grallik had been resting, though. He'd been on his aching feet for hours, moving about restlessly, kneeling sometimes at the side of a wounded knight; one of his talon died and another lay grievously injured and likely would not survive his wounds. All he wanted was to sit on one of the chairs or benches that had been pulled from the demolished buildings, close his eyes, and sleep for a few minutes or have something to drink. After all, he was entitled to whatever water he wanted—he was in charge.

His feet hurt from walking over the rubble. His soft-soled slippers were not much protection from the sharp stones and broken furniture and jagged tools. He didn't wear the hard-soled boots that his fellow knights did; that wasn't the footwear of wizards. But Grallik had been eyeing the dead, and when he found a man of similar build, he intended to appropriate the man's boots to cover his own feet, and damn those who thought him ghoulish rather than pragmatic.

He would rest briefly when he was finished there, perhaps sleep an hour or two if things looked in order. A spell that could stave off exhaustion for days was lost at the bottom of a crevice. He could not recall it without his precious spellbook.

He was so terribly, terribly spent.

Grallik walked toward the slave pens, feeling the slaves watching him. There were only a handful of knights standing guard at the pens. The wizard worried that the slaves might figure out that his wards were absent. If they rushed the knights, they would have a good opportunity to vanish into the wilderness.

But up to that point, the slaves had made no move to escape, so conditioned were they to their horrid existence. The wooden slats of the pen were like the steel bars of a prison to them. The slaves probably still believed that all the wards and glyphs were intact and thought they'd be incinerated by columns of flame if they tried to escape.

Fifty yards to the east of the pens was a mound of goblin and hobgoblin bodies, looking like a big earthen hill in the darkness. They were slaves who had died in the pens when the quake struck, had been carried out of the mines by their fellows, or were killed by the hatori. Some had died quickly, succumbing to their dire injuries. The priests would not be seeing to the goblins for a while, so undoubtedly more of the injured slaves would breathe their last soon.

There were hundreds more dead slaves in the mine, Grallik suspected, and some knights among them. Something would have to be done about all their bodies and the stink building up in the shafts. The shafts would have to be reopened, ore production continued. But clearing the mine was a goal to consider after sunrise. Dealing with the mound of bodies there and then, Grallik had to focus on that problem.

"Guardian N'sera," one of the guards began. "Shall I—?"

Grallik raised his scarred hand. "I need no help with this. Just watch the slaves."

The odor from the dead was strong and overpowering and threatened to topple the wizard. Grallik was thankful he'd not eaten that day, else he'd be retching as he stood in front of the grisly pile. A haze of insects blanketed the mound, the incessant buzzing of the creatures making it hard for him to think. They flowed out around him, gnats sticking to the sweat on Grallik's face and neck and flying into his nose and mouth.

He gagged and crossed his arms in front of his chest, ground the ball of his foot against the hard earth, and reached into his mind for one of his easiest fire spells. He closed his eyes when he felt the flush of the magic, a warmth that was comfortable and welcome. The magic sprang away from him to strike the edge of the pile a dozen yards away. He directed the energy to envelop the closest corpse, a hobgoblin clad in a threadbare tunic that quickly caught fire. Flesh was harder to burn than cloth, so Grallik had to concentrate, picturing a column of beautiful flame, of red, orange, and yellow. Blessed color to contrast with the mud brown of Steel Town. He opened his eyes to see a lick of fire begin to dance along the cloth and catch at the hobgoblin's hair.

The Rebellion

The insects were loud, so he couldn't hear the first few harmonious crackles of fire. But after several moments, the flames spread and the noise of pleasant pops and hisses grew, and the annoying insects buzzed away into the darkness. Grallik felt the heat caress his face, relaxing him. The stench intensified, burning hair and flesh adding to the stink and sending billowing gray-black clouds up in the sky to blot out the stars. The Dark Knights always burned the slaves' bodies, not willing to go to any effort to bury them and not wanting to give them any measure of respect. The goblins and hobgoblins never protested such treatment of their dead—not that their objections would have mattered.

Grallik circled the pyre, sending small lances of flame from his fingers toward the far side. He saw crushed skulls and ribs, partial torsos, and decapitated bodies. A war could not have been more destructive. He'd so far avoided venturing toward the Dark Knights' graves, though eventually that would be necessary if he sought a pair of good boots. He could handle the sight of mutilated slave corpses far better than that of his dismembered brethren.

Satisfied that the pile of hob and gob bodies was burning well, he turned away and abruptly stopped in his tracks.

Goblins and hobgoblins were pressed against the fence, watching the fire. More, they were watching Grallik, their eyes wide and filled with fear and anger and sadness. They looked all the same to the wizard, though his eyes registered the different skin colors—orange, brown, red, yellow, and mottled shades in between. All were a bit drab and weathered looking, like old paint that had faded.

Most had wide-set eyes and broad noses, thin lips and sharp little teeth. Some had tall, pointed ears; others had crooked ones with pieces missing or decorated with shards of bones. Most were thin because the Dark Knights fed them just enough to keep them alive, and their ribs and shoulders were weirdly pronounced. A scattering had little pot bellies, and many had real arm and leg muscles from the heavy work they were forced to endure in the mine. Only one in five or six wore any articles of clothing. As in human society, clothing seemed to carry some measure of distinction, with the older or larger goblins boasting garments that came either from children in Steel Town who had outgrown them or women who had gotten tired of a raggedy garment and pitched it into the pen.

The hobgoblins were simply larger versions with more tufts of hair and even wider faces. Some had large enough teeth to be considered tusks. They came in a smaller range of colors, browns and reds, though they were equally drab and scarred. But they tended to wear more clothes because the hobgoblins served as foremen and stood apart from their more unfortunate brethren.

No two of them looked exactly alike, yet all of them appeared beaten down by years of hard work, malnourished from improper amounts of food, dazed by their hopelessness. To Grallik, they were all one and the same—tools for a job, to be treated with as much care as a sturdy pick or a shovel.

Little more than debris.

Many of the ones staring at him were injured, the stink from their dried blood and oozing wounds reaching Grallik as the breeze shifted. One in a corner drew his notice—a skinny female goblin with dark red skin and a lugubrious face etched with harshness. Her eyes were different, dark and small, set close to the thin bridge of her nose. They gave her a particularly angry expression. The others usually gave space to her, he'd noted in the past. Perhaps, like him, they were bothered by her angry eyes. Grallik had heard her two evenings past, hollering to the guards about a coming disaster. Could she have known about the quake?

How smart was she?

There were shamans among goblinkind. Was she one of them?

Huh! He shook his head. It was not likely but not impossible. He'd never scrutinized any of the slaves, only gave them passing glances when they brought the ore down the mountain. He'd never wondered if one of them carried a magical spark.

It was not likely that Angry Eyes was a shaman. And yet . . .

His throbbing feet reminded him that it was past time to sit and rest. His course took him around the goblin pens and toward chairs lined up where the tavern used to be. Grallik kept his gaze on the skinny red-skinned goblin as he went.

"The earth is not done," he thought he heard her say.

10

FREED SPIRITS

Direfang watched as Moon-eye fawned over Graytoes. The young female sat propped up against a post, hands on her rounded stomach and eyes closed. She looked as if she slept, but the hobgoblin knew she just wanted a measure of privacy. Pretending to sleep despite all the noise and the crowding and the swarms of insects was her only way to get some measure of peace. Moon-eye waved gnats away from her face.

Her legs were swollen, and Direfang could tell that the left might be broken. If it were broken, it would be a clean break, he knew from experience. There were no bones poking out of her skin and no maggots worming their way inside. He was amazed that both legs hadn't been thoroughly shattered and that she hadn't died. But the ground beneath her chamber had been packed with soft dirt, and the dirt had absorbed some of the impact of the timber falling on her. Direfang had carefully carried her out of the mine and down the mountainside. He knew Moon-eye to be a hard worker, and he did not want Moon-eye to grieve too

74

much over the death of a mate and risk punishment.

"Skull men will see to Graytoes later," he told Moon-eye. "Mend Graytoes later. Graytoes will be well, maybe even a little later today." He paused. "But maybe not until tomorrow. The skull men are busy mending the knights right now."

Moon-eye snarled something unintelligible. He'd called to the guards several times, trying to get one of them to summon a Skull Knight to heal his mate. There were other goblins injured worse, but Moon-eye didn't care about them.

"Moon-eye's Heart hurts," he said, stroking Graytoes's arm.

"When the skull men are done with the knights, one will come here," Direfang said.

"Promise?"

Direfang scowled. "No." He patted the top of Graytoes' head then worked his way through the mass of goblins so he could stand at the rail and watch the funeral pyre. He wondered why the Dark Knights chose to bury their dead and forever trap their spirits beneath the earth.

But Direfang had served the Dark Knights for many years and knew that was their way, though he never understood the reasons for it. It had something to do with their gods, the burying and corpse rotting. Perhaps their gods, with their cruel senses of humor, required the barbaric ritual. Direfang had never asked the Dark Knights about it. He was content that the knights, even though they did it unknowingly, properly observed the custom of goblinkind by burning dead slaves.

The goblin and hobgoblin clans had different ways of disposing of their dead, though all accepted the burning that took place in Steel Town. In fact, most of the clans Direfang was familiar with preferred the pyre. Then, after the ashes were cold, friends and relatives of the deceased traditionally would break and scatter any remaining bones, trying to leave nothing intact. Similar things would be done in Steel Town, though not by any ritual, and likely not with relatives involved. The hobgoblin knew the Dark Knights would order the slaves to rake the bones flat and cover them with earth, so the area would not look unsightly. That's what they had done seven years past, when a wasting disease swept through one of the pens and killed more than one hundred goblins before the Skull Knights could stop the malady.

Direfang had been among those who raked the bones then, and he'd volunteered ever since that time to spread the ashes of the occasional lone slave who died because of a beating or mine accident or old age.

The clan Graytoes hailed from preferred to leave its bodies to rot in the woods, bestowing the flesh on carrion birds and the insects, and knowing that larger predators would rip up the corpses, also thereby separating the bones.

Moon-eye was taken from his clan at such a young age that he had no memories of the traditions they had practiced.

Saro-Saro's clan had been known for eating its dead; that was the only clan Direfang was aware of with such a predilection, though he was certain there were others. And that clan, too, scattered the remains of what was not consumed.

Hobgoblin clans on the coasts usually gave the bodies to the seas, knowing fish and other creatures would feast on the dead. Those inland typically cleaved off a limb or the head as a remembrance for relatives, leaving the bodies for scavengers and returning to break and scatter and spread the bones. Larger clans ground the bones and used them in pottery or gardens, honoring the dead by letting them nurture the living.

THE REBELLION

Some of the oldest goblin clans used the rib bones of their dead warriors to fashion pieces of armor, believing that they gained strength by keeping the memory of their heroes and ancestors close. Mudwort once told Direfang that her clan used the leg bones of the dead to beat ceremonial drums and used skulls for bowls. Finger bones were sharpened into fishhooks, for her clan favored extensive use of tools and relied on lakes and rivers for their livelihood. Mudwort knew of many other curious practices concerning the dead but did not speak much about them. She did, from time to time, laugh when the Dark Knights buried one of their own.

No goblin body should be left to rot beneath the earth. And none should be left intact or unbroken, all the clans agreed. There should be nothing for the spirit to return to.

Enemies were another matter. When clan warred against clan, which was rare, or when they fought tribes of kobolds and gnolls, the goblins tried to dig deep and bury beneath the earth the enemies they killed so their spirits would be trapped. It was another way to dishonor their foes.

All the clans Direfang knew of were certain that goblin and hobgoblin spirits—once separated from their dead bodies—would return to Krynn to begin another life.

Everything returned. Nothing was wholly lost.

That explained why Direfang and the others had memories that came to them mysteriously or why they instinctively knew how to do certain things.

It also explained why the bodies had to be destroyed. A spirit would first try to return to its old form, and if that form was whole, regardless of its state of decay, the spirit would lodge there. It would be trapped for decades upon decades in the husk of its former self. And when time finally turned the bones to dust, the spirit would dissipate, lost and tortured eternally.

But if the spirit could not return to its old form because that form had been burned or eaten and the bones strewn about and broken, it would be born again into a new body. Direfang wondered if the spirit of one of the goblins who died in the mine and was burned this night would emerge as Graytoes and Moon-eye's child. He hoped not. He hoped the spirits freed that night would be born to clans well beyond Steel Town and never see the inside of a mountain.

No one knew how long a spirit hovered before returning or how many times a spirit returned.

He wondered how old his own spirit was.

Direfang considered some of the goblins in the camp to be old souls: Mudwort, Saro-Saro, Bentclaw, Hurbear, and a few of those on the pyre. Perhaps those souls in long-ago times believed in gods such as Chislev and Takhisis and would have understood the Dark Knights' silly burial practices. But the goblins believed those things no longer—they were more sagacious.

The goblins and hobgoblins in Steel Town, and in the tribes and clans throughout Neraka, did not revere any of Krynn's gods. They recognized that the gods existed and that they capriciously meddled in mortals' affairs. But goblinkind did not believe that paying homage to any god would send their spirits to some glorious afterlife. Neither did the goblins care to spend their afterlife with any of those gods. Such a fate would be more akin to damnation than salvation.

The gods never did anything good for goblinkind. They never made goblins and hobgoblins and their bugbear cousins strong enough to stand up to Dark Knights and ogres and minotaurs. They never kept goblinkind from being exploited and mistreated by practically all the world's races.

They never kept them from being ripped from their families and made slaves, from being whipped and practically starved, from being forced to mine ore for cruel taskmasters such as the Dark Knights of Hell Town.

And they hadn't prevented the earth from shaking and collapsing shafts down on top of goblin heads.

So because the gods had ignored goblinkind and deemed them worthless of their attention, goblinkind in turn ignored the gods and deemed them worse than useless.

Direfang felt mildly sorry for the Dark Knights, yoked as they were to their foolish gods and rituals, burying their dead so the spirits would be trapped in husks rotting beneath Steel Town's ugly earth. He wondered how many more years he would have to spend in the camp before he died and was thrown into the fire. He watched the flames dance up the bodies and hoped he'd be lucky enough not to be trapped in the mine.

"Cold night, warm fire," a goblin at his side observed. "Good burn."

"Yes," Direfang admitted. "It is a good burn. It will keep the spirits away."

"Away from the mine," the goblin said. "Away from this hell."

Direfang continued to stare at the flames, coughing when the wind shifted and sent the acrid stench of burning flesh across the slave pens.

"Bad smell, the fire. Good that it sends the spirits away," the goblin continued.

"This one will burn a long time," Direfang said. "So many bodies, piled so high. So many dead." The heat from the pyre made him thirstier and made him think about the place in the mine where water poured down the wall, where he drank his fill before carrying Graytoes out. Still, he stood there watching until the fire died down and the pile was reduced to charred, twisted remains. Most of the goblins had watched too, waiting for the ceremony to begin.

Hurbear presided. The goblin, like others of his kind, had a flat face, broad nose, and pointed ears. His mouth was overly wide, however, and filled with broken, flat teeth, which indicated his advanced years. His skin was a dusky yellow; his dull eyes had a film over them. Goblins from the same area tended to have similar coloration, and eight of Hurbear's clansmen, their skin a brighter yellow because of their relative youth, crowded around him.

"The passing comes to all goblins," Hurbear began.

"Let the telling begin!" Moon-eye yelled. "Listen to Hurbear."

The elder goblin made the same speech for each death in the camp. "The shell destroyed, fire cleansed, the spirit reborn." Hurbear made a fist and placed it over his heart.

"Spirit reborn," his clansmen echoed. The largest thumped his belly with the flat of his hand then started up a drumlike cadence, which the other seven joined.

Hurbear raised his arms, fingers spread wide. "Spirits fly above Steel Town. Above pain. Above the great sad. Above clans left behind. Above all things." He turned, nodding to each of the compass points. "The passing comes to all goblins. The passing came to . . ."

"Gray-morning." Direfang claimed the right to speak first, and because of his size and his status as a foreman, none challenged him. "Gray-morning, called 'old mother' by some, hid strips of dried meat stolen from others in ore sacks on trips to the mine. Hungry, Gray-morning would eat before the work began. Hungry always, Gray-morning sucked on rocks and chewed on weeds, begged turnips from the taskmasters. Gray-morning brought smiles. The old mother, the old friend, will be missed." It wasn't a particularly captivating or special eulogy, but it defined the dead goblin and Direfang's relationship to her. Direfang mimicked sticking a meat strip in his mouth and breaking some of it off. "Gray-morning is remembered."

Other memories were not as well spoken but were nonetheless intended as a measure of respect.

"Big Snout smelled bad," a young goblin offered. "Stunk in life, stinks now burning. Stinks worse in death. Big Snout is remembered."

"Growler always scratched. Like a bear, Growler rubbed against the timbers in the mine. Growler is remembered."

"Feshter was lazy. Lazy Feshter slept much, snored much. Lazy Feshter will not be forgotten."

"Blue-lip bore two younglings in this pen."

"Ren-Ren watched the horses. Ren-Ren made horse sounds."

Direfang listened to each remembrance, trying to give each the reverence they deserved, yet finding it difficult to concentrate on only the sad occasion. He was worried about the goblins and hobgoblins who were not in the pens and not on the pyre, those unaccounted for because they were still in the mine.

They were likely dead, but it was not for certain. Some might be caught in passageways and chambers. He'd talked to one of the Dark Knight lieutenants earlier about going back into the shafts to search for bodies and survivors. The knights had missing men too and said that a mission would start at dawn. If goblin and hobgoblin bodies were not recovered quickly, Direfang feared the spirits would return to the dead husks and would be forever trapped in the decaying shells, forever tortured and lost.

"Saro-Saro's brother, Sharp-teeth was. Only brother. Saro-Saro will not forget Sharp-teeth."

"Bright Eyes sang well and told good stories."

"Four Toes feared lightning. Four Toes hated storms and shivered like a youngling when the rains came."

"Igrun was old and carried half-full sacks. Oldest in all of these pens, Igrun was."

Direfang tried to count the goblins and hobgoblins in the pens. But they were moving around restlessly, and they were too numerous—all of them crammed inside rather than some of them working in the mine, as usual. He had neglected to count the number of bodies thrown on the pyre, and so worried that some of the dead would not be named in the ceremony.

Naming the dead and speaking a remembrance was a custom that dated back centuries for some clans. The stories recorded goblinkind's history and were passed from one generation to the next, rarely embellished. The slaves' stories, unlike those in free clans, were short and simple because their lives had been painful and monotonous. But the stories they'd heard before their capture were more elaborate and recalled great discoveries the dead had made, battles won, and strange beasts defeated. The telling was done to catch a spirit's attention, to let it know it was missed and appreciated and, therefore, was welcome back for another life. Mostly it was done to honor the spirit because the gods would not do so . . . nor, in Steel Town, would the Dark Knights.

The sky had started to lighten by the time the ceremony was finished. Not all the goblins had stayed awake to the end, though not for lack of trying. Some of them had been awake for more than a day, and the injured drifted in and out of consciousness.

Mudwort had stayed awake through all of the ceremony, though she did not participate and only part of the time listened. It wasn't that she didn't believe in the ritual; she did, and she had participated in others, though none on the scale of the one that day. Instead she was listening to the earth. When Direfang spotted her and found his way through the press of bodies, he saw that her fingers were thrust into the ground.

Mudwort sat against her favorite post, legs tucked close to her chest and arms at her sides, fingers digging deeper. Her lips were working, though Direfang couldn't hear what she was saying—if indeed she was making any sound. The whispers of those still awake melded into a sonorous, indecipherable hum around them.

She gently rocked back and forth, her eyes closed and head tipped. She stopped moving her mouth for a moment, drawing her lips into a thin line and putting on a pensive expression, then she started mouthing words again.

Direfang watched her, perplexed and fascinated.

The ground seemed to ripple around her fingers, turning into wet clay and smoothing, then hardening, even as Mudwort's expression hardened.

"Doing what?" Direfang said. The words croaked out. His mouth was so dry. He was so thirsty. "Doing what, Mudwort?"

She acted as if she hadn't heard him, but her eyelids fluttered.

"Doing what?" Direfang spoke so loud that all the nearby goblins stopped their chatter and stared.

"Listening," she said finally. She let out a great sigh, and her shoulders slumped. Then she pulled her fingers out of the ground. The holes instantly filled.

11

BLOOD AND WATER

Mudwort's eyes took on an old, rheumy look as she drew her lower lip into her mouth. Her hands hovered inches above the ground, palms sometimes dropping down and touching the earth then pulling back as if scalded. Fingers fluttering and toes twitching, she started mumbling. She shook her head vehemently when Direfang leaned close to see if she was all right.

He spoke to her again, but it was clear she didn't hear him. She cocked her head slightly as though she were listening to something very far beyond the slave pen and Steel Town.

Direfang tried to listen too, straining to shut out the sounds of the goblins moving listlessly in the overcrowded pen and the conversation of a pair of Dark Knights strolling by. The hobgoblin heard nothing interesting, so he waited impatiently for Mudwort to explain what she was doing.

Behind him, Saro-Saro made a clucking noise. "Mudwort is good and smart," he said. "But Mudwort is also mad. There are voices in Mudwort's head no one else can hear.

Good thing the voices only speak to Mudwort. Good that only Mudwort has a sour mind."

Minutes later Mudwort stopped mumbling, though her lips continued to move, and one eyebrow rose sharply as if in surprise. She nodded to Direfang, finally acknowledging his presence, then mumbled something again and kept fluttering her fingers.

"Mudwort listening to what?" Direfang punctuated his question with a snarl, hoping to draw her full attention. "Listening to what?"

"Listening to head voices," Saro-Saro said.

"Listening to nothing." That came from Hurbear, hovering nearby. He shook his head sadly then pushed his way through the press of slaves and disappeared.

"What does Mudwort listen to? Mudwort listens to what?" One of the younger slaves had found her way to the front. Less than three feet tall, already she displayed the stooped shoulders of defeat. Her gray-yellow skin gave her a sickly appearance, but her eyes were bright, her expression curious. She cupped her hands to her ears as if trying to imitate Mudwort. Then she drew her features forward until her face looked painfully pinched. "What is Mudwort hearing, Direfang?"

"Mudwort . . ." Direfang was clearly exasperated.

The red-skinned goblin continued her antics, drawing stares from the closest slaves as she cocked her head this way and that and whispered answers to the voices in her head. The buzz of questions became loud and annoying, and Mudwort finally raised her head and drew her shoulders back and spat at the surrounding slaves, but they wouldn't quiet.

"Mad is Mudwort," one called Brak sneered. "Sour in the head. Saro-Saro is right about Mudwort's sour head. Mind gone bad like old, ugly meat. Mind spoiled and ruined."

"Mad, no. *Dard,* yes," another volunteered, jabbing a

finger toward Mudwort. "Said a bad something was coming to the mine. Said bad, and bad came. Mudwort knew about it. Mad, no. Smart, yes. *Dard,* Mudwort is."

"Mad, mad, mad," Brak repeated, slamming his fist against his palm for emphasis. He was a little burlier than most goblins, and a little more than three feet tall— a veritable giant of his race. His skin was dark orange, marking him as one of the Flamegrass Clan. "Mind dried up. Gone all sour and stinky."

The debate swirled over Mudwort, mingled with random musings about dead companions. Then, suddenly, the chatter was interrupted by a loud thud coming from the stables. Nervous whinnies from surviving horses followed. Then things quieted down again, and the chatter resumed.

"Galgirth's mind was stinky too. But bad that Galgirth died. Spirit come back, maybe, with clear mind in a new body. New body, no stinky mind."

Brak cackled. "All slaves have minds a little stinky. Mudwort's is just smellier than most."

Direfang spoke louder, trying to be heard over the goblins' prattle. "Listening to what now, Mudwort? Certainly not listening to Brak. Listening to what, who, where?"

"Listening," she whispered back. Mudwort's eyes had grown glassy, as if she'd put herself in a trance. She sucked in a deep breath, and her fingers and toes wiggled faster. She started mumbling again, in a singsong rhythm.

"Enough!" Direfang finally grabbed her shoulders and gave them a squeeze. She shook her head to clear her senses, blinking furiously. The brightness came back to her eyes, and she glared at the hobgoblin for interrupting her.

"Listening to what, Mudwort? Who is talking? What is talking?"

She shook her head once more, slapping her knee. "The earth, Direfang! The earth talks and talks. It is angry still. It seethes beneath this place! Like the earth dragon raged after the quake, the earth growls and spits and demands more things to eat."

Direfang knelt directly in front of her, blocking the other goblins so they could not easily see Mudwort, and he drew a finger to his bulbous lips to get her to speak softly, so as not to alarm the others. "Why is it angry, Mudwort? Why is the earth so upset?" His eyes revealed he believed her.

She shrugged. "Not the mine. No, the mine is not upset, and the earth is not upset at the mine. Thought the earth was angry at the mine before, all the digging and stealing rocks, all the hollowing out of the mountain, that was wrong. Earth not angry at the Dark Knights either. Thought the earth was angry with the Dark Knights, too, before . . . when the ground quaked before. Just angry, I think. The earth is just old and angry. Bad, bad angry. Maybe it hurts from being so old. Grouchy like Hurbear. Mad like the earth dragon was."

Direfang scratched the side of his face and opened his mouth to ask another question.

"Angry," she repeated, cutting him off and shaking a finger at him. "Angry enough to shake hard again."

"When?" The hobgoblin spoke in a voice hushed and raspy with fear. "When will another earthquake come?"

Mudwort's eyes narrowed.

All the chatter around them had stopped, and from somewhere overhead came the shrill cry of a night bird. From the center of the camp came the sounds of shovels from the goblins and hobgoblins digging new wells. The bark of Dark Knight orders intruded, demanding the wells be dug faster.

"Tomorrow, it will be," Mudwort said finally. "The earth will quake tomorrow. Or the day after that maybe. No longer than the day after that. Its anger grows." She placed her palms against the ground again. "Grows and grows and grows."

"The day after that," Direfang said, thinking it over. "Tell the earth to wait until then. There are many goblins to bring out of the mine tomorrow." He turned and leaned against the fence, fingers rubbing at the rough wood. "It has to be the day after that if we are to have any chance of saving the ones left behind."

The hobgoblin stood and fixed his gaze on the burning embers from the body pyre then looked past the mound. He spotted a Dark Knight walking the perimeter of the camp, highlighted by the glow from the remnants of goblin corpses.

"The quake destroyed the buildings," Direfang said to himself, reflecting on all that had happened. "Brought down shafts. Killed goblins and Dark Knights and maybe something else. Maybe . . . maybe it killed something dangerous."

The hobgoblin knew about the wards that sounded an alert in case a slave tried to escape. All the slaves knew about them. Some of the wards or glyphs did more than sound an alarm. Some engulfed escaping goblins in flames that shot up from the ground and burned hotter and faster than any fire made by man. Direfang had seen the fatal magic work on several occasions. The threat of those flames terrified the goblins and kept most from even dreaming of escape.

"Yes, the quake destroyed something else," Mudwort said.

The next day, work in the mines began before dawn. Goblins and hobgoblins who'd managed to catch only an hour or two of sleep at best began to clear rubble-strewn passages and shore up timbers and replace crosspieces. They had fewer tools to work with than usual because so much had been lost to the quake. Large buckets made of broken planks from ruined houses were used to bring out rocks. The goblins tipped those makeshift buckets down the mountainside, creating a debris pile to cover up the remains of dead horses and goats.

The shafts were crowded with slaves bringing out rocks, and the stench from their sweaty bodies was intense. Few Dark Knight taskmasters entered the shafts, instead retreating to the mine entrance where the air was a little better and conditions safer. Only one remained in the deeper tunnels, a stalwart from Grallik's talon, and he was quick to whip any goblins who moved too slowly or balked at orders.

Recalcitrant slaves were rare, however, as nearly all of the goblins worked with a fervor that was almost reckless. They were desperate to bring out any of their living brethren who might still be trapped, and equally desperate to bring out any remains so the bodies could be burned and broken before the spirits returned. Also, they worked as fast as possible so they would not be stuck in the shafts for very long. The air was horrible to breathe, and dust filtered down and tried to choke them. And word had spread that Mudwort predicted there would be another quake soon, perhaps that day. Most considered her mad, but there were enough who worried that there was some truth in her babblings, so they wanted to be done with their work and free of the tunnels as quickly as possible.

Nearly three dozen goblins and four hobgoblins were found alive and rescued by sunset, though all were suffering injuries. More than two hundred slave bodies were carried out, and eight Dark Knight bodies were carefully extracted.

Direfang tried to guess how many might still be below—dead or alive. He didn't know for certain just how many slaves there were in Steel Town. He'd had no reason to ask before because the information had not seemed very important. When he asked a taskmaster, though, the query was met with contempt.

"Fewer slaves now than before," the Dark Knight bristled.

"Blessedly fewer Dark Knights too," Direfang muttered in his own tongue. He stood on the mountain trail, overlooking the ruins of the camp and glancing at the slave pens and the blackened circle beyond that marked the burned corpses. More bodies were being carried there for a fresh pyre.

"Fewer goblins and Dark Knights and . . . fewer wards," he continued to mutter to himself in his guttural tongue. "Perhaps no wards at all. Will ask Mudwort to search through the earth . . . listen to whatever in the ground spoke . . . ask the voices if the wards and glyphs are gone. Maybe also ask if goblins—alive or dead—remain in the mine tunnels."

Hours earlier he'd mentioned the wards to Moon-eye and Saro-Saro, that perhaps the quake ruined the magic as it had ruined practically everything else, that perhaps they should test the magic. Both goblins snorted their disapproval, Moon-eye because Graytoes was still hurt and hadn't yet been tended by a Skull Knight. He'd risk nothing if it meant risking her life. Moon-eye was forced to help clear the mines because the Dark Knights ordered it. Not following orders meant a whipping or worse. But if he did his job, maybe the knights would heal Graytoes eventually.

Saro-Saro's reasoning was simpler.

"Slave," he said, pointing to his chest. "Slaves work the mine. Slaves do not try to escape. You know that. Direfang should not think about such things. Direfang is a slave. Thinking such things leads to whippings. Direfang should know that from experience and from lack of an ear."

Direfang had savored the prospect of escape long ago, ten years back. It had taken little convincing then to get him to join with a handful of goblins trying to flee. Because he was young and strong and, therefore, useful in the mines, he wasn't killed. He had been beaten, though, beaten cruelly and horribly, before being healed by a Skull Knight. He'd been reasonably loyal since then, never questioning the Dark Knights, obeying every order, often working harder than he was expected to, even longer than was required. Direfang usually worked until he was thoroughly spent just to keep his mind off his surroundings and situation and off the occasional goblin who tried to break free and was burned by the fiery glyphs or caught by Dark Knights, then tortured and slain.

Work kept him strong and healthy, and three years past, his diligence had netted him a promotion to foreman. Direfang had been tattooed on his shoulder to mark him a foreman. All the dozen slave foremen bore such marks. He thought it uglier than his scars from injuries and punishments, though his fellow slaves considered it a badge of honor.

The Dark Knights currently ruling the camp had likely forgotten his attempted escape; there had been many turnovers in forces, and the hobgoblins all looked much the same to them. If they'd remembered his previous escape attempt, he would not have been made a foreman. He would not have been taken into their buildings for training, and he would not have been given the opportunity to learn the complexities of their language. He would not have been allowed enough looks at their books and maps to gain a rudimentary knowledge of reading.

No, the Dark Knights in the camp probably didn't realize he, too, had tried to escape ten years past and that, from time to time, he still entertained such a notion.

He finally looked away from the camp and slave pens, shook off his musings, and returned to the shafts and worked even harder and faster, driven by the desire to find any slave left alive and to let no corpse rot there.

Twilight was overtaking the sky by the time the Dark

Knights signaled an end to the day's toil. Before the quake, there always had been shifts working nonstop—all day and all night too; the mines were so dark anyway that it didn't matter. But the knights were clearing the tunnels and calling everyone out—perhaps, Direfang thought, because the Dark Knights were spread so thin they did not have enough troops to supervise mining and guard the slave pens all night long.

Direfang held four dead goblins in his arms, his mind so preoccupied he barely registered their weight. He didn't know who they had been in life, their bodies were so crushed, he didn't recognize them. There'd be no one to say words of remembrances for them when the pyre blazed again, but perhaps he could think of something good to say in their honor.

The hobgoblin walked down the mountain trail just ahead of a Dark Knight taskmaster. He could hear the man's shuffling step, so unlike the usual brisk march of the knights, and could hear the man's ragged breathing. The knights had been trimmed in number and beaten down by the quake; the recovery work was hard, and they were not as alert as usual.

The Dark Knights seemed as tired and defeated as the slaves.

"Now might be a good time to consider another escape," Direfang whispered. "Perhaps the only time. The wards and glyphs might be gone. Mudwort might be right. And if the wards and glyphs are gone, there will be no columns of magical flames to burn slaves and stop them from escaping."

The hobgoblin reached the base of the mountain and made his way toward the new mound of bodies piling up. The ceaseless talk of the slaves drifted through the air. Goblins always found something to chatter about. A Dark Knight was barking orders; he was the wizard who'd spent all his hours before the quake melting the ore. Direfang hated that man, but then, he hated all the Dark Knights. The wizard continued to bark orders, and the hobgoblin continued to listen as he arranged the four dead goblins he carried at the bottom of the pile. For some reason, he wanted them to burn first.

The Dark Knight wizard was talking to a Skull Knight. Direfang caught a few snippets. The wizard said it was time to tend to the injured goblins. Then their voices dropped so low, the hobgoblin could not pick out a single word—not until he edged closer.

Someone had found . . . something, Direfang understood. Something important that needed to be guarded.

"Found what?" Direfang wondered as he shuffled to the nearest slave pen. But he did not immediately enter. He leaned against a slat, staring at the huddled, nervous goblins. They still stank of sweat, but it was the sweat of fear, not only labor, so the odor was doubly repugnant. He caught the attention of a goblin who, like him, seemed more interested in the camp activities than in his fellows. "Found something important, what?"

"Water," Folami said, approaching the foreman and poking at Direfang's waist through a gap in the slats. He was tall for a goblin, the top of his head coming up nearly to Direfang's chest. Folami hailed from an ancient clan, and his skin was the color of dry earth. He pointed toward the wizard standing near the center of the camp and licked his lips. "The Thorn Knight there says that water has been found. That's the something important that causes the stir."

12

BLESSED SALVATION

Grallik ordered six knights in his talon—the only ones still healthy after the quake—to pull the slaves back from the well. They'd struck water, and the goblins and hobgoblins were greedily drinking it up and sloshing around in it—fouling the water with their dirty skin and thick sweat.

"Blessed Salvation," one of the knights had dubbed the well.

Two goblins refused to leave the Blessed Salvation, so one of the knights pulled out a whip and started lashing them.

The wizard called a halt to the beating and went over to the well himself, grabbing the disobedient goblins by their arms and yanking them away. The slaves cursed vigorously in the goblin tongue, and though the wizard did not know their stupid language, he could well guess the meaning.

"Keep them all back!" he commanded his talon. "Wound them only if you've no recourse. The priests have enough to do and will not minister to any slaves you whip too harshly. I want no more dead or incapacitated slaves if I can help it. We simply cannot afford that right now. I don't know how long it will take to replace the ones who died in the mines."

The wizard stared thirstily at the water then motioned to a trio of laborers, each man toting ropes and buckets. "Set a perimeter of stones around this . . . Blessed Salvation. Then start filling jugs and take the first to the priests. The injured need water for drinking and bathing. And our dead brethren not yet buried need to be cleansed."

"The horses?" That question came from the stablemaster. "They need water too, else we will have animals to burn along with the dead slaves before the next morning. The horses desperately need water, as much as the priests."

Grallik kept his tone civil because the stablemaster was not a knight and, therefore, not expected to understand protocol. Still, the man needed to be put in his place. "The men come first, Hiram. You'll make no demands on me for the beasts. But I appreciate your concern. After enough water has been drawn for the injured and for all the knights here, you may take as much as you need for the livestock and the laborers."

The wizard turned to see a big, one-eared hobgoblin approaching. "And you will have some water for your fellows . . ." Grallik could not remember the name of the one-eared foreman, though he'd seen him often enough. He never could remember the name of any goblin. "But you must be patient."

The hobgoblin clearly heard the wizard say the livestock and laborers would get water soon enough. Even the horses came before the slaves. The goats and chickens—they, too, ranked above the slaves. The hobgoblin clenched his fists, claws digging into the palms of his hands and drawing blood.

"Yes, sir," the hobgoblin said, giving a slight bow to Grallik. "The slaves last, sir. The slaves are always last."

———— S ————

Direfang volunteered to help put stones around the well, both so he could be near the welcome water and so he could overhear the Dark Knights' talk. Listening was how he had learned their language and how he came to know all of their precious methods and rules. He'd hovered around them, listening and watching, paying close attention, for years and years. And because they found him useful and obedient, they generally paid no attention to him.

"I'll not have the slave shifts working continuously, Marek. I need all the Dark Knights in the camp at night, not any in the mine."

"Guardian? But there are still four knights unaccounted for."

"We have many brothers injured, and it will be days before more Lily Knights are sent here from Jelek or Neraka. Days, a few weeks most likely. We don't have enough healthy men to patrol Steel Town at night *and* supervise the slaves in the mine. The darkness hides much, Marek, and so we need to patrol the slave pens as a precaution. The wards, you know . . ." Grallik steepled his fingers under his chin and lowered his voice, shifting back and forth on the balls of his booted feet. "Many of them are down, useless. We can't afford to lose any more slaves than we've already lost to that damnable earthquake. With all this chaos, and with all our wounded brothers, they might be tempted to try and escape."

"I understand, Guardian."

"But soon, when more knights are dispatched here, either I or Marshal Montrill will set the mine in continuous operation again. You can be sure of that. We must make sure all the shafts are clear and drill a new shaft near where the veins are thickest. In the meantime, we will send an envoy to the ogre chieftain and arrange to purchase more slaves."

The Dark Knight bowed perfunctorily. "Your dinner, Guardian? Shall I bring you something to eat, or will you . . ."

"I will be eating with the wounded tonight, Marek, if I eat at all. And first I want to safeguard this well. Send Trelane and his brother . . ."

"Ostan, Guardian."

"Send Trelane and Ostan to guard this well when they've finished their meal. Then send another knight to start the dead slaves to burning. I've got more important things to see to this evening than roasting goblin corpses."

"Yes, Guardian." Marek pivoted, strode toward the laborers gathering pots and flasks for water, spoke quickly to one man, then continued on toward the Dark Knight burial detail.

The torches and lanterns that illuminated Steel Town flickered in the wind, chasing shadows across ruined buildings and laborers huddled under makeshift roofs with their families. The wind moaned softly, mimicking the sounds of the wounded and accompanying a woman softly crying.

Grallik stared numbly at the camp, his gaze flitting to the tavern owner and his wife, clinging to each other pathetically, then moving on to a knight limping toward the stable. "In a blessed several more days, everything will be operating again in hellish Steel Town," the wizard mused aloud, unaware that the hobgoblin foreman was still close by and listening. "Marshal Montrill will have his command back, and perhaps I will obtain leave to go to Neraka for supplies. For a while there will be tents, just as in the beginning of this place. Tents upon tents, from one end of chaos to the other."

When his work stacking rocks around the well was done, Direfang returned to the slave pens without being allowed a drink.

"No one has helped Moon-eye's Heart." Moon-eye stared at Direfang accusingly. The goblin continued to hover over his mate, alternating between gently touching her stomach and blowing to keep the gnats away from her crusted eyes.

"The skull men still tend to the knights," Direfang said with a deep sigh, studying Graytoes' legs. "Not so bad as yesterday. Swelling is down. Perhaps Graytoes' legs are not broken after all."

The hobgoblin knelt down next to Graytoes and gingerly felt her legs. He watched her face, looking for a reaction. Direfang had learned a little about administering to the sick, again from watching how the Dark Knights did it. She didn't grimace very much when he increased the pressure.

"No, not broken," Direfang pronounced happily. "So Graytoes should lay quiet and rest as long as the Dark Knights allow." The hobgoblin frowned at his own words because he was already making a plan to get all of the slaves moving—as many as would dare come with him later that very night. "Graytoes should rest. Good time to rest."

Moon-eye continued to fret. "Not broken, really?"

"No, not broken." Direfang's breath whistled out between his teeth, showing his irritation at having to repeat himself.

"Baby not broken?" Moon-eye put his ear to Graytoes' stomach. "First baby."

Direfang regarded the pair for a few moments then lowered his voice. "The baby of Moon-eye and Graytoes is not broken. And the baby does not have to be born a slave."

Moon-eye gasped, pulling his chin close to his neck. "Moon-eye slave, Graytoes slave, first baby slave. Moon-eye slave since . . ." He paused and rubbed at his chin, trying to remember just how many years had passed since he'd been a slave and how many years he'd lived in Steel Town. "Slave since . . ."

"Slave since the ogres of the Blood-Claw Chieftain swept into the village," Direfang said, pointing to himself. "Slave since childhood. Slave since fifteen years come the next Dry-Heat." Direfang used the dwarf term for the height of summer, another expression he'd picked up by listening to the people who weren't slaves in Steel Town. "Here since fifteen years come the next Dry-Heat. Fifteen bad years."

The hobgoblin sucked in a deep breath and looked away from the couple. Despite the loss of goblins to the quake, the pens had never before seemed so crowded. Without any shift operating in the mines, all the slaves were gathered there in camp. The awful smell and noise were disconcerting. The breathing, wheezing, snorting—there was no escaping the noise of so many. The pop and hiss of fire was added to the din. The Dark Knights had started burning more goblin corpses.

Graytoes stirred, reaching a hand out and brushing Direfang's knee. "Remember?"

Direfang cocked his head, not understanding.

"Remember the Before Time? Remember being free?"

The hobgoblin nodded. Graytoes and some of the others called their years before slavery the Before Time.

"Don't remember," Graytoes said, her expression sorrowful as she shook her head. "Only remember this. Remember Steel Town only. Memory gone of the Before Time." Tears welled in her eyes, and Moon-eye waved his hands at Direfang to chase him away. "Wish memory not gone, Direfang. Wish the Before Time was still here." Graytoes pointed to her forehead. "Wish the memory was not twisted and sour."

"Direfang should go now and leave Moon-eye's Heart alone." The one-eyed goblin shook his fist for emphasis. "Direfang should not make Moon-eye's Heart feel bad or sad. Moon-eye's Heart has enough broken without breaking heart."

Direfang rose and brushed at the front of his legs. His legs ached. Every inch of him was sore from working so hard bringing out the living and dead then carrying stones to place around the new well. He rolled his shoulders and looked through the sea of goblin bodies, hoping to spot Mudwort. There was no sign of her, and he turned back to the pair.

"The memory of the Before Time is still strong in here," the hobgoblin said, tapping his temple with a long finger. He locked eyes with Graytoes while ignoring Moon-eye, who swatted at him. "The Before Time was better than this, Graytoes. Being free was better. Being free again would be good. Good, too, for Graytoes' first baby to be free."

"Pfah!" Moon-eye again tried to shoo Direfang away.

The hobgoblin went, cutting a swath through clusters of goblins in his search for Mudwort. He finally found her in the center of Hurbear's clan, her red skin a stark contrast to their various shades of yellow.

"Listen," she was telling them. She stamped her foot against the earth. "The quake will come tonight, tomorrow, no later. The ground will shake again and bring down the mountain. It will bring down slaves and Dark Knights and . . ." She stopped when she noticed Direfang looming above them.

"Remember the Before Time, Mudwort?"

She opened her mouth but said nothing. She crossed her arms in front of her, surprised at the unlikely question.

"Remember . . . before Steel Town?"

Mudwort looked upset, not only at being interrupted.

"Remember what it was like to be free?"

Hurbear's clan backed up a few steps, giving Direfang more room.

"Slave since when, Mudwort?" The hobgoblin persisted.

She shrugged, some of her anger and irritation dropping away. She let her arms fall to her sides too. "Long time, Direfang. Slave since . . . too long to remember how long. A slave for many, many years. A long time. Too long."

"Remember before Steel Town, Mudwort?"

Her eyes sparkled in the growing darkness. "Remember, yes. Think about it sometimes. Miss that time, Direfang. It's bad to bring the memories back now. Bad, bad, bad. Such memories are painful and sad and terribly sour."

"Remember what it was like to be free?"

She stepped close and looked up into his broad, scarred face. "Remember, yes. Certainly." Her voice dropped to a whisper, and Hurbear had to draw closer to hear her next words. "Been thinking about it, too. Something else was destroyed with the quake, Direfang."

"How much? How many of them?"

"All of them!" Mudwort stepped back and stared at the ground. "Remember free, Direfang? Remember when—"

"A slave since Ureeg was chief," one of Hurbear's clansmen interjected. He was one of the older goblins in the camp, his skin gray from age. He wore a woman's blouse that dangled to his knees and that was tied at the waist with an old ribbon. The lacy collar fluttered in the breeze. "Slave a long time." He waggled his thumb against his chest.

"That would be . . ." Hurbear pursed his lips and made a guess. "Ten years."

"Twenty," the clansman corrected, holding up the fingers of both hands and flashing them twice. "Ureeg became chief when Toothfew died. Twenty years since Toothfew died and—"

"Longer than that even," Hurbear said, referring to his own years in servitude to the Dark Knights. "Slave forever. Slave always. Slave until dead." The old goblin rounded his shoulders so his back looked humped like a turtle shell. "Feel dead. Should have died twenty years ago."

"Hurbear was not always a slave." Direfang turned away from all of them, looking east. The mound of goblin bodies was steadily burning but was slower than the previous pyre because the wizard had not magically fed it. The wind blew the acrid stink directly toward the pens and made the hobgoblin's eyes sting and water. "Remember, Hurbear? Remember being free? Remember when there were no pens and no whips, and goblins could drink before goats and chickens?"

The old goblin shut his eyes. "Don't want to remember. Direfang should not want to remember. Pain in remembering, as Mudwort says. And nothing good comes from pain." When the old goblin opened his eyes again, he, too, stared through gaps in the press of bodies at the pyre. "Hurbear burn there soon enough, Direfang. Hurbear is old and very tired. All the slaves will burn someday. Direfang, too. Kayod and Quickfeet, Chima and Olabode will burn too, someday. All slaves burn. Then the spirits will be free. Then all will be free."

"S'dards! All in Hurbear's clan are damn *s'dards."* Direfang growled and brushed by the clansmen, goblins parting to avoid being knocked down by the angry hobgoblin. He swung his arms as he went, fists tight and claws again drawing blood against his palms. A few followed him, one of them a tan-skinned goblin who'd been at the camp only a few months.

"Remember, certainly," the tan goblin said. He tugged on what was left of Direfang's trousers, but the hobgoblin did not stop until he reached the boundary of the pen.

Direfang glanced down at the tan-skinned newcomer, recognizing him from the mine but not knowing his name.

"Krumb," he said. "Of the Brokenose Clan."

"A long way from home, Krumb," Direfang observed.

"Came south hunting. Went farther south when chased by a small dragon. Chased right into the ogre hills. Caught then. Slave then." He spat at the recollection. "Hate ogres. Hate Dark Knights worse."

"Should have stayed north and let the dragon feast." Direfang leaned against the top slat and watched the funeral fire, his eyes burning and his mouth painfully dry. He wondered when the slaves would be given water. The water in the well had smelled sweet. The corner of his lip raised when the wind gusted stronger and the stench from the pyre intensified. "Dark Knights will smell this too, the stench will wash over all of Steel Town. Sink into the boots and cloaks and skin."

"Remember freedom," Krumb said. "Memory is fresh."

"Mudwort says the wards are gone."

Direfang didn't get much of a reaction from Krumb, the new slave not yet knowing firsthand about the wards and the columns of flame. But the tan-skinned goblin had already figured out what was on Direfang's mind.

"Escape?" Krumb said the word loud enough that the goblins gathered nearby could hear.

Instantly there was buzz of talk, turning into a debate that grew louder until a pair of Dark Knights walked by on their patrol. The slaves instantly quieted.

When the knights had gone past, Direfang beckoned the small group of goblins closer around him and said, "Escape this very night. Or escape tomorrow, no later. Escape when the next quake comes and the Dark Knights' world once more shakes to pieces. Escape when the Dark Knights must fight the earth and will have no time to catch slaves."

Krumb grinned broadly and scampered away to spread the word.

13

A Slave Since . . .

As the pyre burned steadily, Direfang studied the Dark Knight patrols until he had their dull and predictable schedule memorized. He tried to calculate how many knights were healthy and able to fight—about one hundred, he guessed. There were about two thousand goblins and hobgoblins in the pens.

He'd earlier overheard the wizard say that roughly one-third of the slaves and one-third of the Dark Knights had died in the quake and that another third of the Dark Knights were injured, some severely. Many of the slaves were also injured. One of the Skull Knights would be visiting the pens soon, and those with the mildest injuries would heal quickly.

Two thousand slaves to one hundred healthy Dark Knights. The numbers were in the goblins' favor. Of course the numbers always had been in their favor. The goblins and hobgoblins were just too beaten down to resist. And the threat of the wards and the fiery, killing glyphs, that was a decisive factor.

THE REBELLION

It was nearly midnight, and word had spread through all the pens that Direfang was planning an escape. Only a few dozen volunteered to go with him, and many more tried to talk Direfang and the others out of their foolish notion.

"Slaves always," Thema insisted. "Being a live slave is better than being dead." She was a slight and rather pretty goblin, not yet scarred by too many years in the mine.

"Go out of Steel Town, and you will die," Folami agreed. "Direfang die. Goblins following Direfang will die. All die." Folami was a member of Krumb's clan, and though he had not been a slave for more than a year, he shook nervously as he spoke at the very thought of striking out from the camp.

The whispering and argument had attracted the attention of the Dark Knights, but none knew enough of the goblin tongue to understand what was being said. The four knights who patrolled between the pens and the well watched the pens warily, however, and one of them regularly stepped close and, waving his sword, ordered the goblins to quiet down.

"Won't go back in mine again," Saro-Saro said, his rough voice kept soft. "Mudwort says the world will shake again. Won't be in the mine when it shakes this time. Follow Direfang and die, go to the mine and die. All will die anyway, so follow Direfang. Maybe die faster. Maybe die free."

"The Dark Knights will make all the slaves go back to the mine tomorrow," Thema added. "Heard the knights talk. Heard a skull man say dig and dig and dig until the tunnels open for ore again. Dig and dig and dig until dead."

"Not dig and dig if we escape this night." Saro-Saro's tone was defiant. The cagey old goblin's eyes glimmered with a vitality they hadn't shown in some time. His clan members stayed close, some of them excited at the prospect of escape, a few nervous and shifting, one scratching his arm so hard it bled.

"Escape when the quake comes," Direfang repeated. He

waved his hand for those nearby to be quiet as the knights came close again. When the knights moved on, he continued. "Escape tonight, maybe. Tomorrow, no later than that. Escape during quake. Been a slave too long, been a slave since—"

The hobgoblin stopped when he saw a Skull Knight approaching, flanked by two other knights. They carried a jug of water and strips of black cloth that must have come from the Dark Knights' own tabards and cloaks. One of them carried a pouch with symbols on it, and Direfang knew from the watching the priests before that it contained medicinal herbs.

"Hush all of this talk of escape," Saro-Saro advised. "Quiet for now." He hurried toward the knights, pointing to the deep scratches on his stomach. Because of Saro-Saro's age and standing in the pen, goblins parted for him, and he got to the railing quickly, eager to be the first patient.

"Good Saro-Saro is being helped. Easier for Saro-Saro to escape if healed." This was muttered by an elder female goblin in Saro-Saro's clan.

"Quiet the escape talk," Thema and Folami snarled in unison at her.

"Dark Knights do not understand goblin speak," the elder female hissed.

"A few do." Direfang edged by the trio and was soon at Moon-eye's side. The Skull Knight treated a half dozen goblins before it was Graytoes' turn. None of the knights stepped inside the pen to minister to the injured slaves. They simply reached through the slats to dribble water on wounds, apply a few powders and crushed leaves, and wrap bandages. One beckoned the injured, making it clear that goblins who stayed in the center of the pen would not be treated.

"Help Moon-eye's Heart," the one-eyed goblin pleaded to the knights. The words were in the goblin tongue, and if the Skull Knight understood them, he gave no indication.

Moon-eye hovered close, a hand darting out to reassure Graytoes then withdrawing, not wanting to get in the Skull Knight's way.

Direfang watched the priest, who seemed emotionless. His gloved hands carefully pulled Graytoes closer until she was stretched out parallel to the slats and he could work on her more easily. The priest wrinkled his nose at the smell of the slaves, who washed only when it rained—a rare occurrence there; the pen always reeked with piles of dung. After a moment, the priest turned his head and made a gagging sound.

"Help Moon-eye's Heart. Please help . . ."

"Stop your insipid nattering," the Skull Knight demanded. He spoke in the common tongue of man, but Direfang, alone among the slaves, understood him perfectly. "Step back. All of you back. The smell of you is too strong."

Direfang pulled some of the goblins farther away but made no attempt to tug Moon-eye, who clung to Graytoes.

"By the Dark Queen's heads, this stench . . . it's worse than the last time I came here." Despite his revulsion, the Skull Knight continued to minister to Graytoes. "This one's legs are bruised badly but not broken. Terribly painful, I would imagine." He tugged off one of his gloves and held his hand above Graytoes' legs. A soft orange glow spilled down from his fingers and spread across her hide. "This will make the swelling go down and cut the pain." The Skull Knight looked up at Direfang, knowing the hobgoblin understood him. "You will explain this to them?" He indicated Graytoes and Moon-eye. "This goblin pair? Explain about her legs? She should not walk for a day, perhaps two. You will explain?"

"Yes," Direfang answered.

"She is pregnant," the Skull Knight observed.

"Many of them are," one of his knight attendants said brusquely. "Marshal Montrill favors them breeding.

The young grow fast. Breeding makes more slaves for the mine."

"Yes, when they stop crawling and crying for mama and are old enough to walk," the second knight agreed. "They're not fit for anything until they stop nursing and can stand on their own. Fortunately, that doesn't take too long."

Most of the younglings were kept in the pen farthest south, where their cries were less likely to disturb the Dark Knights' barracks. Graytoes would be moved there when her time came near.

"Good that so many of the females are pregnant now, eh?" one of the knights added. "We'll need more very soon to replace the ones killed in the mine." He, too, wrinkled his nose at the smell. He took a small jar out of a pocket in his tabard, pulled off the cork, and rubbed the salve under his nose. He passed it to his fellows, who gratefully followed suit.

"In fact, it is the pregnancy, more than her bruised legs, that weakens this one," the Skull Knight continued. His ungloved hand rested on Graytoes' stomach. "The child inside causes her distress, the position of it is wrong."

"What say?" Moon-eye leaned close, looking back and forth between the Skull Knight and Direfang. "What say about Moon-eye's baby? Say something about Moon-eye's baby?"

The hobgoblin nodded reassuringly but didn't translate.

"The issue inside of her might yet shift, but perhaps this one's insides simply were not meant to carry a child," the Skull Knight said, as much to himself as to anyone else. He glanced at his attendants. "But she cannot mine in this worrying condition. Not effectively in any event."

"A parasite, she is, then," one of the knights muttered. "Eating, drinking, and doing nothing. But too young to throw on the burning pile from the looks of her. A sorry parasite!"

Some of the goblins understood a few of the words, and those who didn't caught the knight's disparaging tone. They growled softly and spat; some shook their fists. But they made no move to draw closer. Any threatening action might end in a beating. And that would end the healing.

"A parasite, yes, which we cannot have," the Skull Knight said flatly. "My magic cannot change the position of the baby inside her." He splayed his fingers. "But my magic can remove the danger and bring her back to work as quickly as possible."

A sickly green light centered on the back of the Skull Knight's hand and darkened and spread, oozing down his fingers and sinking into Graytoes' stomach. "Watch the slaves and be ready," the priest cautioned. The knights straightened and wrapped their hands around the pommels of their swords.

Graytoes screamed and arched her back.

Moon-eyes shouted, "No!" and grabbed at the Skull Knight, trying to rip him away from his mate. But the priest was too strong and pushed Moon-eye off with his free hand. The green light brightened and covered all of her stomach.

The goblins in that area of the pen grew agitated, many of them shouting questions, some pressing forward and hurling threats at the Skull Knight, if he deliberately hurt Graytoes. Direfang was helpless to intervene. He barked at the slaves, ordering them to stay back and held his arms outstretched to keep them away from the slats of the pen.

"No!" Moon-eye wailed, drawing the syllable out much longer than usual. "Direfang, make the skull man stop! Moon-eye's Heart the skull man breaks! Stop, please, please stop!"

The Skull Knight finally finished, rising slowly and watching Graytoes' belly shrivel. She screamed and screamed as her baby was expelled in a pool of blood, its small form unmoving, dead between her legs. One of the attendant knights picked it up and gestured toward the burning corpse pile.

"This goblin will need to rest tomorrow at least," the priest told Direfang. "Then the day following, if her legs have mended, she can work in the mine a half shift."

"And full shifts all her following days," one of the knights added.

The priest and his attendants moved on, continuing to circle the pen, checking on more wounded goblins and treating some. But they were already weary of the job and announced another priest would be along in the morning to see to the rest.

They left behind a haunting medley of sounds: the crackling of the pyre, Moon-eye's wails and Graytoes' gasping sobs, angry murmuring from groups of goblins. Then a gentle rumbling sound began beneath their feet.

"The quake is coming!" Mudwort exclaimed, suddenly appearing next to Direfang. "The angry earth is talking again."

"Time to be free," Direfang said. He looked out over the heads of the goblins and hobgoblins, to the east beyond the pyre. He took a step in that direction but stopped when someone grabbed his tattered trouser leg. It was Moon-eye.

"You carry Moon-eye's Heart," the one-eyed goblin implored. "Direfang, it is time to leave this Dark Knight hole. There is nothing but death and hate here."

14

HELL TOWN

Then the ground rumbled fiercely, a real shock wave.

Direfang didn't hesitate. He grabbed up Graytoes and barreled into the fence, splitting the slats and rushing through the barrier. At the same time, a giant crevice opened up at the western edge of the slave pen, sucking a number of hapless goblins and fence posts down into the angry earth.

Slaves screamed in terror, and many followed Direfang, who stumbled to his knees as the ground shook harder.

"Take care with Moon-eye's Heart! Don't drop Moon-eye's Heart!"

Moon-eye was close behind. Direfang growled but cradled Graytoes to his chest as he lumbered to his feet. She whimpered, and he couldn't tell if she was in pain or was still weeping over what the Skull Knight had done to her baby. The hobgoblin whirled to the east, doing his best not to jar Graytoes. Slaves swarmed around him. The continually-rattling ground made it difficult to keep his footing.

Goblins surrounded him and raced ahead of him, all

111

panicked and jabbering, all calling out for his leadership. A foreman in the mine, he was someone they expected to give orders and aid, but the only thing he could say was, "Run! Run! Follow! Don't stop running! *Feyrh!*"

All around he heard the knights moving and yelling, but the earthquake was strong, and it was rocking Steel Town.

There were five large slave pens, and Direfang had been in the middle one. Out of the corner of his eye, he saw the Skull Knight and his two attendants. They'd still been out when the quake hit. One of the attendants was on the ground, overrun by goblins. Another was slashing with his sword, his back to the priest, who was weaving a pattern in the air.

He was casting a spell, Direfang knew, and he didn't want to be anywhere within range of the magic. "Faster!" he called to the goblins around him. Graytoes was not such a heavy burden, and she had stopped her whimpering. He fixed his eyes on the tops of goblin heads in front of him, thinking . . . escape . . . freedom.

"Moon-eye . . . where is Moon-eye?" Graytoes reached up to get his attention, touching the hobgoblin's neck.

"Hopefully running fast," Direfang returned, glancing over his shoulder. Moon-eye had vanished in the melee. Hopefully not dead, he added to himself when he heard another wave of screams behind him and an ominous crashing sound.

"The ground eats us!" The frightened voice was human, a laborer or a knight. The hobgoblin wished it to be the Skull Knight who took Graytoes' child. "It swallows us like a beast!"

"Let it swallow the whole town," the hobgoblin muttered to himself, running. Ahead, Direfang saw the goblins part as the earth directly in front of the running crowd heaved and buckled. A crevice opened; then one side of it rose up while the other side collapsed upon itself. Goblins tumbled over the steep side, climbing over each other and falling back down again, shouting and screaming. Another crack formed, opening just wide enough to suck several goblins inside then opening wider and folding on top of the trapped slaves.

Direfang cut a wide course around the gap and kept running.

"Moon-eye," Graytoes pleaded, again whimpering. "Direfang find Moon-eye, please."

The hobgoblin snorted in irritation, trying alternatively to keep his gaze locked ahead and on the goblins pressing so close that they threatened to trip him.

"Moon-eye—"

"Will live or die this night, Graytoes," Direfang finally returned. "Die to the quake or the Dark Knights. Hush."

"Moon-eye—"

"Hush, Graytoes! Hush and live." Direfang had no intention of dropping her and leaving her behind, but he couldn't stop to look for Moon-eye and didn't want to listen to her distracting pleas anymore. He needed to listen for the Dark Knights and to the rumbling of the ground.

———— S ————

Grallik had been resting when the second major quake struck. Pitched from the bench he'd been dozing on, he was nearly trampled by a group of knights rushing past.

"The slaves!" one hollered to him. "They escape, Guardian N'sera! Hundreds! In this quake, they dare to run!"

The chaos that had filled Steel Town when the quake hit two days past paled beside the fresh commotion, Grallik realized as he futilely looked around for loyal members of his talon. The lone wall of the largest barracks shook and dissolved in a heartbeat, right before his eyes. The new well with its ring of stones shuddered, the stones toppling inward and spiderweb cracks emanating in all directions from the hole. The cracks sped toward Grallik as he dashed toward the slave pens. He was nearer to the pens than to the makeshift infirmary, where healthy knights were stationed to help protect Marshal Montrill and the other wounded troops.

The pens were Grallik's priority, and he'd use whatever spells he could muster to impede the slaves running amok.

"Damn me," he cursed under his breath. "Damn me to the bottom of the Abyss for not trying to recast the wards."

The goblins bolting from the pens all appeared to be heading in a wave to the east, where the bulk of his wards and glyphs had been painstakingly and precisely cast . . . and obliterated, two days past, by the churning earth.

Steel Town—Hell Town—had gone berserk. Steam spewed up from a wide rent in the earth to the south. Behind him a woman screamed shrilly. A man called to her, then both voices were silenced after a thunderous crash.

Goblins dashed past and around him, terrified shouts mixed with repeated words Grallik couldn't understand. To the south, in the farthest pen, he saw the mother goblins huddled with their babies. But there weren't as many as the previous day, when he had helped set fire to the pile of dead goblins. So some mothers had already fled, with or without their caterwauling offspring.

Grallik had always feared the greater number of the slaves. He had had nightmares about the slaves rising up and crushing the Dark Knights, and dread gripped him as he neared the closest pen. There were still plenty of goblins inside, but many others were gone and the remaining ones might swarm him. He nearly stumbled as, again, the quake shook the ground.

The quake . . . one of the red-skinned goblins had warned there would be another one. The female goblin with the narrow-set eyes. He looked for her as he went, spotting several with dark red skin but none that he recognized.

"They all look the same, damn them!"

He guessed that well more than half of the goblins were already running away from the camp. He'd stop as many as he could using fire. Fire was his best weapon and the only significant magic that came to him instinctively. Reaching inside himself, Grallik searched for the magical spark that would release one of his more powerful enchantments. Closer, though, he needed to get closer. The mass of fleeing goblins was too far away. Just a little closer, he thought, just a—

The ground rocked violently again, and Grallik fell, the spell disappearing from his mind as he plunged into a crevice. Heart pounding in his chest, he flailed about with his arms and called out for his men. But his voice could not be heard over the noise of the earth, and he was drowned out by the shouts of everyone else in Hell Town. His fingers gripped the edge of the crevice, his body slammed against the side, and the air was knocked from his aching lungs.

Grallik's chest felt as though it had dented from the impact, and his heart continued to pound thunderously. He tried to pull himself up, but the continuing quake made that impossible. His fingers felt numb as he hung on; he could see nothing but blackest night and dark dirt in front of his face. He'd swallowed a mouthful of earth, and spit and spit trying to get the remnants and the taste out.

"I . . . won't . . . die . . . here," he hissed. "I won't! Damn the quake!" Suddenly he was seized by a coughing fit that made him feel lightheaded. "A spell, a spell . . ." There were reliable enchantments in the precious tome the first quake had swallowed. One, he knew, would have been just the right antidote, making him as light as a sheet of parchment and letting him float above the bedlam and out of the crack of earth. If he could just remember it. But he couldn't; he needed his spellbooks with their many spells that would have captured the goblins in invisible nets, that would have trapped them in cages materializing out of thin air.

"Damn my addled brain!"

He knew for certain that not a single one of the glyphs and wards functioned. No flames from fiery columns snared the runners. No high-pitched alarms were sounding. A disaster was upon the place, and he, the temporary commander, the wizard whose magic had failed, was to blame.

He coughed again and felt himself slipping, his fingers grabbing at air as he slid down the side of the crevice and landed in a heap at the bottom, painfully twisting his ankle. Grallik had seen some crevices close up, so he did his best to scrabble up the side to avoid the fate of other victims. He forced himself to focus on his magical skills, searched again for the arcane spark within himself, found and nurtured it, sending the eldritch energy into his fingers.

"Like fire," he breathed. "Be like fire."

Grallik felt his fingers grow warm and sink into the dirt, giving him a better purchase. It was one of the simple enchantments he used to heat the rocks and leech the ore. He used it to heat his fingers so they could bore into the hard earth. Using the spell in that manner was painful to his flesh and reminded him of his youth when he was burned in the home fire. But dying would be more painful . . . and eternal.

With great effort, he began climbing and soon climbed high enough to poke his head above the crevice. A moment later, the rumbling abruptly ceased, and the earth began to fill up the hole beneath him. He struggled over the side, rolling away just as the ground heaved and settled again. Then he forced himself to his feet, crying out when he had to put weight on his twisted ankle. His ankle might be broken, he realized, but he must walk on it. He had to force himself.

"The slaves . . ." Above all, they were Grallik's priority. In charge of Hell Town, he couldn't afford to let any more of them escape. The camp could not function without the goblins. The stain on his career would be permanent.

Suddenly, he felt a renewed purpose. He felt revitalized. He stoked the magical furnace within himself, calling another fiery spell to mind, a cruel but useful one.

"No farther!" Grallik shouted at the slaves as loud as he could. In the same instant, he released the magic, calling up a sheet of flame that rose at the edge of Steel Town and cut through the wave of running slaves, instantly roasting a dozen of them and sending others scattering in a panic.

Grallik didn't enjoy killing the slaves; if nothing else, he sorely required their future labor. The camp didn't need any more charred bodies. But if he did nothing, they all would escape, the camp would wither, and the failure would be his.

The stench from the burning goblins filled his senses, and he had to fight to keep from retching. He coughed harshly as he concentrated on making the wall of fire longer and higher, stretching south to the pyre of corpses, joining with that fire, and turning the area into an inferno.

"I said no farther!"

The wall lit up the whole camp, revealing the scale of the destruction that Steel Town had suffered from the second quake. Nothing stood, not a single wall or post. A cloud of dust, bigger and higher than that from the first quake, shadowed all the knights and laborers who were picking themselves up and shuffling around the camp. Grallik imagined that was what the Chaos War in the Abyss must have looked like.

"Hell," he said. "Hell's come to Neraka."

The fire wall continued to blaze, holding hundreds of goblins back and keeping them from joining their fellows, who were racing away on the other side of the conflagration.

Tears streamed down the wizard's face from the acrid scent of burning bodies and the billowing dirt and the death- and dust-choked air. He glanced over his shoulder:

not even the rubble of his workshop remained. All of it had been swallowed up by the angry earth. The mountain path, which he could see illuminated by bright starlight, had great gaps in it, as though a huge beast from below had clawed at the rocks and cut deep swaths in the path. The three entrances to the mine had disappeared, leaving no trace that they had ever been there.

He turned back to his flaming wall and limped in that direction. In the crush of goblins, he saw one of the Skull Knights thrashing about violently. The priest was grabbing slaves and pounding on them with his fists. Grallik spotted two other knights on the ground near the priest, and as he drew closer, he could tell they were drenched in blood, probably dead.

Grallik, limping, called another spell to mind. Words he'd learned in his earliest years in the Conclave spilled from his lips, and in response darts of flame flew from his fingertips and struck the goblins nearest the priest.

"Away from him!" Grallik shouted. "All of you, back into the pens." Where the pens used to be, he decided, seeing only posts and rails strewn on the ground. It would be a challenge just to corral the goblins and find a means to contain them.

The crowd of goblins backed away from the Skull Knight, who knelt by his two fallen attendants. "Wellon is dead," the priest called to Grallik. "Slaves will die for this, these miserable creatures. They will—"

"There's been enough dying in these past few days," Grallik said firmly. He kept a wary eye on the mass of trapped slaves, continuing to focus his spell on the flaming wall.

Footsteps behind him signaled the approach of a contingent of knights. No matter how many were coming, it wouldn't be enough, Grallik thought. No standing pens, no working wards, too many goblins, half already gone.

The Rebellion

"Guardian N'sera!" The out-of-breath voice came from Marek. "The slaves, what should we—?"

Grallik raised a hand to silence him. *What should we do?* the wizard thought. *I have no idea.* Instead, he answered: "Bring the other Skull Knights here. I know we have wounded brothers, but they've spells that will help quell this slave revolt now." Then, softer, he added, "And this must be our priority, Marek. We cannot afford to lose any more of these slaves."

"Contain the goblins, then see to the wounded," the Skull Knight said, echoing Grallik. "As you command."

"Aye, Guardian! I will summon the other priests!" Marek's footsteps retreated as he shouted for the other Skull Knights.

Grallik concentrated on maintaining the wall. The stench from the burning bodies continued to assault his senses, and coupled with the pain throbbing in his ankle, the wizard was having a difficult time keeping his focus.

"Wellon and Hayson are dead," the Skull Knight reported bitterly. "Both dead to these little butchers. And we were trying to help them! Heal them! Ungrateful monsters."

The goblins were milling about, keeping their distance from the wizard and the Skull Knight but talking too, in their odd language, cut through with clacking sounds and hand gestures. Some wailed at fellows they'd lost to Grallik's fire, and some merely shook their little fists at the Skull Knight.

Grallik suddenly spotted the goblin he'd been looking for, the red-skinned female who had tried to warn them of the coming quake. She had squatted, hands splayed atop the ground, her skin looking molten in the glare of the fire wall. Her lips were moving, but, of course, the wizard couldn't hear her words with all the other racket. As he watched, his concentration divided between maintaining his spell and glancing at her, another goblin came to her side, one with a dull yellow hide and over-long ears.

His mouth dropped open when he saw the yellow goblin squat next to her, putting his hands on the ground too and speaking quickly and anxiously to the red-skinned one. Grallik's flame wall clearly illuminated the little scene, though at first he thought the flickering light played tricks.

The ground seemed to bubble around the two goblins' hands, then a hollow formed that stretched to the wall of fire and, to Grallik's astonishment, tunneled under it. The hollow was just big enough for a goblin to squeeze through, and that was what the yellow-skinned goblin immediately did.

"No!" Grallik yelled, intensifying his spell. The fire filled in the hollow and rose higher, turning white with intense heat. All the other goblins edged past him, trying to escape the intense heat, and he watched with some satisfaction as they clustered in the remains of their former pens.

He looked around for the red-skinned goblin but couldn't spot her. There were just too many goblins, a mass of shifting little bodies interspersed with the occasional taller hobgoblin. Had she escaped through the hollow path too? He prayed to his dark god that she hadn't.

"Guardian N'sera! I need help moving these men." The Skull Knight stood near his fallen attendants.

"You'll have help, but be patient," Grallik returned. He heard footsteps behind him again, at least a dozen armored men from the sound. He ordered the knights to pull the priest's attendants to the center of the camp, to escort the priest away from the goblins, and to gather whatever wood they could find to try to reconstruct the pens.

Only one man questioned his order, a common laborer who'd joined the knights. He wondered whether ramshackle wood would hold the slaves if they saw another opportunity to escape.

THE REBELLION

"We must try," Grallik said in harsh, hushed tones. "Do your best to build something strong. We have to keep the slaves penned in and keep alive the hope of rebuilding this place."

The laborer nodded without enthusiasm. "Hell this place is," he said. "Hell's come to Steel Town."

"Aye, that it has," the wizard returned.

15

WANTING THE BETTER AIR

Direfang had not run so far or so fast since his youth, not since those days long ago, before he was captured by a band of minotaurs braving ogre lands and was sold to the Dark Knights. Once the ground stopped trembling and he was certain the quake was past, he still ran hard and fast, with all the strength he could summon. The ground was relatively flat there, and the sky was clearing, though there were still clouds, especially to the west, where Steel Town and the mine were behind him. Dawn was still hours away, but the lightening sky made it easy for him to avoid holes and cracks in the earth and the rocks that lay strewn in his path.

His legs were much longer than the goblins'. They couldn't keep up with him, and he had long since passed them by and stopped worrying about tripping over them. He still cradled Graytoes, and she still whimpered to him about Moon-eye.

"Stop, Direfang. Find Moon. Please."

He kept running, offering her no reply, wanting nothing

more than to put more distance between himself and Steel Town.

He heard voices strung out behind him, goblins arguing about how long it would take before the Dark Knights would ride out on their surviving horses and search for them.

"Long while," a goblin with a high-pitched voice declared.

Direfang agreed with that sentiment. Though slaves were crucial to the operation of their detested camp, the second quake had caused enough problems in Steel Town to keep the knights and their horses busy back there for some time.

So Direfang continued to run, stretching his legs and delighting in the dull aches that centered in his thighs and in the backs of his calves. His legs had not been tested in that manner for years. His side began to ache after a while, and he held his right arm close to one side while at the same time making sure he kept a good grip on Graytoes.

The young goblin wouldn't stop babbling about her missing mate. Still, Direfang ignored her, kept running.

Foothills loomed ahead to the northeast, where he was heading. There were ogres in those hills—there were ogres in many parts of Neraka—but he intended to hunker down there long enough to rest and think and talk with any of the other goblins who had kept up with him and who wanted to keep following his lead. He would seek Mudwort's counsel in the foothills. He would linger there so she could catch up.

Behind him, sounding like a chorus of whispers because the pounding of his feet and the pounding in his ears were so loud, he faintly heard the frightened calls of goblins and hobgoblins. When the cries diminished and became so soft that he could no longer hear them, he finally slowed his pace and looked over his shoulder. The horde of slaves looked like a brown wave rolling toward him, dirt billowing around their feet, but none moved very fast anymore. He saw two small ones in front stumble and watched as they were trampled by their fellows.

Finally, with a deep sigh of weariness, Direfang stopped and waited for the wave of escaping goblins to reach him.

So many had fled from Steel Town that their movement sounded like a thundering herd. Direfang closed his eyes for a moment, inhaling deeply and registering the scents of blood—Graytoes' and his own. But the sweet air didn't carry a hint of the odor of burned corpses. He didn't smell humans either—the Dark Knights and the laborers and their children. The scent of men was not particularly offensive to him, but he rejoiced in its absence. He opened his mouth and tipped his head back, howling in glee and inhaling deeply again and again as the thunder of goblin feet drew closer.

Within moments, his howls were echoed by the mass of goblins who yelled and screamed with joy to be free of their terrible labor camp. After a few moments, however, several goblins shouted to be heard above the others, one finally successful in catching the crowd's collective attention.

"Quiet!" screamed a pale gray-brown goblin called Spike-hollow. "The Dark Knights will hear! The ogres will hear!" He jumped up and down and finally climbed up on the shoulders of a stocky goblin of a similar coloring. "Quiet!"

The throng fell silent, though there were still murmurs from some. They circled closer to Direfang. The hobgoblin guessed there were maybe a thousand goblins there, maybe half of the slaves who had survived the quakes. He tried to spot Moon-eye, Saro-Saro, and Mudwort, but there were simply too many to sort through. And though the stars were shining down through gaps in the clouds, the goblins were like one thick mass. Direfang didn't recognize any of those he looked for.

"Where do the clans go now, Direfang?" The question came from Spikehollow. His voice was raspy, having used all his energy running and shouting. The question was instantly repeated by other goblins nearby, acknowledging Direfang's leadership.

"Moon-eye, where?" Graytoes craned her neck over Direfang's shoulder, trying to locate her mate.

"South, maybe," Direfang answered Spikehollow. "Maybe all the clans should go south. But right now, let's head to those foothills to the east to rest and plan. Later, south . . ."

"Graytoes!" It was Moon-eye, alive, trying to push his way through the crowd of goblins, but not many knew him or were willingly giving him room to pass. "Moon-eye's Heart!"

"South?" Spikehollow asked. "Why not south now?"

"To safety first." Direfang growled and turned east again, forcing his way through the goblins who had gathered around him and starting to run again as the way cleared. Graytoes called for her mate and tugged at Direfang's hair, begging him to stop so she could rejoin Moon-eye. The hobgoblin snarled, more crossly than he had intended, but did not answer her. Moon-eye was alive; he would follow. There would be time for a reunion when they reached the foothills. At that moment, he wanted more distance from the Dark Knight camp.

Cracks were evident in the ground even a few miles away from Steel Town, showing that the quake damage was not limited to the camp and the mine. In one place a wide crevice sliced through the land, looking like an ugly, jagged scar and causing Direfang to slow his pace and alert the huge crowd running behind him. Beyond the crevice, the landscape was chewed up raggedly, reminding the hobgoblin of Steel Town's garden when it had been freshly tilled. Large rocks protruded there, sharp looking and dirt covered, suggesting they'd been buried until the quake thrust them upward.

The uneven, treacherous terrain would slow any pursuing Dark Knights, Direfang reflected. It certainly slowed him. When he finally made his way past the worst of it, he picked up the pace again. He was unfamiliar with the land that far east and had no idea if there was water running somewhere in the vicinity. But water was what he was looking and smelling for.

What plants there were in that area were stunted. A lone tree to the north was thick-limbed but looked dead. The hobgoblin desperately needed a drink of water, and he knew that the rest of the escaped slaves were just as thirsty. After he reached the foothills, he'd post some lookouts for the Dark Knights, ogres, minotaurs, and anything that might pose a threat. Then he'd search in earnest for water and go back and find Mudwort. He wanted the shaman goblin to talk to the earth again and see if any more quakes were coming.

Maybe, too, he thought, Mudwort could talk to the earth and ask it where water could be found. Why not?

Direfang's feet were bleeding by the time he reached the first slope. His soles were thick from working in the mine but not thick enough to protect him against needle-sharp fragments of shattered rocks that were everywhere on the ground. He climbed up several feet and sat down with a great huff, gently resting Graytoes next to him and waiting for the rest to catch up. From his higher vantage point, he could tell that not all of the escaped slaves had followed him.

Some had fled south, scattering. Others were traveling north, where the mountains were steeper. But well more than half of the escaped slaves were coming his way. He intended to climb higher as soon as he caught his breath. He wanted to climb high enough so he could overlook Steel Town.

That was still too close to the camp to suit him.

As he peered for Mudwort, Graytoes searched the advancing line of goblins for Moon-eye. She didn't whimper for him anymore, apparently satisfied that she'd spotted him once and was certain he was alive and would eventually find her. She put her hands on her stomach and looked up gratefully at Direfang.

"Hate the skull man," she said. "Hate the Dark Knights."

Direfang nodded. "It is fine to hate the knights. It is a good hate, Graytoes."

The air filled with whoops and shouts of joy when the goblins and hobgoblins arrived. They'd forgotten Spikehollow's warning about the Dark Knights and the ogres and felt like celebrating. They seemed to have forgotten everything in their unfamiliar exuberance. Spikehollow tried to quiet them again, but his efforts were wasted.

Direfang buried his head in his hands and waited for the ruckus to subside. Indeed, the ogres would hear those shouts, if there were any nearby, and perhaps they would come to investigate. But unless there was a small army of them, they could do nothing against so many determined, escaped slaves.

"Safe for the time. Safe away from the knights. Safety in numbers," Direfang muttered to himself. "Strong in these numbers. Safe and strong and not stoppable."

An idea began to form.

The hobgoblin patiently waited several long minutes until the celebration died down. The lack of water played a part in the quieting, as many of the goblins became hoarse and rubbed at their throats. He heard murmurs of "water," "free," "Dark Knights," and words he couldn't distinguish.

Moon-eye had found his way to the front. The one-eyed goblin was battered and bleeding, and Direfang noticed that quite a few of those in the front rank were injured too, not only from the quake, but from bumping and clawing each other in their mad dash away from Steel Town. Moon-eye scampered up the rise, put his arm around Graytoes, pulled her close, smoothed at her face with his free hand, and sang to her, an old tune Direfang had heard in his youth. It was the only one Moon-eye seemed to know—the song he had been singing when Direfang and Mudwort found the couple in the mine. Moon-eye's voice quieted the goblins in the front of the throng.

> High sun on the dry, high ground
> On goblins it shines white-bright
> Chases away the bad shadows
> Chases away the deep night
>
> Late sun on the Sirrion Sea
> Turns it a sparkling gold
> Signals a hunt for all goblins
> Keeps out the hurtful, deep cold
>
> Moon glows pale and soft pearly
> Yet goblins have no time to rest
> Moon calls the dark of the evening
> When the night bird leaves the nest
>
> Low sun in the warm valleys
> All goblins watch the orange sky
> Looking for shadows of ogres
> Knowing the time's come to die

There were more verses, but Moon-eye's voice dropped, singing only to Graytoes. But occasionally he looked up and met the gazes of the goblins closest to Direfang.

Saro-Saro was there, wheezing from the effort of running. Hurbear stood next to him, gasping and clutching at himself, alternating between his chest and his throat. The old, yellow-skinned goblin bent his knees, leaned forward, and made a noise as if he were retching, though nothing came out.

Direfang was surprised that Hurbear had made it that far from the Dark Knight camp. Hurbear's legs had so often given him trouble going up and down the mountain trail to the mine.

"Free!" Saro-Saro shouted when Moon-eye was done singing. The word was picked up and repeated by the others, some loudly, some in a normal tone, until it sounded like a chant.

"The ogres!" Spikehollow shouted, finally managing to be heard. Again, he perched on the shoulders of a clansman, so the others could see him. "Quiet or the ogres will hear! Or the Dark Knights will hear! Dark Knights will come and catch Hurbear and Saro-Saro and Graytoes. The knights will—"

"No more knights! No more slavery!" Direfang said, standing, and they all hushed to listen to his words. The hobgoblin felt a little uncomfortable, seeing all of them looking up at him, some holding their breath as if they expected him to say something memorable and momentous.

"Listen to Direfang," Saro-Saro said.

"South," Direfang announced. "Stay together, stay safe, then go south."

"But the ogres?" one of the goblins worried aloud.

"And the minotaurs and the Dark Knights," Direfang added. "Dangerous, all of those creatures, and men."

"What about dragons?" That comment came from someone in Spikehollow's clan. "Dragons are bad. Saw a dragon to the north once. There could be dragons to the south."

"Could be dragons anywhere," an old goblin added.

"Everything dies sooner or later," Hurbear said. "So Direfang says south, and to the south the clans will go." He set his fists against his waist and nodded, signaling his approval of Direfang's plan. "Hurbear's clan will go south with Direfang. The better air is to the south. Better to breathe away from the Dark Knights."

"What lives to the south?" Moon-eye asked. His clan was originally from the northwest, and he'd never been farther south than Steel Town. "More Dark Knights? More ogres?"

"More dragons?" another asked.

"What lives to the south, Direfang?" Moon-eye persisted. "What sort of creatures?"

"Yes, what lies to the south?" Spikehollow interrupted.

They waited for Direfang to reassure them. He said nothing.

"Freedom!" Graytoes answered. "Blessed freedom lies to the south."

They all nodded, murmuring to each other.

"Sleep first?" Hurbear wondered. "Or find water first?"

Direfang shook his head. "Ceremony first," he declared. "Honor the dead burned this night in Steel Town. Then tomorrow, head south, find food and water along the way."

Hurbear cleared his throat and pushed gently at the goblins near him. When he had a little clear space around him, he began. "The shell destroyed, fire cleansed, the spirit reborn." Hurbear made a fist and placed it over his heart.

"Spirits reborn!" the goblins near him repeated. Brak and Folami thumped their bellies with the flats of their hands then started up a drumlike cadence joined by many of the others.

Hurbear raised his arms, fingers spread wide, and he turned west, pointing. "Spirits fly above Steel Town. Above pain. Above the great sad. Above clans left behind. Above all things." He repeated the message as he turned in a circle, nodding to each of the compass points. "The passing comes to all goblins. The passing came to . . ."

"The child of Moon-eye and Graytoes." Again, it was Direfang, claiming the right to speak first.

The remembrances continued for nearly an hour, judging by the position of the stars they could see and the continued lightening of the sky. While the goblins shared the memories of their many dead friends, Direfang only half paid attention. He climbed down from the rise and walked among them, looking for faces familiar to him, eyes locking on the red-skinned goblins in particular. There was no sign of Mudwort, so when the ceremony was finished, he returned to the rise so he could stand and be seen above the crowd.

"Where is Mudwort?" he finally asked, hoping that she finally would be found and come forward.

Her name was passed back through the crowd, and some of the goblins chattered about her.

"Mad, that one is."

"Knew about the quake. Warned knights and goblins, Mudwort did. So not mad, mind not so sour."

"Mind not spoiled and rotten."

"Free because of the quake, free because of Mudwort."

"Caught in Steel Town," one finally answered. An oak brown goblin strode forward. He boasted a crooked nose and a thick, pale scar running across his forehead. "Gnasher of the Fish-Eater Clan," he announced himself. "Saw Mudwort caught. The Dark Knight spell-weaver called forth a great wall of flame, hot as any death-fire. Mudwort dug beneath the fire wall and helped Twitch escape, but then Mudwort was caught."

Another goblin came over. Her skin was the same hue, but more deeply scarred; she was of Gnasher's clan. "Saw that too." She thumped her chest for emphasis. "The wall of flame, it killed many slaves, but not so many as the quakes did. Maybe Mudwort died inside the wall of flame. Should have honored Mudwort in the ceremony. Could honor Mudwort now."

Direfang's aches and exhaustion all worsened in that moment, as if he'd been hit in the stomach by a mailed fist. "Mudwort is caught." He wanted her counsel, needed her to help guide them out of Dark Knight territory by talking to the earth and discovering what stretched beyond the mountains to the south. And he needed her to find water. Mudwort was his friend, the wisest goblin he knew. And though he was free of Steel Town and did not want to go back there, neither did he want to leave her there if she had survived and was still alive. Without his protection, the knights might take revenge on her. And without her wisdom, he wondered how long he would last.

"How many more caught besides Mudwort?" Direfang wondered aloud, the half who did not race to follow him?

"Many. Lots," Gnasher answered firmly. "Lots and lots caught behind the great wall of flame. Lots and lots left behind, still slaves. Lots were burned in the great wall of flame. Lots of slaves screamed and burned and died."

"Slaves no more!" Saro-Saro waved his arm to get the assembly's attention. "Freedom lies to the south. The better air is to the south. Forget the unfortunate left behind."

"South now?" Brak and Folami asked in unison.

Direfang didn't answer. He was listening to the faint call of a hunting bird and the soft growl of a big cat prowling in the hills above him. He registered the feel of the ground against the bottoms of his feet, the wild ground, different from Steel Town. The wind stirred the hair on the back of his neck and spun his own redolent scent around him.

He shook his head after several moments. "South, yes, but not now. First, return to Steel Town to rescue Mudwort and the others. Water and food are plentiful in Steel Town. Clothes and foot coverings too. Things must be stolen. Better that goblins have those good things than men keep it all."

Most stared in shocked disbelief at the hobgoblin. A few

spat and shook their heads as if he were mad. It had taken so much of their willpower just to reach that point of safety. To return to Steel Town was absurdity, lunacy.

"Slaves once, slaves no more," Folami snarled. "Not go back to the slave place ever, ever again, Direfang. No reason to go back there now, ever. Forget the ones left behind."

"Too tired to go back!" Brak agreed. "Too dark. Too tired, and so forget all the others."

The growl of the big cat sounded again, more distant. The hunting bird shrieked again.

"The Dark Knights have weapons!" Saro-Saro protested. "The knights' numbers are less now, but the weapons are sharp. The weapons kill. Saro-Saro will not go back to that bad, bad place. None should ever go back."

Direfang let the protests continue for a few minutes more, then he waved his arms and demanded their attention.

"This time goblins will have weapons too," Direfang proclaimed. "Plenty of weapons to fight the Dark Knights. So it is back to Steel Town for needed friends and needed things. It would be wrong to let the Dark Knights have any slaves, wrong to leave goblins behind." He puffed out his chest, feeling important with the words. "Without any slaves, the mines and the town will be crippled—neither will be rebuilt. So go to Steel Town before the knights gain reinforcements, before the knights can rest and tend their wounds, before the knights rebuild the slave pens. There is no better time to strike at the Dark Knights than now. Defeat the knights, then go south to freedom, where the air is better."

The escaped slaves stared mutely, not one nodding in agreement.

16

RECLAIMING STEEL TOWN

This camp will not be abandoned. I will not allow it."

Grallik paced angrily before the five surviving members of his talon. The quake had taken a horrific toll on the humans too. A deep crevice had opened up at the edge of the infirmary, pulling half the wounded into the gash, along with other knights and laborers and their children. More knights were working desperately to extricate the bodies.

"I am the acting commander of Steel Town, and on my watch this hellhole will be rebuilt." Grallik rubbed his chin contemplatively, avoiding eye contact. "For the glory of the Order, Steel Town must thrive once more. Do you understand?"

"Aye, Guardian," the five answered in unison.

Marshal Montrill had been spared, Grallik learned, but one of the valuable Skull Knights had been killed and another seriously injured, leaving the camp with only two able healers, both no doubt depleted of their magical energies.

"Will you want to dispatch more messengers, Guardian

N'sera?" The talon member asking the question was Kenosh, a middle-aged soldier, originally from Solace, who'd been with the Dark Knights for almost twenty years. Grallik had served with him more than a decade earlier and knew his toughness. Grallik had requested that Kenosh be assigned to his talon when he was promoted to guardian and relegated to that place. "Half the horses remain in camp, only a few are lame and—"

A howl cut through the air, and Grallik looked between his men to see one of the Ergothians setting the broken limb of a tall young boy. The youth thrashed miserably. The priest tried to hold him down while at the same time trying to conjure his healing magic. Behind the priest, a woman shuffled past, dragging a tarp filled with something heavy.

Grallik turned away. "Yes, Kenosh, more messengers will be sent, for certain. We've got no alternative, we urgently need certain materials and more men. But I will not dispatch them until tomorrow or the day after, and I will even send you if you've a desire for more pleasant scenery." He waited for a reaction, and in the interval the boy howled again.

"I will remain," Kenosh finally replied with a grim smile.

"Good. In the meantime, I want a full accounting of the destruction and of the number of men lost and wounded, as well as a detailed list of goods we will need from the outpost in Jelek. And I want a precise tally of the slaves we have remaining as well as those dead or missing."

Kenosh raised an eyebrow at the last.

"To rebuild this town and reopen the mine, we must rely on the slaves. We need to know the number of those healthy enough to work so we can set up new shifts and reassign tasks. I also want a tally of those who are injured but who may not recover fully. Those slaves that would require too much effort to mend, they should be dispatched." He paused. "Too, I need a list of our brothers who can speak the goblin tongue."

"It will be done, Guardian." Kenosh tried to maintain his proud military posture, but he couldn't hide his defeated look.

"But before all of that, my knights, the two skull brothers who are still able and active . . ."

"Siggith of Jelek and Horace Branson, Guardian."

"I must request their assistance now. Kenosh, get them for me."

Grallik watched his talon spread out then closed his sore and weary eyes. The air was still heavy with the stench of burned goblin flesh. Dirt filled the air he breathed, and there was a trace of sulfur, though not as strong as in the first quake. He started coughing again, so hard he doubled over. He didn't stop until he was spent, with his eyes watering so hard it looked as though he had been weeping.

There were powders in vials at the bottom of a crevice that he could have mixed and magicked to chase the horrid odors away. There were potions that would have refreshed him and allowed him to operate as if he'd just waken up from a long night's slumber. But they were all lost, ruined. Though Grallik typically fancied himself a powerful wizard, he felt like a clueless novice. When the clean up was well under way, when the slave pens had been rebuilt, he would travel to Neraka and collect new spellbooks and casting elements. There were many wizards in Neraka, both among the Dark Knights and other organizations. They would help him replace his powders and potions. It would be costly, and at the moment he hadn't a single steel to his name; all of his wealth had disappeared in the crevice. But he would call in favors and make pledges of coin, and he would regain some of his lost magic.

He wrapped his arms around his aching chest and

glanced toward the volcanic peaks, seeing their red tops glowing through the haze. They looked, he mused, like sequins on a lady's dress, set against the darkness. Smoke curled up from them—not unusual, Grallik knew. But there was more smoke than he'd seen before, swirling up into the sky to add to the dismal cloud above Steel Town. It was odd, foreboding.

"By the blessed memory of the Dark Queen's heads," Grallik murmured. A shiver raced down his spine as he glanced from one peak to the next and the next. "What more can happen?"

"Guardian Grallik!" The arrival of the two Skull Knights broke the musings of the wizard. "This is an affront, ordering us here when our brothers are . . ."

"Dying," Grallik supplied the word for the taller man, the one who'd been at the goblin pens when the quake struck and the slaves escaped. The man's face looked skeletal, his eyes and cheeks all the more sunken by dust and dirt.

"Dying, yes," the gaunt man spit.

"Aye, Siggith of Jelek, your brothers are wounded and dying and need your immediate care. But all of us could die and Steel Town will be dust forever if we don't tend the slaves."

Siggith's lips curled into a snarl.

"We have lost too many brothers already," Grallik continued in a more conciliatory tone. "But we can no longer trust the slaves."

"They could rise up again and . . ." Siggith did not finish the thought.

"Wise, Guardian Grallik," Horace, the stocky priest, said. He was an Ergothian with dark and smooth skin. He'd been sweating heavily, and his face was scored with salty streaks that could have been tears for lost comrades. Though Horace's posture was straight, there was fatigue in his eyes, and a sense that the priest was thoroughly overwhelmed.

"I appreciate your devotion to the wounded, Horace," Grallik said. The wizard had seen the priest working to the point of exhaustion. Still, he did not care much for the Ergothian.

Horace had admitted once in Grallik's presence that he joined the Dark Knights only because his brothers did and had pressed him into service, and that he revered Zeboim and never worshiped Takhisis. When his brothers died, Horace requested that the Order to post him on the coast or in Ergoth. Grallik believed that, when the time came, if the Order had other ideas, Horace would quit and likely return to the far island anyway.

Siggith? He was more loyal to the Order, as loyal as Montrill. Grallik had far more respect for Siggith.

"The pens are gone, splinters," Siggith said. "I was trying to heal some of the slaves when the quake struck. For all my efforts, they practically trampled me. I'd flay them all if it was within my power, but . . ." He fixed his gaze on Grallik. "But the camp requires them, as you say. And with the pens in splinters, something must be done to hold them here."

Three men walked past them, their clothes in tatters and their hair so matted and filthy Grallik did not recognize them. One was talking about his wife, who was wounded and near death. He looked up and stared coldly at the Ergothian priest, then moved on.

"The tavern man, his family, and some others are gathering wood now to help reconstruct three of the pens, Horace," Grallik explained. "They'll be using timber from the stables." He had no need to explain his orders but felt compelled to confide in the priests, thinking his openness might make allies of them. "Fortunately or not, we won't be needing five pens this time—not until we've acquired more slaves or recaptured the ones that have escaped."

"Recapture?" asked Siggith skeptically.

"Wooden fences will not be enough to hold them." The Ergothian smoothed at his robe, a nervous gesture Grallik had noted on other occasions. "We cannot spare enough knights to guard the pens. It's a wonder they all didn't bolt when they had the chance. A wonder that we didn't lose all of them."

Grallik considered boasting about his fiery wall that had blocked nearly half from escaping. Certainly they had witnessed the fire. The air still stank of roasted goblin flesh.

"Most of the slaves are dull minded and weak willed, thank Zeboim," the Ergothian continued. "They have been so long under our thumb, they lacked the courage to run."

"Perhaps," Grallik said.

"Or perhaps they fear what's out there more than they fear us. The ogres. Starvation." Siggith let out a raspy sigh. "Minotaurs. We've told enough stories about the minotaurs that the goblins should fear them. Any sane creature would fear the horned race. But you want us to put even more fear into the goblins, eh, Guardian? You want us to . . . convince them that it is in their interest to stay."

Grallik nodded. "For the sake of Steel Town."

The wizard looked beyond the priests and to the glowing peaks. The streams of lava had thickened. It was not his imagination. And the crests glowed brighter than he'd seen them in quite a long time. The vivid color reminded him of the glowing ingots he had culled from the ore.

"Aye, Guardian Grallik, for Steel Town and the Order," Siggith said.

The two priests headed shoulder to shoulder toward the slaves. Already the tavern owner and his son were reconstructing a corner of the center pen, flanked by two knights who aided and shielded them. Ten more knights were on the eastern side, working similarly. Swords out and at their sides, they offered a meager defense against the greater number of goblins. But so far the goblins remained docile.

Some slaves grew uneasy as the Skull Knights neared, a few shouting "murderer" and "youngling slayer" in the common tongue so the priests could understand their insults. They pointed to the gaunt priest. Still, they made no move to escape, though they grouped together and shook their fists. A hobgoblin raised his clawed hands and growled a string of harsh words that none of the knights could translate.

The Ergothian tucked his chin to his chest and started chanting loudly, the melody barely heard above the goblins' chattering and the sound of digging—laborers working on reopening the new well. The priest crossed his arms in front of his considerable chest, then dropped them to his sides. He'd taken his gloves off, and his dark hands were growing pale and shimmering, beginning to look like molten silver.

The gaunt priest copied him, his hands also starting to glow. The Ergothian spread his fingers and pointed them at the goblins. The slaves huddled together defiantly and at the same time they backed away, fear etched on their faces.

The glow spread from the priests' hands, forming two misty clouds that thinned as they spread across the mob of slaves, then slowly descended upon them. The silvery mist shimmered like dew on wet grass, and some of the goblins licked at the vapor, thinking it might be water.

"Steel Town is home," Siggith droned. His words were honeyed and melodic, and the goblins stopped their chattering to listen to him. Most stared unblinking, mouths falling open, but a handful appeared resistant to his charm.

Grallik had seen the priests perform that spell once before, many months past, when a newly-arrived clan of unruly goblins had tried to resist orders to work a double shift. As before, the wizard admired the divine magic and wished he had such powerful enchantments at his fingertips.

"Home is safe," Siggith intoned.

"Home is food and protection and fellowship," Horace said. "There are no ogres in Steel Town."

"Home," one of the younger goblins called out. "Steel Town is home."

"Food is in Steel Town," another barked.

"There are no minotaurs in Steel Town," Siggith said. "Home is safety. Home is water and work. Home is where you belong. Home is where the Dark Knights protect you."

"Steel Town is protection," mumbled a wizened goblin in the front rank. He grinned vacantly, showing only a few intact teeth. "Protection is good. Home is good."

"There are no ogres here," Siggith repeated. "No dragons."

"Yes, home is safe." It was the Ergothian's turn. His voice was deeper and had an edge to it, and most of the goblins covered by his cloud of mist were entranced and started to sway.

If the priests were able to sustain their spell for longer periods of time, it might envelope all of the slaves and bound them all as surely as steel shackles, Grallik reflected. But some of the stronger-minded goblins appeared immune, and they visibly resisted the magic, gritting their teeth and closing their eyes. Some poked at the ones in a trance, trying to rouse them, but to no effect.

"Home," the Ergothian droned, "is a place that slaves should never leave. There are ogres and minotaurs and far, far worse beyond the boundaries of Steel Town. Digging beasts running loose, earth dragons you call them, they are out there."

"Steel Town is home," another goblin called out.

"You must never leave home," the Ergothian said, echoed by Siggith, whose voice was not as commanding as Horace's.

"Wrap your minds around the notion of Steel Town as home!" Horace shouted. "Take home into your hearts. You must never, never leave Steel Town. Death awaits you in ogre lands. You are safe here. The knights protect you."

"The knights will bring you water," Siggith said. He instantly had the attention even of those resisting the magic. "The well is being reopened, and soon fresh water will be brought to you. There is no water outside of Steel Town. And the water we offer here will be cool and good and sweet."

The last statement made Grallik snort derisively. Many goblins knew there were pure, clear streams in the mountains. But there were ogres, too, in those mountains, and both priests mentioned the terrible ogres again and again.

When the priests were finished with their divine magic, the few knights posted as guards had a more docile crowd of prisoners.

The Ergothian Skull Knight reported to the wizard. "Guardian Grallik, the divine incantations we cast are strong and persuasive, but they are not all-encompassing. Some of the slaves will shrug them off before morning, and we will have to refresh the spells. Fortunately most of . . . these pitiful creatures have been cowed by the mines and the whips. The incantation will reinforce their low esteem and dwell inside them for a long, long while." He shook his head as if clearing some cobwebs. "Our spells are taxing and will limit the healing we can perform the rest of this night."

"But the spells were necessary," Grallik said.

"Aye, Guardian." The Ergothian nodded good night and made his way to the new infirmary. Moments later, the other Skull Knight followed.

The wizard stood silent for some time, watching the slaves milling, the tavern man and his son constructing a corner of a pen, and the knights patrolling along the east border of the slave area. He looked for the red-skinned goblin, finally spotting her. She was ruddy with health, though she looked overly thin. Her elbows and knees protruded as if her skin were stretched too tight over her bones. Somehow she'd acquired a scrap of cloth, which she was wearing like a tabard. There was something about her that intrigued him . . . something, not only her ability to predict the quake.

Her head looked too large for her neck, her shoulders exaggerated. She might have been beautiful in goblin terms or horribly ugly. Grallik knew so little about the creatures.

She stared back at him, unblinking and with an unreadable expression. Grallik wondered if she had a name—if any of them had names, for that matter. The other goblins gave her a little space, perhaps out of respect. Were the camp not in such chaos, Grallik thought he might approach her and try to communicate with the slave. He wanted to know how she guessed the second quake was coming and how she had moved the earth under his fire wall so a goblin could escape. Did she really do that? Or had his mind been playing tricks? Could she tell him anything about the strange behavior of the volcanoes?

Did she have some divine spark like the Skull Knights? Was she a shaman to whom magic had been born, as in some men?

He'd been born with an arcane spark, but it had taken years of cultivation to master various spells. It seemed to come so naturally to the Skull Knights and, perhaps, to the red-skinned goblin. The question continued to preoccupy him: Was magic stronger in some creatures? Strong enough that it came naturally and without effort? The red-skinned goblin had no tomes, powders, or talismans, yet she had some power.

"Are you a creature of magic?" He spoke the question aloud, knowing not one of the goblins could hear him.

The rational part of the wizard, that part that had studied under high-ranking Thorn Knights and, before them, Black Robe masters, believed that the most powerful spells—the most powerful spellcasters—were molded by diligent study and practice. But if he'd heard her correctly, if she had predicted the quakes, and if he'd truly seen her part the earth beneath his flames with her fingers, then that red-skinned goblin was a shaman with some sort of primal power.

He felt the brush of something against his scarred hand, and it sent a shiver through him. He glanced down and saw that a silk handkerchief, singed and dirtied, had floated on the breeze and touched him. He blinked and looked back to the slaves. The red-skinned goblin had melted into the throng.

17

SLAVE ROBBERS

Saro-Saro sat cross-legged on a patch of dirt in the shadow of the rise. He scratched at the ground with his narrow, crooked fingers, drawing stick figures and trees then erasing them. He brushed his hands on his threadbare tunic, which had belonged to a child in camp who had outgrown it. Little more than a rag, it was filthy and sweat stained, but it was still better than what most of the goblins wore.

Saro-Saro tipped his head back and sniffed. The air was dry, the clouds high and thin, holding no hint of rain. "Stink," he pronounced. "Not so bad as Steel Town, though." He opened his mouth, waggled his tongue, and gulped in the air. Then he returned his attention to digging in the ground in earnest. Moments later, he was rewarded by finding a thick grub. Like a prize, he held it up and made sure some of his fellows saw his treat. Then he popped one end in his mouth and bit it off, sucking on the juice before finishing it.

The goblins and hobgoblins had spent the day in the

foothills, sleeping, tending to their injured, and searching for food, namely grubs, insects, and roots. Direfang wanted to return to Steel Town for better food, water, and the remaining slaves, but as of the previous night, he had no support.

It was not that the escaped slaves didn't want to rescue their brothers, they just didn't want to do it that night. They'd run far and were suffering, and Direfang's words could not inspire them. Many of them were too exhausted to go any farther, and some simply could not because of their injuries. So Direfang posted sentries, while Moon-eye chattered worriedly about ogres and minotaurs until he fell asleep.

Though they searched hard in the immediate area, they found no water. But there was juice in the grubs and millipedes that were plentiful several inches down in the earth, and that helped.

When the sun started to set and the goblins showed signs of restlessness, Direfang tried again to rouse them.

"Hobgoblins, goblins, are still in Steel Town," Direfang said.

"Mudwort still there," Saro-Saro added.

"Food, water, clothes, all those good things are in Steel Town too," the hobgoblin continued. "All of those things could be Saro-Saro's and Brak's and Folami's."

"Moon-eye's too," Graytoes cut in.

"Very thirsty," Moon-eye added.

"Thirsty," Saro-Saro admitted. "Bug juice is not enough."

"Moon-eye's Heart needs water," said the one-eyed goblin.

"Thirsty, but not stupid. Only goblins with sour, mad minds would go back to that hell place," another countered.

"Not go either," Spikehollow decided. "Maybe stay here and live. Or go south and live."

Rescuing their fellow slaves simply didn't motivate them,

Direfang realized. He had tried to stir them up with words of revenge and retribution, but he got better results with his persistent references to the water and food in Steel Town.

"Thirsty," Saro-Saro repeated, waving his spindly arms around to quiet those nearest to him. He held up the skin of a grub he'd sucked empty. "Hungry for better things."

Direfang tried appealing to their pride. "Goblins can be enslaved but not be defeated," the hobgoblin said. "Now there are too few knights, too many goblins." He talked about how easy it would be to crush the Dark Knights who had treated them so cruelly for so long. It would be easy to take all the water and food and supplies they wanted.

"Unprepared the Dark Knights will be," Direfang said. "So very busy cleaning up Steel Town and tending the wounds of the hurt ones. The Knights will never expect the goblins to come back, fight."

By that time he had persuaded most of the escaped slaves, with only a handful still grumbling their objections to his plan.

Direfang selected thirty goblins from among those who volunteered to accompany him. Then, after thinking it over, he ordered most of the others to follow him and the volunteers at a distance as they made their way back to the camp.

"But not all the way. Not yet. While it is dark, can be quiet and fast," he said. "Later comes the attack, when the clouds are thickest. Be quiet and be fast and be strong."

"Strong and fast!" Brak shouted. "Strong and fast with Direfang!"

"Angry and fast!" Spikehollow added. "Very, very angry!"

"Thirsty!" Saro-Saro barked. "Angry and fast and thirsty!"

When Direfang finally had them whipped into a fervor, he took off at a run toward the knights' camp, not wanting to give the goblins a chance to change their minds and realize it was a very dangerous, perhaps very foolish, endeavor.

Direfang only half believed his own words about how easy it would be to surprise the knights. He had doubts himself whether it was a wise or stupid thing to do, to jeopardize their escape and return to Steel Town. But he thought of Mudwort and it made him sad and angry to leave her behind.

He'd tried to inspire the others just so he would have the advantage of superior numbers. Alone, he didn't have a chance of success.

"My mind sour too, maybe," he mused to himself as he jogged toward the camp, followed closely by the thirty volunteers and, farther back, by the horde of goblins. He mulled over his plan. "Mind is foggy to consider this. Mad? Could be mad." It would have been easier to find a stream in the mountains or to raid a merchant wagon for supplies. But he had convinced himself that he couldn't abandon Mudwort, and furthermore, he had convinced himself all the slaves should be free.

Though he had swayed most of the slaves, not all of them went with him. Moon-eye and Graytoes were still recuperating, and others shuffled away to the north and south along the foothills, refusing to go near the camp and unwilling to wait and see if Direfang would be successful and return. Direfang himself asked the older slaves and the ones badly injured to wait for him by the slope where they would not be a liability to his adventure.

Saro-Saro had argued strenuously in favor of joining Direfang on his rescue mission. Partly that was because the old, cagey goblin was nosy and wanted to see firsthand what would transpire at the camp. He didn't want to hear gossip or legend about it afterward. Hurbear also argued in favor of going on the raid, though Direfang suspected the aged, yellow-skinned goblin would have sidestepped the issue if he could. But Hurbear wanted to look important in front of his clan.

Direfang took pity on him. "Hurbear needs to take care of Moon-eye and Graytoes," the hobgoblin said. "It is important to keep Moon-eye and Graytoes safe. Graytoes hurts badly and must be watched. Hurbear should be in charge here."

That pleased Hurbear, who climbed up the rise to sit next to Graytoes, head up and chin jutted out to look fearless.

"Graytoes be safe here," Hurbear pronounced. "Direfang be quiet and fast. And Direfang will win."

At first the hobgoblin set a demanding pace, then he slowed to a gentle lope, making sure his goblin army could keep up. About two dozen hobgoblins also followed him, though they took up the rear, at Direfang's request, watching their smaller cousins to make sure none stumbled or got trampled. The clouds were still thick, and all of them had to rely on their keen vision to avoid the gaping cracks and piles of rocks created by the quakes. They had to make a long detour around a wide, ugly crevice, but otherwise took the shortest route to Steel Town.

Direfang stopped some distance away, alert to the faint glow of lanterns ahead and the smoldering pile of dead goblins. He held his finger to his lips and glared around at his band of volunteers, passing the word back for everyone to be quiet. Then he gestured to his followers and moved toward the camp.

The cloud cover had grown, and the shadows from the rises were thick and concealing. They could see the new slave pens in the process of being rebuilt. At least six knights patrolled each of the three pens in various stages of repair.

Direfang could smell the many burned bodies even though the wind was blowing toward the camp. He could hear the sounds of men talking and heavy objects being moved around the place. There was little noise coming from the slave pens.

He stared at the makeshift pens. Several hundred slaves were in the pens. Many of them had no interest in freedom, he knew, for they were born there and knew nothing else. Some had vacant eyes. But many had tried to escape with him when the second quake came. They just had not been fast or lucky enough.

"Save the goblins now?" Spikehollow whispered.

Direfang shook his head and edged north, passing the pens and heading toward a ridge on the far side of the camp.

"Save the goblins?" Spikehollow persisted. He tugged on Direfang's trousers and pointed back toward the pens.

"Yes," the hobgoblin replied with a hiss. "But this first. Be quiet." He looked daggers at the young goblin. "Rob first, sow panic, then save the hobgoblins and goblins."

Spikehollow instantly quieted and fell back. The hobgoblin stopped just east of where the Dark Knights had maintained their own burial ground. No one was digging graves at the moment, though a half dozen bodies were stretched out in a line, not yet washed and wrapped, and tainting the air with a sweet but rancid scent.

Direfang was grateful no knights patrolled there. The dead did not need to be protected and could not flee like the slaves.

"Good thing the dead are alone," Direfang said so softly none of the goblins could hear. He crept toward the dead knights, motioning to Spikehollow and the others. At his signal, they started pulling swords and knives from the dead then scurrying away into the darkness to hide.

Then Direfang returned to the closest grave, staying low, and quickly digging at the mound. At a nod, the thirty goblins spread out and started digging at the other mounds.

"Foolish thing the Dark Knights bury the dead with

weapons," he whispered to Spikehollow. "The dead cannot use swords, so it is very foolish. But it is a good thing for goblins, eh?"

Direfang had never wielded a long sword. But he knew the one he retrieved from the first grave was sharper and far more formidable than his claws. He'd watched the knights practicing with such swords and sparring sometimes in the evenings, north of the pens. He believed he could use one well enough. He moved to the next grave and the next, staying low and wary to make sure no living knights came upon them. The other goblins also dug quickly and quietly. When they'd gathered three or four swords each, as well as an armload of long knives, they retreated to where they had piled the weapons.

Direfang ran to where his army waited, whispering news of the weapons they'd gained and the graves they'd gladly desecrated. He brought the goblins and hobgoblins to the pile of weapons and cringed when some of them whooped in joy.

"Quiet," he warned. "There is no surprise without quiet."

The hobgoblins and the largest goblins were given some weapons. It wasn't the weight of the weapons that bothered the goblins—they'd been carrying ore, picks, and shovels for years and could manage the heft of the blades. It was their complete unfamiliarity with the swords that was the problem.

The long knives were another matter, and the goblins clutched them as easily as tools and lanterns in the mine.

"For water!" Direfang declared softly, his voice carrying to the others. "For clothes and goblins left behind!"

"Water," Brak repeated, his eyes glimmering. "For lots and lots of beautiful water."

They stole toward Steel Town, Direfang and Spikehollow in the lead. The Dark Knights had plenty on their minds. They had already forgotten about the escaped slaves.

They hadn't heard the goblins whooping and hadn't considered the possibility of an attack from an enemy outside the camp.

The clouds were thick over the ruins, and though the wind would carry the army's scent, the hobgoblin doubted the Dark Knights would notice the extra smell, not over the stink of sulfur and burned bodies and the dead knights not yet buried.

Direfang headed toward the slave pens, ducking and scuttling like a crab as they drew close. He motioned the others to copy his movements. They tried, but they made a low but steady noise in their number and awkwardness. The dark knights by the nearest pen heard them coming. The knights snapped to attention, one of them pointing to the east.

"The knights see! Run fast and be mean!" Direfang called to the goblins. "Kill the Dark Knights!"

18

WAR WITH THE DARK KNIGHTS

K ill the Dark Knights before the Dark Knights kill Spikehollow!" Spikehollow called.

"Before the Dark Knights kill Brak!"

"For water!" Folami cried. "For lots of water!"

"Beautiful water!" Direfang ran straight toward the center pen, where the Dark Knight guards were lining up to fight the attackers. One yelled a warning to the rest of the camp, then led the others charging the hobgoblin.

Direfang slashed wildly at the first knight—no skill behind his swing, but a considerable amount of strength. All the years toiling in the mine had given Direfang powerful arms, and when he connected with the Dark Knight's waist, he cut through the chain mail and severed the man's spine.

The hobgoblin was so surprised at the effectiveness of the blow that he froze, letting the other knights dart in and surround him. They would have skewered him too, had the rest of Direfang's army not caught up and swarmed them.

Like Direfang, the goblins and hobgoblins boasted no

skill with their weapons, and unlike him, they'd never paid much attention to the Dark Knights' drilling. But their numbers overwhelmed the small group of knights. The goblins knocked the soldiers to the ground without suffering much injury to themselves, and proceeded to drop their weapons and tear at the knights' faces and necks with their teeth and claws. Some goblins wielding long knives stabbed at the knights, over and over until their own leathery hides were soaked and coated with Dark Knight blood.

In the midst of the melee, Direfang was facing off against one knight, ducking beneath the powerful swing of the man's sword. The steel whistled in the sulfur-filled air. When the knight brought the weapon around a second time, Direfang thrust his own sword forward clumsily, just grazing him. But the strength behind the blow surprised the knight, and Direfang kicked at his legs until he toppled.

Dropping his sword, Direfang leaped on the knight, tearing at the man's black tabard and chain coif, pulling them both free and pounding on the knight's face. He pounded and pounded until the bones broke and the man had no face left, was just a mushy, distorted form with broken, protruding teeth and bare skin slick with blood.

Direfang had never killed a person before that day, but within a few minutes he'd sliced through one man and brutally slain another. His savageness ought to bother him, he thought, but he didn't feel any emotion except pleasure. He rose from the second man's body and picked up his sword then bent and grabbed the knight's sword too. A few steps ahead of him was another knight, and the hobgoblin jabbed at the man with both blades, shoving forward and piercing the man's chest.

The goblins were hooting and howling, and by then the entire camp was alerted. Direfang was annoyed that his plan had been subverted so quickly. He'd intended to ambush the knights guarding the slaves, quickly and silently, release the slaves, steal all the water and other provisions they could find in a hurry, and make their escape.

That plan was ruined. Yet all the knights who had been guarding the pens were dead or dying. The goblins were hopping over the bodies and pushing, like a wave crashing, against the rebuilt, makeshift pen that was so rickety it was already swaying. Direfang watched as his goblins smashed it down and yelled at their freed fellows, urging them to run east. The shouts turned angry when most slaves simply stood dumbstruck and refused to move.

"Magic!" It was Mudwort. Direfang spotted her perched atop a still-standing post, waving to him and shouting. "The skull men used magic to deaden minds! The goblins are rooted like trees to this place. Their minds are magicked."

Direfang leaped over fallen knights, slicing open throats as he went just to make sure that some of the moaning, groaning ones would surely die. Then he pressed through the swarm of goblins until he was at the broken pen, knocking a few entranced slaves aside to reach Mudwort.

"Why come back?" The shaman cocked her head and gave the hobgoblin a stern look, yet with a faint smile and grateful relief showing in her eyes. "Come back for Mudwort?"

"Water," he said, shaking his head, unwilling, even now, to declare his friendship. "Came back for water. For all the goblins and for food. Came back for those things."

She grabbed his arm and climbed on his shoulders, her legs straddling his neck. "Water there." She put her hands on either side of his head and forcibly turned his gaze. "Thirsty, Direfang. So very, very thirsty. The shattered well is new again and filled with sweet-smelling water."

Direfang growled softly. He knew where the well was, he'd stacked a ring of stones around the place. But the stones had been tossed away by the second quake, and all around the area, goblins were frantically digging.

"Well collapsed," she explained. "Broken. The quake destroyed the rest of this place along with the well. Everything is broken. Destroyed the insides of the mountain too, the quake did." Her voice was gleeful. "And there." She turned his head again so he could see a row of benches loaded with jars and skins. "Things to carry the very sweet water."

"Lots of things to carry lots of water." Direfang smiled at the thought of bringing water to Moon-eye and Graytoes, and even to Saro-Saro and Hurbear. But first they would have to fight more knights, as dozens came running from various posts around Steel Town, all in arm and leading with their swords.

"Wait here," Direfang said quickly, setting Mudwort down and shouting to the goblins to turn around and meet their nemeses.

Many of the knights were spent, Direfang could tell, their faces dirty and haggard. Still, they looked fierce and determined. Yet the goblin army was surging with energy, all their pent-up hate boiling over and erupting. All but the hobgoblins had dropped the long swords. But many of the goblins had snapped up knives and daggers from the blood-splashed Dark Knight bodies. Those knives were out and flashing as the goblins rushed to meet the knights, and even more, teeth and claws viciously ready for the hated humans.

The first row of goblins fell screaming as the organized and well-drilled knights cleaved through them like farmers cutting down wheat. But before the knights could draw their swords back for second blows, the second and third line of goblins engulfed them. Direfang watched the knights gasp with surprised exclamations of pain, their spurts of blood filling the sulfur-laced air. The quakes had beaten the knights down, and exhaustion added to their misery. They weren't the same hardened troops who had ruled Steel Town before.

THE REBELLION

The knights' feeble attempts to regroup were soon drowned out by their screams and the whoops and shrieks of the goblins. Even Direfang howled in a frenzy. He ran toward the south slave pen, where goblins were clawing and pounding without weapons at the exposed faces of fallen knights. But they showed a discipline lacking in the first battle. They beat one knight after another senseless, but moved on quickly to other foes after making certain each victim was dead.

It was a good, strong army Direfang had assembled.

"Most have muddled minds, Direfang." Mudwort had followed him and was there at his side, pointing to the slaves in the pen area. They milled there with blank expressions and dull, empty eyes that didn't seem to notice the battle. "Most won't leave. Muddled minds won't let the feet move."

But the few who had resisted the Skull Knights' spell were moving, some joining Direfang's army, others fleeing east.

"Hold tight, Mudwort." Direfang placed her up on his shoulders again and rejoined the fray as still more knights materialized and advanced toward the struggle. With Mudwort shouting and pointing to aid him, he swept both swords up and down, as he'd seen the knights do, clearing out a line of knights who had targeted him as a leader.

One knight managed to step past his weapons and slice the hobgoblin's left arm. Direfang reflexively dropped one sword and pulled his wounded arm in close, lurching and nearly unseating Mudwort. But at the same time he brought his right arm around with as much strength as he could summon, the sword cutting through the knight's chain shirt and plunging deep into his shoulder. The blade was lodged there for only a moment, then Direfang pulled hard to free it. Then he brought the sword down again, cutting the man deeply on his head and finally kicking out and bringing him to his knees, weaponless. Before Direfang could finish him, goblins swarmed the fallen knight and started clawing him.

"Could have done this long before," Mudwort said, leaning toward one ear. "Gone after the Dark Knights to win freedom. Should have done this long before. Why not before now?"

"Before there were wards and pillars of flame," Direfang answered. "Before there were more knights and less willpower."

"Yes, and before the ground did not shake." Mudwort agreed, resting her chin on the top of Direfang's head as the space cleared out around them and the fighting moved on.

"This place is ruined now," Direfang said, looking around in satisfaction at his rabid army. "So are the knights. Came back for water, supplies, and other goblins and you. But didn't plan a victory . . . a total victory, like this."

Perhaps one-third of the Dark Knight soldiers had been killed by the first quake, with one-third wounded, and only one-third unhurt. That was what Direfang had heard someone say to the wizard. And that was long hours ago, before the second quake. The second quake had been every bit as powerful as the first, perhaps worse, so the knights were further weakened.

The whole camp could be taken by his ragtag army, Direfang suddenly knew, though at some loss to his force.

"Water!" the hobgoblin shouted, reminding his army of their first goal. He shouted and shouted the word until he couldn't speak. He sorely needed water himself. His legs burned terribly. His left arm pained him too, from where he'd been cut.

The hobgoblin felt a stickiness down his side and realized it was blood dripping from his arm. He couldn't focus on his wounds right then, however, as he spotted three knights heading toward the well, one of them the hated skull man who had magically ripped away Graytoes' youngling.

Mudwort was shouting something and pointing, but he shut her out of his mind and charged the trio, feet pounding behind him to let him know he had plenty of bloodthirsty company. He nearly tripped in his haste, crashing over a fallen knight, but somehow managed to keep his footing and lead with his sword as though it were a pike. Mudwort clung to him.

The Skull Knight, looking sickly pale in the light from lanterns scattered unevenly around Steel Town, turned and squarely faced Direfang, seeming to recognize the once-loyal foreman who had led the slave escape. The Skull Knight moved his hands as though he were weaving lace. A silvery blue glow arced out and struck the hobgoblin in the chest.

"End this fight," the Skull Knight proclaimed. It was Siggith, the priest who had earlier helped charm the goblin slaves into staying in camp, and who before that had murdered Graytoes's baby. "Tell your pitiful soldiers to surrender! Yield to peace, and we will feed you and keep you safe!"

The words sounded so pretty and soothing, they begged to be heeded. Direfang wanted to obey, hear more of the sweet words.

"Steel Town is the only place you'll be safe, hobgoblin. Safe from the ogres and minotaurs. Steel Town is home!"

The Skull Knight's voice wrapped around him like a soft blanket, and Direfang froze in hesitation.

"We will keep all of you safe," Siggith continued.

The silvery blue fingers of light jumped from Direfang to spread to the goblins behind him and closest around him.

"End this fight and find peace, hobgoblin. Embrace peace, all of you. Drop the blades and rest. Welcome home."

Direfang's right arm dropped. "Find peace," the hobgoblin parroted dully. "Peace. Safety. Home."

19

FREEDOM FROM DEATH

No! Direfang, do not listen to the skull man!" Mudwort jabbed her fingers at the sides of the hobgoblin's head. "No!"

"There is peace in Steel Town," the Skull Knight continued, staring hard at Mudwort.

Many of the goblins trailing Direfang had stopped, and the soft thuds that followed were their knives and daggers hitting the ground. But the spell didn't reach all of the goblins, and some swarmed past the ensorcelled ones and headed straight for the trio of knights near the well.

"No, Direfang!" Mudwort clawed at his face, jarring the hobgoblin back to reality. "No muddled mind, Direfang! No time for a muddled mind!" She thumped her heels against his chest for good measure. "Move, Direfang! Kill the skull man!"

A heartbeat more, and the haze in his mind lifted. Mudwort hammered at his shoulders to spur him on. With a deep breath and a shake of his head, he started racing forward again, his mind clearing, bent on throttling the life

160

out of the priest. But Direfang was not able to reach the man because he was surrounded by a deep press of enthralled goblins.

The two knights at the priest's side were still alive and fighting, slashing away at as many goblins as they could reach. Those two were clearly elite warriors, Direfang could see. Their moves were precise, and they flaunted many medals on their tabards. And though they were killing one goblin after the next, they couldn't hold off the mob forever. Again he tried to push forward, gaining a little ground.

Bleeding, snarling goblins who had shrugged off the magic scampered up the men's legs. Some were bashed aside by the knights' shields, but others climbed up their tabards and scratched at their faces. More goblins swarmed the knights until it looked as if a leathery goblin hill had grown by the new well. The Skull Knight was swallowed up too.

Direfang watched all the trio fall before he could get close enough to join in the killing. He tried to call out to Spikehollow, but his throat was still too dry. The young goblin was tearing at the priest and oblivious to anything else.

Instead Direfang turned and lumbered toward the benches with the skins and jars on them. He desperately needed water.

"The blasted wizard!" Direfang cursed in a low voice, as much for his own ears as Mudwort's. He'd found a jar filled with water and drained all of it in one long gulp, regaining his voice. "Not spotted the Gray Robe among the dead, Mudwort. The wizard is the commander now, and must be found and killed in order for goblins to be safe."

The fight continued behind him, and as his right hand closed on a clay jug, he looked around for the man called Grallik.

"Should have been watching for the wizard. Forgot all

about the wizard, Mudwort. In all the blood frenzy and with all the noise, forgot. The most dangerous man is still in camp."

Direfang knew it was the wizard who had birthed the sheet of flame that kept goblins from escaping with him, and who had summoned the priests to muddle all the slaves' minds.

So there was at least one priest left in Steel Town, there was the wizard, and there were still plenty of knights who would be coming to fight the goblins. They wouldn't surrender. They would fight and fight until death.

"With the wounded maybe, the wizard is," Mudwort said, thinking it over. "Protecting the wounded. Protecting Marshal Montrill."

Yes, protecting themselves, Direfang thought. Gathering their forces and making a last stand with the wounded. The wizard would have enough sense not to send all of the surviving knights to confront the ravenous army of slaves.

That was when another half dozen knights materialized on horseback, charging into the mass of goblins thronged around the well. The horses panicked the goblins, as the knights, three of them wielding lances, must have anticipated.

Those lances impaled goblins, lifting the bodies high and tossing them behind the horses as they passed. The other three knights were leaning low and lashing out with long swords in their hands, holding the reins between their teeth and using their knees to guide the horses.

Spittle shot from the knights' mouths as they cursed the escaped slaves and called on the memory of their Dark Queen to aid their struggle. Even the horses seemed in a rage. The animals' eyes were wide and wild, and foam flecked on their lips. They reared back, flailing out with their front hooves and coming down hard, crushing goblins everywhere they stepped. The harsh whinnies, coupled with the clash of swords and the screams of the slaves, unnerved even Direfang.

"Only six horses, six men," Mudwort said. Yet there was a quaver in her voice the hobgoblin had never heard before. "Only six of each. Should not rout Direfang's army. Should not. Cannot." She snorted and jabbed her fingers at the hobgoblin's shoulder. "Should not, but could. Six of each could undo all this. Big knights on big horses are a scary thing."

Direfang roared, a welcome sound in his own ears after his throat had been dry for so long. Giving no thought to Mudwort on his shoulders, he hurled himself toward the horsemen, with Mudwort holding on tight, clamping her eyes shut to keep Direfang's flying hair and the dirt and dust and blood spurting in the air from clouding her vision.

The horses and riders continued their brutal attack. The largest of the knights had two goblins skewered on his lance, the weight tugging the weapon from him when he impaled a third. Releasing it and bellowing, he pulled his long sword just as Direfang reached him. The hobgoblin barreled into the side of the horse with his sword thrust forward. The horse shrieked as the blade cut through its chain barding, and it reared back, trying to edge away, giving Direfang an opening to pull the sword out and jam it in again, deeper, into its belly. Blood showered out and the horse collapsed just as Direfang leaped clear. The beast rolled on its side and momentarily trapped the knight under it.

Mudwort held on so tight, she made it difficult for the hobgoblin to breathe. He spun around behind the fallen horse, pulling his sword free and thrusting it into the struggling knight. Direfang shook his head to get Mudwort to relax her grip. Then he dashed toward another horseman who saw him just in time to swing around and ready his lance.

"Foreman!" the knight bellowed loud enough to be

heard above the battle sounds, recognizing Direfang from the mine. "Foreman! To the lowest level of the Abyss with you and all of your kind! May you be food for the worms by midnight!" Then he lowered his lance and prodded his horse into a gallop.

Direfang didn't balk. He ran straight at the horse and knight, Mudwort still keeping a stranglehold on him. The hobgoblin's bleeding feet pounded across the hard, uneven ground, stone shards and broken bits of things stabbing at his every step. His hand was so bloody from the fight with the other knight, Direfang nearly lost his grip on the sword. It struck his own leg as he ran, the blade scraping him and throwing the hobgoblin off balance. The mishap proved to his fortune, for Direfang lurched just as the knight's lance whizzed by. He didn't avoid the blow completely, though, as the side of the lance caught him and spun him around.

Direfang fell, Mudwort leaping from his shoulders and rolling on the ground to avoid the hobgoblin landing on top of her. The horse reared when the knight pulled back on its reins and brought its hooves down—one clipping the side of Direfang's head, the other just missing. The hobgoblin howled and brought his right hand up to shield his face; his left was still useless from the deep cut on his arm. He howled again, that time in rage, scooping up the sword he'd dropped, jumping to his feet, and swinging hard. Luck guided his aim. Direfang's blade sliced the horse's leg, causing it to retreat.

The world seemed off kilter as he struggled to keep his balance. Raising his sword, Direfang took a wobbly step toward the knight, who was dismounting from the injured horse.

"To the Abyss I'll send you foreman!" The knight gripped the pommel in both hands and bent his knees, assuming a stance that would block Direfang's charge. "To the Abyss, I say!"

But the hobgoblin didn't budge. He was having a difficult time just standing erect. The ache in his skull from where the horse clipped him throbbed inside his head and made it difficult for him to concentrate. The thrumming in his head grew louder and louder, and he barely heard the knight cursing at him. He heard too many goblin voices all around. They sounded like the buzzing of persistent flies. His vision was clouding—everything looking feathery.

"I'll send you and all your pitiful slavekind to the darkest, hottest pit!" The knight began to advance on him when it was obvious that Direfang wasn't going to charge him first.

Around them, the battle raged. The goblins had managed to unhorse two more knights, beating and tearing at them, and were regaining ground by virtue of their sheer numbers. The two remaining horsemen continued to fight on, concentrating on the hobgoblins, who were proving to be more dangerous because of their size and the long swords they were whipping around maniacally.

The hobgoblins surged forward, one accidentally striking a horse and cutting through links in the chain barding. The mounted knight thrust down with his sword, the blade sliding into the base of the offending hobgoblin's neck and killing him instantly. Another hobgoblin stepped in and drove his sword so hard into the knight's leg that it went all the way through and sank into the horse's side. A third hobgoblin, frenetic with a battle fever, finished the knight and the horse, leaving only one knight on horseback.

"Traitorous foreman!" Several yards away, the other knight continued to taunt and spar with Direfang. "I'll die this day, I know it. Perhaps all of my brethren will die. But I'll take you with me to the bottommost pit!"

Direfang offered no retort. It was all he could do to remain on his feet. He felt the weight of the sword in his right hand but couldn't tell if it was raised and pointed at the knight. The knight looked blurry and indistinct to him, like a watercolor painting where all the colors had run together in the rain. All the noises ran together too, words sounding nonsensical and punctuated by the clang of swords.

"Do you hear me, beast?" The knight took a step closer then another step. "Do you hear me, you damnable, hairy thing? I'll see you in the pit!" He wove his sword in a disciplined pattern and, noting that the hobgoblin's eyes did not follow his movements, smiled and pulled the blade high above his head.

"Now!" Mudwort hollered. "Direfang, now!"

In the same moment that the Dark Knight started to bring the sword down, intending to cleave through the hobgoblin, Mudwort dashed in and shoved a dagger into the gap between the knight's leg plates. The knight howled in surprise as his knee buckled. Mudwort tried futilely to pull the dagger free, but it was stuck fast. She leaped back, narrowly avoiding his sword crashing down, thunking impotently against the earth.

"Direfang, kill the knight now!"

Stirred by Mudwort, Direfang lumbered forward, lifting his sword arm as high as he could. The sword came down sluggishly but met resistance. Direfang pushed forward, planting his feet as his sword pierced the Dark Knight's abdomen, and knight and hobgoblin fell upon each other in a heap.

Mudwort darted in close and grabbed at her dagger. She wasn't able to tug it free, but she wrenched it back and forth to cause more excruciating pain for the knight. In a daze, Direfang tugged his own sword free and shoved it into the knight again, satisfied when the blood spilling out washed over his hand. The knight gasped, then lay still. The hobgoblin pushed away from the body and sat, blinking furiously, trying to make some sense of the chaos around him.

"Dead, the knight is," Mudwort said. "Dead, all the horse knights are. It's a good dead." She stood in front of the hobgoblin, brushing at his face. "Hurt, Direfang is. Head sour, eh? But not hurt too bad." She proceeded to describe the action around them: goblins swarming Dark Knights, more goblins snatching up skins and jars and hurrying to the well. Three hobgoblins running with squealing sheep under their arms.

"It is a good madness," Mudwort told Direfang. "More Dark Knight blood soaks the ground than goblin blood. Perhaps the earth will not be so angry now. So much blood, the earth cannot drink it all up. Perhaps the earth will stop shaking."

Direfang held his hand to his aching head then pushed himself to his knees. The world circled around him, and when it finally stopped, he slowly raised himself to his feet and shook out his shoulders then reached down and grabbed the bloody hilt of the long sword and pulled hard until the blade came free.

Things swam into focus. It was as Mudwort described: death and blood everywhere. His head pounded fiercely.

Despite all the pain he felt, the hobgoblin was pleased. They'd managed to rout the Dark Knights with fewer fatalities than might be expected. There were still more knights in the camp, probably gathered at the infirmary.

But they were done for the moment, weren't they?

They'd won their way to blessed, sweet water and to food. Goblins and hobgoblins were leading away goats and sheep and carrying flapping chickens by the feet. One tugged on the reins of a big black horse. Goblins were pulling cloaks and tabards from dead knights, trousers and shirts from dead laborers and their families. Direfang saw Brak stripping the clothes from a small boy, an innocent boy—maybe that should bother him, he who had never killed anyone before that day.

But he didn't feel anything toward the dead human child—only grief for the dead slaves.

He struggled toward the benches, where there were still water containers, pain lancing down his back. Mudwort scampered at his side, mumbling to herself and tugging on his trousers to get him to pause at the body of another dead knight. She retrieved a dagger and tugged free a bloodied tabard, and they moved on.

"Thirsty?" she asked him as she picked up a clay jug. "Cracked." She dropped the jug and picked up another, then pointed to a large stoppered skin. Direfang took it and grabbed another and shuffled toward the well.

Close by, there were only a few more knights fighting, but goblins overran them, killed them quickly, and began looting their corpses. Fires burned here and there from where the combatants had knocked lanterns over on benches and posts.

"Must burn the dead," Mudwort said, noting Direfang's interest in the fires.

"But not the Dark Knights," he returned. He dropped his sword, stretched out on his belly, and dangled his arms into the well, bringing up handful after handful of water and drinking deeply. He splashed water on his face and neck and tossed handfuls on his back. Other goblins ringed the well and were doing the same. Mudwort waited for her turn.

When Direfang had his fill, which took some time, he dipped the skins into the water and held them there until they filled almost to bursting. He stoppered and slung them both over one shoulder, got up, and retrieved his long sword.

"Yes, the dead must burn," he told Mudwort. "Time to see to that."

"Not many dead, though," she said. "Not compared to the Dark Knights."

"No, not too many to burn," he agreed.

Direfang and another hobgoblin set about gathering the goblin bodies and piling them around the benches where the waterskins had been arranged. He ordered Spikehollow and Folami to scour the grounds for other dead slaves, then worked to coax a fire from a lantern burning low. When the bodies started to burn, he headed toward where the slave pens had been. His head still throbbed terribly, and the pain pulsed down his back each time he put weight on his right foot. The thrumming noise in his head and the victory shouts and yelping of the goblins were nearly overwhelming.

"From the death of the Dark Knights, there comes freedom!" A wiry goblin named Crelb was shouting. He stood on a bench, cupping his hands around his mouth for all to hear his words. "Freedom from death! Freedom for goblins!"

Direfang passed by, raising his long sword in salute.

"Freedom, because of Direfang!" Crelb yelled louder. "Freedom from death! Freedom from Dark Knights!"

Some goblins around Crelb cheered, some called the hobgoblin's name over and over until it sounded like a chant. Others at the edge of the crowd barked questions: What would happen next? Where should they go? What was freedom?

Direfang held his right forearm to his head, then dropped his sword arm to his side, the blade thudding against the hard earth. "Yes, what is, what was freedom?" he muttered. "It was years and years ago, and it tasted very good."

"What Direfang say?" Mudwort hadn't heard him clearly.

"Time to free the rest of the slaves," Direfang replied. "The ones with still-muddled minds." He thought about having another drink of water. The dirt- and sulfur-filled air had dried out his mouth very quickly. But more than anything, he wanted to get out of Steel Town, and so he walked toward the huge milling crowd of a few hundred glassy-eyed goblins.

"Minds all muddled," Mudwort said, still at his side. "Badly stuck."

Direfang nudged some of them east and started in that direction himself, expecting them to follow. Then he called for those members of his army who could hear him and waved his sword arm in the air, gesturing east. His other arm was practically useless. His army slowly started to move. But still, the glassy-eyed slaves did not budge, pushing back against the wave of goblins urging them to leave Steel Town.

"This is home," one close to Direfang said dully. "Cannot leave home. Steel Town is safe home. Safe here."

20

The End of Steel Town

This place is dead to us." Marshal Montrill said glumly, lying flat on his back, wadded cloaks propping his head up so he could see the men who circled his makeshift bed. "What the quake didn't destroy, the goblins did."

The air was gray with ash and dust, laced with the sounds of men coughing and moaning and, in the distance, someone hammering. A knight barked orders to his fellows, but the words were drowned out by the crash of something metallic falling.

The men tending the wounded in what passed for the infirmary looked little better than their suffering patients. There wasn't an inch of bandage or clothing that was not bloody and filthy, not a patch of skin that shone clean.

"Aye, Commander," Grallik acknowledged. "It is all finished." The wizard's gray robe was smeared with blood and ashes and tattered at the hem. A dirty stubble marred his face, though no beard grew on the left side where his old fire scars were thickest.

Grallik himself had given Montrill the painful report

of the goblin rebellion, describing the events vividly and leaving nothing out. Some goblins, he told Montrill, still remained in the camp, at the old slave pens, held by the priests' enchantments. It looked as though the goblins who had revolted were trying to force the remaining slaves to leave, but the divine enchantments were strong and the menials were still rooted in place. Grallik did not think it wise to send any more knights to attack the goblins. It would be a suicide mission. He hoped the goblins would all leave, soon and quickly. Besides, few knights besides those guarding the infirmary were healthy enough to fight. That was what he told Montrill, bluntly.

"I hold myself to blame, Marshal Montrill." In truth Grallik did blame himself because he'd posted only a few sentries at the pens after the second quake. He certainly hadn't expected the escaped slaves to return, and he couldn't easily recast any of his wards or glyphs. "We were not prepared."

Montrill said nothing to ease Grallik's guilt.

During the heat of the goblin battle, the wizard had stood on a hillside made of mine detritus, north of Steel Town. He had used a simple spell to render himself unseen and another enchantment to extend his vision into the center of the ravaged mining camp. It had been painful to observe the defeat, the goblins sweeping in and tearing apart everything the Dark Knights had built up during the past three decades.

Yes, the goblins had defeated the knights, even killing three more from Grallik's talon. He had only two men remaining in his own command. The wizard could almost smell the blood from his safe vantage point, mixing with the sulfur that still tinged the air. More than once, Grallik had closed his eyes, sick of the spectacle, the defeat, the carnage, and giving himself over to coughing fits. And more than once he'd considered wading into the fray and unleashing every fire spell he could manage before the goblins could bring him down.

But there were too many goblins, and his magic was close to spent. And he was in charge of whatever was left of Steel Town. It was his responsibility to order the surviving knights to fall back, sending two dozen to protect the wounded in the new infirmary. He doubted the surviving knights could stand up long to the goblin swarm if they chose to pursue their slaughter and turned in their direction.

So he did all he could do. He reviewed the spells in his memory and judged where to place his magical defenses: a wall of white-hot fire here, columns of fire there, an incendiary cloud to choke out those goblins brave and foolish enough to rush the flames. And when the spells were done, Grallik joined the two dozen knights in the infirmary. He was a Dark Knight who swore the Oath every morning, and he picked up a sword—he could well use one—curling the fingers of his fire-scarred hand around the pommel, the leather wrappings of which were already stained with blood.

He had vowed to fight hand to hand and, if necessary, give his life in that hellish, barren place. He truly expected to die there.

But the goblin swarm hadn't spilled toward the infirmary yet and they seemed content to loot the valuables in the camp. He heard the reports: hobgoblins carrying off sheep and goats, goblins and hobgoblins collecting every container in the camp and filling them with water. The red-skinned goblin who'd predicted the quake stabbed a Dark Knight in the knee then rode gleefully around on the shoulders of a hobgoblin who once had been a foreman of the deep mines.

Every Dark Knight death was on his hands.

But there'd been no other option, really, Grallik thought. He stood, hanging his head, at Montrill's side. The commander had awakened from his fever sleep during the massacre, and there'd not been a single Skull Knight available to tend him at that time. The only one left— Horace the Ergothian—had been trying to cast a spell on some of the goblin attackers until he, too, was wounded and fell.

Montrill had tried to get up and join the struggle, but a young knight disobeyed the order to help him rise and instead pressed the commander back onto the bed.

"Men will come," Grallik said. "Twice, Marshal Montrill, I have sent word of the quake and its destruction to Dark Knight commanders in Jelek and Neraka. I have asked for considerable reinforcements."

"But the men will come too late."

"Aye, Commander. Much too late."

Montrill's face was ashen. "Steel Town is dead to us."

"The entrances to the mines collapsed with the last quake." Earlier, Grallik had verified that horrible reality from his perch on the hill. "They could be reopened again, of course, or new entrances dug. But it will take time."

"Years." The word was a rasp Grallik had to strain to hear.

"Aye, Marshal Montrill. Even with slaves—new slaves bought from the ogres and minotaurs—it will take years to set this camp operating again as it used to be."

Montrill closed his eyes, clearly checking his anger. "It *will* operate again, Guardian Grallik, but not under our watch. We have failed the Order, and so this camp will fall to the direction of a younger man with fire in his belly, one who will give this place new life, probably a new name. Perhaps he will name it something grand or something sad to mark the unhappy events of this day. My fire flickers out, my comrade."

Montrill's throat worked, and a young knight stepped forward, tipping a jar of water so he could drink. Montrill swallowed only a little, the rest spilling over his cracked lips.

"You will recover from your wounds, Marshal Montrill." Grallik's voice sounded confident, though he doubted his own words. There was only one Skull Knight left, the Ergothian, and he'd been wounded, perhaps seriously. Grallik had seen him lying next to a dead horse. Where was he now? He looked around.

The supplies were thoroughly ransacked.

Montrill's color was bad, his skin clammy and cold. The fingers of his broken hand were red, an early sign of gangrene, the wizard knew.

"You will recover and be given a new post, Marshal Montrill. The quakes were not your fault. There was nothing anyone in this camp could have done to prevent those quakes."

Montrill nodded, accepting that statement. A thin line of blood spilled over his lower lip and he coughed, his shoulders bouncing against the cot. "Aye, the quakes were beyond our control," he said, pausing again to cough blood. "But the goblins that escaped and returned to attack us, Guardian Grallik, we could have done something about that."

"No, they were too numerous," Grallik countered. He wanted to add: not with the wards and glyphs destroyed, the pens shattered, the many Dark Knights distracted or wounded or dead. "They were an army not to be stopped. Though I admit I should have done more, prepared for any eventuality."

"You will be demoted, of course, stripped of your title and sent to the rank of a common soldier for some time. I, too, will lose stature. A demotion for me looms as well."

Grallik bristled. "There were too many goblins. I couldn't have anticipated—"

"Simple, stupid creatures they are, Grallik," Montrill mused. "Stupid, reckless slaves."

Not all of them, Grallik thought. "One of them was

smart enough to predict the quakes." The red-skinned one, she remained stubbornly in his thoughts. "I heard her tell a guard something bad was going to happen in the mines."

A woman suddenly wailed, and a man's voice tried to calm her. "My son!" she screamed. Then the sound of hammers grew louder and helped muffle her grief. Grallik looked away from the commander, trying to spot the woman and seeing only swirls of dust and shuffling men.

"Superstitious creatures, I say, those goblins," Montrill returned. "Not even a wizard as powerful as yourself could have predicted what the earth was going to do. How could a goblin know a quake was coming? Damnable simple, stupid creatures, the goblins, the lot of them."

Grallik stood there for several long minutes, listening to the crackle of fires throughout the camp, to the plodding of knights nearby as they tended to the wounded, the soft cry of the woman. The goblins were still close, but he had no desire to see how many or know what they were doing. A wind gusted from the west, stirring up the dirt and making the stench of charred bodies and sulfur all the worse.

"In the morning, we leave," Montrill ordered. "Those who can walk will carry those who can't. We march to Jelek, Grallik."

The wizard felt the brutal slap of Montrill's words. The Marshal did not call him Guardian Grallik any longer.

"Grallik, Steel Town is lost and dead to us."

"And we are dead to it," Grallik added.

21

SOME STAY BEHIND

They could have been carved from wood, the goblins standing mute and staring wide-eyed in the cobbled-together slave pens. They didn't register their freed brothers urging them to run. And the one pushed over by Crelb did not even try to rise up from the ground.

Behind them, Steel Town was rubble. Fires still burned, illuminating bodies, broken homes, and a few laborers who risked the goblins' wrath by poking through piles of debris looking for relatives. Direfang had told the goblins to let the humans be. There had been more than enough killing. The hobgoblin was more interested in getting the rest of the slaves organized and out of the mining camp.

"Stay then," Mudwort hissed at the goblins who couldn't shake the spell they were under. "Sheep, go ahead and stay. Sheep, go ahead and die to the Dark Knights left in this place. Die in the mines to the still-angry earth!" She edged by Direfang and wove her way through the entranced slaves. "Die in Steel Town and let the spirits fill the rotting bodies!"

177

Her words finally stirred some of them, particularly mothers with babies who feared the notion of their younglings dying in another quake. If none were left to burn the bodies or scatter the bones, their children's spirits would likely be lost and tortured forever. A group of mothers nervously gathered up their young and tugged them, following after Mudwort.

Still, there were many goblins who had never known anything but Steel Town, had been born in that place and did not know anything except the barren camp and slavery. The unknown frightened them. They refused to leave, huddling defiantly.

"Come east," Direfang told the ones who were ready to follow. He spoke loudly to be heard above the throng, but his words didn't carry much strength. He was tired physically and tired of trying to persuade the weak minded. "Fools, the lot," he muttered, half to himself. "Fools to stay."

The surviving Dark Knights had all but vanished, hiding in the infirmary, Direfang thought scornfully. Their numbers pathetically reduced, the knights had made no attempt to return to fight with the rebellious slaves and—for a time—they would be satisfied with the docile ones remaining.

The hobgoblin flirted with the idea of leading the army to the infirmary and slaughtering the knights down to the last one. But there had been enough death, he told himself again, and he worried that the Dark Knight wizard might be there and might call down fire upon them. Best to leave with their victory, he decided. And best to leave some knights alive to tell the grand tale of the goblin rebellion.

"All right then, stay and serve the taskmasters," Direfang told the still-enchanted slaves, still mute, staring dumbly. "Stay well," he added after a moment.

Direfang gestured, and his army headed out, most of the slaves who were undecided about whether to stay or go allowing themselves to be pushed along with the crowd, in the end leaving only a hundred or so slaves behind. The exhausted hobgoblin asked Spikehollow to take the lead for a while; then he dropped his sword and picked up a hesitant goblin with his good hand, half dragging him along with the rest.

"Stay well," he repeated loudly over his shoulder. "More likely stay and die, as Mudwort says. Stay and be sheep to the few Dark Knights."

Direfang took a last look at the camp, weary eyes sweeping over rubble made hazy by dusty air. He focused on where the tavern had once sat, remembering the music that sometimes spilled out of that building and the knights' laughter that used to make him angry. His gaze moved to a lone charred chair that stood in the center of what had been the store, then to a pile of steadily burning goblin bodies elsewhere. Firelight made pools of blood shine darkly everywhere, and he vowed to find a stream in the mountains so he could wash the Dark Knight blood off his hide.

He wasn't sad to leave that place, nor was he happy. The hobgoblin realized he no longer felt anything about the camp where he'd spent so many years as a slave. He felt no emotion, just emptiness.

At the edge of his vision, Direfang saw a female hobgoblin slap her mind-clouded mate, and when that didn't work, she picked him up and carried him across her back, complaining. Other goblins were doing the same. A particularly burly hobgoblin toted two goblins under each arm. Some of the entranced goblins were coming to their senses, whether by the prodding of their fellows or because the magic was finally wearing off. They acted as if they hadn't seen the battle that had just played out, and they chattered questions to their fellows, who didn't take time to answer.

Still, there remained dozens who refused to accept freedom. Dozens who stayed in their falling-apart pens and did not even turn around to watch their brothers leave.

"East," Mudwort called. "East, Direfang says!"

The word became a new chant that swelled rhythmically. Mudwort climbed on the shoulders of a hobgoblin in the middle of the army. "East, Erguth." She glanced over her shoulder at still-burning fires and at the slaves who clung to Steel Town.

"Fools," she spat. Then she turned her gaze to the eastern horizon, which was slowly lightening. The battle had lasted hours. It was the misty time before dawn. "Wonder what the Dark Knights will chant this day when the sun comes up," she mused. "Wonder how many are left to repeat their worthless oaths and credos. How many will say wasted words in that man's hole? There aren't that many voices left."

Direfang lengthened his stride, wincing with each step of his right foot. He never looked back, though many did, some continuing to call out to friends left behind.

The hobgoblin released the goblin he was carrying to rub dirt out of his eyes. It didn't help, and another rubbing only seemed to make matters worse. His eyes throbbed, his neck was stiff, and his arms felt as heavy as the ore sacks he used to drag from the mine. The pain in his head made it difficult to think.

He locked his eyes on the distant foothills, and for a moment he wished he would have stayed there when they'd first bolted. It would have been easier, certainly less hurtful, fewer would have died—goblins and knights. But they wouldn't have gained the food and blessed water, wouldn't have freed Mudwort and hundreds of others, wouldn't have had the pleasure of slaying the men who had once whipped them.

Pleasure, he thought, almost smiling.

THE REBELLION

Suddenly his mind was flooded with images of the past already receding: the mine and the camp and what he might have been doing that very instant if the quakes had never struck and never destroyed the wards and glyphs and weakened the knights, injuring and killing so many. He would be working in the mines, a foreman but also a slave. He would be struggling under sacks of ore, ordering goblins to dig faster, walking the tunnels to check on his charges. He was feeling something after all. Tears from painful memories welled in his eyes and helped to wash away some of the dirt.

Direfang continued to think of the sad, horrible past, forcing himself to feel deeply in order to give his eyes a washing and a measure of relief from the dirt. He thought of all the whippings he'd received, remembered what it had felt like to have his ear cut off. He walked faster, feeling stronger, reaching the front of the pack and passing Spikehollow. Despite the pain, he kept up his pace, not wanting a single goblin to be ahead of him or see his tears.

"Show no weakness," he whispered.

The sky was gray by the time he'd walked the first mile. It was a murky, misty blanket draped across Neraka. It looked empty, no sun yet, no stars or moons, no clouds. His eyes eventually were washed and felt better. He didn't think about the past anymore. The wave of emotion passed. He welcomed the emptiness again, not wanting to feel anything for a long while.

22

THE STILL-ANGRY EARTH

When they reached the foothills, the goblins feasted on the livestock they'd brought with them and on other supplies they'd hauled out of the camp. They shared their good fortune with the goblins who'd stayed on the rise, and the hobgoblin called Erguth made sure that Moon-eye and Graytoes were among the first to be given food and water. After Direfang drank his fill, he dropped the other full skin he'd carried, then watched as a group of young goblins fought over it.

The hunger was desperate, the feeding frenzied. Not even Folami, Leftear, and Bentclaw working together could control the clans. Within minutes, all of the food and water was gone.

Direfang and Mudwort sat with Moon-eye and Graytoes as goblins picked at the bones of the sheep and goats and lapped at the bloody hides. The oldest goblins had been given the animal hearts as symbols of respect, and they still gnawed on those vital organs while those around them whooped and danced in celebration of their freedom and full bellies.

182

"Worry soon," Mudwort said, pointing at the horde. "Sinks in, other goblins will worry lots too. Wonder where next food will come from, food and water. In Steel Town, everything was provided, though never ever enough of it, no. No hunters in this lot, so there will be worries."

"There used to be hunters among us," Direfang argued softly. "In the time before Steel Town, some hunted."

"Forgotten how," Mudwort said. "Forgot everything except how to mine and carry ore. So soon the worrying will come."

Direfang climbed higher and stretched out on a flat table rock and closed his eyes. He heard Moon-eye softly singing to Graytoes, and he faintly heard Saro-Saro calling to Mudwort, asking her to listen to the earth and discover what lay to the south. Moments later he heard goblins arguing over clothing they'd taken from Steel Town. Erguth the hobgoblin was loudly claiming a pair of boots. Spikehollow could be heard, grandly recounting his part in the knight massacre and boasting a long hank of hair he'd pulled off the head of a merchant who stood in his way. Direfang had no desire to see the prize so kept his eyes closed for a time.

There was a scuffle over a dagger with a horn handle, and Direfang briefly thought about rising and ending all the arguments, demanding that the throng quiet down and let him sleep. Or, failing that, he'd walk up farther into the hills where he could wait until they all dispersed. Quiet might ease the aches in his body and the pounding in his head from where the horse had kicked him. But before he could rise to speak or climb higher, exhaustion claimed him.

Mudwort waited until most of the goblins and hobgoblins were sleeping, their ugly snores drifting up the rise. Not so many goblins had ever slept at the same time in Steel Town because of the various shifts operating in the mines, so the snoring had never been so loud and bothersome.

She climbed higher, beyond Direfang, feeling the midafternoon sun beating hot on her shoulders. The lashmarks on her back had begun to scab over, and they stretched uncomfortably when she reached to grab for handholds. She squeezed her eyes shut after several minutes, willing the pain on her back to go away. She heard her heart pounding and her breath panting and the wind playing across the stone and sending dirt gathered in pockets scattering. She focused on the rhythm of her heart; it was labored. But she calmed herself and slowed the beat, concentrating on the warmth of the sun and caress of the wind, lessening the hurt from the whip marks.

There would be no more whippings, she promised herself. She would never let anyone catch her again and return her to slavery. She would die first. She opened her eyes and started climbing again. Mudwort had expected lots of trees and thick foliage away from Steel Town. She used to scamper through reeds and tall, itchy grass in her youngling years, and she thought the land away from Steel Town might be like that. She had expected mossy stretches and acorn husks crunching under her feet. But when she breathed deep, hoping to smell the heady loam, there was only dirt and stone, the same as she smelled in the mines, and still the hint of sulfur.

She didn't intend to climb too high because that would take her away from the safety of the horde. But she wanted privacy. From her perch, the wind brought pleasant sensations—a trace of flowers that were blooming beyond her sight and the odor of some wild animal that had passed that way, perhaps a mountain goat. The stench from the unwashed goblins was not as strong up there, and she entertained thoughts of striking out on her own for good so she wouldn't have to constantly breathe her smelly brethren.

But there was safety in numbers, she reminded herself, which was why she stopped. She sat on a flat piece of stone, warmed from the sun, and dangled her legs over the side. She placed her hands on either side of her hips and thrummed her fingers against the rock in time with the song Moon-eye had sung earlier. She repeated the verse she remembered.

> *Moon glows pale and soft pearly*
> *Yet goblins have no time to rest*
> *Moon calls the dark of the evening*
> *When the night bird leaves the nest*

Mudwort realized the earth was still angry, though not so terribly angry as it had been when it brought down Steel Town. When she dipped her senses into the stone, she could feel it twitch lightly, hardly noticeable. Things were shifting still in the earth, in ways she didn't understand but could register. Even many miles away from Steel Town—from what had been Steel Town—there were hints of tremors. From cracks in the stones around her and other signs, Mudwort could tell that the quakes had reached out there.

How far?

Had all the world rumbled?

Had all the camps of men and all their cities been turned into dust?

It was a happy image she conjured in her mind, building after building in ruins, humans crushed beneath the wreckage. Ogres, too, buried in their villages, and minotaurs dead everywhere. All the creatures of the world slain, except for goblins and hobgoblins and perhaps a scattering of bugbears. She knew none of that was likely true, that the quake couldn't have affected the whole world, but she let herself daydream for a bit. Then she dipped her senses farther into the rocks directly beneath her and listened hard.

If another quake came, it wouldn't be as devastating as the two she'd already lived through. The earth told her that much. It had vented enough rage, she knew, at least for the time being.

"But the earth is angry still," she reflected aloud. Mudwort was surprised at the sound of her voice, so clear up there when it wasn't competing with other goblin voices. "It will not lie still, the angry ground. It is not yet done."

Mudwort propelled her senses into the earth by imagining that her fingers that brushed the stone were actually burrowing into the ground, by growing eyes with sight so extraordinary she could see far below the ground, by growing huge ears, so she could better listen to the earth murmurs.

At first, she thought it might have been her imagination. She saw layers of stones and strips of sand, looking like painted bands on pieces of pottery. She saw crystals in slabs of rock, including one particularly vivid collection of blue crystals mixed with malachite. In some places the rock was dark, but mostly it was cerulean. Other stones her senses skipped along were familiar: obsidian, chert, and basalt.

She considered catching Direfang's attention and sharing that information with him. But going after the hobgoblin might jeopardize breaking whatever connection she'd made with the deep-down stones. How far could she peer through the earth?

Mudwort pictured herself flowing to the northwest, where the Dark Knight camp once had prospered. A heartbeat later she felt as if she were traveling there, running through the ground rather than on top of it, moving effortlessly, her legs never tiring, her feet never hurting. She heard something as she went, a sound she didn't recognize. It was almost pleasing, a susurrus that calmed her and bid her go faster.

The layers of rock she flowed through were not even,

as she expected them to be. At one time they'd probably looked that way, all even with one placed atop the other by time and the elements. But the quake had broken up the layers and made them more . . . interesting was the word she wrapped her mind around. Shards jutted up here and there, and she passed right through them. A stretch of sand was ribboned with strips of slate. Coarse grains of something crystalline and pale gray were spread across a scattering of obsidian chunks. There was more of the curious blue and malachite mixture.

She could tell she was near the camp or perhaps had rushed by it and was at the mountain with the mine shafts. She saw large pieces of the ore the Dark Knights coveted, one a massive section with thick red veins in it that she knew would yield good, pure steel. It was covered by bands of obsidian and chert. She was pleased it was so deep, so the Dark Knights would not find it and profit by it. That deep part of the earth, at least, was safe from the horrid men.

Mudwort was amazed that she could see colors and feel textures, though she warranted that her active imagination could have been responsible for some of those sensations. She thought she could also smell the richness of dirt that had never been farmed and smell the dustiness of sand and the acrid tang of chipped slate. She would have lingered under the ground for quite some time—or rather let her mind tarry there—had she not felt a startling wave of heat.

Her eyes snapped open and she looked around, thinking that perhaps some goblin had started a fire near her. then realizing that was a foolish thought. She was still alone on her little rock, well above Direfang, who was in turn perched above Moon-eye and Graytoes and all the rest. None of them were paying any attention to her. Those who were not sleeping were still reveling in their freedom.

Moon-eye still fawned over the sleeping Graytoes. Direfang still stretched on his back, his chest rising and falling too unevenly for him to be sleeping. He'd been sleeping before but not right then. So he was pretending to be asleep, she decided, as she and others so often had done in the slave pens. Pretending so he could have peace.

She wiped the back of her arm across her forehead. She was hot; something in the ground had made her hot! A part of her was suddenly frightened, but a greater part was curious. So she closed her eyes again and steepled her fingers against the stone, leaning forward on her arms as if poised to dive into the earth. In a sense, that was what she did, sending her mind hurtling against the stone and wondering why she'd never more fully explored her surprising abilities back in Steel Town. Perhaps the impetus of freedom gave her power, or perhaps it had driven her mad.

"Mind fouled?" she wondered. "Mind broken?"

If her mind had gone rotten and she were only imagining all of it, it wasn't necessarily a bad thing, she thought. She was enjoying it, and it had been a long time since she'd enjoyed anything. If madness was fun, so be it.

Again, she raced through the earth, slowing when she encountered something interesting, such as a tree root so old it had turned as black and as strong as obsidian. The tree that once grew above it was long gone, and Mudwort futilely tried to picture what it must have looked like. Then she continued on her journey, no longer focusing on the Dark Knight camp. She'd tired of that place and of those horrid men. She spiraled outward from her lofty perch.

There were things—goblins, men, animals, she couldn't determine what sort of creatures—moving across the ground, maybe coming in her direction. Perhaps some of the goblins who'd remained in the camp had changed their muddled minds and escaped and were following them. Perhaps surviving laborers were headed to Jelek or the city of Neraka. The things moved with purpose, steadily in one direction, though they did not move quickly.

Then her mind brushed creatures that stirred in the earth to the south, where Direfang intended to go. They were smaller creatures, stirring among the sand and rocks. Snakes, she suspected, because in the past she'd seen several snakes slither out of holes beyond the boundaries of the slave area, sunning themselves in the hottest part of the day and returning to their holes at dark or when a knight walked by and disturbed them. Once, months and months past, she saw the goblin called Brak grab a snake that had slithered too close to the pens. Brak had reached out with his leathery arm and snapped it up, catching it behind the head so it could not easily bite him. Probably he ate it, but Mudwort hadn't watched; her attention had been distracted by something else at the time.

No doubt all the burrowing animals for miles around the Dark Knight camp had been affected by the quake— either killed or displaced, their homes broken just as the buildings in Steel Town had been broken. They were all stirring.

Just how far had the devastation reached?

Mudwort wondered again if any of the ogre villages in the hills to the east had been shaken and battered. She hoped they'd all been destroyed. Because Direfang wanted to go south, perhaps she should concentrate on exploring in that direction.

South.

Farther.

"Ack!"

All of a sudden, she felt a bitter taste in her mouth that no amount of spitting would relieve. Odd that she hadn't noticed the taste before. Perhaps she'd been too preoccupied to notice it building up. But right then it was all she could think about. It had settled firmly on her tongue and made her eyes sting. It filled her nose with a dry, unpleasant scent, and again made her feel unnervingly hot all over.

Curious, that hot, bitter sensation. Mudwort instinctively knew what it meant.

Something very, very bad waited to the south.

23

MORE THAN ONE THOUSAND

Direfang finally slept. For quite some time, he'd been resting, stretched out on the rock, right arm draped over his burning eyes to keep the sun out. He felt almost nothing in his left arm, which a Dark Knight had deeply slashed. He was glad that any pain from that wound was not competing with his other aches, especially with the pounding in his head from the horse that had clipped him. The pounding would not stop.

But he was a little worried about the arm. He'd looked at the wound, which ran inches deep below his left elbow, practically to the bone. He'd wrapped a strip from a Dark Knight tunic around his arm in an effort to staunch the bleeding. The cloth was black and, therefore, did not show any blood, but it felt warm and sticky. He didn't want to think about his wounded arm. He had plenty of other things to be concerned about, such as all the goblins who milled at the base of the foothills and were waiting for his leadership.

When next he woke, it was well into the afternoon, and

his skin felt burned from the sun. He could hear goblins chattering below him, one calling out shrilly that Direfang had woken up again. Others turned their faces toward him.

He let out a great sigh and propped himself up. Dozens of the goblins called to him, the words blending into an annoying buzz before turning into a chant that was picked up by most of the crowd. Krumb and Thema were at the front, repeating his name over and over. He shuddered. It didn't look as though many had left. What had seemed a good idea two nights past, escaping from the Dark Knight camp and returning to free the rest of the slaves, had turned into a nightmare. What was he going to do with all those stupid goblins?

Those goblins, clearly more than one thousand of them—perhaps close to two thousand—had waited at the base of the foothills for him all through the early-morning hours and into the afternoon. The faces he looked down on carried myriad expressions—most of them hopeful and filled with anticipation, some of them worried, eyebrows raised in question. Not many appeared angry, but some glared at him.

He stood, and a cheer erupted.

"Direfang!" the chant grew louder.

Mudwort nudged his leg. She'd crept up behind him. "All look to Direfang," she said. "Commander Direfang. Marshal Direfang. Guardian Direfang." She used Dark Knight titles.

He sighed again, scratching at his chin.

"Say something," she urged.

"What?" he mused to himself. "Say what?"

"Something," she repeated. "Say something important."

He edged forward and raised his right arm, holding the left, still numb, close to his side. "Free of the Dark Knights," he began. He said something else, but his words were lost in the whoops and cries of the throng below.

When the cheers quieted, Spikehollow climbed on Erguth's shoulders and waved a fist. "South now, Direfang?"

"South when?" Gnasher shouted.

They all intended to follow him wherever he went, Direfang realized. He shuddered again, clenching his teeth tight. The previous night, he had said he would go south, and he expected some to accompany him. Others might also go south, wandering on their own. But he never intended that they move as one massive army, sticking together in freedom.

He'd needed their numbers for last night's raid on Steel Town. But he didn't need all of them following him anymore.

He opened his mouth to tell them to split up, go away, that a force the size of theirs would be difficult to feed, perhaps impossible. A force that size would have to raid more human camps, perhaps ogre camps, and would have to capture merchant caravans. More than once he'd thought about the notion of robbing caravans of food and valuables, but how could he lead so many, feed so many?

"Could capture caravans," he whispered. "But goblins would be no better than Dark Knights to hurt others and steal."

"What Direfang say?" Mudwort asked, tipping her ears toward him.

Yet a force that size could not be enslaved easily. Could it? Ogres would indeed think twice about attacking them.

"South together!" Spikehollow called as loud as his hoarse voice could manage. "South with Direfang!"

"South alone," the hobgoblin said softly. "Wanted to go alone, maybe with Mudwort and some others. Not all."

Direfang did not want the responsibility of leading such a massive army. He'd only wanted out of Steel Town—

wanted all of them out of that pit of hell. There were far too
many of them for him to manage. As a foreman in the mine,
he was in charge of shift after shift, but never so many all
at once. But the slaves had always obeyed him, to the point
that he couldn't remember being forced to punish one of
them. Perhaps because he'd supervised so many of them
over the past few years, they still looked to him for orders.
Maybe they'd been slaves for so long they couldn't think for
themselves.

"Lead, Direfang!" Boliver howled.

Maybe they really did need a leader.

They were all free. They could do as they pleased. In
smaller groups, they wouldn't need as much food and water.
In smaller groups they could hide in caves and under over-
hangs in the mountains and in others throughout Neraka and
Khur. Those groups that reached the forests could hide amid
the trees and cool shade, maybe regroup and start villages.

But maybe the ogres would hunt them and sell them as
slaves again.

Direfang knew that slaves were a precious commodity to
Neraka's Dark Knights and, therefore, a lucrative business
for those who caught and sold them.

Smaller groups would be easier for the slavers to catch
and control.

Many of the goblins had held on to the swords and
knives they'd carried away from their battle with the
knights. Those weapons could prove useful in fights with
ogres or minotaurs.

Direfang knew there were tribes of ogres in the hills,
and some minotaurs had moved in from the east. He'd been
captured by ogres years past and sold to the Dark Knights.
He knew ogres to be vicious and formidable, three times
the size of any goblin, outweighing even himself. Yet at that
moment, he didn't fear them as much as he feared leading
more than one thousand goblins.

He could recall the day he was captured with clarity. He could still feel the steely grip of the ogres' hands on his shoulders and legs, feel himself being lifted high and tossed onto the ground with others from his clan and chained hand and foot. He remembered the ogres' pungent breath and their large red-rimmed eyes, their bugcrusted hair and yellowed teeth.

He trembled from the memory.

But then, he realized, his band of rebellious goblins—his army—could crush a village of ogres.

He looked down at them. Their faces were turned expectantly toward him.

"Together there is strength," Direfang said finally. He swallowed hard and suppressed a shudder. "Together there is power," he said. "Together . . ." The rest of his words were drowned out in a cacophonous cheer of agreement.

When the cheering subsided, he heard Graytoes talking. She and Moon-eye had climbed higher and knelt on a table rock below him.

". . . to command all of the goblins, Direfang," Graytoes said. He didn't catch all her words—the cheering was too loud.

But he understood what she meant. It was up to him now. He had to hand out orders, command all the goblins, just like the Dark Knight's Marshal Montrill had ordered around all of the knights in the mining camp.

"South now!" he called to them. "Find food and water along the way. More sheep and goats penned by men. Together there will be strength and power." There was more cheering as Direfang eased himself down the slope, Graytoes and Moon-eye fussing over him, and Mudwort following close behind.

"You have looked to the south?" Direfang asked Mudwort. "What is to the south?" He'd seen her meditating on the rocks and knew she had been talking to the earth.

The red-skinned goblin pursed her lips. "Freedom is to the south," she answered, but she did not meet his eyes.

"Then let us go south now." Direfang began to march, moving his feet in time with the thrumming in his head, his right leg no longer paining him. It was a slow pace for him but one that allowed him to think and to not worry about the older goblins keeping up as he pondered where exactly to lead his eager army.

To the south, certainly, and south would take him along the foothills and deep into the Khalkist Mountains—away from Jelek and the city of Neraka and the major roads where they might encounter significant Dark Knight forces.

Suddenly, Direfang felt thirsty again.

He stared at the ground as he tramped across it, seeing cracks everywhere as though the entire landscape were a dry creek bed that stretched to the edge of his vision. The unevenness of it could have been natural or caused by the quakes; it made no difference to him. The sun continued to beat down on his shoulders, though after a few miles, clouds diminished the heat. At least he thought clouds were responsible until he heard worried murmurs from the goblins directly behind him.

The hobgoblin looked up to see a billowing gray mass pass overhead. It carried with it the stench of sulfur, which he knew well from the mining camp. But it was a slightly different smell, harsher and more painful and at the same time more interesting. It was followed by another gray puff, the tail of which led to one of the volcanoes that towered in the southern half of the country.

The volcanoes belched frequently at night, coloring the darkness with their ribbons of orange, red, and glowing yellow. Sometimes they rumbled, as the ground had done during the quakes. And on more than one occasion, they'd sent so much steam and smoke into the sky that the sun was blotted out for days. There'd been only one significant eruption of the volcanoes during Direfang's stint in the mining camp, and he wondered if another were imminent.

The top of the volcano he stared at was glowing as red as coals at the bottom of a goblin funeral pyre.

"Yes," Mudwort said, answering his unspoken question. "The mountain is angry now like the earth was angry." She grinned broadly, her eyes sparkling. "That mountain will break very soon. Good we go south and thread through the angry volcanoes. Dark Knights will not follow us across such angry ground."

His goblin friend's mind indeed had gone sour, Direfang thought. Mountains could not break. Not even the earthquakes had shattered the mountain that the steel mine was in. They had simply collapsed the tunnels. Still, he shivered as another cloud of smoke and ash belched up from the crater.

"South leads to freedom," Mudwort said. She cackled and rubbed her hands together—something the hobgoblin had not seen her do before.

"Hope Mudwort right," Direfang muttered as he moved ahead.

24

A VILLAGE OF MONSTERS

T hey could have passed for giants, the eight ogres the goblin army swarmed in the mountain pass. Though they were easily nine feet tall and had shoulders as broad as boulders, they'd been caught by surprise and put up only a token resistance before being beaten to bloody lumps by Direfang's goblin horde.

The scene was made more gruesome by the darkening sky and the flocks of birds racing to the east. It had been noon from the position of the sun when Direfang first spied the ogres. But within the passing of a few minutes, all the time it took for the killing, the sky had turned ominously gray and the air cooled.

Some goblins noticed the quick change in the weather but were not overly concerned. Weather was nothing they could do anything about. They were more curious about the dead ogres and what might be in the pouches dangling from their rope belts. Those goblins and hobgoblins who were farther back in the column—and who hadn't even joined the fight with the ogres—were more interested in why everyone had stopped and why the scent of blood was so heavy in the air.

"More vicious here than against the Dark Knights," Mudwort said of the goblins feasting on their ogre enemies. She had reclaimed her perch on Erguth's shoulders and was watching her brethren with a certain amount of disgust. "See the blood? More angry at the ogres than at the foul Dark Knights." She turned Erguth's head so he could look at the largest ogre corpse, which had been practically shredded. "Much angrier, this fight. See?"

Ogres had captured most of the goblins in the first place then subsequently sold them to the Dark Knights in the mining camp. Mudwort detested ogres with all her heart for that reason, but she'd not taken part in the slaughter—instead, she and Erguth had allowed the other goblins to surge past them and join the frenzy of killing and feasting. She was tired of blood, tired in general. And she was much more interested in the changes in the dark afternoon sky.

"It is a good vicious," Erguth returned, eyes fixed on the massive shredded ogre. "A most happy vicious."

"Yes, it is," Mudwort said after a moment. She placed her bony chin on top of his head and watched goblins smear ogre blood on each other's faces. They were painting clan symbols, some she didn't recognize. Some were arguing over choice pieces of the fallen, and over the protestations of others, a barrel-chested hobgoblin claimed a rough-weave tunic that one of the ogres had worn. The garment fell to the hobgoblin's ankles and was spattered with blood, but it was in better repair than most of the garments looted from Steel Town.

Mudwort looked at the sky again and nudged Erguth to forge ahead through the crowd. The mountain pass was relatively narrow, allowing only seven or eight goblins to squeeze through it at one time, resulting in Direfang's army stretching way back and meandering along the trail like a winding river. Word of the ogre deaths was still being whispered along the line, and she heard Brak and Folami and Crelb and others grumbling behind her that they'd been too far back to take part in the glorious bloodletting.

Had Mudwort not been on Erguth's shoulders, the hobgoblin wouldn't have made it to the very front, so tight was the press of goblins wanting their turn at the dead ogres. But she dismissively waggled her fingers at the goblins who blocked their progress, sneering and glaring when necessary. The goblins grudgingly edged aside, giving her a measure of respect and mumbling again about how she alone had predicted the quakes.

From up in the front, Mudwort could better survey the bloody mess. A goblin whose name she didn't know but who had been among those in her pen in Steel Town was using a Dark Knight knife to cut out the heart of one of the ogres.

"For Saro-Saro!" the goblin claimed, marking him as a member of the old one's clan.

Another goblin, a wizened one with a malformed arm, was working on prying open the rib cage of a female ogre and tugging that one's heart out for Hurbear.

Mudwort spotted Direfang several yards beyond the dead ogre bodies. He stood with Spikehollow, Graytoes, and Moon-eye, studying something on the trail. She prodded Erguth more firmly, and the hobgoblin carefully picked his way around the bodies, nearly slipping in a pool of blood, just as more goblins closed in to demand a share of the kill. Erguth showed little interest in partaking and averted his eyes after passing a few particularly gruesome-looking corpses.

"Direfang!" Mudwort called, drawing the leader's attention as Erguth lumbered close.

Direfang acknowledged her with a nod but kept his eyes focused on Moon-eye. The one-eyed goblin was sniffing the trail and running his fingers around the edge of an ogre footprint. Mudwort climbed down and joined Moon-eye. She watched him closely then took a pinch of dirt from inside the print and set it on her tongue. Moon-eye looked quizzically at her then resumed his surveillance of the trail.

Far behind them, the goblin throng had grown noisy, with word spreading farther about the ogre deaths and questions pouring forth about why everyone had stopped. Mudwort shut the noise out and dug her fingers into the earth.

"This way," she heard Moon-eye say. "Carry Graytoes now. Please."

Direfang obliged, picking up the female goblin with his good arm and cradling her close. She could walk on her own and had been doing just that for hours. But Moon-eye was fretting over her and was clearly annoying Direfang.

"Smell it? Smells bad. Ogres came from this way." Moon-eye pointed up a rise, where a narrower trail wound between granite outcroppings. "Scent is fresh and stinky-strong. Smells worse than Dark Knights." He scampered away from the main trail and headed up the narrower one, Direfang following and Mudwort reluctantly pulling back from the earth and again climbing up on Erguth's shoulders. She'd sensed something through the soil, a presence perhaps, and she'd wanted to explore further. But the narrow, upward trail curved east. She wanted to know why Direfang had decided to abandon the southern route.

"Spikehollow, Brak, follow now!" Direfang motioned to those behind him. "Crelb! Forget the dead ogres. Move!"

"Not going south," Mudwort said, catching up. "Going east now. Why?"

He gestured impatiently, pointing ahead. Erguth struggled to keep up with him as Direfang kept moving.

The column of goblins and hobgoblins, spilling out over the sides of the narrower trail as it crested a rise, looked down upon an ogre village. It filled an impressive egg-shaped basin, the Khalkists rising all around it. Larger than Steel Town had been, some of its crude huts, made from wood and stone, were in a shambles, and the earth around the village was slashed with deep, wide cracks between the piles of rubble. So the quakes had been felt even there and had killed some ogres. Across from the goblins, where another trail led, smooth from all the heavy feet that had trod it, was evidence of a funeral pyre. Fat crows picked at the edges.

The ogre town had four dirt roads that divided homes from gardens and livestock and a central communal building that was the largest structure most of the goblins had ever seen. Three big beasts, cows or oxen perhaps, slowly cooked over fire pits in front of it. One building was surrounded by a low stone wall. Mudwort could see four wells and a scattering of flowers around some of the still-standing homes.

"Slaves," Erguth said to Mudwort in a hushed tone. "See there, those buildings, inside? Slaves there to be sold to the Dark Knights." He pointed to the narrow end of the basin, where a high wooden fence with spikes around the outside contained several dozen hobgoblins, goblins, and a few humans—the latter huddling together away from the rest. Mudwort hadn't seen humans enslaved before, and she wondered who—or what—the ogres planned to sell them to.

"Maybe eat them," Erguth said of the humans, seeming to read her mind. "Maybe the ogres eat them."

Nearly sixty ogres could be seen in the village, doing various activities. They had the shape of men, though their heads were overly large for their thick necks, and there were hard-looking ridges across their foreheads shading their dark eyes. Their arms were abnormally long, and the largest of the ogres had ropelike veins standing out from their shoulders to their wrists. No sentry was posted to warn them of Direfang's force. They had never felt threatened in those mountains, so they were oblivious to the army on the crest, the many goblin eyes observing them greedily. The brutes moved around their broken buildings, sifting through the debris, trying to reconstruct some of their homes.

"Rebuilding like the Dark Knights tried to do," Erguth whispered. "Doing a better job too."

"Ugly, stinky ogres." Mudwort was amazed that the Dark Knights considered goblins ugly. The Dark Knights regularly dealt with ogres, and those creatures were much more hideous! How the knights could call anything ugly after dealing with ogres made no sense to her. Ogres were positively revolting.

"Toads are beautiful compared to these . . . monsters," she hissed. She wrinkled her nose and made a gagging sound, certain that she could detect their noxious odor even high up there on the ridge. Only a few had short-cropped hair, and she wondered if those ogres had become tangled in something or had been demoted in rank and so had to cut their hair. Ogres often were proud of their long, smelly, dirty hair. All the ogres below had matted clumps hanging to their waists or below.

"Bugs," she said. "Crawling on heads. Crawling all over." Mudwort imagined that the ogres' hair was infested with them. Some had braids festooned with bones and twigs. One had colorful beads woven into a beard. Most had no facial hair, not even eyebrows. "Stinky monsters, the lot. Stinky, mean." She turned her head and spat, just missing Erguth's arm.

All of the ogres were muscular, and their chests and legs glistened with sweat from the day's heat. Though they wore trousers, only half wore any shirts or tunics. Despite the presence of a small lake at the wide end of their village, dirt streaks, some in elaborate patterns, were conspicuous on their bodies—all over their arms, faces, and chests—and their shoulders were smeared with ash. Mudwort noted patches of ash on the ground and covering some of the rubble. She twisted to look behind her at one of the biggest volcanic peaks. It continued to belch ash and smoke into the air and likely, she reflected fleetingly, was responsible for the gray sky.

"Don't think that is the one that will break," she said to herself. Still, the glow around its crater made her nervous, and she watched a line of lava spill over the side. She couldn't see the bottom of the lava ribbon because a mountain slope was in the way. "Don't think so, but don't know for certain." Once more she climbed down from Erguth and scampered across jagged rocks to get her own view of the volcanoes. "Know for certain at least one mountain will break."

She wrapped her fingers around a spire of rock, instantly feeling the tingle of it. She knelt and felt the ground trembling slightly, so faint she hadn't registered it against the tough soles of her feet. It wasn't the same nervousness or anger she'd noticed before in the mine.

The trembling felt . . . anxious was the word she finally put to the sensation. Mudwort thrust her mind into the stone, hurling her senses downward and passing through layers of rock and dirt, tunnels where snakes and badgers and other things had dwelled but were now absent. Things were moving about in the mountain, creatures sharing the stone's anxiousness and streaming south and east, some burrowing upward and moving aboveground. There were large tunnels too, and Mudwort would have tarried to learn more about them had she not heard the explosion of whoops from Direfang's army.

She glanced up in time to see goblins and hobgoblins spill over the ridge and descend on the ogre village.

25

BLOOD FEVER

Many goblins brandished Steel Town knives, and the hobgoblins with swords held them high while letting out ear-splitting shrieks. Mudwort peered over the edge of the rock spire and watched the surprised ogres react in confusion.

It was a beautiful sight. Mudwort wished she could have watched the battle in Steel Town from such a vantage point. The ogres barely had time to grab weapons—clubs and gardening tools and rocks from the buildings they were repairing—before the first wave of goblins struck. Mudwort cursed the dark sky. If the sun were out, she could see the glorious sight much better.

There were Brak and Folami, charging ahead of Direfang and Spikehollow and barreling into an ogre holding a hoe. Folami shot beneath the brute's arms and rammed a knife into his thigh while Brak grabbed the hoe handle and pulled it free. The ogre roared in anger and flailed with its empty hands, finding Folami's head and wrapping its big fingers tight around the goblin's skull. The ogre picked Folami up, crushing his skull and throwing his corpse toward the approaching Direfang. The hobgoblin howled, put his head down, smashed into the ogre, and sent it to the ground.

"Folami dead." Mudwort shook her head. He was a young, strong goblin, and she used to enjoy listening to his stories—not that she'd ever told him that, but she listened while in the slave pens. She watched as more goblins died, the ogres bashing their heads with clubs and rocks, then hurling the bodies into the still-surging army.

Mudwort looked around to spot others she knew, seeing Moon-eye near Direfang and instantly scowling. "Should not be there." She tsked. "Should be with Graytoes." If Moon-eye shared Folami's fate, Graytoes would be devastated. To lose a baby and a mate could be too much for the goblin to bear. Mudwort did not want the responsibility of looking after a grieving Graytoes, nor should the task fall to Direfang.

"Moon-eye, come here!" Her words were not loud enough to carry down the rise and into the village. But she repeated them twice more, feeling a little better just for saying them. She'd made a token effort to save Graytoes' mate.

The ogres were more formidable than the Dark Knights, she realized after only a few moments. First of all, the ogres were not as tired and broken as the knights had been. There'd been time for them to rest since the second earthquake, and they were larger and stronger than the knights in Steel Town. As she watched, one of the ogres lifted a hobgoblin over his head.

"Erguth?" Mudwort was on her feet, hand cupped over her wide eyes, staring. "No. Not Erguth. Someone else." She didn't know that hobgoblin's name, but from his coloring, she knew him to be a friend of Direfang's. And she saw Direfang racing toward the brutish ogre, Erguth close behind him. Direfang was coated with blood, and Mudwort hoped fervently it was ogre blood and not his own. He'd not yet wholly recovered from the wounds the knights and quakes had inflicted.

Mudwort turned her gaze to another part of the battle and saw Spikehollow lead a band of goblins toward the slave pens, quickly dispatching two guards and starting work at pulling apart the old wood slats. All the goblins had caught the blood fever; the desire to fight was infectious. Spikehollow gestured here and there to various goblins, and though she couldn't hear him, she knew he was barking orders.

Direfang was also ordering goblins around, as was Saro-Saro, who had foolishly joined the battle. Old Hurbear stood on the rise just below her, watching, though after a moment more he started creeping down for a closer look. The goblins fought just as fiercely as they had in Steel Town, but they fought better, Mudwort realized. They followed Direfang's and Saro-Saro's directions with little hesitation.

The goblins were already a better-organized army, Mudwort recognized. They were not as disciplined as the Dark Knights, who had drilled each day in Steel Town, and their weapons were still wielded awkwardly, sometimes ineffectually. But nonetheless, the goblins acting in unison were . . . fearsome.

"Amazing," Mudwort whispered. In her years before slavery, she'd seen goblins work together only for small, specific tasks, such as hunting parties. She looked back to Direfang. She could not locate him for several moments and worried that an ogre might have killed him. She finally spotted him by the building with the stone wall, still holding his left arm close to his side. Crelb was nearby, shouting at him.

The goblins had fought their way through half the ogre village by then and had killed at least twenty of the huge brutes. Ogre children were being herded into houses, and Brak motioned for some of his fellows to pursue them. Mudwort thought it unnecessary to kill the young. She quickly changed her mind when she thought of the ogres who had captured her long ago with even younger members of her clan.

"Kill the ogres," she hissed. "Kill even the younglings." She squeezed the rock spire in her excitement, eyes darting from one end of the village to the next, slapping her foot against the ground when she watched the goblin and hobgoblin slaves spill out of the broken pen and rush to join the fight. Most of the humans stayed huddled, though two skinny men ran away toward the far trail that led east out of the village. The goblins did not try to stop them. The pathetic humans weren't the enemy there.

The spire beneath Mudwort's fingers continued to tingle and pass its anxiety on to her. The ground continued to tremble, still faintly, and coupled with the heady scents and sounds of the battle, she found the moment supremely pleasurable. She sensed creatures still moving above and below the ground and heard the cries of birds that flew to the east. It was difficult to divide her attention between the earth and the battle in the ogre village, but she tried.

The fight did not last as long as the one in Steel Town, and Mudwort was vaguely disappointed about that. It all simply ended too soon. More goblins died there than in Steel Town, but things seemed to even out with the addition of the freed slaves from the ogre pens. She made herself more comfortable, sitting in a shallow depression of earth, and watched as Direfang directed goblins to gather up their dead brethren and burn them, using the slats from the slave pen as kindling.

Saro-Saro had put himself in charge of raiding the ogres' storehouse, which was the building inside the stone wall. Wisely, he did not allow the goblins to feast, but instructed them to spread out the food and wait. Hurbear joined him, sharing in the authority and responsibility.

The Rebellion

There was some chaos, and Mudwort found that more interesting to watch. Brak and other young goblins dashed from fallen ogre to fallen ogre, prying loose pouches and other things of value as keepsakes to mark their bravery in the fight. One goblin used a knife to cut wooden beads out of an ogre's beard. Another cut off an ogre's nose and paraded around with it, holding it in front of his own and laughing.

The goblin army filled the ogre village, flowing through the streets and into the buildings, poking through the rubble and searching through the gardens. Some ate things they discovered, but Saro-Saro was quick to slap them if they were within his reach. The old goblin couldn't keep all of them from looting and eating, however, so he set his clan to passing out the food as the laborers had done in the mining camp.

Mudwort wondered if there might be something tasty for her, such as the three beasts roasting over the fire pits, which Hurbear had placed his clan in charge of. Her stomach trembled along with the ground. She considered leaving her perch on the ridge and getting in one of the food lines. The goblins below would defer to her and let her move to the front. She was very thirsty too, and a visit to that small lake—where many of the goblins were drinking—would sate her.

Still, Mudwort didn't budge. She couldn't say what held her at the top of the rise. She watched Graytoes carefully climb down, following the narrow trail that led to the center of the village. A few older goblins also had stayed back from the fight, either not wanting to risk themselves in the battle or preferring to watch it all unfold. They, too, moved down the trail behind Graytoes. Mudwort should follow all of them, she thought. She should get something to eat and certainly something to drink. She was terribly thirsty again.

What held her there?

"Something," she said. "Something is not right."

Once more she thought about slipping down into the village, not for food, but to find Moon-eye. If she followed Graytoes, she would find Moon-eye soon enough. The one-eyed goblin had an unnatural talent for scenting things, and Mudwort wanted him to come up there with her and smell the air, smell the air from the ridge top without the blood and dirt filling his senses. He might help her puzzle out what was making the earth anxious. He might be able to figure out what is was that followed them.

"Something follows." Mudwort had a twitchy feeling. The earth was telling her that feet walked upon the trail to the north and that they were heading in the direction of the ogre village, following them. She knew the goblin army would be easy to track, but who or what would want to follow so many goblins?

She looked back down the trail, not able to see all of it because of rocky outcroppings and because it curved and disappeared behind a massive upthrust of granite. The gray sky didn't help. She glanced up at the glowing volcano peak. The crater was brighter along the rim, perhaps looking so because everything around it was so dark. It was beautiful.

"A mountain is going to break," Mudwort said. She scratched her head and sniffed, smelling sulfur, just as in Steel Town after the earthquakes. "Maybe that mountain is the one that will break, but maybe not. Maybe soon, though."

She shrugged, rolling her shoulders and getting to her feet. And after staring at the lava stream for another long moment, she started to make her way down the trail. Whatever followed them was not something she wanted to encounter alone.

"Moon-eye needs to help find out what walks behind," she said to herself as she headed down to the scene of the glorious goblin victory.

26

BUGS

Direfang directed one of the goblin clans to pile the ogre bodies against the broken buildings. He had no intention of burning them, as was the practice for goblins; he would not grant them the dignity. Instead, the ogres would be wrapped tight with ropes that Saro-Saro's clan was salvaging so the bodies would not fall apart when they rotted. He wanted the ogre spirits to be forced to return to intact corpses and, thus, be trapped as slaves forever.

"Stay here?" Hurbear asked. "Will this be a village for goblins now? Good home, it looks to be."

Direfang rubbed his chin with his right hand, a gesture he'd adopted since leaving Steel Town. It was a good place, he thought, the village cradled in the Khalkists. It boasted large gardens, which could be tended to yield sweet beans and potatoes, the latter one of his favorite foods, a lake that would always provide water, and livestock that some of the goblins would soon slay if he didn't make his way over to the livestock pens and prevent it. Still, as large as the village was, it wasn't sufficient to support the more than one

211

thousand goblins he'd brought here. It had supported less than two hundred ogres, he guessed from the number of buildings and the number of dead.

"Some, Hurbear," Direfang said. "Some goblins could stay here and rebuild this place. Could build lives here and raise families. A good place, yes."

"Not enough food for all," Hurbear returned, making the same assessment Direfang had. "Enough space, but not enough food. Good space, though. Goats and sheep. Good food. Plenty of water."

"Hurbear want to stay here? Lead the goblins deciding to stay?"

The old goblin shrugged his shoulders exaggeratedly. "Direfang stay too? It is a very good place to live and be happy. And it will smell better when the ogres are gone."

Direfang looked at the lake. It was indeed a place he could call home, he had to admit. He could select which clans to stay with him. Hurbear's, of course, and Mudwort. He looked around for the red-skinned goblin. He could use her counsel right then. He wanted her to speak to the earth, tell him what spread away from the place and what stretched farther to the south. He knew something of the world's geography from listening to the Dark Knights and looking over their shoulders when they were holding meetings. He could read the human language when he worked at it, though he doubted any of the knights had realized they'd inadvertently taught him. He'd read the text on dozens of their maps.

He was interested in staying in or near the Khalkists, which stretched far into Khur and Blöde. He wanted nothing to do with Blöde, however, which was a country dominated by ogres and was known for its contemptible and greedy king. There was a vast swamp to the south that would be easy to lose himself in—and perhaps all of his army. It once had been the realm of a black dragon overlord, but the Dark Knights claimed she was dead. There were lesser black dragons, and they might pose a problem. But there likely were relatively few ogres, and that was a favorable thing to consider.

Too, he'd seen maps of the Plains of Dust, which was a vast area not so dry and desolate as the name indicated. There could be room for many goblin villages there.

"That land would be the best," Direfang said to himself. "The Plains of Dust."

"What say, Direfang?"

"Hurbear can stay and lead," the hobgoblin said. "Stay here in the village that belonged to the monsters. Stay and—"

"But Direfang is not going to stay." The old goblin did not pose the statement as a question.

There were pale reeds in the garden, a plant the hobgoblin was unfamiliar with. He glanced over at them, not meeting the old goblin's eyes. They made the dry shushing sounds in the breeze that had found its way down the slope.

"No. South still," Direfang said, watching the reeds sway. "South to the plains maybe. Hurbear's clan might like the plains too. Or can stay here and make new village."

"Lots of room for goblins in the plains?" Hurbear looked longingly toward the lake then to the lines of goblins forming for their share of food and other spoils. Hurbear was obviously pleased that his clan was taking the lead in keeping the goblins in check around the fire pits and the dwindling beast carcasses.

"Yes, there is plenty of room in the plains." Direfang answered firmly, though he wasn't certain. He'd never been to the Plains of Dust, had only heard some of the Dark Knights talk about the place and had looked at its location several times on maps they'd spread out on a table. If he'd read the maps correctly, there were not many cities marked on the Plains of Dust. "Probably lots of room. More than enough."

"Room for a goblin nation?" Hurbear asked, still staring at the jostling food lines.

"A nation?" Direfang followed the old goblin's gaze and saw that, for the most part, the goblins were acting orderly and not looting the village as haphazardly as they had Steel Town. Some were frantic but not many. "There would be no more goblin slaves in the Plains of Dust, Hurbear. Not sheep anymore, the goblins. Wolves. A nation of wolves, Hurbear."

"Smart wolves," Hurbear added, licking his lips. "And crafty ones. Wolves that are working together now."

"Together? Yes. Perhaps." Direfang suddenly realized Hurbear was right. The goblin clans were working together, much better than before. The attack against the ogres had been more controlled, and so was the aftermath.

The air grew still in the basin, and Direfang looked up at the dark gray clouds scudding across the lighter gray sky. It looked as if rain could be coming, but it didn't smell like rain. He inhaled deeply, the scent reminding him of dying fires.

"Don't want to stay here long," he told Hurbear. "The village is a good place, easy to like. But don't like the sky here. Don't like the smell. And the smell will worsen when the ogres rot. So head south to the Plains of Dust. There will be enough room for a nation there."

The goblins and hobgoblins they'd freed were mingling, some standing in line for food. He saw one helping Brak's clan tug ogres into a pile. The ground trembled slightly, as it had in Steel Town after the large quakes. The trembling unsettled the goblins, but they continued their tasks.

"A nation." Hurbear said, staring intently at Direfang. "Need more goblins to build a good nation, Direfang. More than a thousand here, but still more are needed."

THE REBELLION

The hobgoblin absently nodded. "More goblins for the army and the new nation. More to be found to the south, perhaps, and on the march to the plains. Hobgoblins too. There used to be tribes of hobgoblins in these mountains before the ogres took over and before the minotaurs came. Bugbears would be welcome. Maybe bugbears join this army."

There'd been bugbears of significant number in the mountains long ago, Direfang knew. The greater races of Krynn had worked hard to exterminate them, just as the greater races fought the goblins and caught them and turned them into slaves. Rats, he'd heard some of the Dark Knights use to refer to goblinkind, scum, vermin, bugs—just like bugbears—and worse.

"Goblins used to be bugs for the knights. No more," Direfang reflected, spitting. "No more bugs."

"Yes, bugs!" Hurbear said, sucking in his breath and laughing. "Lots of bugs! Very big bugs! Bug nation!"

Suddenly, at that very moment, as if called forth by their dialogue, gigantic centipedes erupted from the ground between the fire pits and what had been the ogres' communal living area. The creatures had been drawn by the scent of the blood that oozed into the ground and from the vibrations of all the goblins scurrying across their territory. Some were four feet long and as thick as tree trunks, scuttling on their myriad legs and knocking over goblins and hobgoblins.

Screams filled the air around the communal house as the unprepared goblins became snack food for the centipedes. Direfang pounded past Hurbear, grabbing an ogre club and calling for help as he joined others in fighting their new foe.

The goblins in line for food were reluctant to budge and lose their places. But as Direfang started raising his club, as long and as thick as his leg, and smashing one centipede after the next, most were drawn by the fun. The goblins had never seen such creatures, so some started calling out names as they bashed them: "bugs," "monster-bugs," and "ogre babies." Other goblins fled in terror, frightened by their hairy, segmented appearance and legs too numerous to count. Others, almost comically, tried to grab the creatures around the middle and squeeze the life out of them.

Direfang raised his heavy club and smashed one centipede after another as they reared in front of him. Goo splattered in all directions each time he killed one, and he had to slosh through the remains to get to the next creature.

Goblins slipped in the muck, some falling and becoming prey to the creatures that still spilled out of the cracks in the village floor. Goblin screams mingled with the shrill trilling of the centipedes. Above the noise, Direfang shouted for goblins to slice at the beasts' heads, which he had discovered was the quickest way to dispatch them.

The ground rumbled strongly beneath the fire pits, and Direfang hoped that another earthquake wasn't coming to add to the confusion and misery. As he slogged through the battle, thumping bodies, he again looked around for Mudwort.

He was pitched to his knees when the rumbling intensified and the crack that ran to the communal building widened. As the goblin screams grew shrill and painful, Direfang realized that it wasn't an earthquake. Something else was causing the strong vibrations.

The rumbling gradually turned into a sustained growl, with small cracks extending in all directions from the larger ones. The ground near the largest fire pit bulged upward, the earth turning powdery there as the growl climaxed.

That was when a massive centipede head thrust up through the still-widening crack. The centipede, surely the king of all the rest, was as large as a dragon, Direfang thought, as big around as three or four ogres. Its segmented body dropped down onto where the large fire pit had been, the impact causing a thunderous noise and sending goblins flying.

"Death comes!" Spikehollow shouted, his words a mere whisper amid the tumult. "Run from death! Run now!" The goblin spun, dropped the knife he'd been waving, and dashed past Direfang. Even the few smaller centipedes remaining scurried away frantically from the new monstrosity.

"Worse than digging beasts!" Crelb cried.

"Worse than earth dragons," Spikehollow agreed.

Direfang would have joined Spikehollow in flight, but a look at the churning legs of the massive centipede told him retreat wasn't the answer. The huge creature with its many legs would catch up to them in mere seconds. Its trilling sound deafened all those in the vicinity, including Direfang. It jumped up in the air again, showing a stomach as dark as the sky, and dropped straight down toward the hobgoblin.

He swung his club defiantly over his head, fully expecting to be squashed. But then, over the deafening trill and the sound of his heart thrumming loudly, he heard a great whoosh of fire—a fiery column that shot down from the sky, striking the centipede and instantly roasting it. Looking up, Direfang saw its legs flailing madly as the creature was turned into flames. The hobgoblin dropped and rolled away just as the burning creature crashed down onto one of the fire pits. A second column of flame caused the giant centipede to explode, fire roiling across the village.

The stench from the charred giant centipede set all the goblins to retching. Direfang struggled to his knees as he was overcome by choking spasms. When there was nothing left in his stomach to empty, he stumbled to his feet, feeling dizzy and weak from the intense, vile smell. There was no place in the village to escape the horrific odor; burning pieces of its carcass and little flaming piles were strewn as far away as the slave pens, the explosion had been that great.

The hobgoblin fought for breath, tipping his head back and furiously blinking his eyes. The burning air sent tears rolling down his face.

Throughout the village, goblins were similarly picking themselves up and fighting for air, waving their hands in front of their faces, as if that might chase away the incredible stink. Graytoes and Moon-eye clung to each other, gasping. Hurbear curled at their feet, seemingly unconscious.

———— ⌇ ————

Mudwort had been only halfway down the trail toward the village, so she was spared the brunt of it. But a piece of the creature had splattered all the way up there, and she looked at the burned flesh with a mix of revulsion and envy. The fire spells that ended its life had been impressive.

She took another few steps down the trail, breathing shallowly and keeping her eyes on Moon-eye, still intending to draw him back up to the crest. Then she whirled and looked up the way she'd come. No one in the village had been responsible for the fire spells, Mudwort knew, but with widening eyes, she saw who had saved the goblins.

The Dark Knight wizard stood at the crest of the trail that led down into the village.

27

GRALLIK'S FIRE

Three men moved up from the other side of the ridge to stand near the wizard: a stocky dark-skinned priest and two other knights. All four wore tattered tabards and tunics, and the priest's cloak fluttering behind him looked shredded, as if some clawed beast had raked it. Their skin was dirt streaked but slick with sweat. The two knights in armor stood at attention, the light from the still-burning centipede making their plate mail gleam and revealing all the pits and flaws in the battle-worn pieces.

The goblins not deafened or injured by the great centipede's demise spotted the Dark Knights and surged toward the trail, shouting and waving knives. Mudwort rushed halfway up the trail again, arms raised and fingers splayed, shouting too—but not at the knights. She turned and planted herself in the path of the onrushing goblins, shouting at her own.

Her presence halted the goblins. Direfang lumbered into the front, pushing goblins aside with his good arm.

219

"Kill the skull man!" Brak shouted, his voice heard above others'.

"Kill all the knights!" came from a tall goblin in Saro-Saro's clan, pushing up close to Direfang and Mudwort.

"Smear the blood in symbols!" Crelb yelled. "The symbols of Clan Spear!"

A crackling, snapping wall of flame shot up between Mudwort and the knights, stretching well beyond the sides of the trail and lighting up the village below. It was not so tall or so wide as the one the wizard had cast in Steel Town to stop some of the slaves from escaping, and its flames did not burn so hot as to harm the goblins. The fire burned only as high as the knights' waists as they stonily watched the goblins.

"Brave the fire and kill them!" Brak called.

"Stop! Stop now!" Direfang yelled. He planted his feet in front of Mudwort and faced the throng. "Talk to the Dark Knights first." He continued to shout to be heard over a chorus of murmurs and continued cries of "Kill the knights!"

"Why talk?" Saro-Saro edged through the throng. He was hoarse from shouting, and he was coated with goo from the exploded centipede. One of his clansmen tried to pick the most offending clumps off him. "Why talk instead of kill, Direfang? Why not smear the knights' blood in clan symbols?"

The wall of fire crackled louder, and the ground trembled enough for all the goblins to feel it. The murmurs turned to speculation of another gigantic centipede coming—or another earthquake—with one of the hobgoblins in the front shouting that the wizard had clearly been responsible for the quakes in Steel Town and every bad thing that had happened since.

Direfang waited several moments until the horde quieted down a little. "Not kill the Dark Knights . . . yet." He kept his voice loud, but he no longer needed to shout. All were listening, the knights too.

"Why not now?" Saro-Saro persisted. "The clan of—"

"Because the wizard helped by killing the great worm," Direfang returned. He lowered his voice and narrowed his eyes, and he thumped a goblin in the chest who tried to dart past him. "If the wizard had not helped, the great worm would have killed many goblins. The wizard helped. So talk first."

Saro-Saro's lip curled up in a snarl. "Might be more knights on the other side of the trail, Direfang. Dark Knights come to find slaves, probably to buy new slaves from the dead ogres. Dead knights cannot buy slaves." But Saro-Saro's voice and eyes were flat, attesting to his supreme weariness.

Direfang shook his head and turned his back on the army, stepping around Mudwort and making his way up the trail to the four knights, stopping a few feet away from the wall of flames. The hobgoblin leader of the rebellion rotated his neck and clenched and unclenched the fist of his good arm.

"There are no more knights on the other side," Mudwort told the others, whose eyes followed Direfang. "Would have felt more knights stomping on the earth. So no more. Just those." She spit to show her contempt for the men. "Direfang talk."

"Then after the talk, the knights die," Saro-Saro said peevishly. He folded his arms as if he'd just pronounced judgment on them. "Die badly and with pain!"

"Dark Knights are better dead," Mudwort agreed, her eyes flashing. "Dead and buried with trapped, sad spirits."

Saro-Saro thrust out his chin and gestured to his nearby clansmen. "Dark Knights die no matter what Direfang says. Direfang die too, if necessary. Direfang die with the Dark Knights!"

Mudwort looked up the hill at the hobgoblin. She wasn't

quite as ready to sacrifice their leader, her friend. And as much as she hated knights, she was curious why they had destroyed the giant centipede and saved their enemies, the goblins.

Direfang silently regarded the Dark Knights, feeling the heat from the line of flames that crackled between him and them. They all looked fatigued, the stocky priest clearly exhausted and wavering on his feet. He sniffed the air, smelling scorched earth and the ghastly scent of the charred giant centipede, and he brushed at his chest to clear away some of the burned goo that still clung to him. He could smell his own sweat, and the different stench of the men too.

All knights smelled bad, Direfang knew. But those four were especially foul specimens, likely not having bathed in days; deep sweat circles were evident on the wizard's gray robes. Too, dried blood hung heavy on all of them, perhaps their own or perhaps from their brethren they'd left behind in Steel Town. Direfang smelled only the four standing there, and he had heard Mudwort say there were no more. Still, he knew there could be more hidden farther down the trail, waiting for a signal, their scent concealed by the fire and dead centipede and the general stink all around.

How many knights had been left alive in Steel Town? the hobgoblin wondered. At the time, it had seemed a good decision to not encroach on the infirmary, where the last of the knights in the mining camp were sequestered. At the time, Direfang hadn't wanted to risk the deaths of more goblins, and a small part of him had thought it was wrong to kill injured men who could not defend themselves. He regretted that choice as he stood there behind the wall of fire.

"Should have killed all the knights," he muttered to himself. "Not left any alive to follow this army."

"Foreman, we are here to bargain with you!" One of the armored knights addressed Direfang. His shoulders were back and his chin up. He displayed a rigid military posture despite his obvious weariness. "Foreman, you do understand the Common tongue, don't you? We have come here—"

"Direfang," the hobgoblin said.

The armored knight cocked his head.

"I believe he just told us that his name is Direfang." That was whispered by the wizard, who stepped forward, nudging the armored knight aside and taking over the negotiations.

The wizard waved his hand, and the flame wall was lowered to a foot or two above the ground. He looked at Direfang, then past him to the assembly of goblins and hobgoblins down the trail, speaking as loudly as he could.

"I am Grallik N'sera, Direfang. These two men are of my talon, Kenosh and Aneas. They are here because they are loyal to me." Grallik nodded in the direction of the priest. "This is Skull Knight Horace Branson of Ergoth, and—"

"I did not follow Guardian Grallik here out of loyalty," the priest said, interrupting. "My loyalties at this moment rest with myself." He paused. "And perhaps with you."

Direfang continued to regard them with wary curiosity. They were waiting for him to say something, but what they had said up to that point told him little. Goblins and hobgoblins chattered below, some calling up to demand the knights' deaths, one shouting that the skull man should cast healing magic before Direfang killed him. That was not a bad plan, Direfang thought grimly.

Finally, Grallik continued. "Steel Town is dead, Foreman Direfang. Most of its knights are dead, but you well know that. Marshal Montrill, my commander, has died. My talon . . . well, these are the only two men left." The wizard peered around Direfang again, finally noticing that

the red-skinned goblin between Direfang and the swarm
was the one who had claimed the quakes were coming.
"She—that one with the red skin—she is the one who
knew about the earthquakes?"

"Mudwort," Direfang said. He kept his voice soft, not
wanting Mudwort to hear him above the crackling fire. She
might come closer to investigate, and he did not yet want
her counsel regarding the knights. That could be a show of
weakness on his part, in front of all the other goblins.

"Interesting name, Mudwort," Grallik mused. "I wish
to talk to her."

Direfang again met the gaze of each of the knights, lingering on Grallik's dark eyes and not liking what he saw
there.

"I wish to talk to the red-skinned goblin," Grallik
repeated louder.

"Mudwort."

"Yes, Mudwort." Impatience crept into the wizard's
voice. "I want to talk to her. I want to talk to Mudwort."

"The goblins don't do what Dark Knights want," Direfang said. "Any more."

He glanced over his shoulder and saw that Mudwort
had heard her name. She had her head cocked, perhaps to
hear better, but she stayed put. "The goblins call for death,
wizard. So many goblins, how can one foreman stop the
thirst for blood?"

"Aye, no doubt they want to kill us slow and painfully,"
Horace interjected. "I heard them, hear them still, though I
don't understand all of the words. They call for our blood,
don't they? Well, I for one can't truly blame them. That big
hobgoblin there . . ."

"Erguth," Direfang said. He'd heard Erguth, above all
others, calling loudly for the men's deaths.

"He wants to skin us from the look of his gestures,"
Horace continued. "I know a little of goblin-speak. I can tell

you, Foreman Direfang, that allowing your people to kill us is not a good idea. Not for me, not for you." The priest pointed to Direfang's arm. "You'll lose that limb if I don't minister to you. Might lose it anyway. Nasty slice, that. If I do nothing to help, you could well lose more than the arm. The wound is infected, and that infection could take your life. I suspect more of your people could use my aid. I am here to offer my healing aid, even to those who shout for my death."

Direfang growled deep in his throat, and a line of spittle edged over his lip and stretched to the ground.

"I do not lie to you, Foreman Direfang," the priest continued stoically. "I've no taste for lies; my tongue does not wrap around them very well. I am not a kindly man, true, but I am not a liar. Your arm is very seriously injured."

Direfang cursed himself for showing any weakness to the knights. By tucking his left arm close and not using it, he had let them know of his injury. The deep cut was obvious, of course, but without his favoring the arm, the priest might not have known how badly it pained him, might not have used his arm as a wedge against his weakness in the negotiation.

"And you've got a deep gash on the side of your head," Horace continued. He raised a hand and pointed to Direfang's temple. At that gesture, goblins below started shouting, some of them thinking the priest meant to cast a spell. Horace dropped his arm and looked to Grallik, mouthing *I told you this was a foolish notion. Wasted.* "We could die here to these creatures," he hissed, "despite what my magic told me."

"I have confidence in your divining spell, priest," Grallik softly returned. "And I agree with your words. I don't think you, Foreman, or they, can afford to kill us."

Direfang snarled and took a step closer, expecting the wall of fire to rise. Instead, Grallik made a languid gesture, and the flames were suddenly extinguished. At the foot of the trail, the goblins jeered and started to move toward the knights.

28

FIERY TEMPERS

S tay!" Direfang raised his right arm, half turning around and signaling his army to a halt. "Leave the knights alone!" He turned and walked back to Mudwort, keeping his voice loud so both the goblins and the knights could hear him. "The priest offers healing in exchange for safety."

Saro-Saro appeared defiant, opening his mouth to argue, but stopping when Hurbear pushed him. The cagey old goblin stood next to his counterpart. It was clear that Hurbear was wounded, centipede bites all over his arms and chest, and a patch of his hide was scorched where a piece of the burning giant centipede had struck him. He glared at Saro-Saro.

"It is time to see if the priest speaks true," Hurbear said in the Common tongue. The old goblin padded slowly up the trail, his breath ragged. He favored his right side, for he had broken ribs. He passed Direfang but stopped well short of the knights. He raised his arm, waggling his fingers.

"Cure me, skull man," Hurbear demanded.

"I well can. You will see that I only speak the truth, goblin." Horace rolled his shoulders so his cape fell behind him entirely. He held his hands to his sides then brought them to his sword belt, unbuckling it and letting it drop.

All the goblins watched suspiciously.

Grallik unbuckled his sword belt too, but rather than letting it fall, he held it out, slowly walking down the trail with the priest until they stood together in front of Hurbear. Grallik dangled the sword belt in front of the old goblin, who was quick to grab it.

The wind gusted in that instant, pushing aside clouds and showing a patch of blue above in the sky. The stands of reeds in the garden whispered musically, and the faintest scent of flowers on the trail could be detected above the burn and stink of the village below. Then, just as abruptly, the wind dropped and the clouds sealed, making the sky look again like a solid plume of smoke.

"Our weapons will do us no good, Foreman Direfang," the priest explained wearily. "There are simply too many of you. We know that." He raised his voice so the goblins at the bottom of the trail could hear his words. "I know some of your language, not much. But those of you who speak the Common tongue, please translate for those who do not."

The priest waited until the chorus of snarls and whispers rose and fell.

"I offer to heal those of you who are injured, to the best of my ability, until I've nothing left to give. I will heal this one before me first as proof of my pledge."

"Hurbear." The old goblin wanted the healer to call him by name.

"Why?" Saro-Saro shouted, stomping his foot and setting his hands angrily on his waist. "Why help, slavers? What would a skull man gain from such generosity?"

Hurbear translated Saro-Saro's questions for the priest. Grallik nodded, listening, then he walked all the way down the trail, edging past Horace, Hurbear, and Direfang, reluctantly walking past Mudwort, and coming within an arm's reach of the press of goblins, jostling each other for a chance to reach out and grab and choke the wizard.

"We want to help you," said Grallik, "and join with you because Steel Town is dead, my talon destroyed."

"What? Foolishness! Destroy the knights!" a dirt brown goblin shouted.

"Hear what I have to say!" Grallik countered loudly. Though he hadn't understood the words the goblins shouted, he well understood their malicious tone. He waited for Direfang, who had come up behind him, to translate his words. "You'll get nothing from me—from us—if we are killed, if we are dead. But alive, we have value to you."

"Kill the wizard!" Brak cried out. "Kill the wizard now! Don't listen to the slaver's lies."

"Later! Kill the wizard later." Saro-Saro said, raising eyes around him, holding Brak at bay with a harsh glance. "Kill the wizard any time later. Listen first."

Sweat beaded thickly on Grallik's forehead, but his eyes showed relief when the goblins didn't surge forward. The vast army of them waited, nervously, for him to continue.

"I wish to join you, rather than rejoin the Order in Jelek." Grallik swallowed hard at his own words, knowing that, one way or another, he was sealing a fate that he could never have predicted. "I could have let that great worm kill many of you. But I slew the great worm and kept you safe. I did that in order to join your army of ex slaves, help you and," he lowered his voice humbly, "and learn from you."

"Knights killed many slaves in the village." The low, hissing voice came in the Common tongue from directly behind him.

"You are Mudwort," he said respectfully, turning.

She did not know much of the human language, so Hurbear translated the rest of her speech. "Watched the wall of fire burn slaves," she said. Her voice was laced with venom. "Smelled the bodies burn. Heard the slaves scream."

"And your kind killed knights," the wizard was quick to return, trying to keep his voice even. Grallik half-turned so he was addressing Mudwort as well as all the other goblins. "We could argue about who killed more and what was justified, but the argument would be wasted words. All of that is done, and Steel Town is gone. Many slaves are gone. Many knights are gone too. I acknowledge your victorious rebellion."

Behind him, Mudwort brightened when Hurbear repeated those words in goblin-speak. Still, she spat her reply.

"Knights waste words often. Always. The Oath five times. Waste. Waste. Waste. Waste. Waste."

Grallik closed his eyes and raised his hands to the fastening of his robe. In a swift motion, he tugged the garment free, showing a thin, earth-colored shift beneath. His left arm was bare, all of his old scars visible, and many goblins pointed at them. The scars on his neck looked thick and shiny, as did those on his left calf—the shift went only to his knees.

"I suffered too and now I denounce the Order," he announced, the words hard to squeeze from his throat. "To join with you, I denounce the Dark Knights. I am willing—"

"Look at Hurbear!" Saro-Saro gestured up the trail.

High above and behind the wizard, the Skull Knight had been busy tending to the old goblin. Horace was kneeling on the trail, his face even with Hurbear's, working his healing magic.

"Your ribs are broken!" He said it louder so some of the goblins below could hear. "This old fellow's ribs are cracked!"

Hurbear nodded. "Ribs hurt. Breathing hurt. Skull man could mend the ribs maybe. Goblins kill the skull man otherwise. Kill the skull man slowly. Kill and—ouch!"

Horace prodded the goblin gently then turned so the throng could see his fingers glowing orange. There were ooohs and aaahs, shouted questions and curses, but the goblins held fast. "I follow Zeboim," he proclaimed. A great many goblins spat at the mention of the sea goddess, recognizing her name in any language. Meanwhile the glow spread from his fingers to cover Hurbear's side, brightening and sparking like fireflies then sinking in.

Hurbear recoiled, and the goblins gasped, many again calling for the knights to be killed. But a heartbeat later, the old goblin turned to face the horde and spread his arms, grinning.

"Ribs well," he announced joyously. "No pain there anymore." He turned back to face the priest and indicated places on his chest and arms that still hurt. "Mend more and live, truth-speaking skull man. Here and here, hurt here too."

The priest hurriedly complied. When he was finished ministering to Hurbear, he took several steps down the trail and looked to Direfang. "You next, Foreman Direfang. Your arm will take some effort, and as I said, I might not be able to save it."

The hobgoblin hesitated, glancing around at the skeptical faces of others before holding out his good arm and making a strong fist. "No, others first, skull man." He indicated the army behind him. "The worst injuries first."

The priest let out a deep breath. "I am one man," he said softly. "A jaded, selfish man who wants to live to see the next day, and the next and the next." Slightly louder, he said, "I haven't the energy to heal many, not all. Not today."

"As many as possible this day," Direfang returned stoically. "More tomorrow and tomorrow. Then mend this arm. Mend as many as possible and live to see the next day and the next." He looked over the goblin assembly, raising his voice commandingly. "Spikehollow, Erguth, take the knights' weapons." He pointed to the two in armor at the top of the trail. "Then bring the knights down here for more talking."

Direfang slipped to the base of the trail then melded into the ranks of his army. "The knights are useful," he told Mudwort as he passed. To the others, he announced, "Skull men cast spells that kill threatening things, also heal wounds. Useful alive, useless dead, the knights are."

"Keep the knights!" That first voice came from deep in the crowd and soon became a chant. When the crowd again quieted, Direfang headed down, toward the lake, where he intended to quench his great thirst and soak his sore arm. He looked behind him to see Mudwort glaring, but the knights slowly wended their way through the crowd, which had parted to let them safely follow him down to the village.

"See that all the dead goblins are gathered and burned. Make sure that none dead have been missed. Search everywhere," Direfang told a hobgoblin. "There will be a ceremony tonight to honor the dead and keep the spirits away."

"The knights?" the hobgoblin posed. "How shall we treat them?"

"As slaves," Direfang said.

Saro-Saro had been following close behind the leader of the rebellion. He turned to his clansmen, nodding. "Direfang does not die this day," he said. "But Direfang will be watched."

29

KNIGHTLY SLAVES

They dressed the Ergothian priest in the leather leggings of an ogre child, leaving him bare chested. His chain mail was given to the burly hobgoblin called Grunnt, who had distinguished himself in the battle of Steel Town by slaying six knights single-handedly. It was obvious Grunnt found the metal cumbersome and uncomfortable, but he refused to take it off, considering the outfit a mark of honor. Erguth wore the priest's tabard. The tattered cloak had been ripped up and used for bandages, as had Grallik's gray robes.

They let the other two Dark Knights keep their tabards, though Grunnt took their chain mail and the padded armor underneath it, dividing the latter between a few hobgoblins and throwing the armor into the lake—with the knights watching sullenly. The weapons were divided between goblins and hobgoblins, who paraded around with them near the slave pens.

The four knights, fitted with chains and wrist shackles the goblins had found in one of the buildings, were allowed to keep their boots. Grunnt saw how soft the bottoms of the knights' feet were and allowed them the courtesy of the boots while noting it was a courtesy the knights had never given their slaves.

Then Grunnt and Erguth busied themselves searching the village for shoes, boots, and sandals that would fit the hobgoblins. The bodies of the ogre children already had been looted, with goblins claiming the shoes and many of the tunics. A few hundred of the goblins and hobgoblins wore clothing finally, which had been divvied up by clan and age and fistfights. Nothing fit right, save some of the children's clothing that had been looted from Steel Town. And only a smattering of pieces, taken from inside the ogre homes, were clean and in good repair. The only thing that kept a war from breaking out over the clothing was the vow by Saro-Saro and Hurbear that more and better clothing would be taken from other villages, from merchant caravans, and perhaps from shops. Some would even be purchased with coin, rather than stolen.

A reed-thin goblin with a dropped shoulder lit a lantern and set it near the slave pen where the four knights sat unhappily. The lantern was for the knights' benefit, another small concession they'd been permitted because the goblins saw well enough in the dark. It was late, but just how late was impossible to know; the stars were masked by thick gray clouds of smoke and ash. No one had seen the sun set.

"Midnight, maybe, do you think?" Grallik asked, leaning back against a post near the others. The goblins had ruined part of the pen freeing the ogres' captives, but they'd rebuilt a section and tossed the four Dark Knights inside. Four hobgoblins, including Grunnt and Erguth, stood guard.

"I don't think it's quite that late," the priest answered stoically. "But it is night, and the moon is full. I can tell that much without seeing it."

Grallik raised his eyebrows skeptically.

THE REBELLION

"Solinari, Gray Robe, she was nearly round when we left Iverton, and we have marched ceaselessly. So she must be full this night," Horace said with a sigh, as though tired of explaining something to a child. "Every eight months, Solinari is lone and full in the sky. That night is called the Sea Queen's Share, and we priests give to her, our goddess Zeboim, nearly all the material things we have collected since the previous Queen's Share. Well, Gray Robe, all of my material things—my armor and weapon, my tabard, my pouch filled with coins and gems—have been taken from me."

"And so you think the moon is full and that the Sea Queen has already taken her share." Grallik gave a clipped laugh that drew the attention of Grunnt. The hobgoblin moved to the post the wizard leaned against and thumped it.

"Solinari is full," Horace insisted. "If Zeboim favors me, most of my sacrifices will be returned." He leaned back on his elbows, the chain between his wrists long enough to permit that. The sweat on his ample stomach gleamed in the lantern light. His eyes were closed. He was no longer able to keep them open, and his head bobbed. "I'm just so tired, Grallik. It has been too many days since I slept well."

"Since before the quakes for me," Grallik admitted. He also was tired but wasn't about to complain. Too, he'd not been using his magic, as Horace had, so the priest had his sympathy. "I can't remember what a feather bed feels like."

"Only patients in my years before the Order had those." The priest had healed injured goblins until he couldn't stand. Two hobgoblins had carried him into the pen. "I need to sleep, Grallik." Horace eased himself down on his back, not caring that he was lying in mud and waste.

Grallik gripped the railings, his fingernails digging into the old, soft wood. "Horace, you said they would not kill us."

The priest drew his features forward into a scowl. "My divinations appear to be true, Gray Robe. At this juncture, in any event. I predicted that they would not kill us, and they have not killed us. Not yet. And unless one of us does something to provoke them, they will not kill us."

"Yet we are slaves, Horace."

"Aye, that we are. My divinations did not reveal that would happen." He paused. "But that is a subtlety. I asked only whether we would be allowed to live if we joined with the goblins. That is what you wanted to know." His words ended with a slur as he fell asleep.

Grallik nodded, his gesture lost on the sleeping priest.

"This was your idea, Guardian," Kenosh said irritably, continuing to use Grallik's old title. He was one of the two surviving members of Grallik's talon, and he nearly had not followed Grallik there. In the end, he told the wizard that through the years he'd become as loyal to Grallik as he had been to the knighthood, and he did not fancy being reassigned to another talon after the wizard was demoted. "You said our best chance was with the goblins, though I think there is more to it than the simple fact of safety in their numbers. You will tell me your reasons in time, I trust."

The other talon member, Aneas Gerald of Jelek, slept soundly on the far side of the priest. He'd been the most difficult to convince, but he knew that with Grallik's demotion came his demotion, and that was something he preferred to put off for a while, if not forever. In the end Aneas also decided to accompany Grallik and the other two knights, reserving the right to leave at any time. Grallik believed that Aneas would leave at the first opportunity. Perhaps ultimately he would try to curry favor with another post commander by giving him the location of the goblin army and painting Grallik a traitor.

The priest had been the easiest to talk into their venture. Grallik had never cared much for Horace because he seemed to lack the fierce, blind loyalty of the others. Grallik had noted Horace's absence on several occasions when the Oath was recited at dawn. But the wizard appreciated the priest's healing skills and so had set aside that dislike when he asked Horace if he wished to follow the goblins with him.

Horace had said he wanted to return to Ergoth, eventually, but that temporarily he would join with Grallik and offer his curative spells to the goblins. "Healing them, after all, has been my job," Horace had said mirthlessly.

Sitting in the slave pen, Grallik recalled several nights past, sitting in another place—at the southern edge of Steel Town near where his workshop had been and where his tomes of spells had been swallowed by the crevice. Horace sat across from him then, tracing unrecognizable patterns in the dirt.

Horace had closed his eyes, the lids fluttering unnervingly, cheeks twitching. He mouthed words that Grallik could not discern. All of that went on for some time. Then Horace's lips formed a tight line. Still with his eyes closed, he reached into a pocket in his tabard and pulled out four finger bones. By touch, he arranged the bones into a rectangle then cupped his hands just outside them.

"Zeboim, mother goddess, lead us from Iverton. Zeboim, called the Darkling Sea, take us from this camp."

"Steel Town," Grallik remembered whispering, in case the goddess might not know the given name of the place since it was so rarely spoken aloud. "Iverton, called Steel Town."

"Our home is broken," Horace had intoned. "Our brethren dead, our commander dead. Two dozen will leave here in the morning, carrying the wounded. Brother Grallik wishes us to take a different, daring course, mother goddess. He seeks to join the goblins, the creatures we'd cruelly enslaved."

Grallik had nearly interrupted Horace at the word *cruel*.

Slaves deserved no better, he felt, and how the goblins were treated was not truly cruel. It was what their station called for, the wizard believed. Still, he had held his tongue, continuing to observe the Ergothian priest.

"Brother Grallik seeks my company and that of two more knights. Four of us, too few to risk approaching such a force of creatures, foolish perhaps. But a greater foolishness, I think, to take too many other, unwilling knights with us and risk looking like a party made for war. Foolish because we risk the wrath of the slaves and also the Order." Horace then had bowed his head, rearranging the bones slightly. "Zeboim, mother goddess, you know my heart is not with this knighthood. Zeboim, called the Maelstrom, called Rann on my home island, my true brothers are now dead, my true family is lost. And so I will accompany the Gray Robe until you lead me down another path, one that might take me someday back to Ergoth."

Grallik had rocked back and forth, growing impatient with the priest and his religious prattle. The purpose of his magic, the wizard had thought, was to determine if they would live through their first encounter with the angry goblins.

One question!

If the priest didn't hurry, one of the other knights might see them and grow curious and come to investigate. Grallik couldn't risk his plan being discovered. Leaving the Order was not an easy thing, especially given everything that had happened at Steel Town. They'd be marked men, all four of them.

Commanders in Jelek and the city of Neraka would demote him surely. Never in his lifetime would he regain the title of guardian, let alone rise higher than that, as once he'd dreamed. In fact, he could be brought up on charges for losing Steel Town. Punishment on top of punishment! He could not stay with the Order. He could not bear the humiliation.

THE REBELLION

All Grallik wanted was to find the red-skinned goblin and discover what strange magic she possessed. He'd seen her work with another goblin to create a hole beneath his wall of fire—not by digging, but by some sort of spell. The Order was lost to him. All that was left was magic. His tomes were lost to him; he wanted to gain power another way, and the red-skinned goblin offered a new, exciting magic.

"Zeboim, mother goddess, you who are called Zebir Jotun, Zura the Maelstrom, and Zyr, have the goblins scattered?"

Grallik sat rock still. *Finally*, he mouthed.

The priest nodded, eyes closed but moving rapidly behind the lids. "They are largely together, the escaped slaves, but for a few gone to the winds. The goblins, they hold their army together to stay safe and strong. They go south along the spine of the land, the Khalkist Mountains. They leave the danger of Iverton for other dangers, confident in their numbers."

Grallik edged closer. "Will we live, priest?" he whispered. "If we reach out to the goblins and seek to join with them, will we survive? Or is this some foolish, foolish gamble I intend? Ask the mother goddess that, Horace."

The priest grew silent, his hands cupped in front of the new bone formation, muscles in his cheeks quivering. Grallik was about ready to poke the man, but then Horace's lips started moving again. Grallik watched close and made out a few words: Zeboim, Iverton, slaves, breath. Then the priest leaned forward and traced a pattern in the dirt with his right index finger. It was the shell of a turtle, one of Zeboim's symbols.

"Zeboim, mother goddess, the goblin army rages. So many of our brethren the goblins have killed. Brutal, as if a blood fever seized them, pools of blood so thick the land here in this mining camp cannot soak it all up. Retreating blessedly, finally, the army took their kind with them to the east."

Horace himself fell in the fight, next to a horse a hobgoblin had gutted, Grallik reflected. He thought the hobgoblin would gut the priest too and was surprised when the creature moved on. No doubt the priest looked dead or dying and not worth the effort, and it wasn't until long minutes after the goblins had retreated that Horace finally stirred. The priest had tended himself, the familiar healing glow spreading from his fingertips to his own chest and legs, the cuts and wounds magically closing, repairing.

"We can find them, mother goddess, such an army leaves tracks easily followed. If we listen, we might hear them, as such an army cannot travel silently. But if we follow, wise Zeboim, will they kill us? Will their battle fever take hold again? Will we fall to their stolen weapons and their filthy claws? Will they kill the four of us, as they killed so many, many of our brethren? Or will they accept us into their camp?"

Grallik stared at the bones and wondered who they had belonged to, or what. He wondered how bones helped the priest divine the answers to his questions and if the goddess truly spoke to him. He might not have cared for the Ergothian, but he knew him to be a truthful man and the goddess worthy of respect. Grallik glanced at the turtle shell drawn in the dirt. But there was no trace of it any more, the ground hard and cracked where it had been. The priest's spell was taking so long . . .

"They will not kill us, Grallik. The goblins, they will not kill any of us. They will listen to you and to me—though it will require much persuasion, and they will take us into their fold and be thankful for the healing I will give their injured." Horace's face was not as confident as his words.

Grallik jumped to his feet, tugging Horace up as soon as he'd replaced the bones in his pocket. "Then we must leave now, Skull Knight. Get out of Steel Town now and forever."

Horace shook his head. "I am not a Skull Knight, Grallik. Not if I leave with you. Not anymore, so do not call me that. I am, however, always and forever a priest of Zeboim. And I, too, want to leave Iverton and its memories far behind." He brushed at his tabard, trying to clean a splotch of blood. The gesture futile, he finally gave up. "But you are right, Gray Robe. We must leave now, or there will be no leaving."

The priest moved too slowly to satisfy Grallik, and so their course had been plodding as they pursued the goblin army. Fortunately, the army moved slowly too, no doubt because of its size and because it stopped to feast and rest.

One day earlier, Kenosh had discovered the remains of a herd of mountain goats far off the side of the trail. They had covered good ground and found the goblins.

The goblins did not kill them. But, Grallik reflected bitterly, the goblins put them in chains.

"Slaves." Grallik spat the word aloud. Above and behind him, Grunnt made a noise that could have passed for a chuckle.

"Slaves," Grunnt repeated. The hobgoblin pointed his knife at Grallik then at Horace, Kenosh, and Aneas. "Slaves." That was followed by more noises that were a goblin's laughter.

"I'll wager that's the only word in the Common tongue you know," Grallik said, noting that the hobgoblin's eyes showed no hint of understanding what he was saying. "Aye, you stinking, hairy beast, we are your slaves. For now."

Grallik closed his eyes, trying to sleep, but sleep evaded him. His feet pained him. His eyes burned from something toxic in the air. In general he ached all over. Perhaps if he'd felt well, and if his mind had been functioning properly, he would not have rushed off after the goblins. He would have decided on a different course of action. Leaving the Order?

Probably, certainly, that was inevitable, though it was all he'd known for decades.

Going after the red-skinned goblin was a shrewd strategy, he'd concluded. She might offer a possible path to a different future. He tried to find her, peering out across the ogre village through narrowed eyes. There were hundreds of goblins, more than one thousand, he guessed. They filled the basin, most of them sleeping. But many were awake—talking, arguing. Mothers suckled babies. Guards patrolled. From time to time, small groups of goblins, young from the looks of them, came close to the pen to ogle and point and chuckle at the human slaves. But he didn't spot the red-skinned goblin.

Quite some time had passed, and the wizard wondered if it was nearing morning. Then he saw her.

Grallik's eyes snapped wide open, and he moved to the railing. There she was, sitting in the middle of one of the roads that bisected the village. She was with another goblin, a brown-skinned one with an odd-looking, milky eye. He'd seen her with that goblin before, in the slave pens in Steel Town. Friends or family perhaps, Grallik guessed, maybe mates. Clansmen? He knew the goblins came from various clans throughout Neraka, Khur, and farther distant. He'd learned that much from listening to Marshal Montrill talk about the slaves and where the ogres and minotaurs had captured them. But Grallik knew nothing about the goblins' coloration and that skin hue usually marked them as being from one clan or another.

He stared intently, not caring if the two goblins noticed his attentive gaze. The one with the milky, useless eye glanced at him briefly. They were both interested in something on the ground. No, Grallik realized after a moment—not something *on* the ground, they were studying the ground itself.

"Interesting," he said aloud and considered waking

up the priest so he could observe the two goblins too. But Horace was busy snoring, as was Aneas—the two seemed to be making a contest out of it. A glance over his shoulder told him that Kenosh slept too, though more quietly. The man's chest rose and fell so lightly, a casual observer might think him dead. How could they sleep in such filth? The pen stank of goblins and waste and garbage. He had tried to fall asleep but found the situation all too unsettling.

Grallik couldn't see precisely what the two goblins were doing. The light from the lantern didn't stretch that far. But he could tell that the red-skinned goblin—Mudwort, as the big hobgoblin had called her—was tracing patterns in the dirt in front of her and the milky-eyed one. He remembered Horace drawing the symbol of a turtle shell and wanted desperately to know if Mudwort was drawing something similar.

A symbol of her god? Just what did goblins worship?

A symbol of her clan?

He watched her trace designs for another few moments then saw her tip her head back, eyes closed and mouth moving. It was quiet enough in that part of the basin that he could have heard her, except she wasn't speaking audibly. The milky-eyed goblin placed his hands over the area Mudwort had disturbed, palms flat and leaning forward so all of his weight was on his hands. He cocked his head, as if listening to something, and Grallik wondered if perhaps Mudwort was indeed talking in a hushed tone that didn't carry to the pen.

Then the milky-eyed goblin looked up, sniffing the air, and a moment later sucked in great lungfuls of it.

The very thought made Grallik gag. The air reeked. The wizard smelled his own filthy body, his sweat and that of his companions. And the stench of the goblins—like wet mongrels, they smelled. The scent of blood was heavy in the air too, and many things worse than blood. Animals and ogres had been gutted, and goblin flesh had been burned. Ogre bodies were piled here and there, starting to rot.

Grallik had watched them burn the corpses of the goblins, though they did nothing but pile up the bodies of the dead ogres. And the surviving goblins had performed some sort of ritual over the dead goblins they burned. He didn't understand their chanting, but he'd participated in enough Dark Knight ceremonies to know a ritual when he saw one. Come to think of it, he remembered the goblins doing something similar in Steel Town after the quakes, when all the bodies of the dead slaves had been piled high and lit on fire.

So the goblins were more interesting, complex creatures than he'd first believed, and the two who sat on the road pondering the ground were the most interesting and complex of all. They had magic abilities. Grallik could smell their abilities over all the horrid, disgusting odors that hung in the village and that were held cloyingly close by the thick cover of clouds. He could smell the magic.

"Come closer," he whispered. "Please, please, come closer." Finally, the two goblins raised their voices loud enough that their words carried faintly to him. But they were talking in their guttural goblin tongue, and Grallik understood none of their words. Still, he continued watching, his fatigue forgotten as his mind churned.

"By the memory of the Dark Queen's heads!" he breathed. "What they do is not possible! They work together! They combine their abilities! They combine their magic!"

30

SUFFERING PAIN

What does Moon-eye smell?" Mudwort still had her head tilted up, eyes closed not because her magic required it but because there was something in the air that made her eyes sting. She leaned forward and breathed into his face then stretched back and stared at him. "What smell, Moon-eye?"

"Fire," he answered, though the funeral pyres had been extinguished for quite some time. "Fire and stone. Stone smells, Mudwort. The rocks with ore smell different than this rock all around the village. The village rocks smell beautiful, but the rocks deeper and farther away smell as if they are in pain. Pain smells too . . . and suffering."

Moon-eye fumbled for words to better explain everything he was sensing to Mudwort, but she waved him off.

"Understand fine," she said. Then she thrust the fingers of her left hand into the small stretch of dirt between them, her nails plunging in effortlessly, as though she were driving them into warm butter instead of the hard-packed earth.

"The earth itself suffers," she told Moon-eye. "Not right

245

here, but it will suffer bad here soon. Farther away, it feels pain right now, like Graytoes felt pain when the skull man took the baby. And that pain will come closer, move through the earth like worms wriggling. Deeper there is intense suffering pain. Layers of pain and suffering."

A hobgoblin walked past them, toting skins filled with some sort of potent alcohol over his shoulder. He paused and stared at Mudwort, her fingers stuck in the dirt, made a snorting sound at them, then moved on.

"Yes, pain smells strong and bad, Mudwort." Moon-eye sniffed the air again to be certain. "Smells worse than men." He gestured with his head toward the slave pens and smiled at his own humor. "Smell the dead ogres, rotting ogres, tasty sheep and goats and chickens. Smell those things too." He nodded his head toward the far side of the village where the livestock was being kept. "Smell Graytoes too. That is a very good smell. But the pain of the rocks, that smell . . ." He made a face and spat, as if spitting out something spoiled.

"Join in this," Mudwort said.

At first Moon-eye didn't know what she meant. Then he tentatively brought a hand forward, near hers, prodding the hard earth. He recoiled in surprise when his fingers sank in alongside hers. The ridges above his eyes rose in curiosity, then his expression turned instantly grim and serious, his lips thrust forward. A moment later, he leaned close and drove both hands into the yielding ground, just as she had.

"Feels like mud," he said with a slight grin. He moved his fingers easily through the hard earth, reaching out with his right hand and stretching until his fingers touched Mudwort's own buried left hand. "Feels odd . . . but good."

"Smell the world now," Mudwort encouraged Moon-eye. She thrust her right hand deep into the ground and edged forward until she touched his left hand, keeping her hand close to his. "Think strong, Moon-eye. Think and do nothing else except think. See the world now. See the world together."

Moon-eye's mouth dropped open in surprise, but he quickly recovered. "Don't understand, Mudwort! What is this?"

"There is something special about Moon-eye," Mudwort explained. "Felt it a while back, in the slave pens. Could do nothing about it then—slaves then. Do something now, together. Smell the world together, Moon-eye. What do you smell?"

He sucked in a deep breath then another, his good eye widening even more as he explored his power. "Smelling the stone," Moon-eye repeated. "Seeing the stone on the sides of mountains, smooth and pretty, shiny black. More stones are not smooth, though. Look like bugs have bored inside. Holes all over, and those stones feel rough and have felt pain. Are dead now, those stones. Some dead, but felt pain once."

"Feel their pain too," Mudwort said. "It is those rocks that suffered the most, the ones with holes. Warm, those rocks are like the charred wood at the bottom of a fire. Where are these hole-filled rocks, Moon-eye?"

The one-eyed goblin furrowed his brow and sniffed again, putting his face down close to the dirt until his nose brushed it. "Far . . . but not far." He pressed his nose all the way into the earth, then quickly withdrew it. "Too close, Mudwort. The suffering pain is too close, the pain will come here soon. Leave here. Direfang must know now, all goblins must leave!"

Beneath the surface, Mudwort grabbed Moon-eye's fingers before he could pull them out and held them tightly. "Tell Direfang soon, Moon-eye. Together tell him. But there is more to see and smell first. Learn more first."

Moon-eye tried to tug free, but Mudwort's grip was strong. "Look to the south, Moon-eye, where Direfang wants to go."

He fought against her a moment more then relented. "The mountains glow, Mudwort. To the south and west, some mountains glow." There was awe in his voice, his good eye glimmering excitedly. "The one nearest this village, the one seen from the top of that crest. It glows so very, very bright. And others. The ones near Steel Town glow brightest. The not-hurting mountains are to the north of this place."

Mudwort said, "What the quake started, disturbing the sleeping, angry earth—"

"The glowing mountains will finish." Moon-eye completed for her, grinning. "Good, the mountains will bury Steel Town forever."

"But not good that they could bury any more goblins. Here, there is danger too." Mudwort still held his hands tight. "There is more, Moon-eye. See it? See this amazing thing?"

"Yes. But what is it? Beautiful. What is it? Frightening. What is it?"

Mudwort shrugged as Moon-eye stared at the ground, cracks radiating outward from his wrists.

"What is that thing, Mudwort?"

She shrugged again, releasing his hands. "Direfang wants to go south, and that is to the south," she said. "The frightening thing could be there, on the way."

"Could be dangerous," Moon-eye said, though his eye was still glimmering with excitement.

"Direfang does not need to know that," Mudwort said flatly, standing and brushing the dirt from her palms. "Moon-eye thirsty?"

He nodded. "Direfang and Moon-eye's Heart are at the lake."

"Good to be thirsty, then, eh?" Mudwort led the way

down the road, fully aware as she had been all the time, that the wizard was watching her, still watching her.

When Direfang approached the slave pen, the hobgoblin guards were quick to wake up the knights. A dozen goblins had gathered behind Direfang, all of them wielding knives.

"It is Grunnt's turn to sleep now," Direfang told the hobgoblin guard in charge. "Sleep very quick. Soon we go." He spoke in the Common tongue to the knights, who were still rubbing their eyes. "Time grows near to leave this place."

Grallik jumped to his feet, obviously angry with himself for dropping off to sleep in this filthy place. "Where are we going?"

Direfang worked a kink out of his shoulder and dug the ball of his foot into the ground. "South is all you need to know."

"Where south?"

"Just south." Direfang growled and thrust his bottom jaw out. "It is not safe here, Mudwort says. Clearly, it does not look safe." He pointed to the sky, which had lightened a little, though the dark gray clouds remained an ominous sight.

The sky was light enough that Grallik could see the goblins already getting ready to leave the village. They had packs and sacks filled to bulging—skins fat with water from the lake. Jugs were also filled with water, stoppered, and held in nets slung over the shoulders of the stronger hobgoblins. Goats, sheep, and cows were tethered at the base of the trail, and the cows had sacks and blankets draped across their backs. The army was taking everything of value that could be carried or dragged along with them. The livestock would last them a couple of days but little more than that because of the goblins' sheer numbers and ravenous appetites.

The sight of the army ready to march clearly alarmed Grallik, as did the steam rising from cracks in the ground that had appeared during the darkness. All over the village the earth had swelled, as though things beneath the ground were trying to push their way upward, cracks appearing everywhere.

"Thought more giant bugs were coming," Direfang said. "Like the one killed by the fire spell. Not bugs, though."

"But there wasn't any trace of steam when the centipedes attacked yesterday, was there?" Grallik asked. "This is something else."

"Something else. Something bad," Direfang said.

Grallik stepped to the rail and leaned against it.

"Slaves," Direfang said, nodding at Grallik then indicating the priest and the other two knights too. "Slaves will come along." The hobgoblin looked again at Horace, who was still lying on the ground, listening. "Skull man!"

"You want me to tend you now?" Horace brushed futilely at his chest and back, unable to get the dirt and waste off. The priest seemed oblivious to the activity in the village and the steam rising from the ground. He was ready to resume his healing duties. "Aye, Foreman Direfang. And in return I ask that you let me bathe in the lake and drink my fill." Then he looked around, realized the army was preparing to leave, and added, "At least grant me a skin of water to take with me."

The hobgoblin stepped away from Grallik and the priest then turned to address them sternly. "The Dark Knights did not give the slaves in Steel Town any such concessions. Never enough water. The slaves had such courtesies only rarely."

Horace looked surprised at the hobgoblin's vocabulary and command of the Common tongue. The words were not so polished as if they had come from a human mouth. There was a rasp to Direfang's speech, but the language was recognizable.

"Dark Knights held no regard for slaves—no shoes, only scraps of clothes for some but not all. Food not fit for the pigs the knights kept in pens." Direfang growled so loudly, the goblins nearby recoiled. "Slaves asked the Dark Knights for little, and slaves were usually granted nothing."

Beyond the pen, the goblins were forming into clans and columns and lining up to follow the trail out of the village. The steam obscured some of them and made the scene grayer.

"I ask for water and to be clean," said Horace with dignity. "Please, Foreman. I mended goblin upon goblin yesterday, and I will heal more today. I would mend you now while your arm can be saved—perhaps can be saved. In exchange I ask for very little. I ask for water."

Direfang studied the priest. "The skull man uses words well. Uses the word *asks,* not *demands,* says *please.* The skull man knows that words make a difference. So mend this arm, *please,* skull man, and then follow Brak to the lake." The hobgoblin indicated the young goblin standing to his right.

Direfang used his right hand to lift his left arm and set it on the top rail of the fence then nodded to Horace, who approached. Aneas and Kenosh moved up behind the priest. Grallik stayed close by, close enough to watch.

"I will need water or preferably something much stronger, such as ale or rum. Do you have any strong drink here, Foreman Direfang?" Horace wiped the sweat off his face and met the hobgoblin's stern gaze. "Can they, your goblin guards, get me something to cleanse your wound?"

Direfang translated the request to the goblin called Crelb, who hesitated for a moment, not wanting to leave his post. The hobgoblin repeated the message, and Crelb finally left.

Horace spat on his fingers to clean the dirt from them, then prodded the area around Direfang's wound, careful not to touch the actual gash that was purple and swollen and oozing. "You should have let me see to this yesterday. In hours it has worsened."

Direfang offered no reply as the priest continued his poking.

"Does this hurt?"

The hobgoblin shook his head. "Once it hurt then nothing. Yesterday it hurt again but only a little, not much. Today nothing." He looked at the sky and scowled. "The army must leave soon, skull man, hurry with this arm . . ."

"If I want water and my bath, yes?" Horace held his open left hand over the deep cut and gripped the hobgoblin's wrist with the right. His shackles and chains made it difficult.

"Zeboim, mother goddess, this wound is grievous." The sweat on Horace's arm shimmered, and a glowing sheath formed just above his skin. It brightened from yellow to white, and motes of light appeared in the glow. At first the motes were the size of beetles, but in the passing of a few heartbeats, doubled in size and skittered down his arm and over the back of his hand, spilling down his fingers and onto Direfang's arm.

Grallik expected the hobgoblin to show some reaction from experiencing divine magic, but Direfang didn't blink, didn't budge. He stood patiently as the lights sank into his skin. A moment more, and the magical sheath slid off the priest's arm and became part of the hobgoblin's skin. Suddenly Direfang smiled, opening and closing his left hand.

"You are not free of the infection yet, Foreman. Ah, the sentry returns." Horace made a show of the difficulty of moving with his chains, stretching to reach the jug Crelb held out to him. "Foreman, if only you would . . ."

Direfang grabbed the jug with his right hand and passed it to the priest. Horace uncorked it and breathed in the smell. "Oh, this is very strong. And I'd wager very bad tasting. I wonder if it will make things worse." He poured some into his other cupped hand and touched his tongue to the liquid. "Not poison. No, I can tell poison." He proceeded to pour most of the contents on the cut, bathing the wound in the potent alcohol. "I can see bone, here, Foreman Direfang."

Again, the hobgoblin offered no reply.

"The sword that cut you was not clean, Foreman Direfang. Not like a Dark Knight to have his blade dirty, but I suppose it was as much to be expected given the circumstances in the camp." The priest rubbed a little of the alcohol on his hands, set the jug between his feet, and investigated the wound again. "Mother Zeboim, grant me the strength to save this limb."

The rest of Horace's words were foreign to Direfang, though he recognized them as the singsong uttering of a healing spell. The hobgoblin heard the goblin sentries chatter nervously behind him as the priest droned.

"Does the priest mean to kill Direfang?" Crelb whispered.

"No, he is magicking Direfang," Brak corrected. "That is much more likely. Magicking Direfang to let the knight slaves out. Casting a spell on Direfang like the priests cast a spell on the slaves who stayed in Steel Town. But Direfang has a strong mind. It cannot be muddled, will not go sour."

"Don't like magic," another goblin muttered. "Don't like Dark Knight magic most of all. Magic makes the skin itch." Direfang almost smiled, hearing the goblin scratch himself to illustrate.

"I don't suppose you would tell me what they're saying," the priest mused as he worked on Direfang. His hands glowed again, brighter than before. He ran his thumbs along the edges of the wound. The other knights, Grallik included, continued to watch, as fascinated as the goblin guards.

"If the skull man wants to know what the goblins say, the skull man should learn the language."

Horace let out a throaty chuckle. "I suppose Guardian Grallik and I will have to do just that if we're to stay with you. And apparently you mean us to stay, else you wouldn't have put us in these uncomfortable chains." Horace's thumbs smoothed at the hobgoblin's skin as though he were smoothing the wrinkles out of a garment. "Will you supply a teacher for us, Foreman Direfang? Teach us the goblin tongue?"

The hobgoblin stared at his wound. Horace had distracted him with his talk. In the passing of a few heartbeats, his wound had closed, leaving a fresh scar behind. He felt a dull pain, which he welcomed because he'd not been feeling anything in the arm. Pain, instead of numbness, was good.

"Now lean down, will you?" Horace picked up the jug and splashed a little more alcohol on his hands, again making a show of the chains making it difficult for him to work his healing. "Farther. You're too tall otherwise for me to get at that head gash. Hmm . . . looks like you were kicked by a horse."

Direfang noticed that the priest's eyes looked tired and red rimmed, more so than when he'd started. So the magic did exact a price. Horace wasn't pretending. When the priest was finished, he pushed himself away from Direfang. Then he tilted the jug back and took a few swallows, draining it.

"Brak, take the skull man to the lake." Direfang gestured to the empty jug. "That could hold water now. The slaves may have it for their wants." The hobgoblin breathed deeply, feeling better with each passing breath. Then Direfang stepped away from the rail and turned to meet Grallik's gaze. "The army leaves soon, and the slaves with it. The slaves could stay here, but there would be no safety in that." He waved his repaired arm to indicate the village, pointing at the steam coming from some of the vents. "Mudwort says this is a bad omen. Only the blind would call it otherwise. This army leaves very, very soon. Wizard, skull man too."

31

RIVERS

The hobgoblin led the army south along a mountain path that wrapped down and away from the ogre village. The trail was narrow, so only three goblins could walk abreast. To their left, the mountainside rose up at a steep angle and disappeared into a billowing mass of gray clouds. Tugging cows along the trail proved difficult, but the goblins coaxed and pulled their tasty livestock along the side of the trail closest to the mountain. The western edge fell away with the slope to a narrow valley filled with jagged spires.

Direfang would have preferred a faster pace, but he'd been pushing the limit with the army for hours, and many of the goblins and hobgoblins carried packs and satchels filled with treasures and food, and jugs and skins filled with water.

Just how long they'd been marching before he announced a rest, he wasn't certain. There'd been no break in the gray cloud cover, so he couldn't judge the passing of time from the sun. There'd been no change in the air since they'd left. It was still warm, and the slight breeze carried some dust or irritant that continued to burn his eyes. He allowed only a few minutes' rest before he urged the army back to its feet.

The longer they were on the road, the more he grew certain that the clouds were unnatural, an omen perhaps—with a frown, he wondered if the omen might be caused by the Dark Knights. He'd never seen such a gray sky before, and there had been no change in more than a day—just unending gray, not a cloud smelling of water, and all the world smelling dry.

It was Dark Knight sorcery, perhaps. After all, he himself had seen the wizard call down columns of flame. The smoky sky might not be beyond him, his coming to join the goblins a ruse.

The ground shook, not so strong as to impede the progress of Direfang and the others on the trail, but enough to worry even the most dull-witted goblin. Rocks tumbled down, pelting everyone and spooking the livestock. Stone dust fell too, making a gentle, almost pleasant, sound. But when the ground shook again, longer, the dust and dirt that rained down from the mountain above was thick and choking.

Direfang doubled over, coughs wracking him. Mudwort was on Erguth's shoulders, the pair of them right behind Direfang. Erguth leaned against the slope, struggling to breathe. Behind them other goblins and hobgoblins coughed too. They dropped their packs and grabbed for water skins.

"Bring the wizard up," Direfang managed to shout. He turned and looked through the filtering dust, seeing Crelb and gesturing. "Now! Bring the wizard and do it now!" He leaned over farther, breathing deeply, but found the air no better near the ground.

Mudwort climbed off Erguth's shoulders, waving her arms. "Direfang, don't stop, move faster! There should be no stopping here. Move away from this mountain and the other one. Get to new land." She thrust a finger to the west, where a glowing red ribbon cut through the gray. "Direfang, this mountain and the other one are—" When the ground shook a third time, the screams of goblins and the squeals of animals drowned her out. Some goblins fell off the side of the trail, tumbling down the slope and disappearing into a haze of dirt and stone dust that rose in puffs from the valley below.

Another shaking made Mudwort herself stumble, nearly slipping off the side of the trail. Her fingers grabbed the dirt, sinking in, and she pressed her face against the stone. She breathed shallowly and held tight as Crelb pushed past her, dragging the wizard. After a moment she climbed to a safer spot and held her ear to the ground, listening.

"I can do nothing against this sort of disaster, hob—" Grallik began to say as Crelb shoved him forward. The wizard stumbled into Direfang, who was standing straight. The hobgoblin grabbed the wizard around the shoulders. "Foreman Direfang, I cannot stop the mountain from shaking."

"The sky, Grallik!"

The wizard looked surprised that the hobgoblin had called him by his name.

"Look to the sky and tell me what is responsible for this darkness. Did Dark Knight magic do this?" Direfang snarled the question before nearly doubling over again with coughing. "Grallik, what is responsible for the damnable, dark sky?"

The wizard was wracked with coughing too. He grabbed the neckline of his shift and raised it to cover his nose and mouth. "Not my magic, Direfang. I'm not so powerful that I could do this, and I know of no wizard who could. A god, maybe. Perhaps we've all caught the attention of Chislev or—"

Direfang's snarl turned into a roar. "The gods! Never

did the gods help goblinkind, Grallik. So goblins do not recognize the gods. No *god* is responsible. And if not a wizard . . ."

"Another earthquake." The voice belonged to the priest Horace. Brak had led the Skull Knight up the trail.

Brak gave a small, tight smile. "Direfang wanted the wizard, figured Direfang might want the skull man too." Brak's shoulders shook when he broke into a coughing fit.

Dust billowed all around them, as if the dry clouds had settled to the ground. The plink and plop of rocks skittering down the slope drowned out the fearful murmur of the goblins.

"A quake would not so darken the sky, would it, priest?" Direfang spoke loud enough to be heard by the many others around him. Then he cupped his hand over his mouth and nose, filtering some of the dust out. "Zeboim would not darken the sky either, eh, Grallik, priest? So what is responsible?"

When the priest shrugged indifferently, Direfang spun and gestured for the others to follow him south on the trail, knowing that while his long strides would make it difficult for the goblins to keep up, it would also urge them to go faster.

The trail trembled against the soles of his feet, rocks biting into them and adding to the hobgoblin's misery. There was no end to the rumbling as the army scurried behind its leader. Words of panic and the frightened bleats of animals filled the air. Occasional screams cut through the hubbub as goblins slid off the trail and shot over the side.

Mudwort labored to keep up with Direfang, practically running and gasping as she finally closed in on the long-striding hobgoblin. "Wait! Listen, Direfang. Listen!"

He slowed only to pick her up and set her on his shoulders. She wrapped her arms around his neck, then she held her face to the back of his head, finding it easier to talk with the air not quite so dusty against his scalp.

"Listen to the growling, Direfang!" She moved her lips close to one ear. "The mountains growl like maddened bears. Rabid and hungry, the mountains taunt each other. Goblins are caught in the argument between the mountains, Direfang. Goblins will die to the mountains' venomous bickering!"

The hobgoblin frowned, trying to figure out just what Mudwort was saying. He wasn't sure even she knew exactly.

"This quake is longer than the ones before, Mudwort," he replied stoically. "This quake seems to follow us and does not stop. This is not like what happened at Steel Town."

She thumped her heels against his chest, as a rider would knee a horse to get it to go faster. "This is not a quake, Direfang. The quakes started this argument, though. Listened a moment ago to the earth. Listened to the earth explain that the quakes from days ago woke up the mountains."

He slowed but only a little, wanting to be able to hear her a little better. He knew better than to ignore her words.

"The mountains woke up, still tired, Direfang. Cranky and mean, the mountains shake now and spit smoke into the sky. The mountains' bellies are filled with fire." She moved her hands to the sides of the hobgoblin's head and forced him to turn his gaze slightly. "The river of red over there . . . that mountain belched it up. This mountain will—"

The trail bucked beneath them, cracks appearing everywhere. Goblins screamed and called for those in front to run faster.

Grallik and Horace yelled too.

Direfang dropped the satchel he was carrying, raised his hands, and grabbed Mudwort's legs to keep her from falling off. Then he broke into a reckless run, dodging rocks bouncing down the slope and gasping in the dirt-thick air. Goblins and hobgoblins raced behind them, their screams trailing off as they toppled over the side. He wanted to look behind him to see who had been lost, but the air was filled with a brown dust fog, and he couldn't see more than a foot or two in front of his face. He heard a strangled "moo" and a shower of rocks, followed by another and another. He suspected the goblins were pushing the cows and other livestock over the edge because the animals were clogging the trail.

"Knew a mountain would break, Direfang. Should have said something earlier. Did not think it would be this mountain."

It was difficult to hear Mudwort over the groaning mountain and the screams of the goblins and hobgoblins behind them.

"The earth did not say it would be this one. The earth gave no warning the ogre village was not safe. The earth is tricky."

The hobgoblin ran faster still, his chest aching from the exertion, his lungs burning from the dust and the heated air. The hot air! In a few minutes time, the world had grown feverish around them. Direfang pulled Mudwort off his shoulders and set her on the ground, both of them running.

He heard the *chink-chink* of chains and realized the wizard and skull man were keeping pace close behind him, the latter huffing and wheezing like a dying old man.

"Your magic said the goblins would not kill us, Horace," the wizard yelled, spitting out the words. "But your magic said nothing about the volcanoes. They will kill us all."

Volcanoes! Direfang remembered the word the knights had often repeated one night as they studied a large map. The word in goblin-speak was the language's longest: *gosjall-giyera-fajra*, mountains of fiery war. He'd waited on the knights that evening, around the map, bringing them mead and water and honey-covered bread, and polishing the pieces of armor they'd nested along the wall. He'd taken a long time with each task because he had found their words and the map interesting. It had been some years ago, right before he'd been named a foreman in the mine and was taken away from the servile duties of waiting on the knights. But he remembered the maps and what the men had talked about. It had been fascinating.

Direfang recalled seeing nine mountains of fiery war on the map, most of them scattered amid the Khalkist chain, two or three of them quite near Steel Town. Ever since that night, he would often look to the nearest two, sometimes seeing their crowns glowing, sometimes seeing gray clouds hover above them. From time to time, ribbons of red flowed from their tops, and he later learned the Dark Knights called these red rivers lava. The goblins had a word for the red rivers too: *eldura-bundok,* mountain fire.

"This army must keep going south, Direfang. Faster, even if some are left behind. Better that some live than none. The fast ones will live." Mudwort's face was twisted with apprehension as she darted ahead of the hobgoblin. Once ahead on the trail, she started running faster than she ever had before, keeping to the middle and looking straight ahead.

Direfang, impressed by the small one's speed, lengthened his stride but did not overtake her. He decided to let her be the leader for all to follow that day. After all, she had talked to the earth and knew its heart and would know the best path. He valued her wisdom and the counsel she gave.

He heard a pounding behind him, feet slapping against the trail, rocks bouncing down from higher up on the mountain. Chains jangled from the wizard and priest, and no doubt from the warrior knights farther back in the column. Direfang wished he would have removed the chains from the slaves, though he wasn't sure how to do that. He'd seen no keys with the manacles and hadn't bothered to search for any.

"Faster!" Mudwort called, risking a glance over her shoulder.

"Faster!" came cries behind Direfang.

Then the mountain heaved, and the hobgoblin lost his footing, falling forward on the trail and finding himself overrun by a half dozen goblins scrambling over him. He might have been trampled if two pairs of hands hadn't hoisted him up and propelled him forward, the chains dangling from the wizard's and priest's wrists thumping his sides.

"The Maws of Dragons seek to slay us all, Foreman Direfang. While your people will not kill us, the volcanoes certainly will." The priest's face was wet with sweat beads. The trousers he wore also appeared soaked with perspiration.

The wizard was having an easier time dealing with the heat and the strain, but he looked worried and was coughing harshly. "I say not a god nor a man is responsible for this hell, Direfang. It is nature, worse than anything a god or a man could visit upon us. Horace is right; we will all die here. I've no magic that can save us, and he is spent."

The mountain heaved again, and the trail rose and fell as if they were on the back of some great rearing animal. Direfang kept his balance, though he knew many in his army were not so fortunate. Their screams cut through the persistent rumbling and the sound of rocks pelting the slope. He wondered how many had died on the trail, their bodies bouncing against jagged rocks as they tumbled down. And he wondered how long before he took a misstep and joined them.

"Fought too hard to die here," Direfang said through clenched teeth. He fixed his eyes on Mudwort's back. She was ahead of the rest, even the group of goblins who'd passed him, nearly trampling him. Brak was among that group, and Crelb too. The two young goblins were good at running.

The trail turned down at a steep angle. From his vantage point, Direfang saw a great rent ahead, where it looked like the path had been ripped apart with a gaping hole in the center. There was nowhere to go but ahead, the hobgoblin knew, no turning around and going back, no heading down the side of the mountain—not without dying. They must jump the crevice. He couldn't even warn the others above the din. His words would be lost—a useless waste of saliva.

He made a quick decision. He grabbed the wizard and the priest by their arms, half lifting them off their feet. Ahead, he saw Mudwort hurdle the crevice, thankful she landed on her feet and continued her mad run. Of the six who followed her, only five made the gap. Crelb jumped too early, legs and arms flailing in the air and failing to gain purchase. He opened his mouth and a scream emerged, though Direfang could not hear his death cry. The rumbling had grown in intensity and was almost hurtful to his ears. Crelb disappeared into the black hole, and a heartbeat later, Direfang, clutching the two spellcasting knights, who were running wildly in his grip, vaulted the gap and kept going.

"I made it!" Horace gasped proudly.

The wizard said something lost to the hobgoblin, but it sounded like gratitude to Direfang.

"Keep running," the hobgoblin growled, letting go of the two so they could run on their own. "Run and live. Run, skull man and—"

A great *whoosh* swallowed the rest of the hobgoblin's words and rose above the rumbling and screams and pelting rocks. The volcano they raced down had just expelled the tremendous breath it had been holding for decades and coughed up a gout of fire wider and longer than even the greatest red dragon could have breathed. With it came a stream of smoke and ash that shot miles into the air, pushing away the clouds and allowing, for the briefest of moments, a hint of blue sky.

Glowing, fiery rocks were spat out of what had once been the ogre village, some shooting so high up that the goblins lost sight of them. Others arced out in all directions from the crater, horribly burning goblins they hit on the way down. A cinder cloud billowed out as the mountain continued to writhe.

"It bleeds!" Erguth yelled. He'd fought his way up through the panicked horde until he was running directly behind Direfang and the spellcasters. "The mountain bleeds!"

Direfang risked a glance up the slope, registering a thick, orange-yellow ribbon of molten rock erupting over the crater lip and spilling down the side. The glance cost him, as he drew in ash-laced air that sent him into another coughing fit. Horace and Grallik grabbed him, pushing him forward again.

"All of us will die, Foreman Direfang," the priest hissed. "Not even a dragon can match this beast's fury."

Direfang's lungs felt on fire, his throat and mouth so dry he could not work up any saliva. Never had he felt such pain in his eyes. He wanted to offer a clever retort to the priest, to tell him that not all in his army would die that day. But many would perish, he knew, too many.

It felt like hours, but Direfang guessed it had taken only minutes for the front of the column to reach the foothills. It looked like a brown fog had settled in the low part of the Khalkists, but it was dust that hung several feet above the ground. Everywhere the air was filled with dust or ash or both. All of it was difficult and irritating to breathe. Direfang spotted Mudwort and Brak through the haze.

He bent and grabbed the chains that dangled from the

spellcasters' wrists. Leading the human slaves like live-stock, he hurried into the haze, following Mudwort and Brak and hoping those farther back could spot him and follow too.

The mountain continued its upheaval. Faintly, he heard one of the knights call loudly for Grallik and Grallik's answer. Hurbear had somehow made it, as Direfang picked out the old goblin's voice shouting orders to his clansmen. Someone was also calling for Moon-eye, asking if the one-eyed goblin had made it safely down the angry mountain.

Direfang doubted he had. Graytoes wouldn't have been likely to keep up with the brutal pace, and Moon-eye would not leave her, not even to save himself. He pictured the two of them stumbling into the crevice on the trail, not being able to leap over it. Then he thrust the disaster from his mind and yanked on the spellcasters' chains. He shut his eyes, telling himself it would only be for a moment. They were dry and hurting, and he needed a moment for them to be refreshed.

"Look out, Foreman!" Grallik shouted.

Direfang opened his eyes abruptly. Not releasing the chains, he brought his right arm up and brushed his fore-arm against his eyes. Through the haze, he saw another ribbon of red, narrower than the last but coming down right toward them, spilling out over the foothills and blocking their path.

"We are done," Horace said.

Direfang tried to say "not yet," but his mouth was parched. So he tugged hard, nearly pulling the spellcasters off their feet, and charged toward the lava stream, moving faster with each lunging stride. From somewhere behind, he heard Erguth shout for the other goblins to run and jump. Direfang did just that himself, clearing the lava stream, which was not yet very large, while pulling on the chains to yank the knights over the widening lava stream too.

THE REBELLION

Behind him he heard an agonizing scream. Glancing over his shoulder, Direfang saw the hobgoblin Grunnt trip into the lava and shrivel and burn, his cries pitifully dying away.

32

WRINKLES IN THE WORLD

It wasn't just the mountain the goblins left behind that was exploding, it was also the one directly across from it, and at least one other well to the north, that they could see.

"The three are one," Mudwort was saying, trying to make Direfang and Brak understand. The two spellcasters were also standing close by, listening. "Those three, they are one volcano, not three. One volcano with three mouths. The earth says so." She gestured to the south, where a narrow trail led between peaks. It was a trail used mainly by goats and didn't look easy to navigate. A wider, gentler way led to the southwest, but Mudwort insisted that was not the way to go.

Direfang pointed at the southwest route. "The army would do better this way."

She shook her head vehemently, spittle flying from her thin lips. "Maws of the Dragon, the skull man said. One volcano, though, not three, I say. Beneath the earth is a hidden pool of the hottest fire, and it spreads under the three maws,

Direfang. It spreads to the mountains near Steel Town too. The quakes woke up the mountains, stirred the pool of fire, and that is why everything is breaking."

Done with her explanation, she turned from them and dashed away along the narrow, difficult path, not bothering to look over her shoulder to see if they were following. Direfang had dropped the chains of the priest and the wizard. He looked at them, his expression weary.

"Keep up or die," he growled. Then he sped ahead, tripping once, but picking himself up and keeping just behind Mudwort. The other surviving goblins, some just arriving out of breath, shouted to see him disappear—and followed.

Above and behind him, ash, rock, and pumice were spitting high into the air. The ash rose more than a dozen miles. Loud cracks and pops caused Direfang to run with his hands cupped to the sides of his face. The noise was as painful as any of the many burns and small injuries he had suffered on the trail.

To the northwest, the eruption column of one of the volcanoes was filled with twisted flashes of lightning. One more loud blast came from that cone, followed by an avalanche of rock as it began to collapse in on itself. In the process, the volcano disgorged a thicker, darker cloud of ash, and rubble crashed down the breaking slope, accompanied by belching, horrendous-smelling gas and melting rocks.

The air was impossibly hot to breathe, and with each step Direfang gained, he cursed himself for leading the goblin army in that direction. In his effort to avoid the Valley of Neraka and a great concentration of Dark-Knight camps, he'd chosen instead to bring them straight into the belly of the Abyss.

Magma surged and the ground shuddered. Steam belched furiously, so scalding that it incinerated the goblins at the tail end of the army. Lava oozed up through tunnels and broke through the side of the mountain, creating a second eruption point through which gas and ash and melting rocks escaped. A searing, yellow-white river of molten debris spilled out, looking sluggish but picking up momentum and catching more goblins as it furiously wound its way down the mountain.

Had Direfang been at a high, safe distance, he thought he would have considered the vivid river of fire to be beautiful. But the horrors of the Abyss must be nothing near to it, he reflected as he raced on, coughing and sputtering and thrusting the pain all over him to the back of his mind.

Risking a glance over his shoulder, he saw the Dark Knight spellcasters, with a number of goblins swarming around and past them. They flowed like the lava, he thought. But he couldn't see much else. The rest of his vast army was obscured. There were just ash clouds in layers of gray and black, white-hot stone shards flying like snow in a blizzard, and in the distance a shower of red ash. The hellish landscape nearly sucked all the hope from him, but he turned back to see Mudwort, who was remarkably climbing higher and somehow faster, with Brak and Bentclaw only a few feet behind.

His fault; he'd brought them to that place!

His fault for thinking there was greater safety in numbers and that staying together was some prudent measure!

He should have told them to scatter with their clans like bugs running from a disturbed nest. Direfang knew he would have gone south, but not so many of them would have been encouraged to follow, not so many of them would have died. He could still hear their screams amid the crackling and popping, belching ash and gas, and the constant, damnable rumbling. No matter how much he concentrated on the sounds of the volcanoes, he could not blot out the goblin screams.

There was nothing he could do to save the doomed; the exploding mountains were not monsters or men he could fight. And no weapon on all of Krynn could combat them—not even the magic of the priest and the wizard, who doggedly trailed him. The hobgoblin doubted he would save himself.

Direfang could hardly breathe. Everything was so hot and horrible, the scent of ashes and molten rock and burning goblins filling his senses. He could smell pine burning too. Narrow trees grew in patches of dirt throughout the Khalkists, and he could see a stand to his right bursting into fire. Lower, pitch pines burst into flames. Farther to his right, where another volcano had erupted, a white-hot river of lava, wide and surging, rolled down the slope and swallowed more trees. Near it a chunk of stone gave way, then another as a massive rent was ripped in the mountain. With each new rent or gash in the rock, more lava poured out.

Anything in the lava flow's path was doomed, he knew. There was no escaping from that terrible fate.

He realized he hadn't seen a single goat or bird since the exodus from the ogre village. The animals knew, he thought, that the ground was going to erupt, that the Maws of Dragons were going to burst. Why hadn't he noticed the signs and got the army out earlier? Direfang's despair was profound and crippling, and if Grallik had not brushed by him, then Erguth right after, he might have stopped and given up.

"Hurry," Horace wheezed as he drew even with Direfang, impressing the hobgoblin with his strength and determination. "If you die, who's to keep the goblins from killing me?" Then, impossibly, the stocky priest managed another burst of speed and clawed his way up the twisting, narrow trail.

Direfang couldn't reply, his mouth still so painfully dry. But the mountains answered for him, launching gouts of flame into the air, roaring their anger and sending plumes of ash up to join the gray and black clouds.

He remembered the Dark Knights in Steel Town talking about wars and skirmishes and how the sounds were incredibly loud and chaotic and confusing. No battle could match the volcanoes, he knew, perhaps not even the Chaos War the knights were so fond of discussing.

A wind picked up as more lightning flickered in the ash spouts above the two closest volcanoes. The wind keened as it struck the hot ash, and the lava hissed and gave off steam. The wind was strong enough to stir the thick gray-black clouds and let the pale blue sky peek through. And the wind brought with it the slightest draft of fresh air, which Direfang and the others greedily sucked into their lungs.

"Hurry, Foreman Direfang!" the priest called over his shoulder, shaming the hobgoblin with his superior speed.

So hurry Direfang did, his chest and sides aching from the pace and the heat and the choking of the Khalkist inferno.

Ash fell like snow, soft and warm, making it even harder to catch a decent breath. Light as feathers though the ash was, it came so fast and thick that it felt heavy on him. Mudwort ran with her hand cupped in front of her mouth, and Direfang, noticing, copied her. Then he ripped a strip from his trousers and wrapped it around his nose and mouth.

Mudwort paused briefly when the trail vanished, then started picking her way across the rocky terrain ahead, wrapping her fingers tightly as she pulled herself up and up. Direfang saw places where the stone had been scraped, probably from goat hooves. So they were following goats. There were hoofprints in the ash-filled dirt pockets between rocks, and the hobgoblin wondered if Moon-eye was alive and wished he were there. The one-eyed goblin could track goats like no other goblin, and perhaps could point to safety.

There was a bunch of them close behind Mudwort and Brak. The wizard seemed to have little trouble keeping up,

Direfang noted with grudging respect, and a number of goblins scrambled behind him. The priest was struggling to claw his way up. Direfang came up from behind the priest and gave him a boost as he picked his own way forward. He couldn't see very far behind through all the ash and smoke, but he saw goblins crowding up to follow him, one hobgoblin carrying Saro-Saro.

From that mountain, Mudwort led them to another, slightly to the west, then one more. They traveled for more than a day before stopping, falling from exhaustion and sleeping for brief intervals against rocky slopes covered with fine sheets of ash. That far from the volcanoes, they still didn't feel safe. Ash still fell like snow, though not so dense as before, and looking up, Direfang could see splotches of the sky through gaps in the ash-smoke clouds.

Finally he let himself drop, many others joining him.

He slept, though he did not sleep long. Not that sleeping wasn't his desperate desire—there was no part of him that didn't ache or was not bone weary. He could have slept hours and hours, he knew, but they were still not far enough away from the danger and the fire and the falling ash.

Inches thick along that slope, the ash was slippery, and it hid jagged shards of rock that had been hurled far by the angry volcanoes. The ashfall had made the path treacherous. More goblins slept on the slope behind him, single file and curled together. He tried to find familiar faces and clans, but the goblins were all the same color—gray as the ash and the clouds overhead; their bodies and faces were marred, like his, by burns from pieces of flaming rock that had brushed them. Again, he wondered about Moon-eye and others he had not seen for more than a day.

The demonic glow of the lava illuminated the drying streams of melted rock. Ugly and craggy, they looked like wrinkles on an old man's face, wrinkles on the world.

"The Maws of Dragons breathe fire still," Mudwort

told him, coming up to him even as he stirred from sleep. She hadn't slept long either, and she couldn't stop yawning, her fingers shaking from fatigue. "This goblin army—what's left of Direfang's army—needs to march again now. Away from the stone dragons and to a place not far, but safe."

Direfang wanted to ask her where she was leading them—clearly there was a purpose to her course—but still he couldn't manage to get out more than a strangled croak. He'd swallowed too much dust and could barely breathe. His chest felt tight, as though an ogre were squeezing him. He should sleep, just a little more, but Mudwort was probably right—he had to trust in her wisdom—that where they were wasn't a safe place to sleep. He roused Brak and Folami, Saro-Saro and the wizard.

Grallik looked like a walking corpse, his features gaunt and ash streaked, his hair plastered to the sides of his face from sweat and his entire body coated in grit. The shift he wore was tattered and soiled. He looked the part of a slave, reminding Direfang of some of the goblins who'd been pushed too hard in the mines when a thick vein was discovered, and who had worked double shifts and nearly died. Some had.

Direfang gestured to Grallik, who helped the priest up. Horace managed a whispered question: "Aneas and Kenosh?"

Grallik shook his head. "I've not seen them for too long a while." He sagged against the slope and looked at Direfang wearily. "We cannot go on, not without more rest. None of your brothers should travel either. We all need more sleep."

"And water," Horace said.

Grallik narrowed his eyes and stared grimly at the priest. In Steel Town, when the wells had dried up, the priests cast spells to provide water. Horace could do that. "Yes, water,"

Grallik whispered. He pointed to the empty jug that dangled from the rope belt around the priest's trousers.

Horace shook his head. "Not here. I'd be overrun by thirsty goblins. Besides, I haven't the energy. That magic requires some energy." The priest heaved himself forward, following Brak and Folami, nodding to Direfang as he went by. "The red-skinned goblin is right, Foreman Direfang. It would not be good to stay here. I promise I will create water for you soon. But not here. It wouldn't be safe here."

They traveled another full day before stopping. They shuffled along slowly at times, stumbling often, and some of them disappeared over the edge of one trail or another, or were left behind in the dark. No one tried to rescue their fallen fellows, though the lost were mourned. Sadly, their spirits would return to intact bodies to be trapped forever in some rocky crevice filled with ash. But they were too fatigued, too frightened, to stop and do anything about the lost.

Too many had fallen, their bodies never to be recovered, Direfang knew. How many had been suffocated by the ash? he wondered. How many had been burned to death? A good leader would have worked his way back along the column of goblins, boosting everyone's morale and keeping a list of the names of the dead so they could be honored in a proper ceremony.

So Direfang did not consider himself to be a good leader. But he was their leader nonetheless, and he served them by shuffling along and not stopping. If he let exhaustion claim him, if he stopped, the ones behind him would stop also. And if they all stopped, they might not ever move again.

He guessed it was night by the time they came down a cliff side and stood at the base of one more mountain. The air was definitely better there, and only a little ash covered the ground. The clouds were thinner overhead, stars glimmering through wisps and giving some hope to the dazed army. The goblins spilled out into a narrow valley and miserably looked up at the next mountain Mudwort intended for them to climb.

Direfang slumped against a stone outcropping, took a few deep breaths, and collapsed. Around him, other goblins fell. Even Mudwort surrendered to her tortured muscles and dropped down next to an already-snoring Spikehollow. Within minutes, not one of the surviving goblins and hobgoblins were awake.

33

GOLD FOR WATER

Grallik still raged against sleep, though. He searched the recesses of his mind for the spell that would let him brush away his overwhelming fatigue and feel as if he'd rested well for a long night. It was there in his memory . . . almost. He couldn't quite recapture the words and the gestures. He again cursed the loss of his spell tome.

"Horace," the wizard rasped. "Water. Call upon the blessed sea goddess to quench our thirst. The water the goblins had, the food, it's all gone. They lost it or ate it, and I am so terribly thirsty. I'd give you all the gold I've ever owned or will own for the smallest drink of water."

Indeed, Grallik's lips were dry and cracked. The skin on his arms and face not covered by the old fire scars was pocked from hot ash. He raised his fingers and discovered that his eyebrows were burned off. "Water, or we'll die . . . as surely as if we'd been caught in one of those rivers of lava."

Horace was on his knees, swaying and trying hard to

stay awake. His tongue was just as swollen and cracked, and he worked with parched lips to form words that refused to emerge. His fingers fumbled at his rope belt and he pulled the jug loose. Uncorking it, he finished the spell, then took a long pull from the jug, letting precious water run down his chin and neck before passing what was left to Grallik.

The wizard drank greedily, though he had intended to leave a little for the red-skinned goblin. He needed her to survive. If she died of thirst or from the heat, he was certain that all of his misery and suffering—leaving the Order and Steel Town, dragging Horace and Kenosh and Aneas on his treacherous path—would be for nothing.

Grallik turned to see Mudwort soundly sleeping. She wouldn't mind being woken up for a little refreshing water. He shuffled toward her, taking one more drink from the jug. Just one more tiny swallow, he told himself. Without thinking, however, he drained the last of the pure, sweet water, sucking on the lip of the jug to extract the final droplets.

Then he stoppered the jug and placed it near Horace. The water restored some of his energy, so he spent the next several minutes padding around the sleeping goblins in search of the two missing members of his talon. He found Kenosh, recognizing him only because he was a human amid a swarm of goblins. The hair Kenosh had left was in clumps, the places where his scalp was bare were burned. There were more burns on the man's chest, and little of his tabard was left.

At first Grallik thought he was dead because the knight was barely moving, but then he watched Kenosh's chest rise and fall faintly. He knelt and put his mouth to Kenosh's ear. "Brother Kenosh, my heart leaps to find you alive."

Kenosh opened one eye and tried to raise his head.

"No, no. Don't move. Just rest. Horace sleeps, and when he awakes, I'll have him tend your wounds." Grallik gingerly touched a gash on Kenosh's neck and sadly shook his head, looking around for the other. "Aneas . . . where is he?"

Kenosh opened his mouth and spit out grit. Wet ash was caked around his gums. "Dead one day ago, Guardian. He slipped on the trail, went over the side. He didn't even scream, Guardian." Kenosh coughed, closing his eyes. "He suffers no more."

The sky opened up sometime during the night, rain pounding down on the goblins, waking most of them up and rat-a-tat-tatting harshly against the surrounding stone and rocks. The rain refreshed Mudwort, pummeling her but washing away her coat of ash. She tipped her face up and opened her mouth, gulping as much water as she could and not caring that the force of the hard downpour was almost painful.

The waking goblins made joyful hoots and raised their arms and hands to the sky. They hugged each other and carried on, all of them drinking as much as they could with open mouths and filling their empty skins and jugs. Even the three surviving Dark Knights reveled in the intense summer storm. A rare smile played at the corners of Grallik's lips.

"Fair Zeboim, daughter and mother of the seas, we thank you for this gift of life-giving water," Horace prayed. When he was finished, he bathed in the puddles around him while uncorking his jug and letting the storm fill it to overflowing.

Direfang leaned against a natural stone column, wrapping his arms around it and feeling the water flow over him and the rock. He stuck out his tongue and took as much water as he could into his dry mouth. It didn't taste good, flavored with ash and stone dust that still clung to the clouds that hung overhead. But he and the others needed the water so badly, they drank and drank until their stomachs nearly burst.

"Hungry," he heard Spikehollow grumble.

"Later," Direfang said. "Find food later. Just drink and be happy that the Maws of Dragons did not eat everyone." As they had consumed so many in his army, he added mentally. So many dead and gone.

"Not all dead to the volcanoes," Spikehollow returned. "Hurbear's clan headed southwest, where the trail broke away. That clan took the wide trail, and some other goblins followed. Perhaps Hurbear's clan took the better way."

"Perhaps." Direfang shook his head and pointed to the peak that loomed above them. "Mudwort wants to go there now."

Spikehollow scratched at a spot on his cheek that had been burned from ash or rock. "Why climb another mountain, Direfang? Only climb up one side to go down the other. It would be easier just to go around mountain. Yes, going around is a better thing. Tell Mudwort. Make her understand."

Direfang closed his eyes and drank in some more rain. He listened to the goblins talking about lost friends and clan members, about being hungry, about the incredible displays of lava and steam that were still going on to the north. Some talked about being glad they were alive and away from Steel Town, saying they would continue to follow Direfang.

"Stay together and stay strong," Direfang answered Spikehollow. "Mudwort wants to climb this mountain, so we climb."

"Direfang leads the goblins, not Mudwort." Spikehollow snorted contemptuously. He, too, continued to drink in the rain.

The steady patter of rain muted the usual chatter of all the goblins. All the sounds swirled together pleasantly, as far as Direfang was concerned. Spikehollow continued to talk to him, but he only half listened. And he tried, once more, to look around the survivors and pick out familiar faces. The rain had washed the ash and dirt away, but everything was still a mix of grays and browns and scars and burns.

"Direfang!" Spikehollow stomped his foot irritably in a puddle.

"Mudwort must be listened to. Mudwort predicted the quakes," Direfang said softly. "Mudwort knew the mountains would break."

"Hope this next mountain does not break too," Spikehollow said ruefully, closing his eyes and leaning back against the mountain slope, pretending to sleep some more.

Direfang did not have to pretend. Sleep claimed him easily.

After hours had passed without the rain letting up, Direfang woke and made an attempt to take stock of what was left of his army. He could better see them that morning, after a night of rinsing and cleansing. Well, it felt like morning just because he finally could boast a good sleep, but he couldn't say for certain what time of the day it was. There were still only clouds overhead—gray rain clouds and grayer clouds of ash and whatever else the volcanoes had belched up from the earth. His lungs still burned, but the ache had lessened, so he knew all the other goblins and hobgoblins had to be feeling better too. He listened to their chatter, finding some hopeful messages in their conversation. But he also heard a grimness and sadness.

When they'd left Steel Town, there'd been well more than one thousand of them, possibly as many as two thousand. And though some had wandered away during the trek south, the hobgoblin still had more than one thousand following him. He guessed that at best there were five hundred left. Even given that some had gone with Hurbear and his clan, that meant that more than half had been lost to the volcanoes.

The journey toward the Plains of Dust had cost a high, high price.

To his surprise, it hadn't claimed Moon-eye and Gray-toes. Somehow the pair had managed to make it across crevices that other goblins had died trying to traverse. He watched Moon-eye still fawning over his mate, smoothing at her face and singing softly in her ear, the only song the one-eyed goblin knew.

> *Low sun in the warm valleys*
> *All goblins watch the orange sky*
> *Looking for shadows of ogres*
> *Knowing the time's come to die*

Direfang looked up and to the south, seeing through the gloom and rain the glowing, red-orange tops of the three volcanoes and rivers of lava still streaming down two of them. Steam rose up from the craters, the rain cooling the magma.

"All goblins watch the orange sky," he mused. "Knowing the time's come to die." He turned when he heard a scrabbling sound behind him. Mudwort was climbing a mountain path, not much of a path, more a trail for goats. Direfang looked at the ground at the base of the path, noting a circular worked stone, old and with ancient symbols carved in it.

"Don't think there's anything to eat up there," said a hobgoblin called Bug-biter, who had stolen up behind him. Barely past the youngling stage, she stood at his side, also watching Mudwort. "Not even bugs. The rain would have washed all the juicy bugs away. There's only tired legs to be had up there. Tired, tired legs and aching stomachs."

"Safety is up there," Direfang proclaimed, raising his voice and repeating himself loudly so all the goblins near him could hear and spread the word. "The Maws of Dragons continue to disgorge the fire." He pointed north. "Not safe here."

"Maybe it's not safe anywhere," Bug-biter snarled. Still, she lowered her eyes respectfully and nodded that she would follow Mudwort, who was already several yards ahead. Bug-biter let out a great sigh and nudged Brak to join her.

Brak did not move.

Bug-biter threw back her head and howled. "No more dead!" she shouted. "No more dead to the Maws of Dragons and the whips of Dark Knights. No more dead to an angry earth."

She dropped next to Brak, as did Direfang. Despite the rain that had rescued so many others, the hobgoblin was sorry to see the ash thick around Brak's unmoving lips and nose.

"Dead because there was no more air to breathe," Bug-biter said bitterly. She grabbed Brak's left arm and with a mighty tug tore it loose. "Don't want the spirit to come back here to this body." She tossed the arm away, then, with nary a backward glance, turned and climbed after Mudwort.

While most of the goblins were trudging up the trail, Direfang lingered with the three Dark Knights and a small group of goblins who didn't care to budge. He picked up a fist-sized rock and indicated that Grallik should stretch out his chains, then he began striking a link near the wizard's right wrist. After several blows, the link parted, and he worked on Grallik's ankle shackles. Next he turned to the priest's chains then handed the priest the rock and pointed to Kenosh.

Horace started hitting Kenosh's chains, his effort clumsy.

Direfang turned to a small group of goblins huddled together, who were reluctant to head up another mountain. "Safer up there," he insisted. "Above the rivers of fire and closer to good air. Probably no food." He would not lie to them. "Probably nothing at all up there but more rocks. But Mudwort says it's where we should go, and that is important."

One of the goblins crossed her spindly arms in front of her chest. "Tired of climbing, Direfang. Glad to be free, and glad to be alive. But tired of climbing. Why go up the mountain, only to slide down it again on the other side? Easier, Spikehollow says, to go around. Easier is better."

"But look, Spikehollow is climbing." Direfang pointed up the treacherous trail. The goblins were making their way around sharp spires that looked like teeth. "Spikehollow is not going around." He bent and plucked the stone out of the priest's hand and helped him hammer at Kenosh's chain. After a few solid whacks, Kenosh was free. "These men are not going around." He glared at the Dark Knights, daring them to disagree.

Direfang had not been speaking in the Common tongue, so they didn't know what he had said. But Grallik guessed well enough at the meaning and, with a deep sigh, he turned and started up the trail. Kenosh was slow to follow him.

"Skull man?" Direfang spoke in the human language.

Horace ran his fingers over the top of his head and let out a whistling sound between his clenched teeth. "I am not a man built for this ordeal, Foreman Direfang. But I have managed to make it this far. If you want us all to visit Godshome, fine. Just don't expect me to be fast about it."

"Godshome?"

"Aye, Foreman Direfang, that is where the little red-skinned goblin is leading you." The priest took a despairing look up the mountainside, brushed at the burned spots on his trousers, and gamely started moving. "Godshome. A place I suspect no one has visited for more than a long time."

The goblins gathered at the base debated vigorously

among themselves. Then one or two started after the knights with the rest quickly but grudgingly following behind.

"Godshome." Direfang did not like the sound of the place. He didn't care for Krynn's gods because Krynn's gods had never cared for goblinkind. He took one last look around the narrow valley, spotting a soft, orange glow in the distance and wondering if the rivers of fire were coming after them.

"Safer up higher," he told himself. "Safer at Godshome."

34

GODSHOME

It took more than a day to reach the top of the mountain. After a few hours, the rain had turned into a soothing drizzle, and the drizzle didn't stop until long hours after that. At times groups of goblins rested because someone's legs gave out. Direfang carried one of the smaller goblins who'd been reluctant to climb. The knee and ankle of her left leg were swollen, and the hobgoblin said he would ask the priest to mend her ailments once they were at the top.

Direfang kept a vigilant watch to the north, observing the volcanoes. One was still erupting. How could there possibly be any fire and melting rock left inside the earth? he wondered. In the far distance, at the very edge of his vision, he saw more glowing mountains. Six in all, he counted.

Certainly nothing could remain of Steel Town, and the ogre village was also gone, destroyed. Perhaps all the ogre villages in that northern part of the Khalkist range had been obliterated. Had Jelek been swallowed too?

So traveling north might have been no safer, Direfang mused. Just as many in his army—perhaps all in his army—

would have died if he'd chosen that direction instead. It buoyed his spirits a little to think that heading toward the Plains of Dust might have been the wise course after all.

But climbing the mountain they were on . . .

Once Direfang reached the top, he was convinced Spikehollow was right. They should have walked around it instead.

It looked as though the top of the mountain had been smoothly hacked off by a sword—a wide rim surrounded a bowl-shaped depression. And at the bottom of the depression sat a pool of black rock, polished like a shiny mirror and reflecting all the constellations of the summer night sky.

Well, at least they were far enough from the Maws of Dragons and the rivers of fire that they were safe—safe from those dangers, at least. There'd be other dangers, of course.

It might not even be night, Direfang mused. The clouds were still so thick, the sun or moons could not be glimpsed through the gray dark. But if the sky could not be seen, how could the black mirror reflect all the stars back?

A shudder passed from the top of his head to his toes, as he stared at the star formations twinkling up from the mirror surface of the black rock. The goblins around him were silent, spent from the climb, hungry again, captivated and frightened by the sky as reflected in the mountaintop basin. Not one of his five hundred followers spoke a single word. It was as if they were collectively holding their breath. All Direfang heard was the low whistle of the wind and distant *boom* of one volcano, along with the quickened beating of his heart.

He looked around for Mudwort but didn't see her standing on the rim. Could she have fallen somewhere along the trail and no one noticed? No, he spotted her climbing down into the basin, following a staircase made of circular stones similar to the unusual stones he'd noticed at the base of the mountain. Someone, some folk, had marked the trail and that spot long ago. He watched her pick her way down, the path arduous because the steps had been made for someone with much longer legs.

No one followed her, though most watched her. When she reached the bottom, she looked up and locked eyes with Direfang, her gaze lingering on him before moving on to the wizard. She stared at the spellcasting knight for a long moment before turning back to the basin and stepping out onto the black stone polished like a mirror.

She padded out onto the center of the mirrored basin, the stars seeming to dance all around her.

After many minutes of moving around and exploring, Mudwort sat down in the constellation of Morgion, not for any particular reason other than the star pattern looked pretty and was near the exact center of the basin. She didn't know what Morgion was the god of, and she had no desire to learn. She only knew a little about some of the gods and was not aware that all of them had constellations named for them. Indeed, if Mudwort had known in advance that the place was called Godshome, she would have resisted the tug that brought her there.

She had no regard for the gods, practically held them in contempt for ignoring and oppressing her race. Worse, while ignoring goblins and hobgoblins, the gods had bolstered the other races of Krynn—the Dark Knights who enslaved and tyrannized the goblins, the ogres and minotaurs who caught and sold them, the draconians and centaurs who looked upon them as rats to be eaten or bugs to be stepped on and pushed aside.

In short, the gods had conspired against the goblins, creatures they themselves supposedly had created.

THE REBELLION

"Mudwort does not need the gods, and the gods do not need Mudwort," she murmured to herself. "Yesterday heard the skull man call this place Godshome. But no god lives here now, I think. And only one goblin sits in the stars. One goblin uses the magic in this place." She thumped her chest and thrust out her chin. "Only one goblin is with the stars."

Mudwort had heard and smelled the magic of that place back in the ogre village when she touched hands with Moon-eye and scried into the ground. That place tugged at her senses, teasing her with images of the basin and the stars that glittered always, even during the daytime. It had been too powerful of a lure for her to resist, so she'd urged Direfang to follow her and bring his diminishing army.

Moon-eye had marveled at the vision of Godshome too, asking her what "it" was. She'd told him she didn't know because, in truth, she hadn't, not at that moment.

But she knew that the place possessed power.

She was there selfishly, not to help Direfang or the rest of the refugee slaves, but only to sate her own curiosity. She'd never seen or dreamed of such a place, and when it called to her as she sat and spoke to the earth in that ogre village, she knew she had to answer its call. Mudwort wanted the others there merely for company and safety, realizing the security the army gave her. After the goblins and hobgoblins had slaughtered the once-feared ogres so quickly, she knew the army was good protection, even in their dwindling numbers.

If she'd come there alone, it might have been too dangerous. One goblin alone might not stand up to the power of that place.

Mudwort stared into the black surface, seeing her face reflected and haloed by stars. There, she was not an ugly rat. There, she was beautiful, her eyes gleaming and wide. Above all, there she felt strength and power. There was mysterious energy in the shiny dark surface of the basin—not the kind that led to earthquakes or volcano eruptions, but old, old energy of the sort present when the world was born.

Her heart racing, Mudwort placed her hands flat against the mirror black rock and let her senses flow into it.

The surface was at the same time icy cold and scalding hot, the wildly extreme temperatures constantly alternating and making her feel dizzy. She wanted to recoil from the sensation. She'd already suffered so much in the past handful of days. She did not want to sustain any more pain. And yet she forced herself to remain calm. The surface did not hurt her anywhere else except on the palms of her hands—not on her legs, which were stretched out wide, nor her heels, nor anywhere else on her body. Only her hands and fingers felt the violent shifts in extreme temperatures.

Perhaps it meant something, the temperature changes, Mudwort reflected, leaning forward and holding her face near the surface of the black mirrored stone. Perhaps the earth spoke there in a way that was new to her. Maybe the shifts in hot and cold were some sort of old language. So she accepted the agony of the wild-ranging heat and cold, gritting her teeth and trying hard not to cry out. She focused intently on the glittering surface of the rock, trying to push her senses beneath the ground. She was focusing so hard, she didn't notice Moon-eye and Graytoes approach.

Other goblins, too, had wended their way down the stone steps, and the three Dark Knights as well, but only Moon-eye and a reluctant Graytoes had actually breached the surface of the basin, gingerly moving toward Mudwort.

"Moon-eye's Heart will be safe here," the one-eyed goblin whispered to Graytoes. "Moon-eye and Mudwort saw this place when looking into the dirt at the ogre village. Didn't know what it was then, only that it was interesting. Don't know what it is now. But still, interesting." Moon-eye tugged his mate down next to him, sitting across from Mudwort, who only then looked up and registered their presence.

"Saw this place in the ogre village," Moon-eye repeated.

Mudwort nodded. Her hands trembled, so affected were they by the intense heat and cold. She wanted to pull them free, but she found she couldn't. It was as if the palms of her hands had fused to the glossy surface. She opened her mouth to plead to the goblin couple for help, but no sound emerged.

Moon-eye laid his hands opposite hers, fingers touching as they had under the earth in the ogre village. He threw back his head, as if to howl in pain, but he couldn't make any sound either.

After a moment more, the hot and cold vanished. They felt nothing against their hands.

The stone beneath their skin was smooth and the same temperature as the rest of their bodies or the air. All traces of the pain they had felt were also banished. Mudwort looked both relieved and disappointed. There had been magic deep in the stone and inside the pain, and it was gone!

"Together, like in the village?" Moon-eye looked quizzically at her then nudged her fingers when she didn't answer. "Like before? Please. Use the magic together."

Mudwort glanced up, noting the goblins and hobgoblins keeping their distance on the steps. Direfang was still at the top, on the rim of the mountain. The Dark Knight called Kenosh was halfway down the steps and holding fast to a stone post that looked carved, not natural. The Dark Knight wizard and the skull man were at the edge of the basin, both staring, trying to decide but not yet stepping in her direction.

"Maybe the skull man and the wizard need permission," said Moon-eye, noticing that Mudwort was watching the Dark Knights. "Slaves now, the skull man and the wizard must do as Direfang wants."

Then Mudwort looked back at him, locking eyes with Moon-eye. "Together," the red-skinned goblin finally said. "See what is beneath this rock, what is in it, and what it is about."

Moon-eye gave her a lopsided grin as Graytoes wrapped her hands around her mate's arm, cradling close, staring at Mudwort. "Careful," Graytoes mouthed to Mudwort. "Be careful with Graytoes' Heart."

Mudwort felt the stone tingle beneath her, so faint it could almost have been her tired mind playing tricks. It was different than the precursor trembling of the earthquakes or the volcanoes erupting. There was no anger in the sensation that she could detect. But there was a peculiar rhythm to the tingling, like a pulse or someone inhaling and exhaling. The air stirred as if the very basin were breathing deeply. She'd not noticed a breeze before, not down there in the hollow.

Words . . . there were words flowing in the air. Mudwort couldn't understand the strange words, could hardly hear them, but they were there all the same. The susurrus drew her senses down to the shiny black stone and up to the stars.

Moon-eye flew with her.

In their minds' eyes, they looked down from the summit of the mountain, seeing a half dozen volcanoes still glowing to the north, all with ribbons of lava streaming from them. Two continued to erupt, the rivers of fire wide and threatening and filling the valley between spines in the Khalkists. Concentrating their effort, they looked farther to the north, to the place that used to be Steel Town. Only the mountain where they'd once mined ore could be recognized as a familiar landmark. The rest was devastation. They saw not a single stone or man from the camp. The ground was covered by dried magma, a sheet of wrinkled, bubbled blackness. Farther north and to the west, the wasted land stretched. Roads once used by many merchants and the Dark Knights were gone.

To the east stretched more destruction. Hardened lava flows covered scrubland and most of a once-busy merchant route. Horses had been caught in the lava flow, and men too, making strange trapped figures. Mudwort imagined that they'd died fast and horribly, as had so very, very many goblins.

"Lost too many goblins," Mudwort muttered. "Lost not enough men."

"Too many goblins," Moon-eye agreed, sharing her opinion. "Left with a small army now."

Mudwort looked to the south. "Direfang wants to go to the Plains of Dust, wherever that is. Together look there."

"Plains of Dust," Moon-eye said, having learned its name. He squeezed his good eye shut and drew his features together tightly. "See the Plains of Dust. Together."

The air around them stirred again, stronger, bringing more words that none of the three goblins in the center of the mirrored basin could understand. The breeze blew warmer, though not uncomfortably so, and the floor of the basin tingled with a more pronounced rhythm. Other sounds could be heard behind them, goblins and hobgoblins chattering, some curiously and nervously edging down and out onto the basin.

Grallik watched with fascination. He looked up at Direfang, hoping for permission to approach the red-skinned goblin, but the hobgoblin was too far away and not paying any attention to him. The wizard took a deep breath and stepped forward.

35

STONETELLING

Mudwort said there is magic in Moon-eye," Graytoes said, encouraging her mate, alternately looking at him, the goblins venturing closer, and the reflected stars in the mirrored basin. "Use that magic, Moon-eye. See the Plains of Dust."

The landscape Mudwort and Moon-eye looked down upon evanesced, and in its place the Khalkist Mountains rose into view. They flew above the highest peaks, whizzing so fast to the south that the range became a blur of grays and browns.

Graytoes gasped. In the gap between Moon-eye and Mudwort, the field of stars shimmered and revealed the mountains. Graytoes squeezed Moon-eye's arm proudly.

The mountains whisked by and gave way to swampland, a riot of greens the likes of which none of the goblins hovering around them had ever seen. Millions of lizards, practically invisible with protective coloration, darted from under spreading ferns. Vines dotted with large red and purple blooms hung from thick forests of trees as tall as hills. There was water everywhere, most of it covered with a green film and hazes of insects. Mudwort could practically taste the brackishness and smell the loamy sod of the place.

Farther south their vision journeyed, finding a wide game trail that led through the heart of the swamp and past the ruins of a thatch village. Numerous parrots with bright plumage lined the tree branches there, taking flight when the snakes and monkeys came too close. Crocodiles and pangolin lined the banks of rivers. Everywhere insects clouded.

The buzz of goblin talk was drowned out in the ears of Mudwort and Moon-eye by the buzzing of the insect swarms and the growls of hidden creatures not reflected in the basin. They flew farther south, and the jungle finally thinned into a lush, green plain that stretched toward distant hills and woods.

"Said Moon-eye had magic, see? Mudwort was right. Moon-eye *is* magic." Graytoes beamed with pride at her mate, then switched her gaze to Mudwort and again mouthed, "Be careful."

Mudwort stared at the images reflected in the black stone, searching for people and creatures that could do harm to goblins. If that was where Direfang wanted to go, she wanted to make sure they weren't being led into a place as misery-wrought as Neraka and Steel Town had been. She and Moon-eye spiraled upward, observing more of the land from a higher vantage point. There were villages and bands of centaurs and trails wide enough to accommodate wagons.

So there was plenty of land in the Plains of Dust, but it was not a vacant place. The two scrying goblins continued to spiral outward, searching, searching. Moon-eye somehow knew that Mudwort was looking for other goblins. Eventually they located a small band, hunting hares in a copse of birch trees. Later, they discovered a lone goblin hiding out for some purpose at the base of a big black willow.

"Always goblins are hunted," Moon-eye said.

The goblins around them nodded in agreement.

"Direfang says no more," Mudwort returned sharply. "Hurbear and Direfang, and later Saro-Saro, too, talked about a nation of goblins in the Plains of Dust. Said there was plenty of room for goblins there. There is room and food and water."

"Room for a nation." Direfang had finally come down into the basin and joined them, standing close behind the three goblins, gingerly shifting his weight back and forth on the balls of his feet as if the surface were glass and he might crash through. He stood directly behind Mudwort, staring over her and at the images reflected between her and Moon-eye.

Only one spectator stared at something else. Grallik's gaze was fixed on the red-skinned goblin's twitching fingers and on Moon-eye's, where the two goblins touched hands. Together, they had cast some remarkable spell or managed to work some enchantment that neither could accomplish alone.

"How is that possible?" Grallik breathed.

No one answered his question; few heard. They were all staring at the vision in the basin, which was shifting again.

"Where look?" Moon-eye understood that Mudwort was not content with exploring only the Plains of Dust and had moved on.

Mudwort shrugged, not answering at first. "Elsewhere," she said finally. "Look elsewhere until sleep calls."

So, together, they worked the magic of Godshome for hours, discovering remote places of Krynn that likely held no predators for goblins but likewise offered nothing to entice them to settle there. They visited Icewall and lingered to scrutinize the strange walrus people with spears. They looked far, far north where deserts were so white they looked snow-covered and where blue dragons hunted and laired. They crossed a sea and spotted islands far too populated with humans and minotaurs, and they witnessed incredible, tall-masted ships manned by men as dark skinned as the priest.

Most of the others watched patiently, in silence and awe. The Dark Knights never wavered. Some goblins drifted back up and out of the basin. A few began to doze.

They saw a land one goblin near Moon-eye called Northern Ergoth, a rugged land teeming in parts with goblins.

"*Sikkei'Hul,*" Mudwort said, using the goblin tongue. Somehow she, too, knew the name of the place. The goblins there looked organized and fierce, muscular, and they didn't exhibit the whip marks and insignia of slaves. "Warriors," she pronounced them. Then she shifted her vision again.

"The army of Ankhar." Mudwort didn't know the land she looked at, but she heard a nearby goblin whisper "Est-wilde" and saw a band of goblins chasing down Solamnic Knights.

The scene shifted again and again. Finally they saw a forest.

"Qualinesti," Grallik said, putting a name to the place. He stood close behind Direfang, who frowned and raised an eyebrow as if suddenly reminded of the wizard's existence.

"This place," Direfang said, "holds itself familiar to Grallik, yes?"

The wizard nodded, returning his attention to Mudwort and Moon-eye's partnered fingers. "Aye, the forest is familiar to me. Long ago familiar. I lived there once."

Mudwort and Moon-eye slowed their voyage through the woods of Qualinesti, finding small settlements of elves on the coast and the ruins of elven villages toward the heart of the land. Water and game appeared plentiful, and the ground undoubtedly could support whatever crops they wanted to grow.

It seemed empty compared to the other places they'd looked at.

Something about the place struck a chord with Mudwort, and she felt her senses reach out and dip deep below the basin. The sights, sounds, and smells she picked up exploring the Qualinesti trees were heady and overwhelming, and she wrapped herself in the experience and wondered if the place appealed to Moon-eye as much as it appealed to her. Was Moon-eye sharing all her feelings? Did any of the other goblins understand what they were seeing or share her regard?

She thought about the goblins, noticing Direfang and Spikehollow standing nearby on the basin, Saro-Saro with them. It was as though she studied them from a distant point far, far away. There was Moon-eye and Graytoes too, and she saw herself, also. Nearly all of the goblins wore astonished, exhausted expressions—but there'd been no change, subtle or dramatic, in their awestruck expressions since she'd plunged into the Qualinesti wilds and felt the surprising euphoria.

So they were not feeling what she was feeling, not even Moon-eye. She thrust her mind away from the mountain and deeper into the place Grallik had called the Qualinesti Forest. She could hear him, faintly, over her shoulder, talking about the forest, answering Direfang's questions. She half paid attention to what he was saying—in case he knew something that might prove valuable to her.

Grallik said that the elves had abandoned that nation, once their homeland, that a great green dragon had conquered them and chased them away. They had slain the dragon but fled.

She listened to other voices, too, none of them from goblins she recognized and none of them talking about the

Qualinesti Forest. They were goblins whispering as though from far away, goblins scattered in the lands that her mind had visited. They were talking about food and shelter and the heat of the sun. One talked of a mate she'd recently lost.

"Who is there?" one of the spirit-goblins asked.

"Mudwort. Just Mudwort passing through." Mudwort didn't speak those words; they were only thoughts in her mind, but clearly the faraway goblin heard and understood her and answered.

"Mudwort? Where is Mudwort?"

Startled, Mudwort continued moving, fearing if she stopped to converse with the mysterious unseen goblin, the magic of the place might melt away and she'd be forced to stop.

Searching intently again, deeper down in the earth, she noted the earth—bones of long dead creatures, the husks of insects, thick tree roots, forgotten cellars and pits, and more.

Was she still in the Qualinesti Forest? Had she traveled somewhere else? Mudwort didn't know where her senses had taken her without physically leaving Godshome. Her searching was so intense, she hadn't realized another goblin had joined her and Moon-eye. His name was Boliver, and he spread his fingers out to touch those of the other two goblins. Boliver'd helped her days past in Steel Town. Together, they'd willed the dirt to move beneath the wall of fire so a goblin named Twitch and a few others could escape. Boliver had survived the death march of the army and was beside her now.

"Goblins in the village named Boliver Shaman," Boliver told her.

Faintly she heard Boliver speaking to her. A part of her mind was pulled back to Godshome.

"Talk to the stones, sometimes," Boliver added. "Like

Mudwort do. Shaman, the goblins of home clan said. Stone-teller, some named Boliver."

Mudwort preferred to ignore Boliver, but he was trying to help. And in that instant she felt the power of Godshome coursing through her, more than before. Everything suddenly came clearly into focus.

Her mind was still in the Qualinesti Forest. And there was magic in the old forest of the elves. It was one of the true places of power in the world, of secrets in the bosom of the earth.

Godshome was another such place, where the eldritch energy was so vibrant.

But the Qualinesti Forest was perhaps more powerful —she didn't know. All she knew was that she wanted to go there.

The power of Godshome could not be hers. But the power in the Qualinesti Forest, it was something different and perhaps obtainable. Her mind continued to search, coming close, closer, yet never close enough to what she craved.

"Need to be in that forest," she whispered to herself. "In that forest, it can be found, the magic." Louder, she called out to all surrounding her. "The Qualinesti Forest, Direfang!" The excitement in her voice was palpable to all who listened and spread with murmurs and whispering.

"The forest?" Direfang asked, prodding her shoulder, but that was a mistake. Instantly Mudwort's mind was ripped away from the vision of the Qualinesti Forest, and she found herself wholly back to reality, back in the basin, her fingers briefly unloosed from those of Moon-eye and Boliver.

She shook her head and rolled her shoulders, and by her expression let Direfang know that she was not pleased with his stupid interruption of her vision, even after all those hours.

THE REBELLION

"The Qualinesti Forest, Direfang. That is the place for a goblin nation. Not the Plains of Dust." She shook out her hands and crossed her arms in front of her chest irritably. "There are goblins in that forest and goblins elsewhere. Goblins on an island with a stairway of great energy—saw that. Goblins everywhere, scattered. Weak, most are."

Moon-eye pulled his hands back and hugged Graytoes. "Yes, goblins all over the world," he boasted. "Saw the goblins, Direfang, heard the goblins. Those goblins can be called."

"And added to this nation," Boliver chimed in.

"Through stone," Mudwort said. "Talking through the stone, this stone, any stone, the goblins can be called to the Qualinesti Forest. There to form a nation."

Moon-eye stood and pulled Graytoes up close to him.

Graytoes nodded. "It is up to Direfang to build the goblin nation."

The hobgoblin looked up to the western rim of Godshome. Right then there was a break in the clouds, a soft, orange glow spilling through. The glow wasn't reflected fire or lava. It was the sun setting. He remembered Moon-eye's song:

> *Low sun in the warm valleys*
> *All goblins watch the orange sky*
> *Looking for shadows of ogres*
> *Knowing the time's come to die*

"It can be done, this nation."

His own words only mildly surprised the hobgoblin. Direfang recalled from days earlier his conversation with Hurbear, and wondered if the old goblin had made it through the volcanoes. "A nation of goblins. Yes, it can be done."

36

MOON-EYE'S REVELATION

The goblins and hobgoblins worked their way up from the Godshome basin, buzzing among themselves about forging a nation in the old land of the Qualinesti elves, one where every other race would leave them alone. Direfang was one of the first to leave the magical rock, picking up Graytoes and looking at Moon-eye, then pointing to the stairway.

The one-eyed goblin lingered at the edge of the basin. "Catch up," he said to his mate and the hobgoblin. "Want to touch this again, look through it again. Experience the magic. Want to one more time. Be quick, catch up, promise."

Graytoes looked to Mudwort, who rolled her eyes. Graytoes sighed, wrapping her arms around Direfang's neck. "Not stay long, Moon-eye. Days and days and days walk to the forest."

"Not long." Moon-eye waggled his fingers at the pair and sat back down on the mirror black surface, fingers outstretched and mind searching. He vaguely registered

Graytoes calling to him again, telling him to hurry and not to get lost in the magic.

He heard Mudwort call to him too, saying there were plenty of other places of power in the world that they could explore another day. Moon-eye was surprised that the red-skinned goblin was letting him tarry alone at that wondrous place. But the air was still filled with sulfur and ash, and perhaps Mudwort wanted to start the journey to Qualinesti as soon as possible. That was all right with Moon-eye. He'd be quick.

"Yes, hurry!" Moon-eye called. "Not long. Just one more look."

But he had trouble using the magic of Godshome without Mudwort's help. Indeed, he almost gave up when nothing happened right away and he glanced over his shoulder and saw the last of the goblins crest the top of the crater. Saro-Saro and Krumb were at the tail end of the line, the old goblin looking down at him, shaking his head, and gesturing to hurry.

Then, suddenly, Saro-Saro was looking up at Moon-eye because Moon-eye was up in the sky looking down on him. The one-eyed goblin blinked furiously and rolled his shoulders, worriedly withdrew his fingers, and stared down at the vision in the mirror black basin. There it was. The image of Saro-Saro had somehow appeared on the surface of the magical stone.

Of course! Moon-eye thought. He'd seen Saro-Saro at the top, and so was concentrating on the venerable goblin clan leader. And because he was concentrating, an image of Saro-Saro appeared in the basin. He had much to learn about the magic.

"Like the magic," Moon-eye purred. "Love the magic." He replaced his fingers on the surface, feeling his skin turn instantly ice cold, then fiery hot. It took him a few minutes to manage the painful sensations. Then his mind plunged into the earth, searching . . . searching.

He clamped his teeth together and thought about the forest. And just like that, Qualinesti appeared again, though not quite as clear and vibrant as when he and Mudwort were working together. Moon-eye knew the red-skinned goblin had a better command of magic, and he hoped she would teach him some of her wisdom. The air smelled better the more he focused on the forest, as if his nose had poked through the basin, down through the earth, and up into the sky, and had traveled to Qualinesti and was deep into the woods.

A trace of flowers, he smelled. Almost too sweet, he thought. Moon-eye was not used to smelling such good things. The earth had its own odor there too, rich and redolent but neither pleasant nor unpleasant. He listened hard, hearing the squawk of many, many parrots, the growl of something that might have been a big cat, and the shush of leaves rubbing against each other, as if a wind were blowing through the forest.

He could have lingered in the elf forest a long while, he thought; it would be easy to spend a long, happy time there. But Moon-eye needed to hurry to get back to Graytoes, and he wanted to talk to Mudwort about the new things he was seeing.

As he thought of the red-skinned goblin, the forest disappeared. Moon-eye was instantly disappointed, but then Mudwort's face sprang up in his mind—and on the mirror black stone—just as Saro-Saro's had. Mudwort tipped her head up, as if she were searching the sky to find a break in the clouds. She walked behind Direfang and next to Boliver.

"Magic in Boliver too," Mudwort explained to the hobgoblin leader. Boliver's face loomed large on the mirror black surface between Moon-eye's spread legs. The goblin's lips moved, and a heartbeat later, Moon-eye heard his words.

THE REBELLION

"Long way to the forest," Boliver told Mudwort, sounding surprisingly cheerful. "Legs will ache. Stomach will ache. Worth it, though, in the end. Free in the forest."

"Free," Mudwort replied wistfully. "Slaves never, ever again."

Not far behind them, Grallik and the other Dark Knights trudged wearily. The eyes of the wizard never left the hobgoblin leader and the red-skinned goblin shaman. Grallik could scarcely believe his own fate. He had left the knighthood behind forever and had joined the goblin army. He had cast his future with the strange magic of the goblins.

How many goblins had magic inside of them, Moon-eye wondered. Boliver and Mudwort and himself. Others? Not Direfang, but the hobgoblin didn't need magic. He was strong and smart, and that was why he was commander of the goblin army—no, the goblin nation, Moon-eye corrected himself.

How many other goblins could work magic? When Moon-eye thought about the army, a blur of faces rushed past him, most of them yammering or yawning, too many words to pick through.

"Shouldn't be listening anyway," the goblin decided. "Words aren't spoken to Moon-eye. Moon-eye shouldn't be listening. Bad manners."

He thought he'd peek at Graytoes one more time, seeing her cradled in Direfang's arms. He knew he would never tire of looking at her beautiful face and wide, kind eyes. But, he reminded himself, it was better to look at her in person, not in the magic stone. He needed to leave the basin and catch up to the column. Graytoes would be worrying about him.

How far ahead of him had the army gotten?

With that thought, the vision in the basin shifted, and Moon-eye saw Saro-Saro and Krumb trailing a little behind the rest of the line. He intended to move away from that image to something more interesting, so he could see where the ex-slaves were right then. But something he saw riveted his attention.

Saro-Saro was speaking softly to Krumb, and the other goblin was leaning very close to hear, their brows knitted together and noses twitching. They were sharing a secret.

"More words not meant for Moon-eye. Bad manners to listen." Still, he reflected, it would be fun to listen for just a moment, just a brief moment. Then he would leave the wonderful, magical basin and catch up with Graytoes and surprise Saro-Saro and Krumb with his knowledge of their secret. "What saying Saro-Saro? What is secret? What saying Krumb?"

Moon-eye, like many of his kind, was a curious fellow.

"Saro-Saro should lead." Krumb's voice was scratchy, as though there were something caught in his throat, and even with the magic, Moon-eye had trouble hearing all the whispered words. "Saro-Saro should lead the goblin nation."

Saro-Saro nodded, and the old goblin's lips crept up in a sly smile. "Smarter than Direfang, certainly." He thumped his thumb against his chest. "Would do things differently. Do things much better. Not let so many goblins die and starve."

Krumb made a snuffling sound and rubbed his hands together. "Direfang would build a peaceful nation, probably. Make goblins into hunters and farmers and nut gatherers. He is weary of fighting, I heard him say. Weary of fighting, bah!"

"Goblins should be raiders," Saro-Saro said, agreeing, but gesturing for Krumb to lower his voice. "Killers and slavers."

"Slavers." Krumb's dark eyes glistened. His eyes flicked ahead to the human slaves. "And killers, yes. Strong goblins."

Saro-Saro said something else that Moon-eye couldn't hear until the goblin leaned closer to the surface and put his ear to the black stone itself, to the very image of the old one.

". . . kill Direfang," Saro-Saro said. Moon-eye had missed the early part of his declaration. "When the hobgoblin sleeps. With the Dark Knight knife." Saro-Saro carried just such a knife at his waist, Moon-eye saw, a weapon belted on with a strip of cloth that he'd scavenged from the ogre village. The pommel matched the color of the tabard he'd fashioned from an ogre child's shirt. "Can be done, Krumb. In the old days, the one who killed the king became king. Can be done."

"When the time is right," Krumb whispered, nodding. "When Direfang is no longer useful. The mad one too."

"Mudwort," Moon-eye said. "Direfang and Mudwort."

In horror, the one-eyed goblin pulled back from his magical scrying and scrambled to his feet in the mirror black basin. "My friends are in trouble." He felt hot and dizzy, the magic of Godshome tingling through him. He tried to shake it off and start up the rise but walked as though tipsy.

He was halfway to the top before his senses cleared, and he saw no sign of the goblins along the ridge of the mountaintop. Panic gripped him. Had they left him too far behind? He felt his throat tighten, instantly worrying about Graytoes.

How long had he been playing with the magic in the crater? The goblins couldn't have gotten too far ahead, could they?

The sky was still gray and the world in shadows, so Graytoes and Direfang probably weren't able to see to the end of the column. They would think he was marching with them. They wouldn't realize that Moon-eye had not yet caught up.

"Moon-eye's Heart," the one-eyed goblin sighed. "Must hurry. Must warn Direfang and Mudwort." He scampered along the rim of the mountaintop, his fears giving him a surge of energy. "Must tell Direfang about Saro-Saro."

He hurried down a trail he found on the southern slope of Godshome, certain the army had traveled that way and confirming it by taking a pinch of dirt in his fingers and sniffing it for goblin smells. He tripped in his race down the trail, head over feet, and bruised his ribs before picking himself up and gulping dusty air. He smelled the ash still thick in the air, though it was not nearly so strong there as it had been on the other side of Godshome. He smelled blood—his own—and dirt. But the scent of goblins was strongest.

"Not too far behind," he told himself. He peered far ahead, believing he saw a goblin start up another rise, and well ahead of that goblin must be the tail end of the ex-slave army. "Someone else slow." Moon-eye was thankful for that.

A few more deep lungfuls of dusty air, and he was off at a clip, though more careful than before because he didn't want to trip and fall and lose time. There were clumps of grass here and there, not all of them brown, and the dirt was thicker along the trail, almost mud, helping to cushion the soles of his feet. He covered ground so fast that he drew close to the straggler, still far behind the rest of the goblin army. As he came up to the fellow, he spotted two birds in the sky.

"The land is better here," Moon-eye said to himself. "Not so angry and not belching fire." He thought that when he and Graytoes had another child, there would be wondrous stories to pass down to their younglings about their great escape from Steel Town in the midst of an earthquake, and about their victorious battle with the ogres, and all the volcanoes erupting and painting the sides of the mountains with their shiny red ribbons of fire. "Such stories."

It was several long moments more before Moon-eye caught up with the last goblin, who had stopped to wait for him.

"Spikehollow!" Moon-eye stopped, leaning forward, hands on his knees and sides heaving. "Spikehollow waited?"

The young goblin nodded, coming up to him and clapping a hand on Moon-eye's shoulder. "Worried, some were. Afraid the magic of that place might swallow Moon-eye. Almost gave up, but saw Moon-eye running down the mountain. Waited a little, and walked slow. And now together."

Moon-eye continued to gulp in air. "Liked the magic," he admitted. "Liked it almost too much." Then he stood and stared into the other goblin's eyes. "You, Direfang's friend." He touched Spikehollow's chest. "Direfang is in danger. Listen. The magic told me something . . ."

The pair stayed on the trail, letting the rest of the army reach the top of the next rise. Moon-eye told Spikehollow everything—about seeing Saro-Saro and Krumb, listening to them conspire, about the pair planning to murder Mudwort and Direfang and turn the army into a force of killers and slavers.

"Certain this is true?" Spikehollow looked skeptical of Moon-eye's vision. "Certain not dreaming? Magic and dreams, same sometimes, different other times. Maybe Moon-eye breathe too much of the volcano dust? Mind turn sour."

Moon-eye shook his head so hard his entire body seemed to shake along with it. "No, no dream. The magic tells the truth. Direfang is in danger."

Spikehollow nodded. "All right. Must hurry, then." He pointed a thin finger up the trail, telling Moon-eye to go ahead of him.

The sky was a little lighter over the next rise, the cloud

cover thinner. The pair could spot the last few goblins only a few miles ahead of them. They would have to hurry.

Moon-eye took in one more deep breath. "Yes, hurry now." He brushed by Spikehollow and started off at a jog. He wasn't as quick as he'd hoped, but his ribs hurt and his legs ached, and he was terribly tired. "Hurry, hurry. Hurry and—"

A sharp pain in his back suddenly competed with the rest of Moon-eye's miseries. He glanced over his shoulder just as the pain repeated itself again and again. It was the greatest hurt the one-eyed goblin had ever suffered. Spikehollow stood behind him, holding one of the knives that had been stolen from Steel Town.

Moon-eye tried to speak, to ask Spikehollow why he had stabbed him, but he couldn't get a single word out of his choked, burning mouth. His throat was filling with blood, and his back felt on fire. His chest burned too, where Spikehollow had whirled him around and stabbed him yet again.

"Saro-Saro should lead the goblin nation," Spikehollow said grimly. "A nation of wolves, it will be, Moon-eye. Not a nation of sheep."

Spikehollow hissed other things through clenched teeth, but Moon-eye couldn't hear his words. There was a great rush of sound in his ears, like the rapids of a river. Then the one-eyed goblin collapsed on the trail and died.

Spikehollow reached down and cut off one of Moon-eye's fingers, hurling it away so the goblin's spirit could never return to the body. He briefly considered hiding Moon-eye's corpse or pushing it over the side and hoping animals below would discover it and eat it. But he was in a hurry, and he was also stupid, so he loped off in the direction of Saro-Saro and Krumb and the rest of the goblins, proud of what he had done. None of them would be coming back that way, Spikehollow was certain, so Moon-eye would never be found. They would imagine he was following after them and would catch up, but that would never happen.

The goblin wiped at the blood spatters on his arm as he moved ahead. He took in great gulps of air and tried to ignore the pain in his feet from traveling so far over the biting rocks. Spikehollow knew his feet and legs—and all of him—would only hurt more before they stopped. The Qualinesti Forest was quite some distance from there, or so Saro-Saro had told him.

Spikehollow's smile turned into a predator's grin. He would have plenty of time to rest in the forest. All of Saro-Saro's army would rest there before joining together and embarking on the scheme the old goblin was hatching.

In the distance, he saw the silhouettes of the last goblins in the back of the army.

He hurried to catch up.

TO BE CONTINUED . . .

Watch for
THE STONETELLERS

VOLUME TWO
THE DEATH MARCH
Jean Rabe

Coming from Wizards of the Coast in August 2008.

RICHARD A. KNAAK

THE OGRE TITANS

The Grand Lord Golgren has been savagely crushing
all opposition to his control of the harsh ogre lands of
Kern and Blöde, first sweeping away rival chieftains, then
rebuilding the capital in his image. For this he has had to
deal with the ogre titans, dark, sorcerous giants who have
contempt for his leadership.

VOLUME ONE
THE BLACK TALON

Among the ogres, where every ritual demands blood and every ally can
become a deadly foe, Golgren seeks whatever advantage he can obtain,
even if it means a possible alliance with the Knights of Solamnia, a
questionable pact with a mysterious wizard, and trusting an elven slave
who might wish him dead.

December 2007

VOLUME TWO
THE FIRE ROSE

With his other enemies beginning to converge on him from all sides,
Golgren, now Grand Khan of all his kind, must battle with the
Ogre Titans for mastery of a mysterious artifact capable of ultimate
transformation and power.

December 2008

VOLUME THREE
THE GARGOYLE KING

Forced from the throne he has so long coveted, Golgren makes a final
stand for control of the ogre lands against the Titans . . . against an
enemy as ancient and powerful as a god.

December 2009